The Road Back From Broken

A novel by
Carrie Morgan

*Happy birthday, Lyallyn!
I hope you enjoy the read.*

Carrie M

ISBN: 978-1517637927

Cover design by Mark Aro
Interior design by Polagrus Studio

*For my grandfathers, who saw horrible things
during war and took the memories to their graves.*

"The world breaks everyone, and afterward, some are strong at the broken places."

Ernest Hemingway
A Farewell to Arms

Prologue

June 5, 2009
Evans Army Community Hospital
Fort Carson, Colorado

The siren's wail fell silent as the ambulance pulled up.

Jennifer Fitzgerald stood by the Emergency Room doors and watched the paramedics yank the gurney out of the ambulance, its wheels hitting the ground harder than they normally would. The patient squawked at the impact and began complaining in low, slurred tones. He didn't move, though, having one arm secured in a splint and the other handcuffed to the gurney.

Ordinarily Jenn would have been furious with the paramedics for handling a patient so roughly. Had she seen them behaving like that with one of her patients, she would have laid into them right there. But this time, with this patient, she simply stood in bitter silence, her jaw tightening with anger as they wheeled him into the ER.

He hadn't always been this bad. For months she'd told herself he was going through a phase, and that he'd pull himself together somehow, like he always did. That it would get better. But as the weeks turned into months and the long spring of his convalescence

1

turned into summer, it didn't get better.

It got worse.

Four months had passed since her husband's return from Afghanistan, and she hardly recognized him anymore.

Jenn had been across town at Penrose Hospital when she got the call. She'd just ordered a nebulizer treatment for a seven-year-old asthmatic when her phone buzzed in her pocket. The first time, she glanced at the unfamiliar number and thumbed off the ringer, sending the call to voice mail. Before she could even slide it back into her pocket, it rang again—another call from the same phone number. The second call came so quickly on the heels of the first that she knew the caller had hung up and redialed without leaving a message.

"This is Jenn."

She slipped out of the exam room and shut the door with a quiet snick.

"Ma'am, this is Corporal McNamara with the Military Police." Jenn leaned against the wall for support. "There's been an accident and your husband's been injured." The nausea that swirled in her belly when she answered the phone surged into a sickening wave of dread. "We're taking him to the base hospital, ma'am. You're going to need to come down right away."

When she arrived at the Evans ER and saw him on the gurney with a dazed, heavy-lidded expression and an oozing gash above his brow, Jenn knew what had happened.

Her fear suddenly evaporated, leaving behind the stain of anger.

CHAPTER 1

Why is the light so goddamn loud?

Jacob Fitzgerald leaned against the doorway and squinted at the daylight streaming into the kitchen from the living room window.

What the fuck did I do last night?

Pain speared through his left shoulder when he reached up to rub the sleep from his eyes. Every muscle in his body was stiff and sore.

Then he remembered why.

His left hand was wrapped in a neoprene splint that ran from the middle of his forearm down to his knuckles and covered his entire thumb except for the pad and thumbnail. Wiggling his swollen fingers, snippets of the night before flickered vaguely in his mind. His body slamming forward. The loud crunch of twisting metal. The hood buckling and curling against the shattered windshield.

"Fuck."

Shielding his eyes from the sun with his splinted arm, he pushed himself away from the wall and saw his wife sitting at the kitchen table.

Jenn sat her mug down and looked up from the *Denver Post* as he stumbled toward the refrigerator.

"You're up early." He jerked the door open with a wince.

"It's quarter to eleven, Fitz."

He slammed the fridge door shut and turned around, clutching two bottles of water against his chest with his splinted hand. Ignoring her, he twisted the cap off one of the bottles then downed half its contents in three swallows before setting both bottles on the counter. He opened the cupboard and, after a moment of dazed searching, grabbed a bottle of Advil, thumbed it open, and shook out three tablets. Stuffing the pills in his mouth, he drained the rest of the water in two gulps and tossed the empty bottle into the sink.

Fitz searched the kitchen and the living room, his brows furrowed as he tried to discern what seemed off.

"Where's Ryan?" he asked.

Jenn rolled her eyes and watched as he tore a banana off the bunch and poured a cup of coffee. He walked slowly, grimacing in obvious discomfort before collapsing into his chair with an awkward *fwump*.

"Ryan's where he always is at ten o'clock on Saturday mornings."

Fitz's glassy eyes blinked back at her blankly.

"He's got a hockey game, Fitz. Brandon's mom swung by 'bout two hours ago so Ryan could fetch his gear."

His jaw clenched as he silently cursed himself.

Jenn read the confusion on his face but turned away before their eyes could meet. Just one look from him could charm a smile or a laugh from her and she wanted to stay angry. After what happened, she was entitled.

"You don't actually think I let him stay here alone last night while I was dealing with …"

Jenn had sat at his bedside while the ER staff put a butterfly bandage over the cut on his brow and a temporary Neoprene splint on his broken wrist. She'd stared at the uninjured wrist that was handcuffed to the bed rail. Not that the cuffs were really necessary. He'd succumbed to his drunken haze and passed out a few minutes after arriving at the ER.

Fitz picked up his mug and stared into its dark steamy depths. He held the hot brew in his mouth for a second before swallowing, then took another sip.

"The Jeep is—?"

"Junkyard. Insurance company hasn't called back yet, but it's totaled." *I hope you're happy,* she thought, squeezing the bridge of her nose between her thumb and forefinger, hoping to hold off the headache she felt coming on. She knew from experience that readjusting after a deployment was never easy, but this was different. It was never supposed to be this hard.

Fourteen years earlier, when they met in an exam room at Womack Army Medical Center at Fort Bragg, he had been a Special Forces candidate midway through his qualification course and she, a civilian nurse assisting the Army doctor who was stitching up a laceration on his leg.

"Call me Fitz," he'd told her as he calmly received thirty stitches on his shin. The physician tied off the last stitch then left her alone to bandage the smirking soldier's leg.

"Come on." His teeth gleamed brightly behind a crooked, self-assured grin. "Let me take you out to dinner on Friday."

"And why would you do that?" she asked, the sharpness of the question softened by the hint of amusement in her voice.

"To show my gratitude, of course."

She shook her head, looking away as she gathered what she needed to bandage his leg. "That's not necessary, really. I'm just doing my job."

Undeterred, he pressed her again. "Look, you've got a thankless job. I want to change that. Let me thank you by taking you to dinner. It'll be my treat."

Her eyes narrowed and she nibbled the inside of her lip to keep from smiling back.

"*I don't know,*" Jenn said with a coy little shrug as she continued to wrap gauze around his shin. Once she was satisfied that the bandage was secure, she reached for the pieces of medical tape stuck to the edge of the tray.

"*I have a rule against dating patients.*" She applied the first piece of tape, stroked her thumb over it, then looked at him expectantly. "Why should I make an exception for you?"

Fitz's hazel eyes flashed and he licked his lips. She forced herself to focus on the tape and not on his mouth, the warm pulse in her belly a sure sign that her body and her rational mind were at war. Her eyes rebelled, roving his chest, and the moment she saw the way his snug olive T-shirt clung to his muscles, she knew she was done for.

"*Because…*" The teasing lilt in his voice drew her gaze to meet his. "*I'm an exceptional guy, and because you, I think, are an exceptional woman.*"

Jenn bit back a grin, her flushed cheeks belying her attempt to seem indifferent. She knew from the twinkle of expectation in his eyes that he was not going to let her leave the room without giving him an answer.

"*What do you say? Hmm?*"

He watched her fingers as she applied the last pieces of tape to the bandage on his leg, murmuring in disappointment when she let go of his leg and stepped away.

"*You're a man who's used to getting his way.*" Jenn put the medical tape and gauze back in the cabinet. "*Aren't you, Sergeant?*"

"*Not when you say it like that,*" he said with a little pout that quickly faded, transforming into a cocky grin. "*I get what I want because I work for it. The question is, how hard are you gonna make me work?*"

Of course, Jenn did make him work for it but, in the end, falling in love with him was the easiest thing she'd ever done. Six months after they met and just days after Fitz received his Green Beret, they married in Fort Bragg's Main Post Chapel. They moved out to Colorado a few weeks later.

"Goddammit," he spat. "Just got that Jeep, too."

He stared into his coffee, frowning when the liquid rippled as Jenn bumped the table while getting up. "I'm really gonna miss it. Guess it's back to the old Scout." He watched as she put the half-and-half back in the fridge and her breakfast dish in the sink. "It needs the oil and all the fluids changed and all, probably new belts, but—"

"Do you actually think they're going to let you drive on post?"

Jenn glared over her shoulder and flung the last half-cup of stale coffee in the sink with a messy splash. Turning the water on, she gave the pot a quick rinse and filled the carafe halfway. She turned around and slid the pot into place as she flipped the switch to *brew*. The quiet trickle of the coffeemaker was the only sound between them as she began to brew a fresh pot—for whom, she wasn't certain.

"You blew a .13 at the scene. And the blood work at the hospital came up .17 a half an hour later."

"Son of a bitch," he muttered under his breath.

Jenn turned around and leaned against the counter, crossing her arms with a huff. Fitz rubbed his uninjured hand over his close-cropped hair, his fingers curling into his scalp. His splinted arm lay on the table, and she could tell his hand was swollen by how snugly the white-gold wedding band fit around his ring finger.

Her eyes traced the silver ball chain around his neck and the rubber-rimmed dog tags that fell against his chest. The night before he'd left for his last deployment, Fitz had cradled her in the sweaty crook of his shoulder as she slipped his wedding band onto his dog tag chain to keep it safe while he was overseas. When she saw him at the hospital in San Antonio, she couldn't help but smile, knowing from the faint tan line on his finger that he'd put it back on as soon as the wheels went up on his flight to Bagram.

A gritty guitar riff shattered the uneasy silence between them as his phone began to ring.

Jenn swiped the phone off the counter and handed it to him. He glanced at the caller ID on the screen and sighed, then closed his eyes and answered.

"Fitzgerald."

Fitz stood up with a grunt and walked around to the far side of the bar that separated the kitchen from the living room.

"Yes, sir. I understand, sir."

"I can be there—" He looked for his watch, forgetting that his left wrist was in a splint. Turning around, he briefly caught Jenn's eyes as he read the clock on the microwave.

"Forty-five minutes, sir? I'll—" Fitz shook his head, wincing at the twinge of pain from the cut on his brow.

"No, that's really not necessary, sir … Yes, I know, sir, but I'll just ride my bike over and—" He swallowed hard, rubbing his hand nervously over the fuzz on the back of his head. "Yes, sir. I'll be ready, sir."

"Captain Clark?" Jenn asked.

Fitz's tensing jaw was the only answer she needed. "No." He looked down at his bare feet. "Colonel Robertson."

She nodded, struggling to resolve the mix of sympathy, frustration, and anger swirling inside of her as Fitz's shame rolled off of him in waves.

"You best go shower, then."

CHAPTER 2

The sound of the doorbell sent Fitz's heart racing.

Even after two cups of coffee, two bottles of water, and three Advil, his head still pounded like one of those drum corps he and Ryan watched battle it out at Mile High Stadium the summer before.

Standing up from his easy chair, he walked into the foyer and reached for the doorknob, then hesitated. The peephole darkened as his visitor grew impatient. Knowing he had no choice but to face the music, he opened the door.

"Master Sergeant Fitzgerald?"

"Yeah?" Fitz stared at the young man standing before him. The tall, lanky soldier shifted his weight from foot to foot under Fitz's withering gaze, and his swaying frame blocked the sun's rays long enough to allow Fitz to slip on his Oakleys. "And you are—?"

"Rankin," the soldier said, eyeing him suspiciously. "Colonel Robertson sent me to give you a ride to headquarters."

The kid wore a maroon beret rather than a dark green one, which meant he had gone to Airborne School but was not Special Forces qualified. Fitz guessed the kid was from the Group Support Battalion, whose soldiers were the drivers, mechanics, parachute riggers, cooks, chaplains, armorers, and other sustainment personnel upon which the 10th Special Forces Group's fighting men depended.

"Sergeant?" Rankin nodded at the small SUV parked along the curb.

Fitz patted his pockets to make sure he had his keys and wallet, then stepped outside and yanked the door shut. With a sharp upward jerk of his chin, he urged Rankin to move. "Fine. Let's go."

Although he didn't look at Rankin once during the ten-minute drive to HQ, Fitz watched the young soldier drive away before walking into the building. He held his green beret in his hand, repeatedly rubbing his thumb over the soft felt as he made his way down the hall to the colonel's office. Because it was Saturday and the HQ building was empty, the sounds of Fitz's approaching footsteps made the colonel look up before he had a chance to knock.

"Come in, Sergeant."

Colonel Robertson looked away again as Fitz walked into the office. Fitz stiffened, standing at attention as he snapped his booted heels together. "At ease," said the colonel said. "Take a seat."

Fitz relaxed his posture but hesitated. "Thank you, sir," he said nervously, holding his folded beret in his splinted left hand as he tugged his uniform shirt taut with his right. He wore the only Army Combat Uniform he ever kept pressed and ironed, reserved for those times when he had to meet with the brass. He preferred to wear one of his other ACUs, which were as broken in and comfortable as he could make them after twenty or thirty trips through the washing machine.

Robertson's expression was unreadable as he picked up his phone and dialed. He studied Fitz, giving him a long, skeptical once-over as he waited for the other party to pick up. "Yeah," he said tersely. "He's here. All right. See you in a few."

Fitz sat in the chair in front of the colonel's desk, his leg bouncing up and down with nervous energy. A few minutes passed in agonizing silence as Robertson continued to work, the *click-click-clack* of laptop keys tapping out an irritating cadence that made Fitz's head throb. Just as he was about to ask if he could go down the hall to get a drink from the vending machine, Captain Clark, his commanding officer, appeared in the doorway.

Fitz stood up abruptly when Clark walked in the room.

"Sir."

The captain acknowledged him with a nod, then turned on his heel to face Robertson.

"Take a seat, Captain," Robertson said as he snapped his laptop closed. "Let's get started. I've got a 1430 tee-time with Colonel Morrison and I intend to keep it."

Clark sat down next to Fitz, who stared at his hand and stroked a swollen finger over the longest crease across his palm.

"Sergeant," the captain began, his opening punctuated with a sigh that left little doubt that he hated this part of the job. "I'm sure you know why the colonel and I called you in today."

Fitz raised his chin, staring straight ahead as his Adam's apple bobbed in his throat.

"Yes, sir. I can imagine, sir."

Just six weeks earlier he sat in the same chair, having been arrested the night before after a bar fight at a local Chili's restaurant. Colorado Springs police picked him up for disorderly conduct, a Class 3 misdemeanor that also counted as an Article 116 offense under the Uniform Code of Military Justice.

"Six weeks ago, I gave you a verbal reprimand. I asked you to get ahold of yourself and you told me that you would. But now we're back."

"Sir." Fitz acknowledged Clark without so much as a glance.

Robertson reached across his desk for a file folder with a quarter of an inch of material inside, pulling it towards him as he leaned back in his chair. He held his silence for a few moments longer until, finally tiring of Clark's pace, he cleared his throat and shoved the folder aside.

"You're an excellent soldier, Fitzgerald," the colonel said, narrowing his eyes as he studied the man before him. Fitz clenched his teeth under the scrutiny, glad in that moment that he'd taken the clippers to his hair that morning. "With one Silver Star and three Bronze Stars, two for valor, plus three Purple Hearts, you're the most decorated soldier in your company and among the most decorated in the entire 10th Special Forces Group."

Fitz's jaw ticked at the reference to his decorations.

"Look, your team took a tough assignment over there this last go-round, and I know you and your guys saw some of the heaviest action. You earned those medals, no doubt about it."

Cringing at the description of his latest Afghanistan tour, Fitz steeled himself against the memories. "You don't know the half of it." He finally brought his eyes to meet Robertson's. "Sir," he added icily.

Robertson glanced at Clark, whose brows knit together in concern.

"This is not your first strike, Fitzgerald." The colonel tapped his finger on Fitz's personnel file and frowned. "Last time, you got loaded in a bar and ended up in a fight. Now you get lit in the privacy of your own home, which is your business, but then you hop into your car and plow into a utility pole before you've even managed to get halfway to the gate. MPs said you could barely stand when they pulled you out of the vehicle. Says here ..."

Robertson opened the file and scanned the MP's hand-written report about the previous night's events.

"Says here your tox screen showed a blood-alcohol of .17, which is more than twice the legal limit." The colonel closed the file then smacked his hand on the desk. "Look at me, Fitzgerald! You think this is some kind of fuckin' joke?"

Fitz's eyes darkened as he glared back at his battalion commander.

"No, sir."

"You weren't just buzzed. You were hammered. Drunk out of your goddamn skull."

Fitz's face blanched under the colonel's withering gaze.

"Your driving privileges on post are hereby suspended indefinitely," Robertson said grimly. "These privileges will be given back at my discretion upon you demonstrating successful completion of an alcohol/drug education course through ASAP, the Army Substance Abuse Program. You will attend mandatory counseling, also through ASAP, as well as going to AA three times a week for the next six weeks."

Fitz's nostrils flared in anger but he didn't make a sound.

"Effective immediately, you are no longer the Noncommissioned Officer In Charge of Operational Detachment Alpha 0227."

Fitz's eyes narrowed, his breath catching in his throat.

"I could impose a reduction in rank, but I'm not going to. Instead, I'm going to remove your functional authority and dock your pay. To that end, Sergeant First Class Bruniak will be promoted to acting Team Sergeant first thing on Monday morning. You will revert to being your team's Weapons Sergeant. Finally, in addition to the functional demotion, you will forfeit one-quarter of your pay for the next sixty days. You will be reinstated to the normal E-8 rate of pay upon proof that you have met all of the foregoing requirements."

Colonel Robertson crossed his arms on the desk as he leveled a hard stare at the man in front of him.

"Do you understand, Sergeant?"

"Yes, sir."

Robertson glanced at his watch and muttered under his breath. "Even though this latest infraction occurred on-post, the Colorado Department of Motor Vehicles will be informed that you were found driving under the influence, and the state will suspend your driver's license."

"Fuck," Fitz hissed. "How am I supposed to get around, sir?"

The colonel ignored the curse. "As this is your first DUI, after one month you will be able to apply for reinstatement of your Colorado driver's license, provided that you install an ignition interlock device on each of your vehicles. You will have to blow clean before your car will start. That goes for your wife's car, too. Your on-post driving privileges will not be reinstated until you install an interlock on both of your vehicles. You, of course, bear the cost of the interlocks, which I'm told is $500 to $1,000 a year. This is not optional. Do you understand these conditions?"

Fitz nodded once and sighed. "Yes, sir."

"Captain Clark is also going to issue you a Letter of Reprimand. That's two strikes, Sergeant. I could refer you for a court-martial, and hell, maybe I should, but I'm not. But don't be fooled. You screw up again and I'll have no choice but to recommend a court-martial. And let there be no doubt—if you are court-martialed, Fitzgerald, you *will* receive a bad conduct discharge. That means you'll get nothing. You don't get your twenty. No retirement benefits. No GI Bill. No VA home loans. No health benefits. Nothing."

Nothing hung heavily in the air.

"A soldier like you comes along only once or twice in an

officer's career," Robertson reflected as the corner of his lip curled into a faint, almost indiscernible smile that vanished as quickly as it appeared. "I want to see you get your twenty, son. You've earned it. You owe it to yourself and your family to get your shit together."

Robertson pushed his chair back from his desk but remained seated as quiet again filled the room.

This time, it was Clark who broke the silence.

"You can begin AA tomorrow. There's a meeting at 1700 at Saint Patrick's Catholic Church. I'll pick you up at 1630."

Fitz's brows furrowed over his eyes. "But I'm not Catholic," he groused, his voice peaking at the implication. "I'm Episcopalian, sir."

Clark smiled. "Alcoholics Anonymous is non-sectarian. They're just using the room at Saint Patrick's. I'll drive. Save you the trouble of finding a ride."

Fitz knew he had no choice.

CHAPTER 3

The second he walked in the door, Jenn knew it had gone badly.

Fitz tossed his beret on the foyer table, sending a stack of unopened mail clattering to the floor. Without even glancing up to look at her, he ripped open the Velcro flap of his uniform jacket and unzipped it with a stiff, angry jerk. He rubbed his right hand over his face as a low, frustrated sigh rattled in the back of his throat.

She was standing behind the open pantry door when he entered the kitchen, his combat boots making hard noises on the floor. His jaw ticked and each step was slow and measured, as if his limbs were grinding from one position to the next. When she met his eyes, there was none of the tension in their shimmering, green-flecked brown depths that she saw in the sinews of his veiny hands, the cords of his neck, or the bobbing of his Adam's apple.

In his eyes, she saw sadness—sadness and shame.

Jenn looked over her shoulder into the living room, and for a moment simply drank in the way the room looked: the sofa cushions in disarray after their son's Xbox video game marathon the afternoon before, the coffee table littered with dirty glasses and empty beer cans. She glanced at her watch and, seeing that it was a quarter to two, realized Ryan would be home soon.

"Jacob," she whispered.

He blinked, surprised by the formality of being called by his given name.

"I just lost my team."

The words fell from his mouth in a jumble, the cadence of them so indistinct that it took her a moment to decipher what he'd just said.

"What?"

Fitz turned away to look out the living room window at the neighbor across the street mowing the grass. He shook his head, running his hand over his buzzed hair before he finally turned around and brought his eyes to meet hers.

"That's my team, and they just took it away, "he said, spitting each word. "They're giving it to Bruniak. They're making him Team Sergeant. I'm just the fuckin' Weapons Sergeant now."

Jenn paled and a wave of nausea washed over her. She silently chided herself for imagining even the slimmest possibility of a different outcome.

"You had to have known this was going to happen," she replied, unsure which of them her statement was meant for.

Anger flashed in Fitz's hazel eyes. "What the fuck, Jenn? Whose side are you on?"

Her face flushed and her ears reddened. Any sympathy she may have felt just seconds before suddenly vanished.

"How *dare* you say that to me!" she snapped. "How dare you! That's bullshit and you know it."

Fitz looked away.

Jenn jerked open the refrigerator as months' worth of frustration, resentment, and despair roiled inside of her. She pulled out a can of Diet Coke then slammed the door shut and stormed out of the kitchen.

"Where do you think you're goin'?" Fitz called to her as she disappeared up the stairs. "Hey!"

He growled and ran after her, clomping up the stairs two steps at a time until he caught up with her.

"You've got a lot of nerve," she hissed. She cracked open her Coke and slammed it on the edge of the dresser with enough force to mark the finish. "A lot of fucking nerve. After all the hell you've put us through since you came back, how *dare* you suggest I'm not on your side!" She ground out each word, leveling a hard, watery glare at him before ducking into the closet.

Then Fitz saw it.

Their large blue suitcase, the biggest one they owned, lay on their bed, unzipped and half-full.

He stood in shock, his stomach sinking as he stared at the suitcase, its giant maw gaping open, waiting to be filled. Beneath the dull roar of blood in his ears, he heard the scrape and rattle of hangers moving around in the closet.

Hangers clattered again and Jenn emerged hugging a dozen blouses and dresses to her chest. She dropped them on the bed next to the suitcase and stared at the open bag.

"What are you doing?" He tore his teary gaze away from the suitcase and stared at her. Several seconds passed as she just stood there, unwilling to meet his eyes.

"What's going on, Jenn?" His normally rich, deep voice cracked. "Jenn?"

"You don't remember," she said bitterly. "You don't. You don't fucking remember." She sighed, then began to slide her clothes off their hangers and fold them neatly before putting them into the suitcase.

"Remember what?" His throat tightened as she folded a dress, smoothing out all the wrinkles before gently placing it into the suitcase.

It was his favorite of all of her dresses—a sleek black wrap-around piece with white polka dots made of smooth, silky rayon that clung perfectly to every one of her beautiful curves. He remembered the last time she'd worn it for him. It was the night before his last deployment and they'd gone out to dinner, just the two of them. He wiggled his fingers as he recalled tugging on the little sash that held it all together, and how easily the fabric slipped away from her body. His groin hitched at the memory of that night and the way she'd wrapped her legs around him and pulled him close as he sank into her.

"Last night."

Her voice was sharp, her teeth gritted as she picked up the next piece of clothing, folding it into perfectly flat, wrinkle-free halves before tucking it into the suitcase. She finally turned, her eyes welling with tears, her hands clenched into tight fists at her sides.

"You don't remember, do you, Jacob?"

"What? What don't I remember? There's a lot of last night I don't fucking remember, Jenn." He shrugged out of his uniform jacket and tossed it on the floor next to the dresser. "So cut me a break, okay? What did I forget?"

"You were supposed to pick him up." Her voice was thin, almost reedy, as she swallowed against her tears. "Don't you remember? I took an extra half shift from Jacki so I was going to be working until midnight. That's why you were supposed to pick up Ryan at Brandon's."

The ugly, sickening darkness that had been swirling low in the pit of Fitz's belly suddenly crested.

"You were—" Jenn's breath caught in her throat when Fitz's eyes widened with realization. "You were three blocks away from picking up our son when you plowed into that telephone pole!" He winced, each syllable cutting deeply as she shouted at him. "What would have happened if he'd been in the Jeep with you?" Her voice broke as his face contorted in pain.

"Jenn, please," he said in a ragged whisper. "Don't do this …"

The tears that had been brimming in her eyes shook loose and she quickly wiped them away with the heels of her palms.

"You wanna know whose side I'm on? Who lied to the MPs and told them you were on your way to pick up milk and eggs at King Soopers when you crashed? Huh? Do you have any idea what they'd have done to you had they known you'd gone out drunk to pick up your son from another soldier's house?"

She rolled her lips together in a firm line as she remembered talking to the MPs in the hallway while the ER staff took X-rays of his hand and wrist.

"You'd be halfway to an Article 32 hearing and a court-martial right now." She grunted out a sardonic laugh and shook her head. "I covered your ass, Jacob."

Fitz looked at her, stunned.

"You lied to the MPs?" His cheeks flushed with shame at the thought of how far she'd gone to protect him. "I'm sorry," he whispered. "I didn't know."

She took a deep breath, snuffling as she looked at the mix of clothes in the suitcase. Her eyes were raw when she tore her gaze away from the half-packed luggage. "I have to do this, Jacob. I just—"

"Please don't leave me," he begged, reaching for her. She flinched when he curled his fingers around the soft skin of her upper arm. "I'm doing the best I can, Jenn, but—"

"No." Her features twisted into a grimace as she raised her chin and looked him in the eyes. "I've done everything I can to help you." She took his splinted hand in hers, hooking her slender fingers around his larger ones. "God knows I've tried. I don't know what else to do to help you. You have to help yourself."

Fitz let go of her arm and reached for her face, his extended fingers hovering in the air next to her cheek waiting for her to either lean in or pull away. "Don't leave me," he begged, cupping his fingers around her jaw. "I'm tryin', Jenn, but—please don't go."

"I have to. I have to keep our son safe. He didn't choose to be part of any of this."

She fell silent, turning to lean into his hand as she closed her eyes. His big, calloused thumb swept over her cheekbone, drawing a sharp breath and a whimper from her as she gently squeezed the fingers of his injured hand in a silent reply.

"Jenn ..." Her name fell from his lips in a desperate rasp.

"I knew when I married you that your job would force you to see and do things no one should ever see or do." Her voice was almost liquid; the tears in her eyes seemed to seep into her throat. "I love you with everything in me, Jacob, but I have to protect our son. A couple of minutes later and Ryan would have been in that car with you. And if anything happened to him, I wouldn't be able to live with myself."

"I'm sorry." Deep creases cut across Fitz's broad forehead as his red-rimmed eyes pleaded with her. "I just ... I'm so sorry, Jenn."

"I want you to get better." She shrugged away from his hand and reached for his face. "I love you, but the man I picked up from Evans last night is not the man I married thirteen years ago. I want *that* man back."

She stroked her fingertips over the soft brown stubble dotting his jaw. "I know he's in there somewhere, but I can't bring him back. You have to find that man inside yourself. Find him, Fitz, and bring him back."

"Look," he said, wincing as the pads of her fingers traced the edge of his cheekbone. "I'm gonna get help, I swear. Please stay. Please."

"I can't." She wiped away a tear that had dribbled down and lodged itself against the upper edge of his faint afternoon beard. "I have to do what's best for Ryan."

She swallowed and gazed at Fitz, seeing her son's eyes in his father's hazel depths.

"He deserves a summer full of sports and fun, not of waking up in the middle of night hearing his father yell in his sleep, or getting snapped at when his dad has a bad day or night, or *both*, or having to explain to all of his friends why his dad can't pick him up at hockey practice because he lost his driver's license."

Fitz hung his head in shame as the warmth of her fingers slid away from his cheek. Her other hand lightly squeezed his swollen, purple-mottled fingers one more time before letting go.

"I have five days of unused vacation carried over from last year." The words fell messily from her lips as she wiped her eyes with her hand. "And thirteen days accrued so far this year. I've already talked to my supervisor about taking some time off—a leave of absence—once I burn through my accrued vacation. We're going up to spend some time with my folks in Mount Angel."

Fitz's mouth hung open, more in sadness than surprise. "We have a five o'clock flight to Portland." She swore he stopped breathing for a few seconds as his eyes flicked over to the alarm clock on her bedside table. The bright green numbers blinked back at them: 1:45.

Gesturing toward the pile of unfolded clothes sitting next to the gaping suitcase, Jenn frowned and shrugged. "I really have to finish packing. Heather's bringing Ryan back at two, so—"

Fitz grabbed a fistful of her tank top and pulled her to him. A small, strangled sound came from his throat when Jenn's forehead came to rest against his.

"I love you." His whispered words warmed her upper lip as his mouth brushed against hers. "I … I don't deserve you, but I love you."

His lips parted and he angled his head slightly to the side as he pressed his lips to hers. She tensed, hesitated, then melted into him, his mouth grasping at hers as his fingers loosely framed the long line of her delicate jaw.

It was Jenn who pulled away, breaking the kiss when she tasted the bitter note of the previous night's booze beneath the mint of his toothpaste. She allowed him one last nibble on her lower lip before taking a half-step backward.

"You'll come back, right?" he asked.

"I want *you* back." Her voice cracked as her heartbeat throbbed in her ears. "We'll come back when you do."

CHAPTER 4

Captain Clark arrived to find Fitz sitting on his front porch. The captain glanced at his watch and cursed himself for being late, then threw the car into park and climbed out.

Fitz wore a long, deep-pocketed outfielder's glove on his right hand, which struck Clark as odd. As he walked up the sidewalk, the captain mentally thumbed through the roster of the twelve-man detachment and could only recall one of the men, Spaziani, being left-handed. He tried to remember how Fitz held his rifle in the photo that hung in the team room, and he swore that the sergeant had held his rifle's pistol grip in his right hand. *Had to be,* he thought, recalling how Fitz's thick, gloveless index finger had rested flush against the right side of the action, just above the trigger. Clark smirked, pleased with his memory and certain that Fitz was right-handed, which in turn meant only one thing: the glove wasn't his.

Fitz gripped a baseball awkwardly in his left hand and looked up to find Clark standing in front of him. He had free use of his fingers, but because the splint covered half of his palm and his entire thumb, he could only roll the ball into the pocket of the glove and back into his splinted hand again.

"Sorry, sir. Must've lost track of time. Let me, uh, go in and change, okay?"

Clark saw Fitz's keys dangling from a carabiner latched to his belt loop.

"No need. You have your keys. Got your wallet?"

"Yeah, but …" Fitz looked down at the faded Broncos T-shirt he'd fished out of the dirty clothes hamper that morning. "I look like a damn landscaper, sir."

"Well, landscapers go to AA, too, Fitzgerald." The captain's brows arched sharply over his dark brown eyes as he stood at the top of the sidewalk with his hands on his hips. "Look, it's AA, not a debutante ball at the Broadmoor, okay?" Clark wasn't exactly sure if the Broadmoor, a ninety-year-old luxury hotel a couple of miles north of Fort Carson, hosted debutante balls, but he knew from the way the sergeant rolled his eyes that Fitz got the point.

"At least let me put some socks on, sir."

"Nope," Clark said firmly but without any harshness in his voice. "You've got everything you need—keys, wallet, shoes, and sunglasses. Let's go."

Fitz yanked off the baseball glove, setting it to the side behind one of the porch pillars, but he hesitated, palming the wooden step without moving to stand up.

The young captain sighed. "Look, don't make me issue you an order, Fitz. Okay? Come on. Let's just go."

Grunting quietly as he pushed himself off the porch step, Fitz realized how stiff and sore he still was some thirty-six hours after his accident.

"Fine," he growled.

Fitz sat in the passenger seat and stared at his lap as they wound their way out of the Iroquois Village subdivision toward Fort Carson's main gate. The neighborhood looked like a typical suburban development, comprised of block after block of charming if somewhat cookie-cutter three- and four-bedroom homes with fenced backyards and two-car garages. Of course, what made it different was that every home housed a master sergeant, first sergeant, sergeant major, lieutenant, captain, or warrant officer.

Clark drove in silence, occasionally glancing over at the sergeant. *What a mess,* he thought. Three months after assuming command, he had to figure out how to keep the best soldier in his unit from getting bounced after nineteen-plus years of stellar service.

As they waited at a stop sign for a Military Police cruiser to pass by, Clark felt grateful that, for all of the turmoil Fitz was going through, his demotion had been one of authority and not of rank. Had he been demoted from master sergeant to sergeant first class, the Fitzgerald family would have been forced to move out of Iroquois Village into a smaller home in another neighborhood at Fort Carson.

Fitz quietly tapped his finger against the passenger window as they snaked their way through the sprawling Army post. The sergeant was several inches shy of six feet but built like a tank, with short, muscular legs, a long torso, broad chest, strong arms, and large hands. Though he had not yet served with Fitz on a combat tour, Clark imagined him hiking up a rugged mountainside with a heavy load of ammo strapped to his body armor, a carbine slung across his chest, and a machine gun on his shoulder.

"That was my son's glove," Fitz said abruptly, turning to look out the side window at the foothills in the distance. "Sometimes, you know, after dinner, we play catch in the backyard. He's a natural lefty but he's trying to learn to throw right-handed." He looked at his hand, turning it over and studying it as if its lines and creases were suddenly alien to him.

Stealing another glance at his passenger, Clark noted the deep furrow in Fitz's brow and tried to nudge him back into conversation. "So, does your son play Little League?"

Fitz grunted out a laugh. "Nah," he said, the tension in his jaw softened by a widening grin. "Ryan plays hockey, even in the summer. He's only twelve but he plays in the Bantam league—fourteen and under. He was fired up when he made the Bantam league before any of the other twelve-year-olds."

A smile spread across Clark's face at the warmth and love in Fitz's voice.

"He's like me," Fitz said with a smirk. "You know—not tall, but strong as a bull and good on his feet. He's not as big as most of the thirteen- and fourteen-year-olds playing Bantam, but he's quick and he's got a good eye. He was the top scorer in the local Peewee Majors league last year."

The sergeant fell silent again as he stared out the window. Just inside the main gate, on the shoulder of the outbound side of the road, lay the twisted wreckage of a black SUV with a large, brightly lettered sign next to it. "89 Days Since Last Fatal Accident Involving A Fort Carson Soldier," it read. "Don't Drink and Drive."

"Fuck," Fitz whispered, looking away as they passed the wrecked truck. He sighed and turned to Clark. "She left, you know."

Clark did know. The colonel's wife was head of the battalion's Family Readiness Group, and Jennifer Fitzgerald had called her Saturday morning to say that she and Ryan were going to be visiting her parents out of state for a month or so. He and the colonel knew what Fitz would be going home to before they'd even convened the meeting that afternoon.

"Your wife?" He decided to play dumb for the sake of conversation.

"Yeah. Took Ryan with her."

27

"I'm sorry."

Unsure of what else to say, Clark glanced over at Fitz and noticed something out of the corner of his eye. Tattooed into the sergeant's left bicep was a faded replica of the black and red scroll insignia of the 75th Ranger Regiment, which Fitz served with in the early 1990s, before he joined the Special Forces. Clark silently chastised himself for not noticing it before. He'd seen Fitz in short sleeves during morning PT but Clark had been so focused on keeping pace with the men on the three-mile run that he missed it.

Knowing the kind of man Fitz was, he was sure the tattoo was something Fitz had gotten done years ago, probably right after graduating from Ranger School. Rangers tended to be loud and proud, especially the young ones, while the Special Forces guys were usually a bit quieter about their qualifications. Clark had come to admire that quality since moving to Fort Carson and assuming command of Operational Detachment Alpha 0227.

Of all of the soldiers in the twelve-man detachment, it was Fitz who impressed him the most.

Fitz was in many ways the classic career Green Beret: firmly committed, highly skilled, proud of his service but quiet about his status as an elite warrior, and deeply skeptical of newcomers to the unit. Clark had found him extremely intimidating when they'd first met, even though as a captain he outranked the sergeant and towered over him by several inches. Everything about Fitz, from his straight-backed carriage to the glint in his eyes, oozed hard core.

Yet Clark soon found that he and Fitz shared a common understanding of how the detachment should be run. Fitz knew his men, and given the team's record of success during its most recent deployment, Clark was content to leave well enough alone. Likewise, Fitz had little interest in dealing with rules, forms, procedures, politics or the goings-on at the company, battalion, group, or command level. To Fitz, such things were for the brass, and since Clark was one of the brass, these tasks best fell to him and his executive officer. That allocation of responsibility and control seemed both fair and in the best interest of the mission, so they went with it. Clark and Fitz had never actually sat down and openly talked about it, but rather fell into the pattern almost as a matter of instinct.

But as the weeks wore on, it became clear to Clark that, while Fitz was coming in each day and carrying out his duties as required, the rest of his life was coming apart at the seams. It wasn't just Clark; the other sergeants on the team noticed that Fitz had fallen into the uncharacteristic habit of arriving late to meetings, and showed up some mornings looking (as one of the young staff sergeants later described it) like he'd "been rode hard and put away wet."

The enlisted men of ODA 0227 were a close-knit team who kept to themselves, looked after each other, and handled their own, so no one said anything to Clark about it. And while Clark himself had observed Fitz coming in late on several occasions, he knew personally the difficulty of transitioning back into family life and garrison duty after a combat deployment so he didn't give it much thought.

That is, not until he got a call one Friday night from the MPs saying that Fitz was sitting in a cell at the El Paso County jail. Fitz had gotten into a bar fight with two kids from the local liberal arts college and had been arrested for disorderly conduct. Clark remembered thinking, as he hung up the phone, that the college kids should consider themselves lucky to still have all their teeth.

Clark had hoped it was a one-time slip—inappropriate but understandable for a soldier who'd just returned from a tough, ugly combat tour. So he'd counseled Fitz, suggested he look into some stress-reduction strategies, and issued him a Letter of Reprimand. When he received the call that his team sergeant was in trouble again, he knew what he'd hoped was a one-time error in judgment was, in fact, a sign of a much bigger problem.

"You can just drop me off out front, sir," Fitz said as Clark pulled off onto the side street adjacent to Saint Patrick's Catholic Church. "No sense you takin' the trouble to—"

"Nah." Clark pulled into the church parking lot and parked between a Chevy Silverado and a Ford F-150, both of which dwarfed his SUV. "It's really no trouble," he said as he turned off the ignition and opened the door. "Don't worry about it."

Fitz grunted as he sat in the passenger seat with the door open.

"I don't need a babysitter, sir," he scoffed, patting his pockets to make sure he had his keys, wallet, and phone before climbing out. He slammed the door behind him and glared at the captain. "Look, I know I fucked up, okay? But you don't need to walk me in. I'm gonna go." After a moment, he remembered himself and growled, "Sir."

The young captain ignored the comment as he pulled a ball cap over his snug crew cut and tucked his wraparound sunglasses behind his ears.

"Did it ever occur to you that I might have offered you a ride because I was coming here anyway?"

Clicking his key fob, Clark locked the Santa Fe with a chirp and headed for the door, leaving Fitz with a stunned look on his face.

As he reached the door, Clark turned around to find the sergeant still standing by the bumper.

"What?" he called to him. "You just gonna stand there? I guarantee you the coffee here's better than the crap they serve on post. So, come on. Get your ass in here, Fitz."

"Is that an order, sir?" Fitz smirked as he jogged to the waiting door.

"Don't call me *sir* here, okay?" Clark said with a faint smile. "Here, I'm just Brad, all right?"

CHAPTER 5

"Welcome to Applebee's. My name is Keira, and I'll be taking care of you today."

Taking care of us? Fitz thought. He watched her sidle up to their table, his eyes dark and thick-lidded with skepticism. The server was in her early twenties, slender and brunette, her hair held high in a floppy ponytail that bounced from side to side as her attention moved from one soldier to the other.

"Can I get you two something to drink?" She punctuated her question with a faint laugh and turned to Clark with an expectant smile, batting her eyelashes as she gave the young officer a blatant once-over. "We've got a two-for-one special on Coors and Coors Light bottles, and—"

Fitz surveyed the bar and gazed longingly at the long-handled beer taps. The plastic D-rings of his splint made a hard scraping noise against the table as he shifted in his seat. Just an hour earlier, he'd been sitting in a squeaky plastic chair in a Sunday school classroom at Saint Patrick's with Clark and fourteen complete strangers. *"My name's Jacob and, uhhhh, I've got a drinking problem."*

He opened the laminated menu, studying the glossy pictures of wings, burgers, and salads, not because he was hungry, but because it gave him something to look at other than the taps.

"Iced tea," he said quickly, finally looking up again after committing to a non-alcoholic beverage. "Unsweet, with a *bunch* of extra lemons."

A smirk curved Clark's lips. "Same here, but please hold the lemons."

The waitress stared at the two soldiers for a moment, then shrugged and, with a polite if somewhat forced smile and a quick "I'll be right back," turned and walked away.

"Now you've done it," Fitz snorted once the server was out of earshot. "Now she knows that not only will she not get your phone number, but she's not going to get the hella huge tip she was hoping for. She saw the hair and had us pegged for four beers apiece, plus an appetizer and two entrees."

"Yeah, well." There was a flash of edginess to Clark's voice as he tipped up the brim of his Buffalo Sabres cap. "I dated a waitress once. That's how I met my fiancée."

"Huh." Fitz leaned back in his seat and draped his arm over the back of the booth. "I didn't know you were engaged." He hesitated, not wanting to say more because he could tell by the flicker in Clark's eyes that he'd hit a nerve.

"I was." The captain sighed, leaning away from the table as the waitress delivered their iced teas. "Met her when I was at Fort Hood. She was working her way through school waitressing at a Chili's there in Killeen. We dated for a while, and got engaged right before I went to Iraq."

Fitz grabbed the bowl and began squeezing lemon slices into his drink, one by one. "What happened?" he asked with caution, his forehead creasing as he wiped his sticky fingers with his napkin.

"I had a platoon of guys in Fallujah." Clark's voice was dark as he stared into the parking lot. "2/7 Cav, you know? We were right in the thick of it in November '04. There was this one day, five days into the big assault on the town, that was really bad. Between us and the Marines, we lost ten guys. Ten KIAs. 2/7 Cav lost one …one of my corporals. Really good guy, you know? One of my fire team leaders. Smart-ass Mexican kid from San Angelo. A damn fine soldier. His wife'd just had a little boy the month before we deployed."

Clark continued to stare silently out the window. The sun had begun its slow downward slide through the summer sky. Thin wisps of clouds hung over the foothills west of town. He swallowed thickly before going on.

"We were clearing this building. Marine artillery had pounded the shit out of that section of town before we made the big push, but it didn't send the insurgents running. They just dug in, hard. So we were in this building, right? And—"

"Are you guys ready to order?" the server's voice cut in. Fitz shot her a chilling look that made the young woman blanch.

"Sorry," she said meekly, instantly recognizing that she'd walked into the middle of something. "Umm, I'll come back in a little while, okay?"

"Yeah, thanks."

Fitz watched her slender, round-hipped form disappear down the stairs and into the kitchen.

"It was one of those L-shaped staircases, right?" Clark began again, using his hands to illustrate. "You know, two flights and a landing in between? They put the device underneath that intermediate landing and waited until half the squad was already on their way up the second flight of stairs so that they could nail as many of my guys as they could when they set it off."

The captain paused to take a sip of his tea, trying to clear the rasp that had crept into his voice.

"We were on our way up to the second floor when they blew

the IED. The thing tore Hernandez apart when it went off, and really messed up the other two guys who were standing on that landing with him. One guy, Guiliano, lost an arm and his eyesight, and the other one, Carney, who was standing at the base of that second flight of stairs when it went, got his calf and thigh torn up real bad. The docs did what they could to save it, but Carney ended up losing that leg after they got him back to Walter Reed."

Fitz poked at his lemons with his straw, dunking them and watching them float back to the top before dunking them again.

"I'm sorry," he said, frowning as he stabbed at one of the lemons, which made the ice tinkle against the side of his glass. "Spent most of my time in Iraq in the north. Mosul and that area. With the *Peshmerga*—you know, the Kurdish militias. I know it was pretty bad down there." Fitz sighed and shook his head, unsure of what else to say.

Clark stared at the menu in front of him.

"I guess we were lucky. Could've been a lot worse. They didn't put a big enough charge in the thing when they put it together, so when they set it off, the kill zone was smaller than it should've been considering where they laid it. It'd have been a lot worse if they'd have actually done it right."

Fitz swiped his finger through the thin layer of condensation that had formed along the outside of his glass. He opened his mouth to speak but found himself at a loss for words, so he kept quiet.

"It's funny, 'cause it wasn't until I got home—I mean, physically home and back to my apartment that I remembered I lived in a second-floor unit. Steph, my fiancée, couldn't understand why, when we got to the top of the stairs, my hands were shaking so bad I couldn't get the key in the goddamn door. She just looked at me like I was nuts."

Clark winced at the image that clung to the foreground of his mind. "Every time I walked up the stairs to my apartment I saw Hernandez and those guys standing on that landing in Fallujah. It was like a video in my head playing on a loop and I couldn't figure out how to turn it off. I ended up breaking my lease and moving to a new apartment because I couldn't deal with walking up those damn stairs every day. Just freaked me out."

Fitz looked at his captain with soft, sympathetic eyes. He knew a couple of guys from other teams—younger soldiers who were relatively new to Fort Carson when they deployed to Afghanistan—who came back from deployment and found themselves unnerved by the sight of the mountains, which to them were constant reminders of their experience in the lethal valleys of Kunar and Nuristan.

"I started drinking a lot," Clark admitted. "For those first couple of months after I got back, Steph was all excited and threw herself into planning our wedding. We were gonna do it down in Austin, ya know, later that summer. But we started drifting apart. I just couldn't get excited about any of it. Or anything, really. All I wanted to do when I got home was turn on the TV real loud and watch whatever the fuck sports was on while I drank a six-pack, because the horror movie in my head didn't seem to play as loud when I had four or five beers in me."

Fitz glanced down at his left hand, studying his swollen fingers sticking out of the black neoprene splint, and the bright glint of his wedding ring against his skin. He looked up with a self-conscious grimace, but Clark's gaze had turned again to the scene outside.

"She moved out." The captain's voice was hollow and distant. "We argued one night, and when I got home from work the next night, her stuff was gone. She left the engagement ring on the kitchen counter with a handwritten note."

Fitz's breath hitched in his throat as he remembered watching Jenn fill the old blue suitcase with her and Ryan's clothes.

"They teach you a lot of stuff at West Point and in all those field exercises out there at Fort Irwin, but nothing you do—*nothing*—prepares you for seeing one of your guys blown apart."

Fitz swallowed, blinking away a memory.

Clark sighed and continued. "I just … well, I didn't know how to deal with it, so I drank. I drank thinking it'd help me forget. But it didn't. I still remembered, but I lost the love of a great girl because I couldn't find a better way to cope."

A wave of light-headedness washed through Fitz and the color drained from his cheeks. He looked out into the parking lot at a family getting into their SUV, remembering how he'd watched Jenn and Ryan climb into the taxi and the heavy *thunk* of the cab doors slamming shut seconds before it pulled away.

"I don't want to see you lose what I lost. Fact is, you've got a lot more to lose than I did. A lot more."

Fitz watched the SUV's white reverse lights blink on as the truck backed out of the space. "I know," he whispered.

"The colonel wanted to cut you loose, you know." Clark pursed his lips as he reached for his tea. "He was livid when I called to tell him the MPs had picked you up for DUI. I told him maybe we shouldn't be so hasty and asked him to give you one last chance. I made the case for why you were worth it. Yeah, I trotted out all your decorations—the Silver Star, the Bronze Stars, and all the Purple Hearts—and told him that, after nineteen years, you deserved one last chance. Told him the Army owed you the courtesy of one more chance, considering everything you've given the Army."

The SUV drove away, its rosy red taillights disappearing out of view.

Clark tapped the side of his glass and rubbed the condensation between his fingers. "You're lucky, you know that? If we weren't in the middle of a surge facing a big uptick in the operational tempo, you'd be screwed. Fact is, the Army needs every man it can find right now, so local commanders have a little more leeway with handling disciplinary issues in their units. If you catch my drift."

Fitz's heart skipped a beat. "So you're saying the surge is the only reason I'm not being bounced out on my ass?"

The captain answered with a slight shrug. He swirled the half-melted ice around in his glass a couple of times, then raised a single finger. "You've been given one last chance," he told Fitz. "Don't let it slip away."

"Yeah, all right." Fitz nodded as the waitress returned to take their orders.

"You ready?" she asked.

CHAPTER 6

Fitz was hunched under the hood of his 1976 Scout when he heard the quiet ticking of an approaching bicycle. He squinted at the setting sun to gauge how much daylight he had left, then poured the last quart of motor oil into the truck's six-cylinder diesel engine. Stepping away from the bumper, he wiped his greasy hand on an old T-shirt he'd cut into rags, then looked up at the cyclist who had stopped at the bottom of his driveway.

Fitz wasn't sure where he'd seen the man before.

"Can I help you?"

Tossing the grease-smeared rag onto the ground, he walked down with his hands on his hips. As he approached, Fitz glanced down at the man's feet and immediately realized where he'd seen the distinctive blue and green running shoes before.

"You were at Saint Patrick's on Sunday, right?"

The ruddy-faced man pulled off his bike helmet, revealing sweaty spikes of dark red hair. Tucking the helmet under his arm, he grinned and nodded in the direction of the truck.

"I passed by earlier and recognized you but you looked like you had your hands full." The man smiled, glanced at the green fiberglass cast on Fitz's left arm and quickly amended his statement. "Or your hand, as it were."

Fitz raised his arm, turning it over as he wiggled his exposed fingers, frowning at his thumb, which was firmly held in place by the cast's hard mesh. He preferred the splint, but the orthopedist had insisted that he wear a hard cast for five weeks.

Fitz's brow furrowed, knitting low over his eyes as he gave the redhead a once-over.

"Yeah, well ..."

He slid his right hand into his shorts pocket and palmed his phone, as if somehow by touching it he could will his wife or son to call. He ached to hear their voices, even if for only a minute. Though they'd been gone for only two days, it seemed like much longer. The house was painfully empty without them, and it felt strange to sleep in the king-sized bed alone. He hadn't realized how much he missed Jenn's warmth and the way her bottom felt tucked against his crotch as they drifted off to sleep. His chest ached; it had been months since they last slept spooned together.

"What's your name again?"

Fitz struggled to remember the names he'd heard the night before at the AA meeting. It should have been easy, he chided himself, since everyone went only by first names. But his head had been swirling with a thousand thoughts and feelings, and it was a wonder he managed to remember his own.

The man slid off the seat but didn't dismount as he walked the mountain bike a few feet closer to Fitz.

"Jeremy," he said with a toothy smile, extending his hand. At Fitz's arched brow, the man cleared his throat and withdrew his hand. "Captain Jeremy Daniels, if you want to be formal about it. Everybody in the group just calls me Remy, though. My wife and I live 'round the corner there, 'bout half a block down on the right."

Fitz's eyes quickly swept down to the bright gold band on Remy's left hand, then flicked upward again. He wondered if perhaps the young man wasn't as young as he'd initially thought. "A captain, huh?"

Remy smiled. "Yeah," he replied, wiping his sweat-covered brow with the back of his forearm. "4th ID, 1st Brigade. I'm with the 1st Battalion, 66th Armored. Just moved up from Fort Hood last month."

Fitz tried to cross his arms but, remembering the cast on his left wrist, sighed and let his injured arm rest on his hip as he turned his backward ball cap around and pulled it snug over his eyes.

"So you're a tanker?" Fitz tried to visualize the lanky, rusty-haired captain riding in an Abrams tank, his head and shoulders sticking out of the turret. He grimaced, glad that, for all the travails of the infantry, he didn't spend his days riding around inside a hot, cramped, noisy tank or Bradley armored personnel carrier.

Remy shook his head and laughed. "Heavens no," he said with a grimace of his own. "It's a combined arms battalion, both armor and infantry." He paused, anticipating the next question. "I'm the battalion chaplain."

Fitz's mouth fell open in surprise. "Oh."

Remy smirked, amused at the all-too-common response.

"Why do you guys always do that? It's as if I said I was with the MPs or something." Fitz's soft-eyed curiosity hardened into a scowl. Realizing his error, Remy quickly corrected it. "I didn't really mean 'you guys' like … It's just that when you tell other soldiers you're a chaplain, it's like saying you're a proctologist or something."

Fitz stared blankly, only the slightest cocking of his brow giving any indication at all that he was even listening.

"You know what I mean." Remy rolled his eyes and sighed. "I'm sorry. I know I should be better about names, considering my line of work, but remind me again …?"

"Isn't AA supposed to be all anonymous and shit?" Fitz asked, moving his arms awkwardly as he again tried to cross them in front of his chest.

Remy raised his hands innocently. "You disclose what you want to disclose. I just assumed since we're neighbors and all, we might—look, if you don't feel comfortable with that, by all means. I didn't want to presume, I just ..."

Remy seemed to be a couple of years older than Captain Clark, but three or four years younger than Fitz, who guessed by his rank that Remy's path from college to seminary to the Army was not a direct one. Fitz sensed that the outgoing chaplain genuinely wanted to be friendly, so he decided to expose himself a little.

"Jacob Fitzgerald," he said quickly. "But pretty much everybody other than my mom and dad call me Fitz."

Remy extended his hand again and, this time, Fitz accepted the offer and shook.

"Nice to meet you, Fitz." Unable to contain his curiosity, the chaplain raised his brows expectantly. "So, you're, uh—?"

Fitz hesitated, but decided that since he'd already given his name, he might as well reciprocate and disclose his unit.

"2nd Battalion, 10th Special Forces Group. I'm, uh ... a, uh, master sergeant." He stuttered, clearing his throat at the sudden strangeness of having to identify himself by rank for the first time since his demotion. While he still held the same rank and was still technically the highest-ranked enlisted soldier in ODA 0227, losing the leadership of his team gutted him.

Silence hung between the two as each man sized the other up. A big Dodge truck roared past then Fitz, unable to stand any more of the awkward quiet, finally spoke up.

"Wanna, um, come inside?" His forehead crinkled with uncertainty and he wondered if he was making a mistake.

Remy smiled. "Sure." Swinging his leg over his bike's crossbar, he dismounted then hesitated as he looked over at the porch. "Mind if I park my bike—"

"You can stick it in the garage." The shiny black and silver Diamondback, with its fancy bar-ends and front suspension forks, seemed too immaculate to have been broken in on a trail yet. "I'll close it up and it'll be safe."

Remy rolled his bike into the garage and leaned it against the wall next to Fitz's own. The chaplain gave the blue-framed, mud-splattered Kona an approving nod and followed Fitz into the house. Remy's heel caught the corner of the recycling bin and the loud clattering of clanking glass stopped the two of them in their tracks. The bin was stuffed beyond capacity with half-crushed cans of Coors Light, empty bottles of Corona, and several empty liquor bottles.

Fitz turned around, blushing when he saw Remy staring at the heaping bin.

"I threw it all out."

His eyes darted between the chaplain and the recycled empties. "I, uh, poured the rest of the Cuervo and the scotch and the better part of a six-pack down the drain. I mean, before I went to the meeting yesterday. I didn't drink it, you know—not after …"

Remy crowded Fitz to hurry him through the door into the utility room. Closing the door behind him, he followed the sergeant into the kitchen as he casually looked around. "Hey, you don't need to justify yourself to me. I'm not here to check on you. I was just passing by and stopped to introduce myself. Seriously. That's all."

Fitz shrugged and walked over to the refrigerator. He yanked it open and stood in front of the open door as the cool air misted over his sweaty skin, then leaned in and inventoried the contents.

"Let's see, I got ..."

Remy wandered into the living room and Fitz blushed as he realized what an unholy mess the house had become in just a couple of days. An open pizza box lay on the coffee table in front of the TV, empty but for a couple of stale, half-gnawed crusts, and a trio of Chinese takeout cartons sat on the island between the kitchen and living room. A half-dozen empty cans of Diet Orange Crush filled the kitchen counter, waiting patiently to be taken out to the recycling bin as soon as there was room for them.

"Sorry," Fitz said with a sheepish grimace. "I, uhhh ... I sorta need to go grocery shopping, but since I can't drive, you know, and riding a bike up to the King Soopers and back with groceries is kind of harder than I thought it'd be with the cast and all, I—"

Remy waved off the apology. "Are you kidding me? Please. When my wife comes back from visiting her mom and dad, she always tells me it looks like a tornado ripped through the house. She says I go from zero to bachelor in three days."

Fitz's broad, muscular shoulders relaxed at Remy's admission.

Fitz turned back to survey in the contents of the fridge. "It's been a long time since I was single and not living in a barracks with a meal card. When I was in college, I lived in the dorms on the meal plan, then I enlisted and lived in barracks until I got out of the SF school. I was a brand-new sergeant when I went off to Fort Bragg to train for Special Forces, and me and Jenn got married right after I finished the qualification course, so I never really lived as a bachelor, on my own, with an apartment and a kitchen and shit."

The chaplain smiled faintly at the sudden gush of information and gestured toward the open refrigerator with his chin. "So, whatcha got there, buddy?"

"Not a fuck of a lot," Fitz replied with a grunted laugh.

Reaching in, he grabbed two cans of Diet Orange Crush and handed one to Remy, then shut the fridge door with his foot. He leaned back against the counter and studied the chaplain for a long moment before cracking open his soda.

CHAPTER 7

Remy sat on one end of the plush, wide-armed sofa and allowed his attention to settle lazily over the two things in the room worth observing: his companion, Master Sergeant Jacob Fitzgerald, and the Rockies-Mariners game on the big-screen TV.

Fitz sat on the opposite end of the sofa with his legs propped up on the coffee table and his casted hand resting on his lap. Every so often, his narrowed eyes would widen as an infield play came together and he'd swing his feet off the coffee table, reach for his Orange Crush with his healthy hand and shake the other at the TV.

"Son of a *bitch!*"

The Colorado shortstop scooped the ball off the dirt and side-armed it to second in plenty of time to permit a double play, which fizzled when the second baseman bungled the throw to first.

"Fuck!" Fitz slammed his soda on the coffee table in frustration. "What the *fuck,* guys? Goddammit!"

His outburst fell silent when he saw Remy staring at him.

"Sorry, I, uhh …"

Embarrassed, Fitz quickly turned back to the game to avoid a disapproving glare from the chaplain. Remy laughed, dismissing Fitz's concern with a wave of his hand.

"It's okay. I try to avoid taking the Lord's name in vain, but I'd be lying if I told you I didn't curse up a freakin' storm when my Cards blow one like they did against the Rockies the other day."

Fitz blinked with surprise and swung his head around. "What? You're kidding me. You're a friggin' Cards fan?"

"You say it like it's a venereal disease."

A wicked gleam flashed in Fitz's eyes. "Not sure there's an antibiotic that'll work for that one, though."

"Smart ass."

Remy glanced at the score on the screen as the broadcast dropped away for a Budweiser ad. The Rockies led 3-1 at the top of the seventh inning.

"So wait, you're from St. Louis?" Fitz asked.

"Nah, I grew up in southern Illinois—Carbondale, actually. My dad's a forestry professor at the university there." Remy shrugged at Fitz's arched brow. "Yeah, I know. Anyway, Carbondale's about two hours southeast of St. Louis and five from Chicago, so the Cards were my team growing up."

Fitz smirked. "Yeah, well, if Pujols' bat doesn't heat up, your Cards aren't gonna do shit this year. Their on-base percentage is crap." He brought his drink to his lips only to find a small sip remained. He stood up abruptly and waggled his empty can. "Want another?"

"Yeah, sure," the chaplain replied, pleased by the flicker of laughter in Fitz's eyes.

The sergeant fished another two sodas out of the fridge and, in a sudden moment of inspiration, remembered he had a jar of salsa. After some rummaging in the pantry, he emerged with a smile, his arms raised triumphantly as he brandished an unopened bag of tortilla chips.

Remy beamed. "Nice!"

"Yeah, right?" After struggling a little due to his injured hand, Fitz managed to open the salsa jar and took a precautionary sniff before dumping the contents in a bowl. He grabbed the bag of chips then paused, realizing he had more to carry than he had healthy hands to carry with. "Crap," he grumbled, looking up with an awkward grin.

Remy walked over and grabbed the chips and salsa. "Lemme give you a hand."

Fitz smiled gratefully as he sank onto the sofa and handed Remy a fresh soda. He hesitated for a moment as he watched the chaplain scoop salsa onto his chip and shovel the whole thing into his mouth.

"Umm, I'm assuming this isn't breaking the rules, right? You know, that it's okay 'cause we're in AA together?"

Fitz's voice peaked, his brows knitting together as he puzzled over the issue in his mind. In the nineteen years he'd been in the Army, the only times he had ever hosted an officer in his home was during the backyard "hail and farewell" parties he'd held for outgoing members of his Special Forces team. Hanging out one-on-one with an officer like this had always been deeply taboo.

Remy reached for his soda. "You're worried about fraternization?"

"Well, yeah, seeing as how you're an officer and I'm enlisted."

"Well." The chaplain thought about it for a moment before a knowing grin spread across his face. "We may be toeing the line a tiny little bit, but—"

"But?"

Remy winked. "I prefer to think of this as ministering to my flock."

"So I'm part of your flock now?" Fitz scrunched his nose, unsure of how he felt about that. "Exactly what flock is this I'm a part of?" He glanced up at the TV to check the score, then turned back to Remy with a curious expression on his face. "So, what? Does this mean you're gonna pray with me or something?"

Fitz's question hung heavy in the air between them. Neither spoke as the TV commentator pointed out how many pitches the Rockies pitcher had thrown and wondered aloud how much longer the manager would keep him in before calling the bullpen.

When the game broke to a commercial, Remy reached for the remote and muted the sound. The chaplain's raised brows creased his broad, faintly freckled forehead.

"Do you want me to pray with you?"

Fitz reached down and drew his fingertips along the side of his calf. The odd, almost delicate gesture caught Remy's eye as Fitz's fingers curled into his calf, mapping the skin, the pads of his fingers skimming over an archipelago-like pattern of scars that dotted his leg. Since he'd been sitting on Fitz's left, Remy hadn't noticed the scars. But he knew what they were the second he saw them.

In the five years since he'd accepted a commission as an Army chaplain, Remy had ministered to the needs of scores of wounded soldiers whose bodies were peppered with metal after being wounded by IEDs. He'd seen far worse injuries than Fitz's, but he also knew that those soldiers who emerged with minor shrapnel injuries often bore deeper wounds beneath the surface. As he watched the sergeant's long, thick fingers stroke the slowly fading pink scars, a swell of sympathy crested inside of him. He was still lost in his own thoughts when Fitz's voice broke the silence between them.

"Will it help me get my family back?"

Fitz's shimmering eyes met Remy's. His hand began to tremble and he growled, pressing his fingertips harder against the scars as if by doing so he could rub them out of existence.

"I want my family back. I miss them so much."

"I know you do." Remy's heart ached for Fitz, even though he wasn't exactly sure what happened that had caused Fitz's family to leave.

Fitz swallowed hard, the sharp bulge of his Adam's apple dipping low in his throat. "I'd pray if it meant He'd help me get my family back," he said. "God, I mean. I just—"

"God won't bring your family back," Remy interrupted. "Only *you* can do that, Fitz. But prayer can help us uncover the strength we need to overcome the challenges around us."

Fitz gently rolled the inside of his lip between his teeth. "I dunno," he muttered, rubbing his hand over his tired eyes.

Remy studied the fading pink gouges splattered on the side of Fitz's muscular calf, knee, and thigh. After a moment, he tore his gaze away from the scars and looked up.

"You know, it takes a lot more courage to ask for help than it does to go it alone."

Fitz's brows arched hopefully over his glimmering eyes. "So you'll pray for me?"

"No, I won't." The firmness in Remy's voice gave way to a soft, friendly smile. "But I'll gladly pray *with* you."

CHAPTER 8

The afternoon sun bore down hard on the fourteen-man patrol as they walked the maze of streets that wove between the mud-brick houses.

They'd been patrolling for two hours and Fitz knew from the way the Afghans' rifles sagged as they scanned the streets that fatigue was beginning to take its toll. Although his moisture-wicking thermal undershirt kept the fabric of his jacket from chafing his skin along the edge of his armored vest, the day had proved warmer than expected and Fitz wanted nothing more than to get back to their outpost so he could shed his gear and feel his skin breathe again. Knowing they still had a couple of hours left before they could call it a day, he reached for the push-to-talk radio switch clipped to his vest so he could tell his medic, Peterson, to halt the patrol. Maybe a short break would help to re-center the Afghans' focus.

He'd had just pressed the switch to talk when he was suddenly blinded by a flash of light and thrown to the ground in a shower of gravel, sand, and heat.

Dust hung heavy in the air, burning Fitz's eyes as he sat up and winced at the searing pain in his right leg. He blinked and shook away the haze, glancing down to see his leg torn and bloodied, peppered with sand and shrapnel. He extended his leg, hissing at the pain that clawed from his calf straight up to the base of his spine. The agony made his muscles tense in unison, which only made his wounds hurt worse. He raised his arm, his cry swallowed by a throaty grunt as he saw bits of gravel, shards of blackened metal, and something white sticking out of the bloodied tears in his camouflage jacket. For a second, he wondered if he was looking at the exposed surface of a compound fracture of his arm.

The distant sound of his own heartbeat warbled through the ringing in his ears as he tore his gaze away from his shrapnel-dotted arm and looked down the block where the explosion came from. Two of the Afghan troopers who had been walking some twenty feet behind Peterson lay in the dust, their heads tilted back and their mouths open, though he couldn't hear their moans through the buzzing in his ears.

"Peterson!" he shouted, using his rifle to drag himself to his feet.

"Peterson, where are you?"

Fitz bolted upright in bed, his breaths coming in pants, his heart hammering in his chest. He squeezed his eyes shut and tried to settle his pulse by slowing his breathing the way he'd been trained to do, slowly exhaling between lips formed into a tight "O." A bead of sweat dribbled down his spine.

"Kumak koneen!" the Dari-speaking voice cried out in his head. *Help me!*

Forcing his eyes open, Fitz made out the dark outline of the bed, the dresser, and the mirror. The sheets beneath him were creased and damp. He turned toward the dim light of the waning moon shining through the window behind him.

"Shoma khoob mesheen," he heard himself call back as he got up and stumbled forward. *You'll be okay.*

Fitz nearly fell into the bathroom, catching himself with his healthy arm as he leaned hard against the doorway. He flicked on the light with the edge of his hand, blinding himself. Holding his casted arm over his eyes, he stumbled toward the vanity and leaned over the sink. His vision slowly adjusted and he turned away from the light, his gaze falling on the taut sinews of the arm that held him over the sink. The brown hair that floated over its thickly veined surface wasn't dark enough to conceal the familiar trio of pink scars and the shadow of faint pitting that dotted his skin.

As he stared at his arm, the echo of his own voice played an endless loop in his mind.

"Peterson!"

Pushing away from the sink with a grunt, Fitz turned around and yanked open the mirrored door of the medicine cabinet. He stared at the shelves full of seldom-used lotions and hair products, many of them bought from a coworker of Jenn's who sold Avon on the side. Now she was a thousand miles away, hidden away in the sleepy hamlet of Mount Angel, Oregon, where her retired parents lived.

"Peterson, where are you?"

The cacophony in his mind continued as he looked down at his bare legs and the gnarled skin on the side of his calf that had been flecked with shards of hot metal and what looked like bits of chalk.

"Peterson, where are you, goddammit?"

He squeezed his eyes shut, trying to chase away the image of pulling some of the larger pieces out of his leg, only to see the wounds fill with blood as he held the fragments between his fingers.

"Peterson!"

His gaze fell on a plastic bottle from Walgreens. Swallowing thickly as his heart began to race again, he pulled the bottle off the shelf and read the label. *Percocet,* it said. *10mg/325 mg tablets.* His name was on the bottle, but he puzzled over the prescriber's name for a few moments until he remembered the narrow-faced, beady-eyed Army doctor at Fort Sam Houston who performed the last of the surgeries to extract steel shards embedded near the radial artery in his forearm. He frowned, frustrated that, despite the weeks he spent in Army hospitals, he couldn't remember the names of his doctors.

He stared at the bottle, his hand trembling as he debated whether to open it.

The call for help came through not as a shout but a faint, almost liquid murmur. Fitz wasn't sure if it was his, the trooper's, or someone else's. "Lootfan ba man kumak koneen!" Grabbing his rifle, he lunged forward toward the bloody scene a few meters down the street, ignoring the shrapnel that twisted into his flesh as he moved.

Fitz held the bottle in his left hand and tried pushing and turning at the same time with his right, but without the use of his left thumb to hold the bottle securely, he was unable to get enough leverage to open it.

There was blood everywhere—on the ground, on Corporal Saleh, on the trooper beside him who thrashed around in the dust as four of the other Afghans who had been standing near Fitz came forward to attend to him. The corporal's cheeks were covered with a black, feathery adolescent beard, and Fitz wondered how much of the blood on Saleh's face was the corporal's and how much was what was left of Peterson and the Afghans who'd been standing behind him. Fitz steeled himself, focusing on Saleh and his gaping shoulder wound.
"Shoma khoob mesheen," he told him, cupping his hand around the Tajik's fuzzy jaw. "You're gonna be okay. Okay? Shhh …"

Frustrated, Fitz set the bottle on the counter and pressed down on the cap, trying to press and turn at the same time but the bottle slipped again, stubbornly resisting his attempts to open it. He held it down with the free fingers of his left hand but the bulky fiberglass cast got in the way, so he switched hands, holding the bottle against the counter with his healthy hand, but again found he lacked enough palm to get a solid grip without the use of his thumb.

"Fuck."

He threw the bottle against the mirror, listening to the tablets clatter around inside as it rolled off the counter and came to rest next to the bathtub.

He glared at the stubborn orange bottle with an angry scowl, walked over to the toilet and took a piss.

Then, glancing one more time at the bottle on the floor, he crawled back into bed.

CHAPTER 9

"I thought you were just my ride to the store." Fitz glanced sideways at Remy with a crunch-browed expression of exaggerated annoyance. "Since when did you become my nutritional counselor?"

Remy dropped the last peach into the plastic bag, twisted the top and tied a loose knot, then set the bag in the cart next to the apples. "I prefer to think of it as ministering to the whole person." The chaplain grinned and waggled his brows teasingly as he walked alongside the cart.

"Ahhh, right. Is this one of those 'the fastest way to a man's heart is through his stomach' kind of things?"

Remy forced Fitz to stop the cart by stepping in front of it. "Not really."

His attention was drawn to the bin of neatly stacked pomegranates tucked between the pineapples and the mangos. "Ah! These things are great for you."

He reached for a plastic bag, his blue eyes glittering with enthusiasm. "They're high in folate, which is one of the B-vitamins, and vitamin K. I saw an article in *Men's Health* last month that said that regular consumption of pomegranate increased salivary testosterone, which in turn—"

Fitz stared at the stack of shiny fruit, their color forming a red haze before his eyes.

The fruit-seller called out in Kurdish as Fitz walked by his stall. "Hinar!"

The old man had sliced a pomegranate into quarters, pulling the peel apart to reveal the bright scarlet berries inside. He ran up to Fitz, bubbling excitedly in Kurdish and Arabic about the taste of the tart fruit that, according to the Holy Qur'an, flourished in the gardens of paradise.

Not five minutes later, as the patrol exited the bazaar and rounded the corner into a residential block, a massive explosion sounded from the opposite end of the market, sending Fitz and his men diving for cover. They ran back into the market, the far end of which was no more than a dust-choked pile of flattened stalls filled with the broken, bloodied bodies of the dead and the howling, twisting forms of the wounded.

Making his way through the bazaar looking for survivors, Fitz found himself face-to-face with the pomegranate vendor. The old merchant's warm brown eyes stared back in perfect calm, his shattered skull spilling forth its contents in grim imitation of the fruit he'd offered to Fitz just minutes before.

"No pomegranates." Fitz's voice was flat as he nudged Remy away from the fruit with the front of the shopping cart. "See over there, Padre." He jerked his chin toward the next row over. "Looks like they're running a special on cantaloupe."

Unable to resist rolling his eyes at being called Padre, the Unitarian chaplain quickly refocused.

"What's wrong with pomegranates?" He casually browsed the stack of honeydew melons in front of him as he waited for an answer. "They're truly one of nature's superfoods."

"I don't like 'em, all right?" Fitz closed his eyes and turned away from the glossy, red-skinned fruit, not caring how harsh his answer sounded. "I got my reasons. Just—no, okay?"

Remy noted both the firmness of Fitz's rejection and the vagueness of his explanation as he conceded the point with a gentle nod. They continued along, harvesting a week's worth of fresh fruit and vegetables before moving on to the meat department.

They were standing in front of the refrigerator case debating the relative merits of beef versus pork ribs when Fitz's phone began belting out waves of rough heavy metal riffs. He fished the phone out of his pocket and answered without even looking at the caller ID.

"Hey."

Fitz blushed as he walked away from the shopping cart. The chaplain surveyed the various packages of baby back ribs, searching for the one with the least visible fat and the thickest cuts of meat, setting several aside where the butcher cut the meat too close to the bone. Though his eyes were focused on the Styrofoam packages of pork, he couldn't help but glance over every so often as he eavesdropped on Fitz's side of the conversation.

"I'm okay." Fitz winced, his muscles tensing as if he were bracing himself.

"Yeah, I'm at King Soopers right now." Remy heard the faint warble of the caller's voice through Fitz's phone and guessed he was being scolded.

"No, I, I haven't been driving … I know, okay?" Fitz swallowed and rubbed the palm of his healthy hand over his hair. "No, Jenn, the chaplain I've been working with … Yeah, that's the one … He drove me to the store. Yeah." He fell silent, listening intently to the voice on the other end of the line.

"I know he is. Can I talk to him? Please, Jenn?"

Fitz turned around and waited for his son to take the phone. His eyes met Remy's and he held the chaplain's gaze for a few seconds before he drew a shallow, nervous breath and looked away.

"Hey, buddy."

Trepidation bled through the sweetness in Fitz's voice.

"How's it goin'?" Fitz put his finger in his ear to isolate the sound of his son's voice, his shoulders hunching as if he were trying to crawl into the phone itself. "Mom said you found a summer rec league up there in Salem that had an open slot."

Fitz listened, nodding and murmuring affirmatively at the voice chirping in his ear. "I'm glad you get to play hockey up there this summer." His tone was wistful as he finally turned around to face Remy and the refrigerator case. The chaplain tried to affect a look of curiosity and surprise in the moments before the sergeant looked away again.

"Do you like your coach?" Fitz paused and waited for an answer. "You like the guys on your team?"

After a couple of seconds of what Remy could only imagine was reticent near-silence, Fitz prompted his son again.

"Hey," he said in a soft, soothing tone. "I got some stuff I have to deal with here, buddy, to take care of, but I promise I'll come up to visit you and Mom as soon as I can, okay? Maybe we can go camping when you get back, before you start school? I'm thinking St. Mary's Falls Trail, just you and me, huh? We can take our bikes up to the top. Whaddya think?"

Fitz's shoulders rose as he took a deep breath, then slumped again as his son's reply warbled from the handset.

"Okay," Fitz whispered into the phone. His chin dropped to his chest with a defeated sigh. "Hey, Ryan. Wait."

Remy's breath hitched in his throat as anguish and self-loathing rolled off Fitz in dark, heavy waves. Fitz's fingers wrapped tight around his phone, dwarfing the device.

"I love you, son. I miss you like crazy, buddy." He hesitated, then cleared his throat. "Be good for your mom, okay? I'll see you soon." Several seconds of silence passed on his end. "Okay, all right. Look, I just—I guess I'll talk to you later."

He closed his eyes and covered them with his casted hand as he listened. "I love you, Jenn," he said quickly, almost preemptively. Another moment went by before he added a weak, "G'bye."

The call ended with a quiet beep as Fitz stared at the screen and sighed.

CHAPTER 10

Nights were the worst.

The days without Jenn and Ryan stretched into weeks, but Fitz couldn't get used to being alone. Each night he felt unsettled and exposed in their king-sized bed, a wide expanse of cold, empty sheet his only companion as he listened to the house's stony silence.

Gone was the sound of Jenn's tiny snores and the little murmurs she made when she moved in her sleep. Absent was the warmth of her body, the gentle curve of her belly a silent but sensual reminder of the life their love made. He longed to feel the cushion of her bare bottom against his as they slept "cheek to cheek," and to feel her roll over and curl herself around him in the twilight when the chill slipped in through their half-open window.

Sometimes, when restless frustration finally drove him from his bed, he'd stand at the top of the stairs and listen for the telltale sound of Ryan playing Nintendo long after he was supposed to be asleep. Fitz missed all of the mundane little noises that made the Army-issued two-story a home, even the faint *clickety-clickety-click* of his son's willful disobedience.

He hated the silence.

Some nights, he didn't even bother going to bed. He'd watch

TV, letting ESPN SportsCenter drone on into the night until the monotony of hearing the day's baseball scores for the fifteenth time finally nudged him into slumber.

Whether he finally dozed off in bed or on the sofa, sleep never lasted long. An hour or two after succumbing to the heavy haze of exhaustion, the dreams came to poison his rest. His mind filled with visions of human confetti dotting the blood-strewn sand, the rattle of flying gravel hitting the side of a Humvee, and the chatter of small-arms fire. Sounds and images flooded his mind until the blinding flash and deafening punch of the IED tore him from sleep with a raspy, terrified shout. He would struggle to catch his breath, gulping down air as he rubbed his sweat-slick arms, trying to wipe away the prickly sensation that made his skin crawl.

The warm night of July sixth was one of those brutal nights, one that found him awake and gasping for breath as his eyes fluttered open in the dim light. Fitz pulled himself free of the tangle of twisted covers and sweat-creased sheets with a tired grunt, and swung his legs over the side of the bed.

For a minute he just sat there, silent and unmoving as he tried to relax and re-center himself. Aware of his heartbeat swishing in his ears, he closed his eyes and felt his diaphragm drop and his ribcage open as he drew in a breath. He let his mind settle on the upward slide of his diaphragm as that breath flowed out. *Open chest, breathe in,* he told himself as he forced his unsettled mind to focus on his body's most vital function. He felt his breath pause, hanging naturally in the space between inhaling and exhaling, then slowly, training his mind completely on the place behind his navel, he drew his belly inward and slowly let that breath out.

Fitz pushed himself off the bed with a quiet groan and made his way toward the soft green glow of the bathroom nightlight. He flicked the light on and cringed at the brightness as he leaned on the doorframe for support.

He frowned at the face he saw in the mirror, dragging his fingers over the shadow of stubble on his jaw. Staring at his pale, weary reflection, he saw in the pallor every minute of sleep that had escaped him over the month since he last drank himself into dreamless oblivion. He wanted that oblivion—wanted to slip into a slumber so deep the dreams wouldn't come, and to fall asleep quickly, before his restless mind had time to worry if they would.

With a sigh of exhaustion and disgust, he jerked open the medicine cabinet. His eyes fell on his target, and he reached for the orange pill bottle, clutching it like a prize as he read the label.

Percocet.

The letters whispered in a friendly swirl of soft, quiet voices, beckoning him to accept their invitation.

His heart raced as he stared at the bottle and remembered his previous attempt to open it the week before. Fitz wondered if he could saw through the plastic with the carbon-steel blade of the Gerber knife he kept in his assault pack in the closet. He held the bottle in his fist, yearning for a few sweet hours of sleep unmolested by the dreams that had plagued him for so long it seemed a lifetime ago that he last dreamt of anything good.

He squeezed the bottle until the edges of the plastic dug into his palm, then turned it over in his hand as his fingers opened like a flower's petals. His breath hitched, trapping a curse high in his throat as he stared at the black letters inked into the smooth skin on the underside of his forearm. *Jenn. Ryan.* He had gone out the Friday before, leaving the Rockies droning in the living room as he grabbed his old North Face daypack and headed out the door. Three hours later, he'd wheeled his bike back into the garage with his wife's and son's names penned in a Gothic script on his throbbing forearm.

He mouthed their names as he read them. Shaking his head, he walked out of the bedroom and jogged down the stairs.

Fitz set the bottle on the kitchen counter and pulled open the junk drawer next to the sink. Surveying the jumble of contents, he brushed the clutter aside and smirked when he plucked a small, rubber-handled hammer out of the mess. Twirling the hammer in his hand, he remembered the last time he'd used it—to hang up the framed Joe Sakic poster he and Jenn gave Ryan for his birthday the year before.

Shrugging away the thought, he put the hammer down and picked up the bottle of Percocet. He placed it on the edge of the counter, its cap hanging just over the lip as he turned it with his healthy hand, twisting it open with a satisfying *snap*.

Fitz stared at the open bottle for a second, then shook the four white tablets into the palm of his hand. He picked one up and rubbed it between his fingers, noting the powdery residue the pill left on his calloused fingertip. Fitz set the tablet on the counter and picked up the hammer, holding it over the pill with a slight waver before swinging the hammer firmly and crushing the pill beneath its forged head.

A swirl of nausea coiled in his belly as he looked at his handiwork.

The pill hadn't pulverized the way he'd hoped it would, but rather, it broke into several chalky pieces. His lip curled in disgust as the blood murmured in his ears, then he brought the hammer down again, crushing the pieces with a second, angrier blow. Grabbing a second tablet, he followed the same procedure, repeating it again and again until all four tablets—forty milligrams' worth of pharmaceutical-grade narcotics—had been crushed into dust on the kitchen counter. Setting the hammer aside, he scooped the opiate powder into the palm of his hand and held it up to his nose.

Fitz knew it was enough to put him down for the count. He'd be deliciously high for a little while, then a sink into a good seven or eight hours of dreamless sleep before waking up again.

But he *would* wake up again. And it would all be waiting for him—everything that had haunted him the night before would be there in the morning. The nightmares in his head would still be there, ready to claw him out of sleep the next time his eyes fluttered shut. His gaze narrowed as he studied the loose, featureless powder, its white color as empty as the dreams he wanted to fill his nights with.

Empty.

The word itself pulsed through his gut. He remembered the Ranger next to him calling out *"I'm empty!"* as they huddled against a wall in Mogadishu, taking fire from a Somali position across the street.

"I'm empty!"

He recalled the way the blood soaked into the sand as it oozed out from under his comrade's helmet.

"I'm empty!"

Fitz flung his open hand into the stainless-steel sink and watched the drug billow into a cloud of dust before falling like snow to the bottom of the sink.

He thought back to that day's reading from the book of *Daily Reflections* he got at his first AA meeting.

"The chief activator of our defects has been self-centered fear."

He looked down at his trembling hand and gritted his teeth, making a fist hard enough that his knuckles turned white and his nails dug into the meat of his palm. He recalled a quote from Patton that he'd read somewhere but had forgotten about until Remy reminded him of it the night before:

"Courage is fear holding on a minute longer."

Turning his hand over, Fitz slowly opened his fist and noted the powdery residue wedged into the creases in his palm, then looked at the tattoo drawn across the widest part of his forearm.

He leaned over the sink and turned on the faucet, rinsing the dust off his hand before grabbing the sprayer and washing forty milligrams of snortable oblivion down the drain. The trickle of the drain reminded him of the afternoon Jenn and Ryan left for Oregon, and the gurgle he heard as he poured out every ounce of alcohol in the house, including the two unopened bottles of Jack Daniels he'd bought the night before he crashed the Jeep.

Shaking himself out of his haze, he turned and yanked open the fridge to retrieve a can of Orange Crush. He leaned back against the counter with a sigh, popped open the can with a quiet whoosh and saw the faint glow of dawn warming the twilight.

CHAPTER 11

The dirty guitar riff nudged at Fitz through the veil of sleep, prompting him to grunt into his pillow. It wasn't quite loud enough to wake him fully. At least, not initially.

His phone rang again, the opening bars of Metallica's "I Disappear" jerking him wide awake. He'd finally dozed off around one, thanks to a double-dose of the melatonin supplement he'd picked up at a health food store after doing some internet research on non-prescription sleep aids. The hormone proved a godsend the night of July fourth, when he took three melatonin capsules along with a hundred milligrams of Benadryl to knock himself out so he would sleep through the fireworks. Every night since then, he'd used a combination of melatonin and Benadryl to help him fall asleep and, for the most part, it worked.

The phone rang a fourth time.

"Fuck me," he growled into the pillow. "Shit."

He rolled onto his belly and reached for the nightstand. Curling his fingers around the vibrating, blaring phone, he squinted into the darkness, glancing at the clock on the top of the dresser to check the time as he rolled onto his back and answered.

"H'lo?"

"Jacob." A faint female voice croaked in his ear. He heard a strange thickness in the voice that made him sit up in bed and rub the sleep from his eyes. "It's Mom."

He squeezed his eyes shut, shaking his head as he tried to tug his mind out of the dense fog of sleep. "Um, what? Wait, what's going on, Mom? It's like, 3:30 in the morning—"

"Jacob." Her soft voice broke between the syllables. Fitz pressed the phone hard against his ear as he struggled to hear her. "Your father, he's …"

Fitz swallowed and felt a dark foreboding in his belly. "Mom, what's wrong?"

Several seconds of staticky silence hung between them. Finally, he heard her sniffle.

"Your father is dead."

Fitz's heart skipped a beat. His mouth opened but he couldn't speak, the shock so immense. He finally caught his breath and swung his legs over the side of the bed. He curled his toes against the carpet as if the friction alone could prove he wasn't caught in the middle of a surreal nightmare.

"Are you—?" He glanced up at the window and saw the waning half-moon, then looked down at his bare legs, which looked gray and pallid in the moonlight. "Mom, are you okay?"

She made a sound, a sort of strangled sob, then breathed a ragged sigh.

"He fell asleep with his clothes on watching the Yankees game. I went to wake him up so we could get ready for bed and I … I couldn't wake him up, and …" She faltered, and Fitz heard her draw another hard, jagged breath. "They just left with him and I just don't know what to—I mean, I don't know what to do."

"I'm coming, Mom," he told her, his reassuring voice wavering slightly as his heart began to race. "I need to, uh …"

He looked around the room, wondering where the spare

suitcase was, then looked at the stiff neoprene splint that held his wrist snugly in place. Wiggling his fingers and the tip of his still-immobilized thumb, he felt grateful that the doctor had removed his cast so he didn't have to figure out how to fit the carefully tailored sleeves of his Class A uniform coat over it.

"Look, Mom. Lemme pack up some clothes and stuff and I'll be up there in a couple hours, okay? We'll figure this out, all right?"

He listened for her answer but heard only waves of static.

"Mom?"

"Yes." She punctuated her rasp with a sniff and a shuddered sigh. "Please drive safe, honey, hmm?"

Fitz bit back a smile at hearing her bid him the same farewell she had since he got his driver's license. "Okay, Mom. I'll see you in a bit."

He ended the call.

He sat on the edge of his bed, staring at the way the cool moonlight reflected off the curls of hair on his thighs. *He's gone,* he thought. *He's actually gone.*

A wave of regret washed over him as he realized two months had passed since he last went up to see his parents in Littleton, an hour north of Fort Carson. They'd talked about buying a three-pack of tickets so he, his dad, and Ryan could see the Rockies play a series against the Cubs in early August, or catch a three-game stand against the Giants at home later that month. Now, they'd never get to do that.

His belly swirled with shame as he wondered what his father would have thought to find out his son had been demoted from team sergeant and threatened with a court-martial, and that his grandson's summer trip out to Oregon had less to do with the boy spending time with his maternal grandparents and more to do with getting away from his father.

He stared at the dark Gothic lettering on his forearm, tracing the words *Jenn* and *Ryan* with his eyes before he noticed he still held the phone in his hand.

He pushed himself up off the bed and stumbled toward the closet, unsure if the spare suitcase was still tucked in its usual place the back or if it was out in the garage. Seeing the empty shoe-rack on the floor, he suddenly realized he wouldn't find the spare suitcase in the back of the closet or in the garage. It was in Oregon, with his wife and son.

Then another thought occurred to him. *I can't drive.*

"Fuck."

He thumbed impatiently through his phone's contacts and found Remy's number under "CHAPLAIN."

Fitz stood next to the closet and listened to the line ring and ring, certain it would roll over to voice mail. He'd begun to wonder how much it would cost to get a cab from Fort Carson to where his parents lived in the southwest Denver suburbs. *A lot less than I'll pay if they pull my ass over for driving on a suspended license,* he thought. He was about ready to disconnect when the line finally picked up.

"It's the middle of the bloody night," the chaplain's tired, grouchy voice growled into the phone. "Som'in wrong?"

"I need a ride."

He pulled a pair of heavy cedar hangers off the rack, clutching his dark blue dress uniform coat and gold-trimmed blue trousers to his chest as he walked over to the bed. Gently setting the uniform on the tangled mess of twisted quilt and wrinkled sheets, he took a deep breath and stared at the uniform.

"Right now? I mean, umm …" Remy's voice grew louder, and Fitz imagined the chaplain had padded out of his bedroom to avoid waking his wife. "Hey, how 'bout I call you in the morning, okay?"

"I gotta get up to Denver. Like now."

Fitz flicked the light on and walked back into the closet, looking on the top shelf for the black leather jump boots he wore only with his dress uniform. He edged up on his toes and reached for the boots, which had acquired a thin layer of dust since the last time he wore them.

A pregnant pause hung on the line. "Wait a minute." Remy's voice was clearer and more awake. "What's going on, Fitz?"

Yanking an old duffle bag out of the back of the closet, Fitz swallowed the knot in his throat and walked back out into the dim light of his bedroom. He stared at the well-worn bag, which his son had used for years before Jenn bought him a newer, bigger one in honor of Ryan's move from Peewee hockey to the Bantam league.

"Fitz?" The chaplain's voice jerked him out of his thoughts. "You there?"

"My dad died."

Fitz dropped the duffle bag on the bed and ran his hand absently over the back of his head, overwhelmed by the dozen different things he knew he'd need to do once he got up to his parents' house.

"I gotta get up to Denver to help my mom. I just sent in the paperwork for my license reinstatement last week, but since they say it takes the DMV twenty business days to process the request, it's gonna be at least a couple more weeks before I get to take my driver's test with the interlock on the Scout." The words tumbled from his mouth in a breathless rush. "I don't know how I'm supposed to—"

"Shhhhhh," Remy whispered. "Slow down. I'm sorry about your dad, I really am. Most important thing now is for you to be there for your mom, okay? Why don't you just pack the things you need, all right? I'll drive you up there—it's not a problem. I can be at your place in, I dunno, twenty minutes? Is that enough time?"

Fitz rubbed his eyes with the heel of his hand as he looked down at himself, standing in the middle of his bedroom in a pair of boxer briefs. "Yeah, okay. I'll, um, leave the front door open. Just come in when you get here. I'll either be in the shower or, you know, packing and shit, and—"

"Don't worry about it," Remy said gently. "It's fine. Take your time. Do you have a suitcase?"

"Yeah," Fitz answered quickly. "I'm okay, I—"

"What about a garment bag? For your Class A's?"

Waving off the suggestion, Fitz said, "I think we have one around here, in the garage somewhere, but—"

"I'll lend you mine."

"But—"

"It's no problem." There was a hushed shuffle on the other end of the line, then a quiet squeak followed by the unmistakable spray of a shower being turned on. "Go. Get your stuff together, okay? I'm gonna take a quick shower and shave and I'll be over in a few. You sure there's nothing else I can bring?"

Overwhelmed by the suddenness of it all, unnerved by having to ask for help, and unsettled at not knowing how he was supposed to feel, Fitz shook his head as he paced between the bed and the closet.

"No, I'm fine. I'll see you in a bit, I guess."

The last thing he heard before the line disconnected was the rattle of a shower curtain being drawn back.

CHAPTER 12

Fitz knew the chaplain was there before he even turned off the water.

Living on the edge of danger for months at a time had taught him to listen for the small sounds around him. He'd heard the low creak of footsteps through the hiss of the shower's spray. Leaning his head against the cold tile wall, he let the warm, soothing spray pummel his back and drew in one last deep breath of steam. With a groan, he finally gave in and cut off the water, yanking the curtain back and reaching for a towel.

It was a strange novelty to bathe without a plastic sheath to keep the cast dry. His hand and wrist ached, and while he still had to wear the splint for another week before he could begin physical therapy, he was glad to finally be rid of the cast. Ignoring the stiffness in his knuckles, he gently rubbed the towel over his chest and wrapped it around his waist, then reached for the splint. As much as he hated it, he hated being on light duty even more, so he'd followed the letter of the doctor's instructions. He was determined to join the rest of the team when they went out in the field for a training exercise at the end of the month—the first since their return from Afghanistan in April.

Fitz swiped his hand across the fogged-over mirror and studied his reflection. Stroking his hand over his stubbled jaw, he debated whether to shave, then shook his head and sighed. He looked down at the names of his wife and son tattooed on his arm, muscles twitching as he clenched his fist. He knew he would have to call them, later, and the prospect of that call made his gut churn.

When he walked into the bedroom, Fitz found Remy standing next to the bed staring at the small stacks of folded clothes. A well-worn pair of running shoes lay next to them along with a tiny pile of balled-up athletic socks, a solitary pair of black crew-length dress socks, and his faithful pair of dusty black jump boots in sore need of a spit-shine.

The clatter of Fitz snatching his watch off the dresser jerked Remy to attention. He turned around and glanced over his shoulder.

"Hey." The chaplain had an odd lilt to his voice as he saw the sergeant standing before him wearing nothing but a towel. "I, uh …"

Remy had spent countless hours with Fitz in the five weeks since the troubled Green Beret had walked into the Sunday AA meeting at Saint Patrick's. Once a week, he drove Fitz to the supermarket, and on Tuesday and Thursday evenings and Sunday afternoons, he picked him up on the way to AA. On Saturday evenings, he'd drop by for a few minutes, usually just long enough to make sure Fitz was doing all right. It was more than most AA sponsors did, but Fitz was more than just an addict that Remy was sponsoring in a Twelve Step Program.

Although Remy understood why Jenn had left with Ryan, his heart ached for the man she left behind to sort through his problems on his own. The chaplain had made it his mission to ensure that Fitz wouldn't have to endure the journey alone.

But for all the time they spent together, it wasn't until Remy saw Fitz half-naked that the full scope of what the man had been through and what he was capable of enduring became clear. In addition to the shrapnel scars on his right arm and leg, he bore a half dozen other marks on his shoulder and upper chest that Remy hadn't seen before, each one a testimony to a toughness and strength of will that had kept Fitz alive through battles the chaplain could only imagine.

Remy's cheeks flushed when he realized he'd let his gaze linger too long on the towel-clad sergeant. The two exchanged a brief, awkward look.

"Sorry," Fitz apologized as he closed his watch clasp with a sharp snap. "I should've showered and then packed but I ..."

He fished a pair of underwear out of a drawer, then rubbed the towel over his crotch before casting it aside and stepping into the faded plaid boxers.

"I wasn't sure where my tie was—you know, for my Class A's—and once I got to looking for it, I, um ..."

Fitz's voice trailed off as Remy studied the neatly pressed uniform coat draped over the edge of the bed.

The chaplain stared at the coat, reading its chevrons, stripes, bars, ribbons, badges and other insignia for what it was: a resumé of Fitz's accomplishments during his nineteen years of service. Below his master sergeant's chevrons, six gold service stripes on the cuff of his left sleeve testified to his longevity, while the eight Overseas Service Bars on his right cuff symbolized four years served in combat zones abroad. The left chest was heavy with five rows of ribbons, a few of which he recognized: the Purple Heart with two oak leaf clusters signifying that Fitz had been wounded in combat on three separate occasions; a Silver Star and a Bronze Star with two oak leaf clusters, both of which bore a *"V"* indicating he'd been decorated at least twice for valor in combat.

Above the ribbons, was a blue Combat Infantryman's Badge, and beneath them, badges that testified to his Ranger, Military Freefall Parachutist, and Special Forces qualifications. On the coat's right breast, below the pocket, was affixed the screaming eagle insignia of the 101st Airborne, which Remy knew represented Fitz's very first combat experience back in 1991. Above the pocket was the symbol of the U.S. Army Special Forces—two arrows crossed over an upthrust dagger with the motto *De Oppresso Liber:* "Out of oppression comes a free man."

In a few short seconds, Remy had learned more about Fitz's military career than the reticent sergeant had disclosed in the five weeks since they first met. Remy felt a bit like a voyeur, though, surveying the dress uniform, which, in its silent glory, laid bare the accomplishments that its wearer would never admit to.

Fitz walked silently over to the bed and began to place his neatly folded clothes into the old hockey bag. He packed like a soldier—quickly, neatly, and efficiently, not surprising for a man who spent months at a time living out of a duffel bag.

Remy noticed that Fitz wore jeans, which seemed odd given the warm summer night and the high of ninety forecast for the following day. He wondered if perhaps Fitz's mother hadn't seen his scarred leg yet, and that by wearing jeans he hoped to keep it that way. The quiet between them was broken by the *fwip* of the duffle's zipper and the chaplain tucked that notion away for further thought.

Remy pointed at the garment bag leaning against the dresser. "I brought that for your Class A's."

Fitz's eyes were dry but narrowed with a tension that spoke to the myriad emotions coursing through him.

Reading his ambivalence, Remy walked over and grabbed the garment bag. "How 'bout I take care of that and you finish getting dressed, okay? I packed us a thermos of hot coffee for the trip up since nothing's really open now."

"Okay." Fitz rubbed his eyes with the heel of his hand and padded back to the closet.

Remy held up the dark blue coat, feeling its impressive heft, before gently laying it into the unzipped garment bag. He ran his hand over it, smoothing out the fabric before folding the sleeves across the chest. He placed the white dress shirt in next, then laid the lighter blue, gold-fringed trousers on top and draped the black necktie around the trouser hanger. He gave the whole outfit one last look before zipping the bag closed.

Glancing over his shoulder, Remy saw Fitz pull a green-and-blue plaid madras shirt over his head, then reach into the bathroom to swipe his shaving kit off the counter and flip the lights off.

Drawing a long, tired breath, Fitz tucked his shaving kit inside his duffel and zipped the bag. He stood there for a moment, staring silently at the battered duffel, then shook his head and looked up at Remy with a shrug.

CHAPTER 13

They were several exits up Interstate 25 before either of them said a word.

One thing Remy Daniels learned in seminary was that sometimes the best thing is to leave a person to his silence, at least for a little while, as they struggle to get their mind and heart around a difficult situation. And while he had known Jacob Fitzgerald for only a few weeks, he knew Fitz was a man who prized his self-reliance.

Remy knew Fitz was more accustomed to giving help than asking for it. Seconds after answering his phone that morning, he sensed from the waver in Fitz's voice that the sergeant was lost and unsettled. It took a substantial measure of courage on Fitz's part to swallow his pride and call in the middle of the night to ask for a ride. A less courageous man—one who wasn't fully committed to straightening up his life and getting his family back together—would have hopped in the old Scout, blown a clean, alcohol-free breath into the electronic ignition interlock, and driven up to Denver himself, suspended driver's license be damned. Fitz could have done that, and the overwhelming odds were that he would never have been pulled over.

But he didn't, and Remy admired him for it.

It wasn't until they passed the exit for Garden of the Gods that Fitz finally spoke.

"Fuck."

He leaned back against the headrest and rubbed his hands over his face. "This fuckin' sucks." His fingers curled into his hair, clawing at his scalp in frustration. "Just … sucks …"

Remy looked at him, hoping to head-off a meltdown by helping Fitz stay grounded in the present. "What did your mom tell you?"

Fitz swallowed, his Adam's apple bobbing in his throat as he turned to stare out the window.

"Not much. Just that she tried to wake Dad up after he fell asleep watching the ballgame, and …" He drummed his fingers on the armrest. "She couldn't wake him up." His voice was low and even as he spoke, each word deliberate and vaguely distant. "The paramedics couldn't revive him."

Remy suspected from Fitz's fidgeting that he was roiling with emotions he hadn't even begun to sort out.

"I'm not sure, but it sounds like maybe a heart attack," Fitz added. "Dad's had heart problems for a number of years. He had a pretty bad heart attack about five years ago, which did some permanent damage to his heart. Had a bypass, then had a pacemaker put in a couple of years back."

"Your dad was retired military, right?" Remy remembered Fitz mentioning once that his father had been stationed at Fort Campbell.

"Not retired," Fitz corrected him. "Ten year stint, from '66 until '76. He got caught up in one of the last rounds of RIF'ing after Vietnam."

Remy knew of the Reductions In Force the military implemented in the early 1970s to shrink itself down to a manageable peacetime size as the U.S. drew down its forces in Southeast Asia. All branches of the armed forces were affected, both officers and enlisted ranks, when hundreds of thousands of men were unceremoniously dumped into the civilian workforce.

"What'd your dad do after the war?"

Fitz reached for the climate control knob and turned down the air conditioning. "His last billet was at Fort Carson, and—"

"Carson?" Remy bit back a laugh. "Really?"

A smirk curved the corner of Fitz's lip as his shimmery, green-rimmed brown eyes swiveled to meet Remy's quick glance. "Yeah. But he spent most of his career at Fort Campbell. That's where they sent him right after he and Mom got married in '67."

"Airborne?"

Fitz shook his head. "Air cavalry, actually. Or, well, it became air cav—airmobile—in late '68 as the whole concept of helicopter-borne infantry really took shape. Dad was right on the leading edge of that whole thing."

He squinted as he mentally scrolled through his father's service history. "Anyway, he was a troop commander in the 2nd Squadron, 17th Cavalry. He went to Vietnam in December '67, right before the Tet Offensive, and came back in late '68. He got sent back in late '69 for a second tour. My mom was four months pregnant with me."

"Really?" The chaplain's brows scrunched over his eyes. "So he was deployed when you were born?"

Fitz's jaw shifted and he pursed his lips into a firm line. "Yeah."

He stared off to the east, where the morning twilight clung to the dark horizon. The inky sky reminded Fitz of the morning Ryan was born, just a week after his return from a six-month deployment in Bosnia. His heart ached remembering the twice-weekly calls home to his pregnant wife—he'd hated himself for missing nearly the entire pregnancy.

Fitz shrugged away the memory.

"I was two months old when he came home from his second tour."

Remy sensed something dark simmering on the edge of Fitz's voice and, figuring the best way to keep him from brooding was to talk, pressed on with genuine if somewhat strategic curiosity.

"Is that when you guys moved out to Fort Carson?"

"Mmm-hmm. In late '71, Dad was given a company command in the 3rd Battalion, 12th Infantry here at Carson. After that, he moved to a staff position at 4th ID's 2nd Brigade, and finally got promoted to major and moved over to the 1/8 Cav to be the battalion executive officer. By '76, there were too many majors and not enough open slots for lieutenant colonels, especially for those who didn't go to West Point, so Dad left the Army."

Silence again crept between them as Remy's blue eyes flicked from left to right, reading the mileage signs along the highway and noting the speed limit, watching for one of the Colorado State Patrol cruisers that lurked along the median on this stretch of I-25, ready to pounce on speeding truckers or drunks in the wee hours of the morning.

Fitz muttered softly as a semi roared past them on the left.

"Mom and Dad liked Colorado so much they decided to stay," he explained. "Mom's folks lived in western New York—she grew up near Ithaca—and Dad was from Staten Island, but their folks had both passed away, so there wasn't anything keepin' 'em back east. Dad landed a gig with Martin Marietta, in their aerospace division, so we moved up to Denver."

"He became a rocket scientist?" Remy realized the query came off a bit more flippant than intended. He sighed with relief when he saw a faint smile quiver Fitz's mouth.

"Not exactly. He was in marketing. See, in the mid-1970s, the aerospace industry was moving toward reusable space vehicles, and—"

"Oh! Like the Space Shuttle?"

"Exactly." Fitz smiled the first genuine grin Remy had seen since picking him up. "The Space Shuttle project started years before the first one took flight in '81—they started building the first vehicle in 1975, and the conceptual engineering for it began as far back as the late '60s. Dad worked at Martin for years, doing all kinds of proposals for all kinds of shit, a lot of it for NASA and the Air Force. Kind of funny, really, because us Army guys are always talking shit about the Air Force, then my dad gets out of the Army and spends the next twenty years in the private sector kissing the Air Force's ass and trying to get 'em to buy stuff."

"So he wasn't an engineer?"

"Oh God, no." Fitz laughed. "Dad's degree from SUNY Buffalo was in history. See, Martin needed guys who could talk defense-speak, who knew how guys in the military made decisions, and who could help them put their bids together to appeal to the Air Force guys and ex-military guys at NASA who were awarding the contracts for rockets, space vehicles, missiles, guidance systems, and all that other shit. Dad, being a former officer with a respectable golf game, was a perfect fit."

Remy smiled. "What was his handicap?"

Fitz whirled his head around and shot the chaplain a look. "Fuck if I know," he snorted. "He tried to talk me into golf lessons when I was like twelve, but—"

The chaplain snickered at the flash in Fitz's eye. "You don't strike me as a golf kinda guy."

"Not quite." Fitz turned away again and stared dreamily out the window, scratching his chin at the first hint of dawn along the horizon. "If it didn't involve smashing things, smashing people, or both, it wasn't a sport I could get into. Golf's really not my style. Too genteel, if you know what I mean."

Remy waggled his fingers around the steering wheel as he tried to imagine a teenage Fitz. "So I'm going to guess you played ..." He hesitated, then turned and gave the other man a long once-over. "Football in the fall, right?"

Fitz crossed his arms over his chest. "Yup."

Remy settled his gaze on the interstate ahead, tapping his finger on the steering wheel with a pensive murmur.

"Well," he said, "since you like smashing things but you don't like golf, I'm going to assume that means you played baseball in the spring."

"Uh-huh. Okay, Padre, I was a three-sport letterman. So, what did I play in the winter?"

"Too short for basketball." Remy leaned away to soften the blow when Fitz swung a quick punch into the meat of his arm. "Ouch. So, lemme see—I'm not sure what sports your school had, but since you went to high school here in Colorado, I'm guessing wrestling, hockey, or swimming were the other options. No indoor track, right?"

"Um, no."

"You don't have a swimmer's body." Fitz's eyes flicked to the left and narrowed sharply. "What?" Remy coughed. "You don't. Besides, you're too hairy."

"Swimmers shave, you know."

"So you *were* a swimmer? I'm impressed. I always thought those guys had nerve, running around in Speedos in front of all the girls. Plus, you know, shaving—"

"Hell will freeze over before I'd be caught in a Speedo," Fitz declared, his brows sloping low over his deep-set eyes. "The only woman I want seein' my junk is my wife, 'kay?"

"Your wife's the only woman who's seen your junk?" A teasing grin hung off Remy's lips as he said it, knowing it wasn't true. The Green Beret was a good-looking man, if somewhat rough around the edges, and Remy was certain Fitz had dipped his pen in a number of bottles of ink before settling down with Jenn.

"Hardly," Fitz snorted. "But seeing my junk is a privilege afforded to only one woman at a time. And for the last thirteen years, Jenn's held a monopoly on that, which suits me perfectly well. I don't share her, and she doesn't share me."

The chaplain smiled. "So you weren't a swimmer."

"No," Fitz said, his voice suddenly darker and more glum as he turned to stare out the window again.

Remy silently chastised himself for mentioning Fitz's absent wife. "I got it," he said firmly, hoping to put the conversation back on the rails. "You were a wrestler."

"Huh," Fitz grunted back noncommittally. "And why do you think that, Padre?"

Remy took his eyes off the road briefly to study his companion's profile for a minute. The Toyota's instrument panel cast a dim glow over Fitz's face and accentuated the sharp angle of his cheekbones, the vague cleft in his chin, and the overhang of his heavy brow.

"Low center of gravity," he said as he brought his eyes back to the road. "You're strong, quick and…"

He recalled the afternoon Fitz talked him into checking out a rock-climbing gym on the north side of Colorado Springs. They stood in the back of the room and watched a half-dozen chalky-fingered climbers scale a wall using only the tiny fist-sized hand- and toe-holds to leverage themselves. The usually quiet sergeant had bubbled with enthusiasm as he explained how the climbing wall worked.

"You have an intuitive sense of your body's location in three-dimensional space." Remy glanced over to catch Fitz staring at him with one brow sharply cocked. "So, yeah, I'm gonna guess you were a wrestler."

They passed a highway sign advising that they were ten miles from Castle Rock. After the sign disappeared behind them, Fitz turned away from the window. "I held the Colorado state record for the fastest pin for a while before a kid from Loveland broke it in '94—"

Remy's eyes widened. "No shit, really?"

"Yep," Fitz replied with a smug grin. "Five seconds."

"Remind me not to ever get in a tussle with you," the chaplain said with a chuckle. "Though I'm not sure why a Speedo is too revealing but a singlet isn't. It's not like either one leaves much to the imagination."

Fitz glared back at him in heavy-lidded disbelief. "Whatever. I always wore a jockstrap under mine." He paused for a moment. "Between my dad and my wrestling coaches, I didn't really have much of a choice in the matter."

His thick brows furrowed over his eyes and he looked away without another word. He watched the faint glow along the horizon deepen and reveal a bright sliver of sun as dawn broke the twilight. Remy swore he could almost hear Fitz thinking as he sat there still as stone with his arms crossed in front of his chest, but the chaplain drove on and left his companion to his thoughts.

The sun had risen all the way above the horizon when Fitz finally drew a long, deep breath and spoke.

"He was really pissed when I dropped out of college."

Startled by the suddenness of the statement, Remy shook his head. "What?" It took a couple seconds for his brain to catch up with his ears. "You mean your dad?"

"Yeah," Fitz said. "He thought CSU was a good place for me. I remember him telling me that."

"CSU?"

"Colorado State. Up in Fort Collins, maybe a half hour south of the Wyoming border. My grades were good enough to ensure me admission, so it was the only school I applied to."

"But you dropped out. Why?"

Fitz scratched his jaw and shrugged. "I wasn't the college type. I'm a hands-on kinda guy, you know. I like doing stuff, going places. In junior high and high school, I always had Scouts and sports to keep me from getting all twitchy, but when I got up to CSU, I didn't really have that kind of outlet, and I got bored. Dorm, dining hall, class, dining hall, dorm. Rinse and repeat. Same shit every day. The whole thing was a drag. I had barely started the spring semester when I decided I wouldn't be registering for fall classes. Mom was disappointed but Dad was *pissed*. I mean, I'll never forget the look he gave me when I came home at spring break with all my shit in the back of my truck and told him I needed to put it all in storage 'cause I was shipping off to basic training."

"Why do you think he was so …"

Remy paused, wondering how exactly the elder Fitzgerald had reacted to the news that his son had enlisted. Had he yelled, or did he give Fitz the cold shoulder? Remy wanted to know how that conversation had gone, or if father and son had even had a conversation at all, but Fitz just stared into his lap and cracked his knuckles loudly.

"Why do you think he reacted like that?" Remy asked.

Fitz scratched his jaw and shrugged.

"I don't really know."

CHAPTER 14

Remy sensed Fitz's growing tension as he pulled up in front of the house.

He shut off the ignition and frowned. Fitz sat in a daze, his knuckles white as he gripped the sides of the donut box that he'd held on his lap since they stopped for a dozen and a carton of coffee along the way. The smell of dark roast had filled the Highlander's cabin as they passed through Littleton en route to the Ken Caryl Ranch development where Fitz's parents lived.

"Hey." Remy's voice was gentle as he surveyed the brown two-story set back some forty feet up from the street. "We're here, buddy."

Fitz closed his eyes and nodded, pressing his lips together in a firm line.

Remy pulled the key from the ignition. "You okay?"

"Yeah." Fitz glanced down at the yellow-and-blue box in his lap. "Can you take these?"

Remy grabbed the box and studied Fitz, who reached down to grab the container of coffee he'd been holding between his feet. "Look, I'll be fine."

"I know you will." Remy opened the door with an encouraging smile and stepped out of the car.

Fitz walked up the steps and onto the front porch, each footfall a little more confident than the last. He reached for the doorbell but hesitated, his finger hovering over the glowing button for a few seconds before he pushed. A faint *ding-dong* rang inside the house and thirty-year-old hardwood floors creaked as his mother made her way to the door. Seconds lengthened into what felt like minutes as she turned the deadbolt and unlatched the chain. The heavy wooden door opened slowly to reveal a small, sun-weathered face with red-rimmed brown eyes and silver-streaked blond hair.

"Jacob." She reached out to touch his face as he leaned in and hugged her to his chest with one arm.

"Mom." Fitz rubbed his bear paw of a hand across her shoulders as she snaked her slender arms around his back. "I'm sorry," he murmured into her hair. "I'm sorry I wasn't here to—"

His apology was cut off by a sob that shuddered through her before being muffled by the cushion of his chest. She hugged him tightly as she tucked her nose into his shoulder and cried, her grief rolling off of her in waves that he absorbed.

"Shhhh." He cupped his hand around the back of her head, stroking her hair as the sobs faded into quiet hiccups. She slowly unthreaded her arms from around him and stepped back.

Diane Fitzgerald was a small woman with narrow shoulders, slender wrists, and thin, delicate fingers, who stood just a whisper over five feet tall and weighed barely a hundred pounds. She drank in the sight of her son, a proud smile curving her lips as she saw her husband's strength—if not his height—in Fitz's broad frame.

"Oh." She noticed Remy standing behind Fitz. "I'm so sorry." Her muttered syllables fell sloppily as she sniffed and wiped the tears from her eyes with her fingers.

"Mom." Fitz's voice was gravelly as he reached for her hand and gestured toward Remy with a jerk of his chin. "This is Chaplain

Daniels." Remy acknowledged her with a smile and a tip of his baseball cap. "I asked him to give me a ride up here."

Diane's brows furrowed. "A ride? But—"

Remy stepped forward to offer Diane a polite handshake. "Jeremy Daniels, ma'am," he said, cutting in to save his friend from a conversation he wasn't ready to have. "But everyone just calls me Remy."

She accepted the chaplain's handshake, gingerly at first, relaxing a little at his gentle touch, then clasped her other hand around his, squeezing it lightly before letting go. She looked into his eyes, which seemed even bluer after he moved out of the sun and under the shade of the porch.

"I'm awfully sorry for your loss, ma'am."

Diane winced then looked away as if the comment cemented a reality that hadn't quite sunk in yet. For several moments, she stood there with a stunned daze in her eyes, finally regaining her bearings with a couple of unsettled blinks.

"Thank you, Remy." Her voice was ragged as she turned toward the open door. "Why don't you boys come in?"

Fitz nodded silently and pressed his fingers softly against her back as he followed her inside. Remy pulled the door closed behind him, watching as Diane, a tiny wisp of a woman, led her son, a short-legged but long-torsoed mountain of muscle, into the kitchen.

"Brought you some of LaMar's dark roast, Mom."

"You didn't have to do that. I was about to put a fresh pot on."

"I know." Fitz unscrewed the cap on the to-go carton. "But this way, you don't have to. You can have a fresh batch of your favorite stuff and no messy grounds to deal with." His chest tightened as he looked at her reddened, puffy eyes. "Come on. Why don't you sit down? I'll pour us all some coffee and get some plates, okay?"

Remy laid the box of donuts down on the end of the table, opposite from the place-setting where a pair of balled-up Kleenex sat next to a half-empty mug of coffee. He watched as Diane took her seat, studying the way she held her mouth, her lips trembling as she tried to hold her emotions in check.

Fitz returned to the table with two steaming mugs of coffee in his right hand and another in his still-splinted left. He handed one to his mother, who accepted it with a tired smile, then set the other two on the table, gesturing for the chaplain to take one while he turned and fetched plates. Once Fitz had finally sat down, Remy opened the box of donuts.

"What'll it be, ma'am?" Remy ignored the quizzical look from his friend, who was unused to hearing him speak with a polite Midwestern lilt. "Fitz here told me you liked the apple-filled jelly ones. I like those, too. They remind me of my mom's Dutch apple pie."

Diane nibbled her lip as she studied the box. Her finger hovered over a sugar-dusted jelly-filled before she plucked a maple-iced French cruller out of the box.

"Actually," she said, placing the pastry on her plate. "Roger was always the one who liked the apple jelly donuts. I prefer the raspberry-filled kind myself." Her neutral expression twisted into a frown and she closed her eyes, covering her face with her hand as she drew a shuddering breath.

Remy stared at the box of donuts and wondered how long it would be this way, where every single thing, no matter how trivial or mundane, would remind them of their loss. He'd seen countless families go through the grieving process in the wake of a loved one's unexpected passing and knew from the slack in Fitz's jaw and the glassiness in his eyes that his friend was struggling to grasp what had happened.

Diane, on the other hand, had been given little choice as endless minutes passed while the paramedics tried in vain to resuscitate her husband. Remy imagined her listening as they radioed back to base and conversed with the on-call physician before terminating their life-saving efforts. She'd have watched her husband wheeled into the back of the funeral home van and waited as the vehicle pulled away, following its progress with her eyes until the red glow of its tail lights disappeared around the corner.

But for his son, it seemed that Roger Fitzgerald's passing didn't full sink in until Fitz saw his father's favorite jelly donut passed over, unwanted and undisturbed, staying in the box with the old-fashioneds, crullers, and cinnamon twists.

CHAPTER 15

Plopping into a chair on his parent's deck, Fitz stared at his phone for a minute before taking a deep breath and pressing the call button. He leaned his head back in the chair, staring at the cloudless sky as he listened to the drone of the phone's ring—once, twice, three times. Glancing at his watch, he saw that it was a quarter past ten and was debating whether to leave a voice mail, send a text or, or call back, when the line finally picked up on the fourth ring.

"Hello?"

He knew from the way she said hello that she'd answered without even looking at the caller ID. He'd been so focused on whether she would answer that he suddenly found himself at a loss for what to say.

"Fitz?" A couple of seconds lapsed and his heart fluttered as he struggled for words. "I'm sorry, but I'm having trouble hearing you in here. Must be the bad reception."

"Hey," he said uneasily, standing up from his chair and walking over to the edge of the deck. He leaned into the railing and rubbed his hand over his hair as a pair of joggers loped along the trail behind the house. "Can you hear me?"

In the background, he heard the clack of sticks and the hiss of skates cutting across the ice. She was in the stands at a rink somewhere watching their son play, and he frowned at the thought of how long it had been since he'd seen Ryan on the ice.

"Yeah. Barely, though. You know how shitty the reception is in these rinks. Can I call you back tonight, after dinner? Mom and Dad are taking Ryan to see the new Harry Potter movie, and I'll—"

"My dad died."

A wordless beat passed between them as the sounds of hockey were silenced by the tweet of a referee's whistle.

"W-what?"

"Dad's gone." His voice was low and raspy, more breath than words as it crackled across the line. "He had a heart attack last night. I'm up here at the house with Mom."

"God, Fitz," she whispered. "I'm so sorry. God, I can't believe it. I'm so—oh my God, I just—are you okay?"

"Umm…" He glanced over his shoulder and saw his mother flitting between the kitchen and the utility room, doing her usual morning chores. "I'm okay, I guess. You know, considering."

He sighed and brought his attention back to the greenbelt with its endless stream of Saturday morning cyclists, joggers, and walkers. "I guess it hasn't really sunk in yet—that he's really gone, you know? I mean, he was talking about getting tickets to see some Rockies games and all. I don't know. It's just kind of surreal."

"I'm sorry, Fitz."

The din in the background quieted down and he suspected she'd walked out of the stands to the corridor in front of the locker rooms. Amid the silence that hung on the line between them, so faintly dotted by static it sounded like breath, he imagined her pacing, pressing the phone to her ear as she hunched around it. "How's your mom doing?"

"As well as can be expected, I guess. I think she's still stunned by it all. Shell-shocked, you know."

"Of course," Jenn said quietly. She paused and drew a ragged breath. "Ryan's playing right now, but I'll tell him this afternoon, after lunch. When do you think …?" Her question trailed off, as if the mere mention of the word *funeral* would cement the reality of it in a way that nothing else would.

"I don't know yet. Probably mid next week—Wednesday or Thursday. Mom and I are going over to the funeral home after lunch to sort out the arrangements. Got Chaplain Remy looking into an honor guard." He paused, anticipating her unspoken question. "He drove me up here. I still haven't gotten the paperwork back from the DMV."

Jenn hesitated, letting go of a quiet sigh before she spoke. "Well, as soon as you know—"

He didn't wait for her to finish. "Mom and I are gonna try to confirm the date this afternoon and then I'll start looking at flights for you guys." He swallowed thickly, unnerved by the strange irony that his father's death would reunite him with his family after five long weeks of separation. "I, um, can I call you tonight?"

"Yeah, that's fine."

Though over twelve hundred miles separated them, he could hear the gears turning in her head. "I'm really sorry, Jacob." The intimacy of her using his first name tugged at something deep inside of him. "I'm sorry about your dad, and I'm sorry we weren't there when—"

Fitz shook his head. "It's okay," he said, cutting off her apology. He hesitated for a moment. "Does it make me a bad person to say I'm glad I'm going to get to see you two again?"

He swore he heard her smile on the other end of the line. "No." Her voice held an unexpected brightness. "It doesn't make you a bad person. We've missed you."

"I ..." His breath hitched and anticipation twittered in his belly. "I miss you, too. More than you can imagine."

Another long moment of staticky silence passed between them.

"I can imagine." He heard the sounds of skates and sticks again and knew she'd climbed back into the bleachers. "I'm really sorry, Jacob. Call me tonight? Or sooner, if you—"

He heard the *fwoosh* of the sliding glass door opening behind him. "I'll call you tonight, okay? I love you, Jenn. Tell Ryan I love him, too."

"I will," she said, her voice cracking at the edges. "I love you, too."

CHAPTER 16

Diane Fitzgerald opened the sliding door and walked out onto the porch, clutching her mug to her chest as she sat down next to her son. She took a small sip of coffee and set the cup down with a quiet clink. Fitz looked up with a faint scowl that softened when his eyes met hers.

"It's supposed to get to ninety-two today, honey." She studied him, slouching in a patio chair wearing stonewashed jeans, a faded Madras shirt and a pair of Chaco sandals. "You'll be more comfortable in shorts."

"I'm fine," he grumbled, rubbing his palm on the thigh of his jeans as the sun's warmth saturated the denim. "I'm used to wearing a lot more than this when I'm out in the field."

She reached for her coffee with a frustrated sigh, holding the mug in both hands as she stared into its creamy brown depths. Fitz pulled his Nuggets cap low over his eyes, curving the well-worn brim with his fingers. She breathed another sigh more resigned than the first, then turned away and let her gaze settle on the verdant foothills to the west.

"You needn't be so self-conscious about it." She spoke quietly, focusing on the mountains, though she watched him out of the corner of her eye. "Your father had scars, too, Jacob."

"Not like these." Fitz yanked off his cap and tossed it onto the glass-topped table. "Not like mine."

"He was wounded in combat, too." Her voice was delicate and measured, as if she were easing into a memory. "Twice."

"I know," he snapped, frowning at the sharpness of his tone. He closed his eyes and took a moment to center himself. "He earned two Purple Hearts, one at Song Be and another at Fire Support Base Ripcord in the A Shau Valley. I know all that."

Diane tapped her finger on the handle of her mug as she studied the weathered grain of the sun-washed cedar deck that her husband and son built over the course of two weekends thirteen years earlier. He was a newlywed then, and she remembered sitting on the lawn below with her daughter-in-law watching the men work.

"Jacob, did you ever wonder why you were an only child?"

Fitz's brows knit low over his eyes as the corner of his lip curled in confusion.

"What are you talking about?"

"You know your dad was shot at Song Be." Her cadence was slow, almost contemplative, as she spoke. "In the arm during a firefight. It wasn't a severe injury; they didn't even send him home. He was taken to the battalion aid station to be patched up and was sent right back out into the jungle a couple days later."

Her voice was edged with aggravation, more than Fitz expected to hear from her nearly forty years after his father's return from Vietnam. He couldn't remember the last time his mother spoke to him about his father's wartime service. The subject was one his parents tended to avoid as he was growing up.

"The second time, though ..."

The gravity in her voice made Fitz straighten in his chair. He'd seen the scars once, when he accidentally walked in on his dad wearing only a pair of white briefs. Even then, as a boy, he intuitively knew that the scars were from his dad's time in Vietnam, but Fitz never asked how he got them and his father, for his part, never offered to explain.

"The siege at that firebase, Ripcord, went on for nearly a month. Almost the entire month of July. Your father's unit was sent in to help break the siege. The Army wound up abandoning the post, but only after seventy-five men were killed, and almost five hundred were wounded—including your father."

That much was familiar to Fitz, not because anyone had ever told him what happened in in the A Shau Valley, but rather because curiosity drove him to research it himself.

"Your father was medevac'd after being hit with shrapnel from a mortar a few days before the Army withdrew."

"I remember the scars. I saw them once, here." He pointed to the upper inside part of his left thigh.

"That was only part of it," Diane said vaguely, then fell silent. She stared into her mug, swirling its lukewarm contents around. "Your cousin Andrew has cystic fibrosis. You know that, of course."

"Yeah, obviously. But what does that have to do with Dad and Vietnam?"

"Both your father and your Uncle Ralph were carriers of the CF gene," she explained. "It's not uncommon for carriers to express certain mild abnormalities, among them a congenital absence of a vas deferens."

"Wait, what?" Fitz coughed, squirming in his seat as he squeezed his eyes shut and tried to shake the unwanted image from his head. After a moment, he opened his eyes, a confused look on his face. "But wait, how can that be? Dad … well, he got you pregnant with me, so he must've had all of the, uh, equipment working right. Right?"

Diane smiled at her son's discomfort.

"A man needs only one of each—a testicle, a vas deferens, and a seminal vesicle—to do the job. On his second tour in Vietnam, while leading his men at Fire Support Base Ripcord, your dad caught shrapnel in his groin."

Fitz winced, well aware of what it felt like to be peppered with hot shrapnel. "Jesus. So that's what the scars on his thigh were from?"

"They surgically removed the shrapnel from his thigh and pelvic cavity but they ended up having to remove one of his testicles, too."

The pained expression on Fitz's face melted into one of sympathy as he realized his father's war wounds were more disfiguring than he had imagined. "Was he, I dunno, able to, uh—?" His cheeks flushed as he stammered, unable to ask the obvious question that hung between them.

Diane didn't skip a beat. "He retained all of his function, but his infertility was due to being a carrier of the mutated CF gene, which we only found out about, I don't know, seven or eight years ago, when your dad was having those breathing problems and they couldn't quite figure out why. They ran a battery of tests, and one of them was for cystic fibrosis. Turns out he was just a carrier, and didn't have the disease. But the fact that he carries the mutated CF gene explains why he was born with only one vas deferens. And the one he did have got severed on his second tour in Vietnam. Vietnam gave your dad a vasectomy, more or less."

"And cost him a ball," Fitz chimed in grimly.

"Yes. I know your father always felt, well, un-whole, I suppose, after he came back. He was self-conscious about what he looked like, though I doubt other men in a locker room paid enough attention to his scrotum to notice he only had one—"

"Mom." Fitz rolled his eyes. "I get it, okay? All right? I get it."

For a minute, neither of them said anything. They both stared off into the distance at the mountains, each content to be in the company of their own thoughts. Sweat dampened the crotch of Fitz's jeans and he knew she'd been right about the shorts, but before he was willing to admit as much, his mother broke the silence again.

"I know things happened to you over there. And I know you carry the scars of the things that happened over there. Things you don't want to talk about. And I'm not going to push you to talk about them. But I want you to know that you're not the only Fitzgerald man to come home from war with scars, or to feel self-conscious about them."

She met her son's warm hazel eyes with a smile. "I just—well, I just want you to know that. You don't need to hide your scars from me, Jacob. I was an Army wife for ten years." Her last words came out in a croak as the emotions she'd been holding in bubbled up from within. "Your father and I were married for forty-three years. I know all about soldiers and their scars."

Diane's pale brows arched expectantly, creasing her forehead as she tried to read her son's tired, heavy-lidded expression.

Fitz sighed and shrugged. "So I should go in and change, then, huh?"

"You'll be more comfortable. Go inside and change. I'll make us some tuna fish sandwiches for lunch."

He wasn't hungry, but he sensed her offer of lunch was less about satisfying his body's metabolism and more about finding something to keep her mind occupied.

"That sounds great, Mom."

CHAPTER 17

Fitzgerald men weren't always the strong, silent type.

But Jenn knew that when life's pressures ratcheted up, Fitzgerald men turned inward and smoldered, brooding behind a stony wall of anger that could only be penetrated by one thing: the patient determination of a Fitzgerald woman.

Like his father and grandfather, Ryan Fitzgerald was a brooder.

He'd always been that way. Even as a toddler he was prone to spells of quiet, angry pouting. Jenn wondered if it had something to do with being an only child whose father's job sent him away for weeks or months at a time, leaving no one at home to complain to about life's injustices except for the person responsible for the inequity: Mom.

She suspected it was deeper than that. Perhaps his shy, inward-looking nature traced back to the fact that he was born eight weeks early. Jenn recalled a study in the journal *Pediatrics* indicating that adults who were born premature were more likely to be socially inhibited and introverted than peers born full-term.

"He's so tiny," Fitz whispered, palming the glass with his left hand while clasping Jenn's with his right.

"I know." Her voice cracked between syllables as she looked at their

day-old son through the window of the Neonatal ICU.

"Hey." Fitz pushed away from the glass and gently pulled her toward him. "Look, he's going to be fine. Little guy's going to have to cool his heels here in NICU for a few weeks while his heart and lungs get stronger. But he's going to be fine. He's gonna be okay."

Jenn watched their son in his incubator. Weighing just three pounds, twelve ounces, the boy's tiny red face was masked by an oversized ventilator and he wore a diaper that looked cartoonishly large in comparison to the skinny little legs sticking out of it.

"Maybe if I hadn't worked so long. Or maybe if I'd—"

"Jenn."

Fitz cupped her jaw with his hands, swiping his thumb across her cheekbone to wipe away a tear that had fallen there.

"Listen to me. You didn't do anything wrong. Sometimes these things just happen. There's no reason why, and there's nothing you could've done to change things. A lot of women work all the way up to the day they go into labor. Women in a lot of places literally give birth in the fields—they squat down between the rows of lemon trees or whatever and have their babies, then get back up and keep on pickin' fruit or whatever they were doing. Now, where their husbands are during all of that, fuck if I know, but ..."

Smiling through her tears, she tried to move her face away, but his cradling hand held her firm.

"Look at him." Fitz's hand fell away as he turned back to the glass that separated them from their son. "Look at him in there, wiggling those arms and legs around. He's a little fighter. He's not giving up, Jenn."

"Of course not." She nodded and wiped her eyes with her fingers. "He's his father's son."

"That's right," Fitz said, tapping the glass with his finger. "Short and hairy, just like me."

It surprised them to see their newborn son's tiny body covered with fine, downy hair. The lanugo, the doctors called it, was part of normal fetal development and not uncommon in babies born pre-term. The doctors assured them it would go away within a couple of months.

Jenn rolled her red-rimmed eyes and slapped his arm. "That's not what I meant. What I mean is, he's brave and stoic. He's quiet and doesn't flinch when the nurses tend to him. Reminds me of a certain someone I know."

Fitz smiled. "It's funny," he said, staring fondly through the glass at their son. "Since the afternoon I called you from Zenica and you told me you were pregnant, I've been calling him Little Bitty. Even when you'd tell me the baby was the size of an orange or a grapefruit or a cantaloupe, it was still Little Bitty. You know, in my head, since we decided not to find out if we were having a boy or a girl." He laughed, then turned to her with a smile. "But we need to give Little Bitty a name, 'cause at some point, he won't be so little bitty anymore. And besides, it could get awkward at school."

Jenn laughed. "Maybe a little."

Her smile faded when she glanced back at their son. With Fitz having left for Bosnia just before Christmas and returning stateside only six days before the contractions began, they never got around to deciding on a name.

Fitz snaked his arm around her waist and gave her hip a gentle pat. "Whaddya think?"

She looked at him with eyes that were suddenly more clear and bright than they had been just moments before.

"Ryan Jacob Fitzgerald." The name fell from her lips without hesitation. Fitz's hazel eyes flickered with recognition. "I want to name our little fighter for his father, who's never shied away from a fight."

Fitz bit back a smile. "Ryan," he whispered, turning back to the tiny boy in his incubator.

"Our son."

The ride from Mount Angel up to Portland was silent, as was the wait in the gate area in Portland, the entire flight from Portland to San Francisco, the ninety-minute layover at SFO, and the entire flight from SFO to Colorado Springs. The only exception was a briefly mumbled "Sprite, please," when a flight attendant asked Ryan what he wanted to drink an hour after leaving San Francisco.

Ryan spent the day alternating between hunching over his Nintendo or listening to rap-metal on his iPod while reading a hockey or mountain bike magazine.

The fifteen-minute cab ride from the airport to the house was similarly quiet. From time to time, Jenn would glance over at him, but the moment she'd catch his gaze, he'd turn away.

All in all, during the more than eight hours it took them to get from Mount Angel to Fort Carson, Jenn and her son shared eye contact for all of ninety seconds.

Ryan's silence wasn't new. He had been pulling away for months, starting in the weeks following his father's return from Afghanistan. When Fitz was discharged from the hospital at Fort Sam Houston and sent home to Fort Carson, he was quiet, withdrawn, and lethargic. Ryan respected that his father needed to heal from his injuries, and so he gave his dad extra space. But even after the stitches were removed and the shrapnel wounds began to heal, Fitz remained in a shell most of the time. Four weeks after his discharge from the hospital, the rest of his company returned from deployment and the doctors at Fort Carson released him for restricted duty. Jenn had hoped—for both Fitz's sake and their son's—that things would start to fall into place and life would return to normal.

But it didn't.

Each day, Fitz got up and went to work, came home, changed

out of his ACUs, and plopped himself down at the dinner table where he ate in relative silence, saying little if anything other than a grunted, half-interested "Fine" in response to, "How was work today?"

Each night, he put his plate and silverware in the sink with a loud, careless clatter before relocating to the easy chair in front of the TV set with a beer—or three or four. He remained glued to the screen through three periods of hockey and both intermissions. Fitz wouldn't even turn away during the commercials.

For the first couple of weeks, Ryan tried to squeeze into the tiny spaces where it seemed there might be a place for him in his father's life. He sat on the couch and watched the game, asking questions and making comments about it—questioning the refs' penalty-calling, chatting about the various players' scoring stats, asking Fitz what he thought of a given roughing call or whether the Avalanche would be able to tie up the game and send it into overtime—but Fitz seldom answered with more than a mumble or a grunt.

Unable to penetrate the protective wall his father had thrown up, Ryan gave up and withdrew behind a wall of his own.

So by the time he and Jenn arrived in Oregon, Ryan was sullen, angry, and impossible to reach. In Oregon, things seemed to get better. Jenn found a youth hockey team in Sherwood, about forty minutes north of Mount Angel, which was one player short two weeks into the summer because one of the boys had moved. Finally able to invest his energy into something other than his Nintendo, Ryan began to open up a little, and the hard edges of his anger slowly began to soften.

All of that progress came to a screeching halt the afternoon Jenn told him that his Grandpa Fitz had passed away.

They were driving from the rink back to her parents' house

when she told him. Of course, she knew the news would be hard to take, but she didn't expect him to react the way he did.

"I hate him," he growled, his emerald eyes welling with tears. "I hate him." He turned away and stared out the side window, the jaw of his round, youthful face set hard as he sniffed away tears.

Jenn's brows furrowed. "Why do you hate him?" She struggled to understand why her son would hate his grandfather for dying. Or being dead. Granted, the news was shocking and hard for her to believe, too, but Ryan's reaction puzzled her.

"Ryan." She pressed him again. "Why do you hate him?" She wanted to get inside his head the way she hadn't been able to do for months. Teenagers could be reticent and, at times, reclusive, but Jenn knew her son's walls were too thick and impenetrable to attribute just to precocious rebellion.

"I hate him." He ground his words out with his teeth, unwilling to tear his eyes from the trees along the side of the highway. "I hate him, because it's his fault I didn't get to see Grandpa Fitz before he died. Now I'll never see him again, and it's all Dad's fault. I hate him."

His words echoed in her thoughts during the entire journey back to Colorado.

She understood Ryan's anger, but hearing it, and seeing it in the pinched tension that gripped her son's still boyish features, was something different entirely.

They stopped by their house to pick up three things: the mail (since Fitz had already been up in Littleton for several days), their formal clothes (a dark blue suit for Ryan and a black sleeveless dress and shawl for her), and the Scout. Jenn listened as her son moved through the house with loud, stalking steps, the hooks of the hangers scraping the bar as he jerked his suit out of his closet. She heard him curse when he opened the fridge and found it empty except for a carton of milk past its expiration date and a couple of cans of Diet Orange Crush.

"Do you have what you need?" she asked him, sifting through the stack of mail as he nodded curtly on his way to the garage.

"We're taking the Scout," she called out to him. "Not my car."

Ryan's mumbled reply was drowned out by the sound of the door slamming behind him.

The 1976 Scout had been Fitz's project for as long as Jenn had known him. One of the earliest sport utility vehicles, the white truck bore faded blue and red stripes to commemorate the nation's bicentennial. Fitz bought the truck when he was a senior in high school, and the knobby-tired brute had followed him from Littleton to Colorado State and then to Fort Benning and Fort Bragg before finally making the trip to Fort Carson in 1996.

Ryan reached for the grab handle and pulled himself into the passenger seat with a grunt. He patted his hand on the bulging pocket of his cargo shorts where he'd tucked his trusty Nintendo player, then fastened his seatbelt.

Jenn climbed in, frowning as she struggled to get comfortable. The truck was big—too big as far as she was concerned—and it felt awkward compared to the snug comfort of her Camry. But Fitz asked her to bring the Scout up to Littleton to allow him to finish the last bit of work he was doing on it, and so he'd have it in case the DMV paperwork came through while he was helping his mother sort through his father's affairs.

She was about to turn the key when she suddenly remembered the ignition interlock that Fitz had installed on both vehicles. The device was about the size of a TV remote and was attached to the dash with a thin strip of Velcro. Jenn studied it for a moment before plucking the handset off the dash with a sharp, startling rip.

Ryan watched her bring it to her mouth, push a button then

blow into it. She pulled the device away from her lips and waited a couple of seconds, then a green light flashed and the device beeped quietly as it registered an acceptable blood-alcohol level. Jenn stuck the handset back onto its Velcro mount and turned the key partially. She waited for the old diesel's glow plug light to blink off, tapped the accelerator, and turned the ignition as the Scout roared to life.

"I hate this stupid old truck," Ryan grumbled. "It's slow and clunky. I liked the Jeep."

"Me, too." Jenn pursed her lips as she backed the Scout out of the driveway. She knew from the engine's growl and the vibrations she felt through the accelerator that the truck was running better than it had in years. "But the Jeep's gone, honey, and this is gonna be our second car for a while." The check from the insurance adjuster went straight to the bank to pay off the balance they owed on the Jeep, and the few hundred dollars left over after that was spent installing the ignition interlocks.

Neither of them said a word as the old Scout growled out of Fort Carson's Main Gate and snaked its way toward the interstate. The tightly wound tension of a question begging to be asked hung in the air between them, and it wasn't until they finally merged onto the highway that Ryan finally spoke.

"Is that a breathalyzer?" He pointed at the handset.

Jenn's brow cocked upwards. "Sort of. What—I mean, how did you know that?"

Ryan rolled his eyes. "We learned about 'em in health class last year. We watched a video about drinking. They showed a guy getting pulled over by the cops and him blowing into a thing that looked like that."

She vaguely remembered him coming home from school with a flyer informing parents that the students would be going through a

D.A.R.E. drug and alcohol course. Fitz was medevac'd from Afghanistan the very next week and her recall of that period was little more than a blur.

"I'm not an idiot," Ryan stated flatly. "Dad got in that crash 'cause he was drunk."

Jenn drew a steadying breath. "Yes, that's right."

"So's that to make sure he doesn't drive drunk?"

"That's exactly what it's for," she admitted. "But even though it's just your dad who got the DUI, anyone who drives one of our cars has to take a breath test before the car will turn on."

"Oh," he said, surprised by that revelation. "So is this gonna keep Dad from drinking?"

The question slugged her right in the solar plexus.

"Well, your dad's been attending classes on how not to drink. And they took away his driver's license. The only way he gets it back is by having these things—ignition interlocks—put on both of our cars, so that whenever he wants to drive anywhere, the car won't start unless the driver blows into it and proves there's no alcohol on their breath."

Ryan's brows furrowed. "I don't understand why he has to take a class on how not to drink. I mean, it seems pretty basic to me."

Unsure of how to respond, she shrugged and focused her eyes on the road. Five weeks had passed since she and her son went to Oregon and left Fitz alone. She wasn't proud of abandoning her husband when he needed her the most, but she'd been at the end of her rope. At the time, she didn't know if there was any other way to protect Ryan and force Fitz to see the severity of the situation. Fitz seemed to be doing better now, although the voice of reason in the back of her mind cautioned her against expecting too much.

"Your dad loves you, you know."

Her voice was low and quiet as she glanced over at her son, who had his father's straight, pointed nose and long eyelashes.

"He loves you, Ryan, and he's been working very hard to get better." She paused, remembering the sympathy and interest Ryan had shown in Fitz's physical injuries when he visited his dad at the Army hospital in San Antonio. "It took a while for Dad to heal from the shrapnel, even after they took out the stitches. It's just taking a bit longer for his mind to heal, too."

A frustrated sigh rattled in the back of the boy's throat. "I know. It's just not fair. None of it's fair."

"I know it's not." She pushed hard on the Scout's stiff accelerator to pass a slow-moving semi in the right lane. "It's not fair at all."

CHAPTER 18

Fitz heard the rumble of the Scout's engine as it approached.

He'd decided to take a nap after meeting with the minister to discuss the funeral service, but managed only to lie down, not sleep. Despite Remy's encouraging words when he'd left that morning, Fitz's nerves crackled with anticipation at the prospect of seeing his wife and son. Plopping down on the bed in what used to be his old bedroom, he tried to settle his mind and the calm anxious swirl in his belly.

When he heard the Scout pull into the driveway, he jumped out of bed, threw on a fresh shirt, slipped on his sandals, and jogged downstairs to meet them at the door.

Fitz's gut roiled as the doorbell echoed through the house.

He saw their shapes through the mottled glass window in the door, but he hung back as Diane rushed into the foyer. She glanced over her shoulder and gave him a reassuring smile, then opened the door.

"Jennifer," she said, opening the door wide as she took in the sight of her daughter-in-law and only grandchild. "And Ryan, my handsome boy. Come in, come in." Her voice was strong and bright, belying the sadness and unease that lay tightly coiled inside. "You two must be exhausted after such a long flight."

Fitz stood at the base of the stairs as his wife returned his mother's embrace with a smile. As soon as Jenn escaped Diane's hug, he stepped forward and opened his arms, tiny creases of worry etched into his brow as the seconds it took for her to approach seemed to stretch into hours.

She walked to him, resting her head on his shoulder when he pulled her snug against his chest. After a moment, she snaked her arms around his waist and hugged him back, nuzzling his neck.

"I missed you, baby," Fitz whispered in her ear.

"I missed you, too."

She turned her head and pressed her lips to the soft, smooth skin on the edge of his jaw.

When Ryan mumbled something to his grandmother, she patted Fitz on the hip and pulled away. He stood there, seemingly frozen, as his gaze shifted over to their son, then back to her. His brows arched over his watery hazel eyes with uncertainty as he waited for Ryan to make eye contact.

"Ryan …?"

His voice had a vaguely questioning upward lilt as he wondered if his son would even acknowledge him. He waited for the boy to look up from his sneakers, and when at last Ryan did, Fitz released a long breath and slowly opened his arms, beckoning Ryan to him.

The boy leaned in cautiously, coming just close enough for Fitz to pull him into a hug.

"I love you, son," Fitz murmured as he rubbed his hand up and down Ryan's back. "I missed you, buddy." He cupped his big hand around the back of Ryan's head and felt the softness of his hair. Closing his eyes, he remembered the afternoon nine months earlier when he'd stood in the gymnasium giving his son one last hug before he left for Afghanistan. He remembered how Ryan's fingers had curled around his rifle sling and the pinch of his son's embrace before he pulled away and fell into formation with the rest of his company.

The two women held their breaths as the scene played out before them. The wincing, stiff-armed boy relaxed when his father gently tousled his hair. Ryan's jaw moved as he turned into his father's shoulder, and while the women couldn't hear what he said, they felt an unexplainable relief when Fitz nodded and gave him one last protective squeeze before letting go.

It was only after Diane finally spoke that the tension in the room dissolved. Relieved sighs filled the space where awkwardness had just been.

"Lemonade, anyone?"

CHAPTER 19

Fitz watched Jenn slip out of the spare bedroom where Ryan was sleeping. She lingered for a moment, then shut the door behind her with a quiet snick and made her way toward Fitz's old room.

He stood at the top of the stairs, his arm draped over the banister, transfixed by the sight of her walking down the hall. The TV warbled quietly in the master bedroom and he wondered if his mother was awake or if she had left the TV fill the quiet void of a loved one's absence—just as he himself had done on so many nights.

Jenn passed by, her steps slowing slightly when their eyes met. Fitz swung his arm off the banister and followed her, hanging by the bedroom door as she slipped in and kicked off her sandals. Fitz closed the door behind them, flinching at the sound of the latch. It had been five weeks since they were last alone together and the tension in the air grew more acute with each passing second. He felt strange standing before her, but a need deep in his chest drew him to her, despite the wave of nervousness that swirled low in his gut.

"Jenn ..."

He walked to the window where she stood, her arms crossed in front of her chest, her gaze focused on the dimly lit jogging path that ran behind the Fitzgerald home. The waning moon was little more than a thin crescent behind the Ponderosa pine that wavered in the breeze.

"Jenn."

He was close enough to smell the peppermint oil shampoo in her hair. His trembling hand hovered next to her arm, his fingers curling toward her skin as she drew a breath, but for several long moments, he didn't touch her.

"When did you do it?"

The syllables were light and crisp as his hand finally came to rest on the warm, smooth skin of her upper arm. Her breath hitched, but she didn't pull away.

"The ink, I mean."

Fitz squeezed her arm gently, his touch so slight that she barely felt the pads of his fingers.

"Friday before last." His words fell raggedly as a flash of nervousness surged through him. "You hate it, I guess." His voice sank and he braced himself for criticism.

Jenn shook her head. "No, I—"

She fell silent, closing her eyes as she breathed in the faded scent of his menthol shaving cream and sandalwood aftershave. If she buried her nose in the crook of his shoulder, she'd smell *him*—his sweat, which would bring a flush to her skin the same way it did the day they met. But she hung back, unsure if she wanted that. A part of her was still angry, more about how his actions had hurt their son than for her own pain.

But another part of her, the part that loved him and always had, wanted him back, however and to whatever extent she could have him.

It seemed a lifetime ago when he slid the ring on her finger in front of the altar in Fort Bragg's Main Post Chapel.

"To have and to hold," they told each other on a cool Carolina morning before dozens of friends and family. "From this day forward, for better, for worse, for richer, for poorer, in sickness and in health, to love and to cherish, till death do us part."

But as bad as things had been since Fitz came home from Afghanistan, she knew he hadn't always been the dependent one who needed the support, the help, the shoulder to lean on.

"I don't care if we can't have another baby," he told her. "God, Jenn, you gave us our son, and with the two of you in my life, I don't need anything else."

She melted into him, letting his arms swallow her up in his embrace as she sobbed. Nineteen weeks into her second pregnancy, she'd miscarried. A neighbor who came over to return a borrowed baking dish found her on the floor of their kitchen in a pool of blood. The doctors at the base hospital said that if she'd have been left for another ten minutes, she would have bled out. The borrowed dish saved her life.

"I know you wanted this little girl," he murmured into her hair. They'd just found out the baby's sex during the ultrasound the week before. "I wanted her, too. We both did. We loved her."

She felt him swallow, his Adam's apple moving against her ear as he drew a jagged breath.

"We love her still. And I love you still. If you want another child, we can adopt. If you don't, well, that's okay, too." She squeezed her eyes shut as he pulled her closer to his chest. "I love you and I love Ryan, both of you, with everything I am. You two are my whole world. I'm sorry this happened but, baby, I love you. I love you so much."

He held her as she cried, forever it seemed like, stroking her back and kissing her hair as his own silent tears shuddered through him.

Jenn placed her hand on Fitz's, closing her eyes as she stroked the bumpy web of his veins with her thumb. Opening her eyes again, she looked up as he suddenly released her arm.

"No," she murmured, searching for the familiar in his face. It had been so long. "I don't hate it. I just ..." Her voice trailed off in uncertainty and hesitation.

"Just?"

His voice was tense and the sinews of his arm quivered as she reached for him. Her long, slender fingers wrapped around his wrist as she slowly extended his arm toward her, tracing the Gothic letters with her fingertip, barely touching the ink-drawn skin as his muscles moved underneath. Years ago she had read *Angels and Demons* and its sequel *The Da Vinci Code,* and she remembered the "ambigrams" mentioned several times in the story.

She wondered how Fitz came up with the ingenious script that read *Ryan* one way and *Jenn* the other. A smile crept across her lips. Fitz often surprised her by the things he knew and knew how to do. She was the one with bachelor's and master's degrees in nursing, but he, a college dropout who took years to earn his degree by correspondence, always found a way to figure things out—difficult things, strange things, random things she never would have imagined he'd care enough to *want* to figure out.

"I love it," she told him, her lips parting in a smile. "I just—I'm just surprised by it. You got the other one—" She gestured toward the faded black and red Ranger regiment insignia on his left bicep. "You got that before I even met you. I didn't think you'd ever get another one."

A shiver ran through Fitz as her finger ghosted across the underside of his forearm. "I only had one arm." He lifted his gaze to meet hers. "With the cast on this one, I pretty much had one arm. It felt ... well, it felt the way my whole world felt when you and Ryan left. Like a part of me had been taken away." He remembered what his mother had revealed about the injury his father suffered in the A Shau Valley. "Like I wasn't whole anymore."

She heard the quiet fracture in his voice. "I'm sorry." She stroked her whole hand over the tattoo. "But I had to. For Ryan."

Fitz tried to swallow the knot in the back of his throat. "I know you did. I'm sorry, I just—"

Jenn tapped the tattooed skin one last time with her fingertips. "I know." She brought her hand up to his jaw and knew from the light dusting of stubble that he had shaved that afternoon, right before they came up from Carson. He'd shaved for *her*.

His hand cupped her hip as he closed his eyes and turned into her touch, softly trapping her fingers against his shoulder with his jaw.

"I was afraid I'd lost you." He slowly opened his eyes and took in each curve and line of her face, letting his gaze pool in her pale gray eyes. "When you left, I wasn't sure you'd ever come back."

"But I told you I would," she said thickly. "I love you, Fitz."

Her voice cracked on the word *love* as his fingers pressed possessively into her flesh. The faint yellowish light of the bedside lamp made his shimmering hazel eyes seem browner.

"You *know* that."

Fitz's lips parted and Jenn was sure he was going to say something. But he didn't. Instead, he took a breath and squeezed her hip, then leaned in and kissed her.

At first it was tentative, just a soft plucking of the lips, but then a quiet growl sounded in the back of Fitz's throat. Jenn's lips moved in response to the flick of his tongue between them. Heat flashed through her body as he licked into her mouth, his tongue meeting hers as her lips moved against his. He tasted smoky, like coffee left on the burner too long, its bitter edges softened by a spoonful of sugar. Breaking off the kiss, she let him walk her toward the bed, watching as he stared back with dark, dilated eyes.

Their eyes stayed locked as they hesitated, each waiting to see what the other would do. His gaze seared her the way it always did and Jenn remembered how he'd looked at her the night she first gave herself to him.

Her reverie was broken by a quiet grunt when Fitz reached for the hem of his faded T-shirt and peeled it off, discarding it on the floor behind him.

"Jenn."

He cupped her jaw in his hand and swiped a callused thumb under her chin. The flicker of his green-haloed eyes and the gentle touch of his work-roughened hands never ceased to enchant her, even more so that night because it had been so long since she'd had the chance to see him like this. His mouth hung open and she felt the warmth of his palm against her jaw. She angled her head into his touch, mewling in disappointment when his hand fell away. Jenn reached for him, and he leaned in even closer to her, close enough that his breath tickled her upper lip.

"Jenn." Her pulse throbbed in her ears as he struggled for words. "It's, well, I just—"

She didn't wait for him to finish. There was time enough for words later, but right then, in that moment, she needed him, needed *this*—to know that no matter what had changed about him and between them, the flame that kept them going over the years was still there, flickering brightly.

"No," she whispered.

She closed her eyes and placed her hand on his chest, smiling at the throb of his heartbeat beneath her palm. She raked her fingers through the hair on his chest before she worked her way up to his neck, briefly stroking the cold metal chain that held his dog tags.

Her fingers paused as she passed over a slight indentation just below his collarbone. Fitz flinched when she touched his scar, but her fingers continued their gentle arc from his chest across his shoulders to his arm. She drew her finger along the curves of his muscles, down along one of the veins that snaked over his forearm to his hand before finally coming to rest on his white-gold wedding band.

Fitz let her rub his ring a few times before he looked up and captured her fingers with his thumb, holding them tightly as she stared into his eyes. Releasing her fingers, he took the hem of her lemon yellow tank top and pulled it up. A crooked smile crossed his lips as he slipped it over her head and let it fall to the floor.

"God, you're beautiful," he whispered, dragging his index finger from the notch at the base of her neck down to the shadowed cleft between her breasts.

She groaned quietly as her hand slipped down to his belt. After working it free of the buckle, she tugged it through the belt loops, swiping a finger over the edge of his navel as she pulled it free. Smiling at the way his muscles tensed at the contact, she paused just long enough to let him unclasp her bra before thumbing open the waistband of his shorts.

Jenn's eyes widened at finding him naked beneath his shorts and she reached for him, her body flushing in anticipation. His hips thrust into her as she closed her hand around him, and he sucked in a sharp breath, the contact coming as a shock after not being touched for so long. Soon, his hands and fingers were everywhere, quickly stripping her of her skirt, bra, and panties, desperately seeking bare skin. Bringing his lips to her neck, he licked and nipped at her delicate skin, firmly enough to make her shiver but not hard enough to leave marks.

He walked her backward, pushing her onto the bed. Moving up her body on his hands and knees, he planted kisses on her belly, brushing his lips across the gentle curve of her abdomen. He licked her navel, murmuring unintelligible endearments into her skin, stroking his fingers along her side as she twisted against the sheets. He turned his attentions lower, dragging his lips over the three faint scars left by her emergency hysterectomy. Nine years after the miscarriage, the marks had faded to shimmery reminders of the difficult times they had faced together.

Fitz hovered over her, his entire body alive with hunger and taut with anticipation, yet he suddenly hesitated. Her chest tightened as her thighs pressed against his square, bony hips, and her breath hitched high in her throat.

It had been so long.

Too long.

Too long since he'd loomed over her like this with flushed, glistening skin, his eyes glimmering and dark with desire. Jenn scraped her nails down his back as her lips mouthed an inaudible plea. He closed his eyes and rocked his hips against her but despite her urging, he still hesitated.

"Please, Jacob …"

She swept a hand across his chest, flicking his nipple with her nail, drawing a groan from him as he finally sank into her.

As he began to move, she remembered the last time they were together like this. It was the night before he shipped off to Afghanistan—nine months earlier. The memory of that night flickered through her mind as they made love. Each time he moved, she rolled her hips up to meet him, dragging her nails down his sides the way she knew he liked. He leaned into his forearms as he rocked into her, wincing a little as her heels dug hard into the backs of his thighs. She sighed as he pressed his lips to her throat, the hum of his murmurs tickling her skin before he turned his head and moaned as they came apart together.

CHAPTER 20

A light breeze blew through the window, cooling the flushed skin left bare by the sheet draped carelessly over their lower halves.

Fitz propped one of his arms on the pillow behind his head while hugging the other loosely around Jenn, who lay with her head on his chest. He dragged the pads of his fingers between her vertebrae, caressing her sweat-slicked skin. When she curled her body more snugly against his side in response to his touch, he smiled. She stroked her thumb over the space in the middle of his chest, right below his dog tags, picking up the hair with the edge of her thumb on the upstroke then smoothing it down. Their caresses fell into sync as they enjoyed the comfortable silence.

A hooting owl startled them from their daze.

"There are more of those here now than there were when I was growing up," Fitz stated. "Owls, I mean. I'm not sure why. Maybe all the development brought more critters for them to eat. I dunno."

Her thumb stilled as she glanced up at the open window, then she continued her stroking.

"Which ones sound like horses?" she asked.

He turned his head, a strange look on his face. "What?"

"The owls, I mean. You know, like ..." Jenn made a whinnying sound high in her throat, which brought a snort of laughter from Fitz. "Oh, come on. That's what they sound like."

Fitz snickered and pressed a kiss to her forehead. "I think it's kinda hot when you make animal noises."

"Hush, you." Jenn slapped his chest and rolled her eyes. "I'm serious, though. What kind are those?"

"Screech owls, I think. But that one—" He paused, waiting to see if the noisy owl would sound off again, but the bird held its silence. "That one we heard's probably a barred owl."

Taking a cue from the owl, they remained quiet for another few minutes before Fitz nuzzled her hair and spoke, his whisper warming her scalp with each word.

"So, does this mean we're back?"

"Back?"

Back where? she wondered. *Back to what?* She pursed her lips, focusing on the curve where Fitz's waist swept toward his hip to avoid his gaze. *The iliac furrow,* she thought, distracting herself with a silent survey of his anatomy. She traced the sharp curve formed by a ligament as it ran along the edge of his hip to the pubis bone. She'd missed his body and the freedom to explore it, more than she had been willing to admit during the weeks they'd been apart, and the long, lonely months before that when he pushed her away.

Unnerved by her apparent discomfort, Fitz turned and kissed her forehead, letting his lips linger there.

"You and me, I mean. Does this—you know, tonight—mean we're back to where we were before?"

Jenn blinked.

"We'll never get back to where we were before." She rubbed her lips against the downy hair on his chest, grounding herself against the anxiety pooling in her belly. "That place where we were? It doesn't exist anymore, Fitz. Those people we used to be? I don't think they exist anymore, either."

The gentle rise and fall of his chest stilled beneath her cheek.

"I haven't had a drop to drink since that night." His voice was clipped as his hand came to rest on the small of her back. "I watched that cab drive away, Jenn, and I went inside and poured it all out. Every fucking ounce. Every beer. The Cuervo. Both bottles of Jack I'd bought at the Class Six. Even that unopened bottle of expensive Caol Ila single malt I picked up on the way back from Tblisi a couple years ago. That half a bottle of white wine you had in the fridge. I even threw out the cough medicine in the pantry." He closed his eyes and took a deep breath, swallowing hard as he loosened his hold on her. "I got rid of it all. Every drop. I gave it up. All of it."

"I know," she whispered.

His heart pounded beneath her hand.

"But what about the Percocet?"

A dark wave of foreboding washed over her and every muscle in his body tensed at her question. "A few days after we left for Oregon, I remembered that I'd left it in the house, but when I got there this afternoon and looked in the medicine cabinet, it was gone."

Jenn knew that there was no need to voice the question that had gnawed at her all afternoon. Dread swirled in her gut as she prayed that her fear wasn't true. She sensed his hesitation as his skin become dotted with goosebumps and his hand trembled against her hip.

A minute passed before he said a word.

"When I gave up the booze …"

His voice was thick and edged with trepidation.

"It got harder to fall asleep, you know, because I couldn't just drink myself into a stupor on the couch. Some nights, I couldn't fall asleep at all. I tried lots of things. I'd go for a long run in the evenings, hoping to tire my ass out, but that kind of made it worse, so I'd try a six-mile run every morning, but that still didn't help. I tried Tylenol PM, which seemed to help a little, but I had to take three times the recommended dose to feel even a little drowsy. Then I figured out that the 'PM' in Tylenol PM was actually Benadryl, so I'd take three of those instead, just trying to knock my ass out so I could get some kind of sleep before the …"

He squirmed, shifting his hips against the sheets as if the very thoughts in his head made his skin crawl. Jenn wondered what it was that troubled his dreams. She had her suspicions, but Fitz had said almost nothing about what happened over there. Even now, five months after his return, she knew little more than what they told her when she got the call: that he'd been injured by an IED that took the lives of Sergeant First Class Matt Peterson and four Afghans they were on patrol with.

She remembered the dazed expression on his face when she first saw him at Brooke Army Medical Center in San Antonio. His eyes were glassy and unfocused, his pupils mere pinpoints from the fentanyl they'd given him for pain and the benzodiazepine used to sedate him during the flight from Germany. Gauze was wrapped snugly around his right arm and leg, and a half-dozen other bandages dotted his right shoulder, upper chest and hip. Doctors told her that, in addition to the shrapnel injuries, he had also suffered a significant concussion—a *blast neurotrauma*, they called it—as a result of the pressure wave created by the IED when it detonated.

"The dreams," she prompted him with a whisper, stroking her fingers across the soft nest of hair on his chest. "I know."

Fitz took a deep breath and sighed as he hugged her closer.

"There was this one night." His lips were just a fraction of an inch from her hairline, close enough for her to feel each syllable on her brow. "I got woke up by another one of my dreams, and, well, it was so damn real that even when I got out of bed, it was still in my head, you know? Like a movie, but it kept on playing even after I woke up. I couldn't get it to stop, you know, couldn't flush it out of my head. It just kept going and going."

He swallowed and Jenn turned her head slightly to press a kiss to his chest. She knew, could *feel*, how hard this was for him.

"Somehow, I remembered I had the meds they gave me after my last surgery. And so I went into the medicine cabinet, but with my hands shaking and the stupid cast on my hand, and I guess being as freaked out as I was by the dream, I couldn't get the damn bottle open. I really wanted to, though." He swallowed again and Jenn heard a liquid quality in his voice as his emotions bled into each and every word. "But I couldn't get the bottle open. So I put it back."

"But I looked, Jacob. Today, and it wasn't there."

"I know." His tone was flat except for a twinge of something she sensed was guilt.

"A couple weeks after that, it happened again. I'd finally managed to fall asleep, but after a couple of hours I got woke up again by one of my dreams. I get these dreams a lot—four, maybe five nights out of seven? A lot. Anyway, that night I was just exhausted 'cause I'd had a real bad streak of like nine nights in a row where the dreams would wake me up. I looked like shit."

Fitz looked down at her with a little grin and gave her arm a squeeze.

"A lot worse than I look now. Anyways, I went into the medicine cabinet again and grabbed the Percocet. I had four ten milligram tablets left—a total of forty milligrams' worth, right?

Enough to knock me on my ass for a good six or seven hours."

"Jacob." Her eyes welled up as she imagined him standing in front of the bathroom mirror with dark circles under his eyes, drenched in a cold sweat. "Jesus, baby." She sniffed, trying to hold back her tears as she waited for him to admit what he'd done. Her mind raced as she wondered what to do next, who to call, and what would happen if she told someone at Carson—

"But I couldn't do it. I looked down at your and Ryan's names tattooed on my arm, and looked at myself in the mirror, and I knew I couldn't do it." He kissed her hair, snuffling away his tears as he held her tight against his chest. "God, Jenn, I just wanted to *sleep*, to forget about it all for a while, to be able to just get through a whole fucking night without seeing and hearing and thinking about it all, and I really wanted to do it, but I knew I couldn't, because if I did that, I'd be letting you two down. Again."

Jenn smiled and wiped her eyes with the palm of her hand. "So what did you do?"

"I went down to the kitchen. Into the junk drawer where we keep the little hammer we use to hang up pictures and stuff, you know? And I smashed those little fuckers into a powder. Then I rinsed 'em down the sink." He grunted out a sardonic laugh. "What's the street value of that shit, babe? Two hundred bucks? I dunno. But, anyway, I washed it down the drain and threw the bottle in the trash."

"Really?"

"Yep," he said, unable to hide the flicker of pride in his voice. "Never touched it. God, I wanted to like you wouldn't fuckin' believe, Jenn, but I didn't. I looked at this …" He let go of her and brandished his tattooed forearm where they both could see it. "I looked at your name, and Ryan's, and I knew I couldn't. I just couldn't do it."

"I'm proud of you." She looked up and kissed the soft skin on the underside of his chin, the only part of his face she could reach from where she lay.

"Thanks." He blushed at her praise. "Sleeping's still a bitch, but Mr. Melatonin is my friend, and he helps a bit. Him and his buddy, Benadryl. I apologize in advance if I have one of my shitty dreams and wake you up tonight."

Jenn ruffled his chest hair. "Like that's anything new, hmm?"

Fitz kissed her forehead. She purred, then squealed when he suddenly pushed her off of his chest and rolled over so he was straddling her, leaning over her with a smile the likes of which she hadn't seen from him in nearly a year.

He nudged her knees apart and took his place between them with a crooked grin.

"There's one thing better than melatonin, you know."

CHAPTER 21

Dust hung in the air, covering every inch of their skin, caking their tongues and throats as Fitz and the men behind him shook off the numbing haze.

"Kumak koneen!"

Voices called out from the end of the block, begging for help as their overlapping cries flooded into Fitz's mind as a jumble. He heard the murmur of Afghan voices and the scraping of boots against sand, but it all sounded so distant and strange as the throbbing in his head pounded away behind his eyeballs.

All he could think about was the burning.

Everything burned—his arm, his leg, his neck, his shoulder, in a dozen places from his shin up to his armpit—and everything hurt, everywhere, as if he'd had the shit kicked out of him by a gang of guys twice his size, been set on fire, and thrown into a ravine.

"Shoma khoob mesheen," he reassured them as he struggled to his feet. "You'll be okay. It's gonna be okay."

Jenn reached for him, skimming his shoulder with the pads of her fingers. His skin, like the sheets beneath him, was soaked with sweat.

"It's okay," she whispered, her breath hitching in the back of her throat. "Shhhhh, Jacob, it's okay. You're safe, we're fine, and it's gonna be okay. Shhhhh."

Fitz shivered. The bedroom window was open, but even with the cool morning air wafting against his sweaty skin, he still should not have been cold.

"Shhhhh…"

She assumed he'd been dreaming about the IED attack, but she wasn't sure.

She was never really sure. Before—even before she and Ryan had left—he never let her in on exactly what happened over there. He never shared the memories that made it hard for him to fall asleep. He never spoke of the dreams that woke him in a cold sweat. He never let her get close for long enough to ask.

The specialists at the Army hospital in San Antonio told her he'd survived an event that was deeply traumatizing, both physically and mentally, but, given his training and experience, they were confident that he would come around once settled back into family life.

But Fitz never settled in, and he never opened up. For the first few weeks after he got out of the hospital, the pain from his injuries made even basic activities like bathing and moving around the house a struggle. As the physical wounds healed, his mood began to sour. He pulled away from his family and disappeared into himself. For months, he dug in and hid behind an impenetrable wall of booze and silence, hardly saying more than a few dozen words to her or Ryan on any given day.

But now, despite the sad occasion for their reunion, he seemed to be better—not perfect, and not the way he was before the IED, but still, better—and more open than before.

Maybe he's turned the corner, she thought as she slowly snaked her arm around his waist and held his shaking body to her chest.

"It's okay. Shhhh."

She whispered soothingly against the back of his neck, wondering as she held him whether it was helping or whether he'd panic and lash out in his sleep, as had happened a couple of times before. Eventually, though, his ragged, heaving breaths eased, he stopped shaking and slipped once more into what she hoped was a dreamless sleep. After listening carefully to the rise and fall of his breaths and the quiet snore that passed between his lips, she joined him.

"Hope you don't mind."

Sergeant First Class Matt Peterson leaned over the bar with a grin as he accepted a new pint of Fat Tire from the kid working behind the taps.

"I told my roommate he could join us when he got done with his softball game up at Skyview."

Fitz tipped back his Sierra Nevada and drained the last of it in two swallows. "Sure, Doc. No problem. As long as he doesn't expect me to buy his beers."

Peterson laughed. "Figures, you cheap son of a bitch—but no, I'll cover his." He rolled his eyes, raised his brimming glass, took a careful sip, then set it down on the bar. "Always were a cheap fucker."

Amusement twinkled in Fitz's eyes as he wondered why Peterson shared an apartment. The medic did pretty well with an E-7's salary and bachelor housing allowance, plus jump pay, hardship duty pay for the two months they just spent on an advising mission in Mali, and a Foreign Language Proficiency Bonus. Fitz figured Doc simply didn't like living alone and opted for a roommate since it was impossible to keep a pet given how frequently they had to deploy or go out in the field for training. But it still struck him as odd.

"Cody, right?" Fitz tried to recall the name of Peterson's roommate, who worked as a paramedic for the Colorado Springs Fire

Department.

"Yeah." Peterson grinned as he glanced down at his watch. "He said it was an early game this week so he should be along anytime now."

Fitz's stomach growled. He'd just reached for the appetizer menu when Peterson's stool scraped against the floor. Turning around, Fitz saw the medic's eyes light up as he stood and gave a hearty one-armed hug to the tall, raven-haired newcomer.

"Hey." Peterson's voice was soft as he tousled Cody's sweaty hair, leaving it a clumpy mess of black spikes that stuck up in a dozen directions. Swatting Peterson's hand away, Cody rolled his eyes and surveyed the taps.

"Fat Tire?" he asked, pointing to the rich amber ale in Peterson's glass. Peterson grinned and nodded, then gestured for the bartender to bring him another of the same. "Hell, this might be the best beer I've had all week."

Fitz picked up his empty bottle of Sierra Nevada and waggled it in the air at the bartender who acknowledged him with an upward jerk of his goateed chin. "So, did you guys win your game?" he asked with a lopsided grin, tapping the empty bottle against his lip as he peered over at the firefighter.

Cody looked at Fitz with narrow eyes, then laughed.

"Nah." He snatched his beer from the bartender's hand as soon as it came within reach. "Our cleanup batter had to switch shifts with another guy so we had to shuffle the lineup. The first baseman can't hit worth shit, so—"

Fitz smirked. "Oops."

Cody stared into his beer for a second, then looked up with a sheepish grin and shrugged as he brought the pint glass to his lips. "Yeah, Fire Station Number 7 actually got blanked tonight. Shut out."

He took a long sip and set his glass down with a heavy clank.

"Moynihan had to switch shifts 'cause his boy's screwing up in school and his wife couldn't get off work to make the parent-teacher conference so, yeah, guess that's the breaks. We're playin' Station 5 next week. Last time we played those guys we hammered 'em by five runs, so—"

Peterson reached over and clapped Cody on the back, then gave his shoulder a quick squeeze. The firefighter leaned in a little and nudged his housemate in the arm. The pair clinked glasses then drank, and for a few seconds, Fitz was certain the two of them had forgotten he was even there.

Fitz woke to the screech of hydraulic brakes and the grinding crunch of a garbage truck compactor.

He shaded his eyes with his hand, grimacing at the unfamiliar bedside table and the wrinkled peach-colored sheets draped over his hip.

Fitz rolled away from the sun, wincing at the twinge in his lower back, then saw the reason for his soreness. His eyes roamed the curve of Jenn's shoulder and followed the long line from her armpit along her side to where the swell of her hip disappeared beneath the sheet. Before him lay a plane of creamy skin dotted with faint freckles where the sun had left its marks.

Fitz moved closer, bringing his hips right behind hers. The sheet pulled away, exposing his back to the warm morning sun. He kissed her shoulder, brushing his lips across her skin as he nudged her bottom with a gentle thrust. Jenn groaned softly and reached back to touch his thigh, skimming her fingertips over the soft brown curls on his legs. Her caress sent a tingle racing up Fitz's spine and he leaned in, pressing wet kisses against the back of her neck.

Encouraged by her giggles, he snaked his arm around her waist and drew a quick circle around her navel with his finger, distracting her with kisses as his hand migrated downward.

"God, woman." Her left leg slid forward, granting him the access he craved. "You drive me crazy, you know that?"

Her response was a murmured chuckle followed by a gasp when he sank into her, oblivious to the rustling in the kitchen below.

They made love, awash in sensation: the sweet, musky smell of sex; the unique softness of warm skin that's been cocooned in bed for seven hours; the whispered movements woven of unhurried enthusiasm. Fitz's arm wrapped a little tighter around her waist with every rolling stroke. When they broke, they did so in near silence, his cry moaned into the damp skin of her shoulder followed by hers, muffled by the pillow as she shattered around him.

Minutes passed wordlessly. Their flushed, sticky bodies slowly peeled apart and sprawled out in a bed that had been his twenty years ago. The noises of morning filtered up to their bedroom as the unmistakable hiss of a cracked egg hitting a buttered pan signaled the beginning of the day.

Jenn rolled over to face her husband, who lay on his back with one arm propped behind his head as he held the sheet against his belly with the other.

"You need to talk to him. Ryan, I mean."

Fitz sighed, braving the light from the window to avoid her eyes. "He hates me."

"No," she insisted, scraping one of the creases in the sheet with her fingernail. "He doesn't. But he thinks he does."

Fitz's jaw tensed as he turned to her with a scowl. "What's that mean? If he thinks he hates me, that means he hates me."

She stroked her thumb against one of the deeper scars, a jagged two-inch-long pink line that ran from his elbow across his bicep. "He doesn't hate you, Jacob. He's angry. He's angry and he's hurt.

He feels like his dad doesn't love him anymore, and nothing I tell him can convince him otherwise."

He sucked a sharp breath between his teeth as her finger traced a path along another grooved scar. "I really fucked up." He pulled his arm away from her defensively.

"You should talk to him. Really sit down and talk to him. Just the two of you, father and son. He's not a little boy anymore. He's a young man and he needs his father. He needs someone to look up to. At some level, subconsciously maybe, I think he knows that. He just wants to spend time with you, Fitz—to *be* with you." She paused to glance at the alarm clock on the nightstand. "I need to run out to King Soopers this morning and pick up some things," she said, changing the subject. "And order some food for Wednesday afternoon."

Fitz chewed his lip. He remembered the uneasy look in his son's eyes when they walked in the house the day before.

"I'll drop you two off at the pool." A faint smirk danced across her lips when he looked at her strangely. "I packed both of your swim trunks when we went by the house yesterday."

"Okay, but you'll still—"

His voice wavered and Jenn gave him a reassuring smile.

"I'll run by King Soopers. I'll do what I need to do, bring the groceries back here, then your mom and I will grab our swimsuits and join you at the pool. That'll give you an hour or so to yourselves."

Butterflies fluttered in Fitz's belly.

"Why am I nervous about taking my boy to the pool? I've been dropped into a hostile country behind enemy lines with nothing but an assault pack and a rifle, but I'm freaking out about taking my twelve-year-old to the fucking neighborhood pool. What kind of fucking asshole am I?"

"You're not an asshole." Jenn pressed a kiss to the round, firm edge of his bicep. "It'll be fine, I promise. Just …"

His brows knit suspiciously. "What?"

"Don't be afraid." She brushed her lips across the pockmarked skin of his arm. "Don't be afraid to bare yourself to him—the way you did to me. We're in this together—you, me, and Ryan. Let him in, Jacob, the way you let me in." She looked up and saw a flicker in the watery depths of his hazel eyes.

"You're his father. He loves you and he admires you. So let him in."

CHAPTER 22

"How many eggs you want, Ry?"

The question caught Ryan by surprise. After a moment, the boy looked up at his father and shrugged. "Three, please."

A proud grin cut across Fitz's face. "All right, then." He reached into the cabinet to grab two large pans, one for eggs and one for bacon.

Ryan sat at the table, flipping through the copy of *Hockey News* he'd retrieved the day before from the stack of mail, trying his best to ignore the noise behind him. Every so often, he'd glance over his shoulder at his father, watching him flip the bacon in the pan and tuck the bread into the toaster. He couldn't remember the last time his father made a breakfast that consisted of anything other than cold cereal.

"Over-easy, right?"

"That's fine," Ryan grumbled, his brow arching at the question. Since when did anyone care what *he* wanted? He rolled his eyes and returned to his magazine. His father's demeanor was pleasant and chatty, suspiciously so compared to what he'd grown used to, and Ryan didn't know what to make of the shift, which struck him as weird and more than a little unnerving.

Breakfast was a quiet affair between father and son. Each dug into his eggs, toast, and bacon with fervor. Each time Fitz sought eye contact, Ryan did his best to avoid it. The strained silence between them was made less awkward by the animated conversation between Ryan's mother and grandmother, who were seated next to their respective sons brainstorming a list of groceries to tide the family over until after the funeral. When the women left the kitchen, each gave Fitz an odd look as they passed by—one that reminded Ryan of the kind his mom gave him after his hockey team gave up a goal.

Fitz stood up and grabbed their dirty dishes, determined to wash them before the yolk congealed into the yellow cement that only dried egg could create. The carton sat open on the counter, its empty pockets proof the half-dozen eggs the two of them had wiped out in a single breakfast. Seeing his father preoccupied with rinsing a stubborn smear of gooey yolk off a plate, Ryan slid his chair out quickly, eager to put some space between them. The screech of the chair against the hardwood floor made him wince, but when his father didn't turn around, he figured he had a clean getaway. *Maybe he won't notice,* he thought.

"Hey, Ryan," Fitz called out, stopping him on his way to the stairs.

"What?" Ryan snapped. Ignoring his son's insolent tone, Fitz set the dish in the drying rack, wiped his hands with a towel, then tossed it on the counter. Ryan slinked back down the stairs.

"Why don't you go up and put your bathing suit on? Mom's gonna drop us off at the pool on her way to the store."

"I don't want to go swimming." Ryan stuffed his hands in his shorts pockets and stared at his feet, refusing to meet his father's gaze.

"You don't have to swim," Fitz told him. "But we're gonna go to the pool so we can get outta Mom and Grandma's hair for a while, okay? They've got some stuff to take care of and then they'll join us at the pool."

"I don't need a babysitter, *Dad*." The last snide syllable stuck like a knife in wood.

"I know you don't." Fitz swallowed nervously as he put the butter and raspberry jam back in the fridge. "But …"

Fitz hesitated, recalling his wife's words that morning. *Don't be afraid to bare yourself to him.* For twelve years, he'd tried to make his son's life as normal as possible, shielding him from the ugliest parts of a soldier's life. But in the end, he couldn't, and Fitz wondered if in trying he'd done more harm than good.

"Maybe I just want some company."

Ryan looked up. That was the last thing he would ever have expected to hear after months of the silent treatment. Ryan's eyes narrowed with deep skepticism as he tried to make sense of it inside his head.

The whole thing was confusing.

Ryan recalled the afternoon before his dad's last deployment. The two of them had gone out for pizza then played catch in the backyard for a little while before Ryan went over to his friend Brandon's house for the night so his parents could have some "alone time." He remembered the sad, resigned look on their faces when they picked him up the next morning. The three of them went to IHOP for breakfast, which allowed them one last chance to spend time together as a family before heading to the gymnasium for Bravo Company's deployment ceremony.

The Dad he had pizza and played catch with that warm October afternoon, and who he hugged and said goodbye to the next day wasn't the same Dad who came back. After the last few awful months, Ryan wasn't sure he would ever see the old Dad again.

He wondered if this was just an act his dad was putting up until after the funeral, when he'd return to the usual routine again. Ryan wasn't sure, but he was tired of getting his hopes up only to be disappointed over and over again. After the embarrassment of his last birthday, he stopped expecting his dad to be anything other than an asshole.

He heard his mom's footsteps coming down the stairs. "Fine."

"Great," Fitz replied as Jenn walked back into the kitchen. "Go get changed and maybe grab a couple towels from Grandma's linen closet, hmm? Lemme just finish up here and I'll go change, too, then we can head out, okay?"

The boy's eyes were tense, his mouth held in a hard, suspicious line as he nodded slowly. "Yeah, okay," he muttered before disappearing into the foyer.

Jenn turned to Fitz. "You should go up and get dressed, too." She snatched the half-and-half out of his hand and tapped him lightly on the backside.

"All right already," he groused as he made his way to the stairs.

"Don't forget there's water shoes in the suitcase and sunscreen in the medicine cabinet," she called to him. "Ryan hasn't spent much time in the sun this summer—he'll burn, Fitz."

"Got it, Jenn!" he hollered back from the top of the stairs, his voice edged with an audible smile.

CHAPTER 23

It was still early when Jenn dropped them off at the neighborhood pool.

Fitz watched as the Scout pulled away, following it until it disappeared and the growl of its engine faded from earshot.

Once the Scout was out of sight, Fitz turned and watched Ryan walk along the edge of the pool. The boy surveyed the long line of empty lounge chairs before finally dropping his backpack and towel on the one nearest the diving board. Toeing off his sandals, Ryan shook his head at a couple cooing over an infant in water wings in the shallow end and scrunched his nose at the elderly woman walking laps across the middle of the pool. He had just peeled off his T-shirt when his father's voice approached from behind.

"Don't forget your water shoes. I put 'em in your backpack."

Ryan swung his head around with a dark scowl. "I'm not a baby, Dad," he snapped as his father dropped his things on the chair next to his.

"Never said you were."

Fitz heard the anger in his son's voice, but he tried not to show his anxiety as he draped his towel over the back of the chair and slipped off his flip-flops. The concrete felt strange and rough beneath his feet, an acute reminder of how long it had been since he'd spent any time hanging around a swimming pool. He stared at his feet, wiggling his toes on the pavement, remembering a younger Ryan splashing around in this very same pool two summers ago, not long after Fitz returned from a previous six-month-tour in Afghanistan.

"Mom says you're doing really great in hockey."

He waited to see if the compliment would make Ryan look up, but the boy kept his eyes focused on the pool.

"I'm just thinkin' that it'd be a real bummer if you rubbed the skin off the bottoms of your big toes the way you did last summer when you spent three hours playing Marco Polo at Justin's birthday party."

With only a roll of his eyes to acknowledge his father's point, Ryan grabbed his knapsack, set it on his lap, and unzipped it roughly. After some rummaging, he yanked out a pair of mesh water shoes and slapped them on the pavement.

"You gonna wear some, too, Dad?" Ryan inspected his goggles for a moment before snapping them on and propping the eyepieces atop his fluffy brown bangs. "Or is this something you just get to tell me to do?"

"I brought mine," Fitz said, forcing a smile. "I gotta go back in the field in a couple of weeks, and the last thing I need is to rub the pads of my feet raw. So, yeah—I'm gonna wear mine."

"It feels weird swimming in them," Ryan complained as he slipped into the bright blue mesh shoes. "It's like wearing flippers."

Fitz offered an apologetic shrug, sensing that a "Do as I say, not as I do" approach would blow up in his face. "I know, but it beats the alternative."

He unzipped his own backpack, noticing how small and flimsy it was compared to the tactical packs he was used to humping in the field. He retrieved his own water shoes and a sweat-stained, sun-faded Colorado State ball cap, then looked up to catch his son watching him before the boy turned away. Fitz pulled the hat low over his eyes and tucked his sunglasses behind his ears to rest on the brim.

"Hey." Fitz's verbal nudge prompted Ryan to look up. "Did you put your sunscreen on?" The boy replied with a minute shake of his head. "Here, let me get your back, okay? Then you can do the rest."

Once the sunscreen was applied, Ryan ran to the edge of the pool and cannonballed in, sending a huge spray of water in all directions. His head and shoulders bobbed above the water, then disappeared again as the boy drew a deep breath and dove under, swimming all the way down to the bottom of the pool's deepest section. After a few seconds, he surfaced, nearly leaping out of the water before doing it all over again.

Fitz sat on the edge of his lounge chair and watched with fascination as Ryan forced himself to stay underwater longer each time he dove down. He preferred the deep end and had tackled swimming like he did everything else—fearlessly and head first, never doing anything by half-measure. As Fitz sat and quietly watched his son swim alone, he saw a part of himself each time Ryan's rubber-soled feet disappeared underneath the water.

Ryan dove twelve feet down to the bottom, swimming underwater from one side of the pool to the other before surfacing again. When he came up for air, red-faced and gasping but with a goofy smile hanging off his lips, Fitz knew that, regardless of what had happened between them since his return from Afghanistan, they shared a certain stubbornness and drive.

Jenn's plea again echoed in his mind.

"He just wants to spend time with you, Fitz—to be with you."

Fitz stood up, yanked off his hat and sunglasses, then took a long, slow breath, steeling himself for what came next.

"Don't be afraid. Don't be afraid to bare yourself to him."

He gave himself an encouraging nod and reached for the bottom hem of his T-shirt. Dismissing the anxious swirl in his belly, he peeled his shirt off, tossed it on the back of the lounge chair and turned around.

He watched the young couple at the shallow end of the pool as the woman handed the baby to her husband. She turned and looked up at Fitz, meeting his eyes briefly before giving him a casual but obvious once-over. He felt exposed, the rosy constellation of scars and gouges that streaked his arm, leg, side, and shoulder laid bare to her as he stood there. When he finally looked away, Fitz felt her eyes linger on him.

Her gaze was the reason he usually wore jeans when he went off-post. Scars like his were a common enough sight at Fort Carson that he never felt the stares. In the southern part of Colorado Springs nearest the post, Fitz felt comfortable enough to wear shorts or a tank top on a hot day. But once he ventured into places where soldiers were more of an oddity, he covered up to avoid the looks.

Fuck 'em, he told himself. *You're not here for them. You're here for him.* He drew a deep breath and let it out slowly, trying to exhale all of his anxiety and irritation before turning to face his son.

Fitz walked to the edge of the pool. Ryan was in the corner of the deep end, taking a break from his dive-swim-surface routine. The boy watched Fitz toe the rounded tile lip of the pool, his scowling eyes softened by curiosity. The cool clear water lapped quietly against the wall, and Fitz let his mind sink into the gentle, almost metronomic, sound. His hazel eyes flicked up to meet his son's green ones before he leaned forward and dove in. He swept his arms in front of him, leaving the tiniest possible splash in his wake as he disappeared underwater.

A couple of seconds later, Fitz's head popped up a few feet away from Ryan. He swam over to the side of the pool, draping his arms over the edge while he settled into a comfortable spot. Closing his eyes, he felt the cool water lick against his nipples as the late morning sun warmed his arms and shoulders.

Ryan studied his father, a faint smile on Fitz's lips as his head lolled back against the round edge of the pool. It was the first time he'd seen his father this way since, well, he wasn't exactly sure because Fitz had spent the better part of the six months prior to his last deployment in the field training. In the months before he went overseas, he'd venture out into the field for a week or two or three, not only at Fort Carson but also at a Colorado National Guard high-altitude aviation facility west of Vail and at Fort Wainwright in Alaska. Ryan remembered the hand-carved totem pole his dad had brought back from Alaska a month before he shipped off to Afghanistan.

He kept treading water, scissor-kicking every so often to avoid drifting too close to the edge of the pool, and tried to remember the last time he had seen his dad without a shirt on. It had been a very long time. Even at the hospital at Fort Sam Houston, Fitz wore a thin, blue hospital gown that covered his chest and upper arms.

Ryan looked at the scars on his father's right arm, following them as they wove like little pink rivers across his arm, threading in between the pebbly skin underneath the flat, wet hair on his forearm. It seemed weird that, even though Ryan had seen them dozens of times, this was the first time he had actually paid close attention to them. The shortest one, just an inch long, followed the outside edge of his dad's forearm from his wrist across the top of his forearm. Another, almost parallel to the shorter one and only slightly longer, picked up in the middle of his forearm and snaked toward his elbow. The last was two inches long and cut across the underside of his elbow and up to his bicep. Ryan remembered how, when the wounds were still fresh and healing, his dad would wince every time he bent his arm.

"Did it hurt?"

Ryan blurted out the question, his eyes wide with surprise at hearing his thoughts escape his head in an awkward tumble. His heart skipped a beat as he swam a couple of feet farther away, certain that his father would be furious that he'd asked about *it*.

It was the thing they never talked about—that *he* never talked about—even though *it* was the reason Fitz came home from Afghanistan eight weeks early—the reason he spent two weeks in a hospital in Texas, the reason that he acted angry all the time. *It* was the reason everything at home had turned upside down.

Ryan's breath hitched when his father's eyes snapped open. Fitz stared at him with a blank, unreadable expression, and the boy wasn't sure what to make of it. His heart thundered in his chest as he waited for Fitz to say something, anything, to save him from the uncertainty of it all.

Fitz tried to read the intent in Ryan's pinched, narrowed eyes, but he was at a loss. The connection he used to have with his son had been more or less severed, and he wasn't sure he would ever be able to repair it. He was afraid, sure that if he said the wrong thing, he would ruin everything between them and lose what remaining bond might still exist between them. The sour taste of fear rose in his throat.

"You mean the ..."

He swallowed, his Adam's apple bobbing as he remembered

Jenn's words and knew she was right. *"He's not a little boy anymore."* He looked at his son and saw the man Ryan was going to be emerging from the fading boyishness of his face, which Fitz realized was longer and more slender than it was when he deployed overseas ten months earlier.

"You mean the IED?"

Fitz's voice caught on the *e*. His memory of that day was tucked away in an overstuffed footlocker in the back of his mind with the rest of his wartime memories. He'd spent years trying to keep the footlocker locked down and secure. He felt its lid slowly creak open as he focused on his son's face and the brightness of his teeth, which, by some genetic fluke, were almost perfectly straight.

"Yeah," Ryan whispered, his nostrils flaring with unease. He nibbled the inside of his lip and swam a little closer, wincing as he braced for the response.

Fitz hesitated before answering. "Yeah, it hurt."

Ryan pressed the point, his innate curiosity getting the better of him.

"Was it loud?"

"I don't remember what it sounded like," Fitz admitted, drawing a sharp breath as a wave of dizziness washed over him. "It must've been loud, but I don't remember the sound. I just remember the pressure and the heat. And the flash. It happened in an instant." He snapped his fingers for emphasis. "The force of it was so powerful it blew out my eardrums."

The boy's brows leaped at that. "Really?"

"Yeah." Darkness tugged at Fitz from deep inside. As much as he didn't want to talk about it, he knew Ryan deserved to know—especially now, after all the three of them had gone through together because of it.

"I was 'bout forty feet away when it went off."

Fitz pushed away from the wall, pointing to the far end of the pool where the young couple with the baby had been. They were gone, replaced by a mother with a boy who looked about three and a girl he guessed was a year older.

"Like about the distance from here to where the lady and the kids are."

Ryan looked over at the woman and the two little kids splashing around, then turned back to his father.

"Were you, like, just out walking around and stuff? I mean, when it went off?"

Fitz's cheek twitched and he looked down, trying to focus himself by watching the water lap at his chest and feeling it move over his arms and through his fingers.

"Yeah." His raspy voice caught in his throat at the memory. "We were out on patrol—a mixed team of Americans and Afghans—in a little village called Kelalbat, in Kunar Province. It's in the northeastern part of the country, in the mountains near Pakistan."

"Did the medic fix you up? I mean, after the bomb went off?"

Fitz wasn't surprised by the question. Ryan's friend Brandon's dad was a medic in the 4th Infantry Division's 12th Infantry Regiment. Between that and Jenn's occupation as a nurse, Ryan was naturally curious about a medic's role. Still, the question struck a nerve and Fitz's gut churned as he tried to formulate an answer.

"No." A pair of piercing blue eyes glittered in Fitz's mind as he remembered the big Swede's toothy smile and booming laugh. "The bomb got him. He—" Fitz's voice cracked and he swam back toward the wall, grabbing onto it, struggling to catch his breath. "Peterson," he whispered. His pulse throbbed in his neck but he tried to ignore it. "You met him at the picnic last summer, remember?"

Ryan nodded. "Yeah, I remember. He seemed like a really nice guy."

Fitz sensed from the flicker in Ryan's eyes that the boy had more questions and that he was debating whether to ask them. He understood Ryan's ambivalence because he felt it in reverse. While he didn't want to stifle his son's curiosity, Fitz was tired of talking about Kelalbat and the IED, but he didn't want to silence Ryan after finally getting him to talk. And so the two bobbed quietly in the deep end of the pool, each treading water as he wondered whether to say more.

The metal gate creaked and with it came salvation.

Ryan and Fitz turned and saw Jenn and Diane approaching, clad in bathing suits and sarongs. Father and son swam to the side of the pool nearest their chairs and grabbed ahold of the rounded edge. Each wore a weary, sheepish smile as the women made their way toward the chairs draped with familiar-looking towels.

Fitz stole a glimpse of his wife's long, slender legs as she walked by, but Jenn caught him leering and rolled her eyes. Setting her tote bag on the lounge chair next to his, she turned to him with an arched brow that begged for an answer to an unspoken question. Fitz pressed his lips together in a firm line and nodded.

Diane watched their silent exchange out of the corner of her eye, then winked at her only grandchild, a soft, sweet smile on her lips.

"Did you bring lunch?" Ryan asked. "Ya know, 'cause I'm kinda hungry."

Jenn chuckled at the cheeky question and answered with a teasing gleam in her eyes. "Guess you'll have to get out of the pool to find out."

Fitz clung to the edge of the pool as Ryan clambered up the ladder. Water ran off the boy's husky frame in long sheets, drenching everything in his path.

"But you're not getting anything until you dry off, young man!" Jenn threw a towel at him.

Fitz finally let go of the nervous breath he'd been holding and laughed, then swam his way to the ladder to join them.

CHAPTER 24

Fitz scowled at the five balled-up wads of paper scattered on the table in front of him.

Together, they testified to the two hours he'd spent staring at the yellow notepad in frustration, waiting for inspiration to strike. The moment the doorbell rang, he jumped up, threw his pen down, and jogged into the foyer before anyone else could get there.

He opened the door to find Remy standing under the porch light. Dressed casually in jeans, loafers, and a polo shirt, the chaplain carried a small duffel in one hand and a garment bag in the other. Fitz greeted him with a grateful smile, then ushered him into the waiting arms of his mother, who drew Remy into a warm hug.

"Nice to see you again, ma'am." The chaplain shot Fitz a wide-eyed, solicitous look but in return got only an amused snort.

"Have you eaten dinner?" Diane didn't wait for Remy's answer before nudging him toward the kitchen. "I just put the leftovers in the fridge. They're still warm."

Fitz shook his head and grinned at his mother's incorrigible hospitality, then took Remy's bags and disappeared up the stairs. The house's fourth bedroom, which had for years been Roger Fitzgerald's home office, had an old but comfortable foldout sofa bed. The afternoon after her husband's death, Diane returned from the funeral home and set herself to tidying up the dusty office so the sweet-faced chaplain could stay with them rather than at a hotel. Fitz knew that playing hostess to Remy would give his mother a little joy to distract her from her grief, and, for his part, he was grateful to have his friend around.

By the time Fitz returned to the kitchen, his mother had the chaplain seated at the table across from Fitz's notepad and paper wads. The microwave dinged and out came a plate piled high with roast chicken, peas, carrots, pearl onions, and potatoes au gratin. Remy tucked into his late dinner, no doubt encouraged by the pair of maternal eyes that watched to ensure he didn't leave the table hungry.

A few minutes later, Jenn emerged from the utility room with two perfectly pressed white dress shirts on hangers. She set the shirts on the hook on the back of the utility room door, then turned her attention to their newly-arrived guest.

"You must be Remy." She walked up to the table and stood behind Fitz, putting her hand on his shoulder as she greeted the other soldier with a smile. "I apologize for not coming out earlier, but I was in the middle of starching the shirts when you got here." She smirked as the chaplain swallowed and quickly wiped the gravy from his lip. "I guess Diane's already seen to it that you're properly fed and watered."

Remy stood up from his seat and reached across the table to offer her his hand. "Yes, ma'am. And you must be Jenn. Fitz's told me a lot about you."

Fitz glanced up from his pad of paper, arching his head back to look at his wife. "I was, uh, going to introduce you two, but—"

"You're a bit late, hon." Jenn noted the still-blank sheet of paper in front of him and tempered her teasing by gently squeezing his arm. "The iron's still hot," she told Remy. "If your shirt needs a touch-up, I don't mind. It'll just take a couple of minutes."

The offer took the chaplain by surprise. "Oh, umm …" He raised his hands in protest. "It's not necessary, really."

"It's no trouble, really. I'll go upstairs and fetch it out of your room."

Remy grabbed his plate. "Really, I'm sure you've got plenty to deal with tonight, and tomorrow's going to be a long day for all of you—"

Diane interrupted with an exaggerated gasp, snatching the plate out of Remy's hands. "I'll take care of that, chaplain." She twirled quickly from the table around the island to the sink. "Why don't you two boys go outside on the deck and let us ladies tidy things up here?" She glanced over her shoulder with a coy glint in her eyes. "I'm sure you two have lots to catch up on."

Fitz set his pen down. "You heard her, Padre." He pushed his chair away from the table with a playful twinkle in his eye. "I swear, if I stare at that blank sheet of paper anymore, I'm gonna lose it." He yanked the refrigerator open and retrieved two cans of Diet Orange Crush, pausing to press a quick kiss on the top of his mother's head before making his way to the sliding glass door. "Come on. We're being kicked out for a little while."

He slid the door open, stepping aside to let Remy pass as he paused to meet his wife's gaze. Fitz gave her a thankful nod before following the chaplain onto the deck. Joining Remy at the deck railing, Fitz handed him one of the sodas.

The chaplain turned the can over in his hand, hesitating before cracking it open. "I always wanted to ask you the reason why you drink diet pop and not the real stuff. You never really struck me as the diet pop kind of guy."

Fitz laughed. "The reason is inside ironing your shirt. When

Ryan got old enough to drink soda, Jenn decided the only kind she'd allow in our house was the sugar-free kind. I can't really taste the difference, so it's all the same to me."

"You do realize that there's nothing in this stuff that's actually natural, right?" Remy's brow crinkled as he read the ingredients. "Citric acid, malic acid, potassium benzoate, sodium citrate, aspartame—they're all additives ..."

"What are you talkin' about?" Fitz huffed, glancing down at his own can. "Right there it says 'natural flavors.' That's right. *Natural.*"

Unconvinced, Remy rolled his eyes. "If there was anything remotely orange in Orange Crush, don't you think they'd just come right out and say it? Like Orangina—it'd say it's nine percent juice or whatever. There's nothing natural in this at all except maybe the water. And maybe not even that."

Fitz shrugged then took a long swig before setting the can down on the railing with a muted clunk.

"I been drinkin' this stuff since Craig Morton was the Broncos quarterback in '77 and they got hammered by the Cowboys in the Super Bowl." He grunted a laugh. "They had the best defense in the NFL that year—Randy Gradishar, Tom Jackson, and Lyle Alzado. The Orange Crush, you know? They were awesome."

His voice took on a dreamy quality as he reminisced.

"Dad scored tickets that year to the AFC divisional playoff game between the Broncos and the Steelers." Fitz's eyes narrowed as he looked out onto the greenbelt. "I'm not sure how he nailed the tickets. Probably got 'em from a vendor at work or something. I dunno."

Remy smiled, pleased to hear Fitz talking openly about his father.

"The game was on Christmas Eve, and getting to go to that

game was my Christmas present that year. I remember it was cold—maybe thirty-five, forty degrees at kickoff? I was a seven-year-old kid, what did I know? I was so excited, it could've been ten below with a forty mile an hour crosswind and I'd still have been on cloud nine. Dad got me all bundled up in a scarf and mittens and I had on my old orange-and-blue Broncos stocking cap with the goofy little pom-pom on the top. Remember those?"

"The old polyester knit kind, right? They were itchy and useless in the cold but they looked cool. I remember having a Bears one like that."

Fitz snorted. "Anyway, the Steelers had a fuckin' fantastic defense, too—this was back in the old 'Steel Curtain' days, with Mean Joe Greene and L.C. Greenwood, Ernie Holmes and Dwight White. So you basically had the two best defenses in the league going at it at Mile High on Christmas Eve. I mean, what better Christmas present could a kid have?"

The chaplain smiled at Fitz's enthusiastic ramble.

"I sure can't think of one," Remy admitted. "That's a pretty special thing you and your dad shared." He paused for a beat, looked at the can in his hand and smiled. "You'll always have that memory with you." He studied Fitz's profile as he leaned over the railing. "You know that? Always."

"Yeah." Fitz took a long, deep breath and sighed. "I'm supposed to give the eulogy tomorrow, and I don't have a clue what to say. I was never good at speeches in school. I nearly crapped my pants giving the toast at my cousin's wedding a couple years back. I mean, what am I supposed to say?"

Remy's brow furrowed. "I don't know, but these things usually go best when you speak from the heart."

"Okay." Fitz rolled his eyes. "That has got to be the least helpful piece of advice ever, Padre. Seriously. What the hell am I supposed to say tomorrow? I been sittin' at that table staring at a notepad for hours and I got *nada* to show for it."

"Well." The chaplain gave a little shrug and set his soda on the deck railing. "Just from what you've told me about your dad, seems he was always encouraging you to excel. To do things, even if they were hard. To stick with it and to be a leader."

Remy paused, remembering the conversation they had in the car on the way up from Fort Carson.

"I know you said your dad wasn't thrilled about you dropping out of CSU, and maybe he wasn't excited about you going in enlisted, but I'd bet dimes to donuts he was pretty damn proud when you graduated Ranger School and when you got your Green Beret."

Fitz's pout softened into a reluctant smile. "Yeah, I guess."

"Maybe your dad would've rather you'd been an officer like him. Or maybe he'd rather you'd have stayed out of the Army altogether. He wouldn't have been the first Vietnam vet to feel that way. But I'm pretty sure he was proud as hell of you—because even though you wear stripes and not bars, you're a leader. The men you serve with look up to you. And the officers you serve under— they count on you, and they know you'd go to hell and back for your men. That's leadership. The real kind. The kind that matters. I think your dad knew that. And I think he was proud of you for it."

Fitz rubbed his tired eyes with the heel of his hands, trying to hide his blush. "You really think so?"

Remy's brows arched high over his pale blue eyes, which looked almost green under the warm porch light.

"I know so."

Fitz leaned back against the railing and sighed, his shoulders slumped as he closed his eyes and summoned up the strength to go inside and give the eulogy another go. He stood like that for a minute until Remy finally clapped him on the back and shepherded him into the house. Once inside, Remy left Fitz in the kitchen to write while the chaplain went upstairs to shower.

On his way to the bathroom, Remy paused to listen to the murmur of conversation in the kitchen below and noticed a framed photo of Fitz and his father on the wall at the top of the stairs. From Fitz's hollowed-out cheeks and the sharp bulge of his Adam's apple, Remy guessed it was taken after Fitz's graduation from basic training. Every soldier loses weight during basic training, and judging by the picture, young Fitz was no exception. The shot was obviously posed and while Roger Fitzgerald's purse-lipped smile seemed somewhat forced, Remy noted a proud gleam in the eyes of both father and son despite the palpable underlying tension. It was strange to think that just weeks after the photo was taken, Fitz shipped off to Saudi Arabia to fight in his first war.

Remy was so deep in thought he nearly collided with Ryan as he rounded the corner and stepped into the bathroom.

"Oh, whoops." Remy held his shaving kit against his chest like a football as he studied the startled young man standing before him. "Sorry. Please, you go first."

The blushing boy pushed his floppy bangs away from his eyes with a quick shake of his head. "No, sir, you're a guest in our house. I mean, you know, in my grandparents' house, so, uh, really, you should go first, sir."

"Okay," Remy said with a nod. "I promise I'll be quick."

He watched with a faint smile as the boy turned and walked away, glancing over his shoulder at the chaplain before disappearing into his bedroom. Remy thought about the three generations of Fitzgerald men. The sound of laughter downstairs shook him out of his daze as he quietly slipped into the bathroom.

True to his word, Remy showered quickly. He threw his clothes back on and rubbed most of the water out of his hair, then knocked quietly on Ryan's door. He watched through the crack as the boy jumped to his feet and tugged earphones out of his ears, tossing them on the bed before he answered the knock with a sheepish grin.

Remy leaned against the doorway, smiling at the tinny sound of music that pulsed from the boy's earphones. "Told ya I'd be quick."

"Umm, yeah. Thanks."

Ryan brushed past him on his way to the bathroom, but Remy lingered, studying Ryan's short-legged, long-torsoed form. Based on the photos he'd seen of Fitz as a young man, he was fairly certain that Ryan would grow up to be a green-eyed, wavy-haired version of his father.

Remy was sitting on the foldout sofa bed with a Bible in his lap, still thinking about Ryan and Fitz, when the door creaked open behind him. He turned around and found Ryan's lightly freckled face peeking in from behind the door, his eyes narrow as if bracing for a scolding. Seeing Ryan's reticence, Remy set his Bible aside and beckoned him to enter with a gentle wave of his hand.

Ryan closed the door behind him but hesitated, stuffing his hands in his pockets and staring at his bare feet as he curled his toes against the creamy wool carpet. The boy's lip curled slightly as he looked up and gave Remy a cautious once-over.

"So, you're my dad's new pastor?"

Remy pursed his lips and considered the question. "Not exactly. I'm really just a friend who happens to be a minister."

"Oh." Ryan's brow furrowed. "So you're not the chaplain in my dad's unit?"

The twinge of caution in the boy's voice reminded him of the afternoon he met Fitz. *"A captain, huh?"* The boy didn't just resemble his father physically: he clearly shared his father's skeptical nature.

"Actually," Remy replied with a faint grin, "I'm the chaplain for the 1st Battalion, 66th Armor. 4th Infantry Division."

The boy's eyes lit up. "My friend Brandon's dad's in the 4th I.D. He's a medic in the 4/10 Cav."

Remy winked and nodded approvingly. "Ah, a BlackJack. Very cool. I know the chaplain in the 4/10 Cav. We served together in Iraq."

Ryan fell silent again as he crossed his arms and turned to glance out the window at the house across the street. As open as he'd seemed just moments before, Ryan seemed to have withdrawn again.

"Your dad told me you two went to the pool this afternoon."

Ryan uncrossed his arms but his brows remained deeply furrowed. "Yeah."

There was a downward lilt to the boy's voice as he shook his head, crossed his arms again, and turned back to stare out the window. Remy observed Ryan's tense, protective body language and wondered what things had been like for the boy, having his world turned upside down first by his father's deployment and a few months later by Fitz's serious injuries, and again by his father's drinking and the chaos of having to leave after his father's DUI.

Sensing Remy's eyes on him, Ryan pushed away from the wall and walked over to the desk. He plopped into the office chair and looked up at the chaplain with a sigh.

"He told me about the IED."

The chaplain's eyes widened. "Really?"

Ryan shifted uncomfortably in his seat. "Yeah. I mean, a little," he muttered.

Remy leaned against the sofa cushion. Part of him wanted to hear about the conversation at the pool, but Ryan's reticence moved him more than the sharp tugs of his own curiosity. He was drawn to the boy's shimmering green eyes, which were neither a cool gray-blue like his mother's nor a warm hazel like his father's, but somehow a unique mix of both. Remy smiled, recognizing Fitz's restlessness in the way Ryan had started swinging back and forth in the desk chair.

"Your dad's never told me about the IED."

Ryan's chair-twirling stopped. "Really?"

"Nope. Not once."

A puzzled look crossed the boy's face and he began to swing the chair again.

"You know what I think?" Remy pursed his lips and thought for a moment. "I think your dad trusts you in a way that he doesn't trust me. That's why he confided in you."

Ryan blinked as a faint, almost indiscernible smile curved his lips. "Seriously?"

Remy waggled his rusty red brows and nodded. "Definitely. The things he told you aren't the kinds of things he tells other people, not even his friends. Actions speak louder than words, right? Well, the fact that he did that—you know, that he confided in you like that? It shows how much he trusts you."

The chair stilled and Ryan suddenly sat up a little straighter, his lips quivering as he bit back a proud smile. "Really?"

"Absolutely. There's not a doubt in my mind."

CHAPTER 25

Fitz stood in front of the mirror and ran his hands over the front of his dark blue uniform coat, flicking away an invisible piece of lint.

He glanced down at his feet, hoping that the forty minutes he'd spent spit-shining his jump boots the night before were enough to make them appear flawless to the naked eye. With a quiet sigh, he put on his beret, placing it so the Special Forces insignia sat just left of center and the fold hung over his right temple.

"You look great."

Jenn sidled up behind him, resting her chin on his shoulder and tracing her fingers over the service stripes on his cuff.

"You know …" She turned him around to face her, smiling as she drank him in. "I definitely like the blue better. Looks crisper, I think, than the old green Class A's did." She reached up and fingered the snug knot of his tie, adjusting it slightly before stroking a finger along his smooth, clean-shaven jaw. "Reminds me of our wedding day, seeing you dressed up like this."

Fitz's eyes gleamed and a quick smile curved his lips, but it quickly disappeared. He pressed his head against the warmth of her hand and closed his eyes.

"You'll do fine." Jenn stroked her thumb across the prickly hairs over his ear, smiling as she remembered watching him take the clippers to the back and sides the night before. "You're going to do your dad a great honor today."

Fitz frowned. "I feel like I'm this close to coming to pieces," he said, indicating with his thumb and forefinger as. His hand trembled in the air between them. "I just don't know—"

"No." Jenn cupped both her hands around his jaw and pulled him close so the stiff felt of his beret grazed her forehead. "You'll be strong today, Fitz. I know it, but …" Her voice trailed off as she gathered her thoughts. Stepping backward, she brought her hand down and brushed her fingers over the six rows of ribbons on his chest.

"It's okay to show that there's a heart under here," she whispered. "No one's expecting you to be a hard-core Green Beret today. Just a loving son who lost his father."

Fitz swallowed thickly and stared at his reflection in the mirror, wincing at the tingle in the hinge of his jaw that warned of tears.

"I guess," he whispered.

The drive to St. Matthew's Episcopal Church went by in a haze, and it wasn't until the rector, the Reverend Ben Hopkins, gave Fitz a slight nod that the reality of the moment became immediate again. Squeezing Jenn's hand for strength, he turned and kissed his mother's cheek, then took a deep, fortifying breath and stood up from the pew.

He tried to ignore the throbbing in his ears as he approached the pulpit, acutely conscious of the hard, sticky noise his boots made against the wooden steps. Fitz looked out from the wooden podium over the dizzyingly large sanctuary and saw dozens of faces—some teary-eyed, others bleary-eyed, and still others pensive, dazed, or bored—watching him expectantly. Tapping his thumb nervously against the side of the podium, he reminded himself that every one of the people staring back at him was there to honor his father.

"My father—" His voice broke as his breath hitched between syllables.

Catching Jenn's gaze, Fitz recalled her words from that morning. *"You will be strong today. I know it."* He pursed his lips and closed his eyes for a moment, letting her words wash over him before he opened them again, a faint smile parting his lips when she nodded encouragingly.

"My father told me once that, 'A lot of men can lead, but not every man who leads is a leader.' My father was a *leader.*" Fitz's voice grew stronger as he continued. "All my life, I've looked to my father as an example of what it means to be a leader."

He felt exposed and raw in front of the sea of faces before him. *Breathe in, breathe out,* he told himself. *One breath at a time.*

"There's a saying in the Army: 'Mission first, troops always.'" His voice deepened as he moved into familiar territory, but still he hesitated, letting his gaze sweep over the crowd, gathering some strength from their patient, interested eyes.

"That was my dad. Dad knew that sometimes being a leader means pushing people to do things they don't want to do, to go farther than they think they can go. He was this way when he was in the Army, whether as a brand-new butter bars lieutenant leading a platoon in Vietnam in '68, or as a company commander in '71 when he got back from his second tour. After he left the Army in '76, he went to work for Martin Marietta and became a leader there, too."

Heads nodded in the audience as Fitz ticked through the decades of his father's life.

"Even at home…"

Fitz's voice thickened again as he glanced at his mother clutching an embroidered black shawl around her shoulders as she listened, her eyes pinched with bottled-up pain.

163

"At home, Dad's leadership was less about driving me to do one thing or the other, to be anything in particular, but more about encouraging me to be as good as I could be at whatever I chose to do. He pushed me to excel, to be better than I thought I could be, to be more than I would've thought I was capable of."

He stroked his fingers over the snugly trimmed fuzz on the back of his head, letting the prickly feel of it momentarily distract him.

"At the time, I kind of thought he was a slave driver." He paused, smiling at a memory. "But as I grew older, I saw Dad's pushing for what it really was—not pushing me in a particular direction, although Dad *always* had an opinion that he wasn't shy about expressing."

A few chuckles crackled forth from the gathering, and Fitz felt some tension melt away as some of the straight-lipped faces finally smiled at him.

"It wasn't so much that he was pushing me in a *particular* direction, but rather that he pushed me to excel in whatever direction I chose. He didn't want to think for me—he wanted me to learn to think for myself. He didn't want to decide for me—he wanted me to learn to make my own decisions. And while I know I've made a lot of decisions over the years that Dad didn't agree with, and done things he would have done a lot differently if it were up to him, I know I wouldn't be where I am today if it weren't for Dad's leadership. I always knew that as long as I tried my best, I would never be a disappointment to my dad."

Fitz paused, girding himself for the last few moments of his tribute.

"I think that everyone who met Dad felt that little push, the subtle or not-so-subtle nudge. Regardless of what you were trying to do, he pushed you to be the best 'whatever' you could be. If you accepted that invitation—if you were willing to *try*—then there was nothing my dad wouldn't do to help you attain that goal."

He swallowed hard, suddenly feeling choked by his necktie.

"That was my dad's gift. He showed the kind of leadership and love and trust that lifts people up and propels them forward. That's Dad's legacy, one that I can only hope to live up to as I make my way through this life. To be the kind of leader and the kind of father that my father was."

Scanning the crowd, Fitz felt a flash of uncertainty and wondered if his words had done his father justice. He walked back to his seat, pausing to press his hand to the flag-draped casket, curling his fingers against the fabric as he passed by. As soon as he took his seat, the rector began to speak.

"We must always remember that neither death, nor life, nor angels, nor demons, nor things present, nor things to come, nor powers, nor height, nor depth, nor anything else in all creation, will be able to separate us from the love of God in Christ Jesus our Lord."

Fitz stared at the cedar casket, his gaze blurring at the sight of the brightly-hued flower arrangements that encircled the casket.

"O God, whose mercies cannot be numbered, accept our prayers on behalf of your servant Roger, and grant him an entrance into the land of light and joy, in the fellowship of your saints…"

Father Ben's voice entered Fitz's mind like a distant horn bellowing through fog. The sanctuary echoed with words of Scripture and prayer meant to give comfort to the bereaved, but Fitz felt empty, his thoughts loose and disorganized as the liturgy swirled into a murmur only slightly louder than the blood roaring in his ears. From time to time, he was tugged out of his haze by the press of his mother's hand against his thigh, her slender fingers absently stroking the wool of his uniform trouser until she caught herself and stilled again.

"For our brother Roger, let us pray to our Lord Jesus Christ who said, 'I am Resurrection and I am Life.' Lord, you consoled Martha and Mary in their distress. Draw near to us who mourn for Roger, and dry the tears of those who weep."

The limousine ride to Fort Logan National Cemetery was a quiet affair. Fitz sat next to his mother, while Jenn and Ryan sat behind them, and the four of them rode in silence, each one wrapped in their own thoughts as the procession wound its way from the church to the cemetery.

The limo pulled up along the curb behind the hearse in front of a section of graves along the western side of the cemetery. Fitz turned around and looked at his wife and son with a weary, somber expression. Jenn leaned forward and pressed a light kiss to her husband's cheek that made him close his eyes and sigh. He checked his beret in the window's reflection and glanced back at his son. Ryan's eyes were red-rimmed and watery, his teeth clenched and his jaw rigid as he tried to keep his emotions hemmed in. Fitz reached back and gave him a comforting pat on the knee.

"I'll see you guys in a bit, okay?" He gave them one last nod before stepping out of the car.

The five other pallbearers had gathered in two organized lines behind the limo, waiting for him. Two were friends of his father's: Major General Kevin Thompson, who served with Roger Fitzgerald in Vietnam and had just retired after spending two years as the commander of the 82nd Airborne Division; and Mark Weatherford, a retired Air Force colonel and colleague of Roger's from Martin Marietta. Two were members of the honor guard furnished by the local unit of the Colorado Army National Guard. Remy, who agreed to be the sixth pallbearer, gave Fitz a comforting pat on the back as he fell in line behind the others. The chaplain arched his brows, silently asking if Fitz was okay. Fitz nodded and gestured toward the waiting hearse.

He was a son, burying his father, but Fitz was also a member of his father's own honor guard. Despite the emotions roiling inside of him, he had to carry himself with military bearing as they brought his father to his final resting place among the rows of other men and women who'd served their country dating back to the Civil War.

Fitz drew a deep breath, coiling his emotions inside of him so that he could carry out this one last honor for his father. The hearse door opened to reveal the flag-draped casket. A staff sergeant from the National Guard asked the pallbearers to fall into formation. Three of them, Fitz included, had served as military pallbearers before, and the others had attended enough military funerals to capably assist. The guardsmen served as the lead pallbearers on each side of the casket, allowing the others to follow their cadence.

The six men moved as crisply as they were dressed, turned out in white gloves and perfectly pressed dress uniforms. The officers wore peaked caps with embellished brims befitting their ranks, while Remy and the guardsmen wore simple black berets and Fitz, his distinctive green beret. As they carried the casket between the rows of tombstones to the gravesite, Fitz's mind dissolved into the rhythm of his movements. Each foot fell perfectly in sync with those of the man in front of him, and his eyes were fixed straight ahead. The rows of stone formed a corridor, its walkway carpeted in wispy Kentucky bluegrass. Fitz kept his emotions in check by focusing his gaze on the collar of the man in front of him, but when their steps slowed and they set the casket onto the platform over the open grave, his heart sank and he blinked away tears.

He took his place between his mother and his wife while the

priest intoned the prayer that committed Roger Fitzgerald to his final resting place. The rector's voice was strong and carried clearly through the late morning air, but just as it was during the church service, the words reached Fitz's ears as little more than a murmur.

"Everyone the Father gives to me will come to me; I will never turn away anyone who believes in me."

Fitz's breath hitched as the breeze picked up and caused the flag to flap against the sides of the casket.

"In sure and certain hope of the resurrection to eternal life through our Lord Jesus Christ, we commend to Almighty God our brother Roger, and we commit his body to his final resting place."

Trying to maintain a veneer of emotionless decorum, Fitz clenched his jaw at the word *final*.

"May the Lord bless him and keep him. May the Lord make His face to shine upon him and be gracious to him, and lift up His countenance upon him and give him peace. Amen."

The benediction made Fitz shiver as he remembered receiving that same blessing in a crowded, dusty tent chapel in Saudi Arabia in February 1991. It was the night before he and the other men of the 187th Infantry Regiment loaded into Black Hawk helicopters and air-assaulted into Iraq during the very first hours of Desert Storm's ground phase. Like most of the men in his platoon, he'd been nervous about going into battle for the first time. Never a particularly religious man, he surrendered to the gravity of the moment, closing his eyes as the battalion's Catholic chaplain placed his hand on the crown of Fitz's head and recited the same priestly blessing.

Unsure whether the Lord had really protected him when he went to war or whether he'd just been lucky, Fitz hoped that God would look after his father, and that He would not forget his mother, who was now suddenly alone after forty-three years of marriage.

The voices of the crowd rose up and joined that of the young, round-faced priest as the service concluded with the Lord's Prayer.

"Our Father, who art in heaven, hallowed be thy Name, thy kingdom come, thy will be done, on earth as it is in heaven. Give us this day our daily bread. And forgive us our trespasses, as we forgive those who trespass against us. And lead us not into temptation, but deliver us from evil. For thine is the kingdom, and the power, and the glory, for ever and ever. Amen."

Fitz's gloved hands trembled as the mourners' voices faded. The priest looked skyward as he spoke the final invocation.

"Rest eternal grant to him, O Lord. And let light perpetual shine upon him. May Roger's soul, and the souls of all the departed, through the mercy of God, rest in peace. Amen."

Father Ben stepped back, yielding to the two guardsmen who stood over the casket as a third soldier slowly raised her bugle and began to play "Taps."

The peaking, plaintive melody sent a chill down Fitz's spine. As the last notes faded, he focused on the flag draped over his father's casket and the two soldiers who stood next to it.

The guardsmen picked up the flag and tugged at its corners, making it taut and flat. They side-stepped away from the casket while holding the flag aloft, folding it in half lengthwise and repeated the process, tugging it taut again, before folding it in half again.

One of the soldiers turned his gloved hand to make the first triangular fold, repeating the process hand-over-hand until the flag became a folded triangle of white stars on a blue field. The junior guardsman stroked the flag's corners to ensure they were tight and pointy, holding it snugly while the staff sergeant in charge of the detail tucked the last inch of material into the tight triangle. The staff sergeant saluted the flag, then the sergeant turned the flag over and presented it to his superior before he, too, saluted. The sergeant stepped back and to the side as the staff sergeant approached the row of chairs where Fitz and his family sat.

Fitz bit his lip as the soldier knelt on one knee and presented the folded flag to his mother.

"On behalf of the President of the United States, the United States Army, and a grateful Nation, please accept this flag as a symbol of our appreciation for your loved one's honorable and faithful service."

"Thank you." She clutched the flag to her chest as the staff sergeant rose to his feet and saluted her.

Fitz wrapped his arm around his mother's narrow, bony shoulders and pulled her close, kissing the top of her head as she shuddered against the ribbons on his chest.

"Shhhhhh," he whispered into her hair. "I know."

He closed his eyes as Jenn threaded her fingers through his gloved ones and squeezed.

CHAPTER 26

When the last of the guests who had come to pay their respects to the family finally left,

everyone retreated upstairs to change out of their formal clothes.

For his part, Fitz was glad to get out of his Class A's. The wool-blend coat and trousers were hot and didn't breathe worth a damn, and by the time he'd taken them off, his shirt, undershirt, and boxers were damp with sweat. Tired, sticky, stinky, and sore, he shed his uniform and slipped into the shower, cranking up the water as hot as he could stand it. He let the stream pummel his back, as if by doing so he could wash away the malaise that had gnawed at him since the guardsman tendered the folded flag to his mother.

He closed his eyes, pressing his forehead against the cold tile wall as a chill ran down his spine.

"What?" he snapped, rolling his eyes at the tow-headed medic. "What are you talking about? I've walked point the last two times."

"I thought you were one of those 'lead from the front' kinda guys, Boss." Peterson's lips curved into a smirk and he waggled his brows. "Come on. I'll flip ya for it."

"Whatever. I think you want me walking point so you can stare at my ass."

"You think?" Peterson barked a laugh. "No doubt about it, Fitz. You have a very nice ass, but face it, pal: you're not my type. Too hairy. You should consider waxing that shit. Maybe then I'd reconsider."

"No one's waxing a goddamn thing." The low growl in his voice was contradicted by the twinkle of laughter in his eyes. "I'll have you know my wife loves my hairy ass."

"So you say." The medic adjusted his rifle sling so his weapon would lay across his chest at a more comfortable angle. "C'mon. We gonna flip for this shit or what?"

Fitz dug for the lucky Colorado state quarter he always carried in his right hip pocket.

"You know, I could just order your waxed ass to walk point." Holding the quarter between his thumb and forefinger, he shot Peterson a pointed look. "Heads, you take point. Tails, I do. Got it?"

Fitz tossed the coin then grabbed it in midair, slapping it onto the back of his hand. The two men exchanged a long look before Fitz moved his hand to reveal George Washington's thick-necked profile.

"Guess I'm on point," Peterson said with a weak shrug. Then he grinned. "Gives you a chance to look at my ass for a change, huh, Boss?"

"I'm not gonna be lookin' at your pasty white ass, Peterson. I'm gonna be too busy watching for snipers and IEDs. The intel we got last night wasn't particularly encouraging. Reports of Taliban infiltrating from the south over the last three nights. I'm tellin' ya, Doc, this valley's a fuckin' powder keg."

"Day at a time." Peterson retrieved his tactical gloves from his thigh pockets and pulled them on. "That's all we can do, right, Boss?"

Fitz glanced down at the rifle slung across his chest and stroked his *finger over the cool metal of the action. "Yup," he said, buckling his chin strap. "Day at a time."*

The water had run cold by the time Fitz got around to rinsing off. He hadn't bothered to use shampoo. Since he wore his hair in a high and tight, there wasn't much to wash, so he just rubbed some Irish Spring into his barely-there hair, dispensing with shampoo altogether. He rinsed his hair then shut off the water and just stood in the shower, his head tilted against the tile as he let the water roll off of him. After a minute, he stepped out of the tub and reached for a towel, rubbed it over his crotch, then wrapped it around his waist and walked out with the hope that his mother wouldn't catch him dripping his way back to his bedroom.

Fitz walked in to find Jenn sitting on the bed in capris and a tank top with a book in her lap.

"What's this?" She held up the slender leather-bound volume.

"Oh." He unfurled his towel and quickly rubbed it over his chest and under his arms before tossing it on the floor near the closet. "Found that in the basement while going through a box of Dad's Army stuff."

He retrieved a pair of shorts from his duffle bag.

"I was looking for a copy of his discharge papers for the funeral home guy. Why the hell Dad didn't keep a copy in a folder in the office, hell if I know." Stepping into his shorts, he zipped them up as he met Jenn's gaze with a crooked grin, hoping she'd noticed he hadn't put on underwear.

"Fitz," she groaned with a dramatic roll of her eyes. "You really are incorrigible."

"Mmm-hmm." He bit back a laugh and pulled a T-shirt over his head. "That's why you married me—'cause I'm a challenge."

Setting the book back on the bedside table, she stood up and sauntered over to him, slipping her fingers under the waistband of his shorts and pulling him toward her.

"Really?" Her voice dropped a half-octave as she resolved to retaliate for his teasing. "Are you sure it's not because you are a scintillating conversationalist?" She swiped her fingers over his navel, then gently pushed him away.

"You love it when I scintillate you," he snickered. Jenn laughed, glad to see his sense of humor emerge again after months of humorless gloom.

"So you say." She shook her head and turned around. "Come on."

Fitz felt short of breath and the room suddenly closed in on him as Jenn walked out the door and vanished down the stairs.

"So you say. Come on. We gonna flip for this shit or what?"

When Fitz finally walked into the kitchen, Jenn knew from the paleness of his slack-jawed face that something had happened. The lewd, snarky grin he teased her with upstairs was nowhere to be seen. Her gaze met his as he walked past, but the expression in his hazel eyes was shaded and unreadable. He didn't seem angry, but worry still coiled in the pit of her belly. He seemed sad, distant almost, and she didn't know why.

He yanked open the refrigerator and pulled out a can of soda, then kneed the door shut. He cracked the can open, pausing for a moment before he tipped it back and took a sip. Whatever had come over him now rolled off of him in tense, dark waves.

"Are you okay?" Jenn reached for his arm and grazed his wrist with her fingers, silently coaxing him to meet her gaze. "Jacob? Hey."

His brows arched over his eyes as he opened his mouth to speak, then hesitated. The longer he lingered in silence, the more demanding her fingers became, pressing into his skin and stroking the hair that covered the groove-like scars on his forearm.

"What's wrong?"

Touch had always been her way to draw him out, and the one thing he had always been helpless to resist. She watched his eyes flutter shut and wished that her fingertips could tease apart the knot inside of him.

"Fitz?"

He opened his eyes, then covered her hand with his, stilling the fingers that stroked his arm. Rubbing the top of her hand with his callused palm, he shrugged.

"Just tired, is all. It's been a rough couple of days, you know?"

She knew there was more he wasn't telling her. But she also knew he had probably opened up as much as he could in that moment. From his touch and his willingness to be touched, she sensed there would be more—more opening up, more healing. But for now, this was all he could offer her.

"I know."

His hand slipped away from hers and he pulled her into a loose embrace. He clasped her against his chest, her face nuzzled into the crook of his neck as he pressed his lips to her hair as he breathed in the smell of her.

"I'm sorry," he murmured, his breath warming her scalp.

Unsure what he was apologizing for, she kissed the side of his neck. "It's okay," she whispered, rubbing her hand across his back. They stood there, leaning into one another, until the quiet equilibrium was broken by the sound of heavy feet clomping down the stairs.

"Oh, um."

Ryan blushed as he stumbled into the middle of an intimate moment between his parents.

"Sorry, I, uh—"

Fitz and Jenn pulled apart, their eyes glistening as they looked at their son.

"What is it, Ryan?"

Noting that he had reverted back to shorts and a T-shirt, Jenn instantly regretted not having gotten a picture of him in his suit while she had the chance. Like his father, Ryan hated any outfit that required him to tuck in a shirt or wear a tie, and it was rare to have both of them dressed up at the same time. She wondered if she could coax her boys into dressing up again in the fall so they could have a real, honest-to-goodness family portrait done.

Ryan looked down at his feet, stuffing his hands into his pockets, his nerve wavering as his parents watched him expectantly.

"What's up, buddy?" Fitz prompted him.

The boy glanced up and met his father's eyes for a moment before looking away again.

"I ... well ... I was wondering if we could go back to the pool today. It's still afternoon and, I mean, do we have to stay at the house all day because of, you know, the funeral, or—?"

Jenn smiled as her son struggled to formulate his request. This uncertainty was new. Before, when Ryan wanted something, he asked for it, often all too pointedly. But after Fitz came home injured and withdrew into himself, rejecting both Ryan's and her entreaties for affection or attention of any kind, Ryan stopped asking for things. Headstrong and rebellious like his father, he simply took what he wanted and ignored what he didn't. But now, in his vulnerability, he was trying to redraw the lines that used to exist between him and his father.

Fitz blinked with surprise. He bit his lip, obviously eager to accept the proposal and yet visibly nervous at the prospect of being left alone with his son again.

"Maybe your mom wants to come with us?" He turned to Jenn with a solicitous crease in his broad, tanned forehead.

Jenn looked at her watch and glanced toward the stairs.

"Someone should really be here when your mom wakes up from her nap. But I can drop you two off at the pool, and you can just call when you want to be picked up. How's that?"

Father and son turned and looked at one another. Ryan's brows arched over his cool green eyes, silently pleading with his father. Knowing full well he'd denied his son so much of what he needed for so long, Fitz took a breath and nodded.

"Okay."

Twenty minutes later, Fitz and Ryan were back where they were two days earlier, except this time the full intensity of the afternoon sun warmed their shoulders as they toed off their sandals and slipped into their water shoes.

Ryan's limbs rippled with impatience as a group of younger kids played Marco Polo in the middle of the pool and two boys closer to his own age took turns at the diving board. He headed for the diving board, rolling his eyes when Fitz hollered at him not to run. He waited for the boy who had just jumped in to clear the area beneath the board before taking a loping start and bouncing high off the board, flipping once before slipping head over heels into the water.

Fitz jumped to his feet and clapped.

"Yeah! Nice!"

Ryan had struggled to master the front flip the previous summer, and seeing his son accomplish something that had eluded him for so long filled Fitz with pride. "Way to go, buddy!"

The commotion attracted the attention of the other two boys who had been diving. One, the taller of the two, was climbing up the ladder and out of the pool as his redheaded companion prepared to jump. He turned and looked at Fitz with a scowl, annoyed at having his use of the diving board and the pool's deep end curtailed by the newcomers. The boy's eyes widened when he saw the web of scars on Fitz's right arm. He froze, unable to do anything but stare until he became aware of the weight of Fitz's gaze, by which time he'd entirely missed his friend's backflip.

Ryan clung to the ladder and glanced over his shoulder to see what the tall boy was looking at. As Ryan followed the young man's eyes, his jaw tensed and he heaved himself out of the pool, striding over to the diving board steps where the boy stood staring.

"What're you lookin' at, huh?" Ryan stepped into the other boy's personal space. When he did, the boy tore his eyes away from Fitz and looked at Ryan with surprise. "Didn't your mom and dad teach you it's not polite to stare?"

Ryan nudged the boy to the side as he climbed the steps onto the diving board.

The tall boy's eyes shifted between Ryan, Fitz, and his companion. "I didn't mean anything," he said quickly. He saw that the thick-necked man with the buzz cut and all the scars had stood up from his chair and was watching them. "I was just—"

"Yeah?" Ryan interrupted, propping his hands on his hips. "Well, my dad got those scars fighting insurgents in Afghanistan. So instead of staring at him like a stupid jerk, you should say *thank you.*"

Without a further word, Ryan rocked back on his heels, ran to the end of the diving board and leaped, throwing his body into a tight front flip before his feet pierced the water's surface.

Fitz's chest swelled with pride again as his son swam back to the ladder and hoisted himself out of the water. The other two boys, having suddenly lost interest in their game of competitive flips and cannonballs, retreated toward the middle of the pool and left the entire deep end to Fitz and Ryan.

After watching Ryan dive and swim for a few minutes, Fitz finally peeled off his T-shirt and tossed it onto his chair. He dove in, scarcely leaving a splash as he disappeared beneath the water. Fitz swam along the pool's bottom, rushing up to the surface to appear right behind Ryan as the boy reached the ladder on his way to execute another flip off the diving board.

"Hey."

Ryan clambered out of the pool and turned around, his red nylon swim trunks clinging to his body in a way that made Fitz smile. Though still a boy, Fitz could see his son was a bit longer-limbed and filling out in certain places that left little doubt that puberty was just around the corner.

"I'm proud of you," Fitz told him, reaching up and patting him on the calf.

Ryan replied with a shy grin before jogging back to the diving board. Fitz draped his arm across the ladder as Ryan walked out to the end of the diving board, which sagged slightly under his weight. This time, though, Ryan turned around so that his back was toward the water. After taking a moment to focus, he brought his arms up over his head, then bent his knees and jumped, curling his body into a ball as he flipped backward into the pool.

Fitz threw his arms up in celebration, pushing away from the wall and swimming over to meet Ryan when he surfaced.

"I did it!" His eyes glittered in triumph.

A wide grin spanned Fitz's face as he ruffled his son's wet hair, sending it sticking up in a dozen messy spikes. "You sure did. That's awesome, buddy."

Unused to his father's effusive praise, Ryan blushed and swam to the wall nearest their chairs. "There's a pool in the next town over from Mount Angel that Nana and Poppy go to. I've been working on it all summer."

All summer.

Proud as he was of his son, and impressed as he was with the boy's determination to master the feat all on his own, the phrase stung. It was a sharp reminder of all the time he'd spent away from his family, and of how long he had alienated himself from them after returning from Afghanistan.

"All that hard work paid off," Fitz told him, trying to ignore the pang of guilt.

Ryan rubbed his hand over his hair to flatten its wild, wet spikes. "Thanks, Dad."

Silence passed between them as Ryan caught his breath and Fitz chewed on his thoughts.

"I'm sorry," Fitz blurted out.

Ryan furrowed a puzzled brow. "What?"

"About your birthday. And about the way things were, you know, when I got home. I'm sorry I didn't …"

Fitz looked at his son, who stared back with expectation and caution in his eyes.

"I'm sorry I didn't handle it better. I let you down. You *and* Mom."

The surprise in Ryan's face melted into an open-mouthed frown as he recalled the Sunday afternoon a week before they left for Oregon. His mom organized a birthday party for him at Fargo's Pizza, inviting eight of his friends from school and hockey to join them for pizza, cake, and retro video games. He'd been looking forward to it all week, especially to seeing his dad display his mastery of *Street Fighter II* in the arcade.

But when it was finally time to go, Fitz had passed out in the easy chair, a six-pack's worth of empty beer cans littering the end table next to him. Though it normally took more than a six-pack to get loaded, Fitz had a head start since waking up hungover from a bender the night before. Jenn and Ryan didn't even bother trying to rouse him. They just left him there, passed out and snoring, and tried to salvage the rest of the afternoon as they made an excuse at the party about Fitz being called in to work at the last minute.

"I was really mad." Ryan's voice cracked as his words took on a liquid quality. "You were over there for four months and then, when you came back home, after you got out of the hospital, you didn't want anything to do with me." He clung to the edge of the pool and stared at the tile, avoiding his father's gaze as the hurt he'd felt for months finally bubbled over. "I thought I'd done something wrong."

"You didn't," Fitz whispered. "I just—"

"It doesn't matter, because that's what it felt like." Ryan's words tumbled out of him in an uncontrolled gush. "You always would tell me, before you deployed, that with you gone, I was the man in the house and that I had to step up. Then you came home this time all busted up, and so I tried to be strong and brave and grown-up the way you wanted me to—not just while you were in Afghanistan, you know, but while you were in the hospital and even after you got home. I tried to help out even more than usual, 'cause I knew you'd been hurt and all and your friend …"

Fitz's eyes shimmered with tears, and his lips parted, not to speak but as if he were struggling to breathe.

"You lost your friend." Ryan watched his father's eyes close in remembrance. "And I knew all that, so I tried to be good, to help Mom and do extra chores and do what I could to help you, since you were still banged up. I tried to be what you wanted me to be, like you told me before you left, about being a man. But none of it mattered. You didn't want to talk to me or even look at me." The last dozen syllables fell messily from Ryan's mouth as tears welled up in his eyes. "It was like I wasn't even there."

Fitz rubbed the tears from his eyes with the heel of his hand.

"I'm sorry," he croaked. "It was just … I really don't know how to explain it, but … I guess I just felt so—"

"Sad?" Ryan offered helpfully, his brows curved over his tear-rimmed eyes. He bit his lip to keep from crying.

"No, just …"

Fitz looked away, trying to find a word that would capture what he had felt like.

"Empty."

The lone word fell as a whisper. Fitz stared at the mountains in the distance, remembering his unexpected relief when he discovered that the landscape of Kunar Province was more or less identical to the western half of Colorado.

"I just felt empty. Like there wasn't anything good left in me anymore. I couldn't stop thinking about it. Everywhere I looked, everything reminded me of it. Of what had happened, you know, over there. I drank beer and watched sports all the time, 'cause I tried to fill my head with noise and distract myself to keep from thinking about it. But it didn't work."

Ryan's eyes softened. "When I'm upset about something, Dad, you always want me to tell you about it. Why didn't you talk to us? Me and Mom, I mean. You always say we're a team, the three of us. 'Team Fitzgerald,' right? So why didn't you talk to us about it?"

The afternoon breeze suddenly picked up and Fitz felt a chill as the gust left his skin dotted with goosebumps.

"Let's get out and dry off, okay?" He jerked his chin toward the ladder. "Before we both turn to little prunes."

They dried off and settled onto their lounge chairs to soak up some rays before the sun began to dip behind the mountains.

"Why didn't you talk to us, Dad?" Ryan asked, his voice gentle yet insistent.

"I didn't want to burden you with it."

"But you did anyway ... by not telling us."

"I know." Fitz covered his eyes with his hand, unable to meet his son's gaze. "But I didn't want to talk about it at all. Not to you, not to Mom, not to anybody. I wanted to ... I just wanted to forget. To leave it behind."

The boy drew his legs up to his chest and folded his arms over his shins. "But you couldn't," he said. "Forget it, or leave it behind. Could you?"

Fitz looked away and stared at the beads of water trapped in the hair on his legs. The wet, matted hair stuck to his pockmarked skin.

"No," he admitted, ruffling his hand over his shin, pausing briefly as his finger skimmed over the long-faded scar in the middle of his shin that was a permanent reminder of the day he met Jenn. "No, but I didn't want to stain you with it, either. The ugliness of it. It was worse than the worst thing you've ever seen—worse than, God willing, you will ever see. Worse than the worst horror movie you've ever watched, even the really bad ones you watch over at Brandon's house 'cause you know your mom and I would never let you watch 'em."

Ryan blinked. "You know about those?"

"I'm a father," Fitz replied with a grin. "I have ways of finding things out."

Ryan heaved a sigh of relief when he heard the chuckle in his father's voice.

For a minute, neither one of them said anything. Fitz sensed the boy's uncertainty from his fidgety silence. He could guess the questions the twelve-year-old had since he, too, had thought about such things. After seeing the *Rambo* movies as a boy, he'd wondered if Vietnam was really like that.

Something tickled Fitz's leg and he reached down to rub his calf, letting his fingertips skim over the pebbled skin that was streaked and speckled with slightly depressed pink scars. Jenn knew what the scars were, and the kinds of shrapnel the surgeons pulled out of him. She spoke to his doctors, looked at his X-rays, and reviewed his medical charts at Fort Sam Houston while he drifted in and out of a fentanyl haze.

"See these?" Fitz pointed at the chain of scars on the side of his calf. Ryan looked first into his father's eyes before his gaze settled on the scars.

"Yeah." Ryan's voice was edged with uncertainty as he watched his father's long, thick fingers stroke across the slow-fading scars. Fitz's callused forefinger skated over his leg before coming to rest on an inch-long scar midway up his calf.

"This one was from a piece of metal," he explained. "From an old Soviet antipersonnel mine that they rigged up to make the IED." He pointed to several other scars higher up on his thigh. "These ones here were also from metal fragments."

Ryan's breath stilled as he watched his father's finger move from scar to scar.

"And these..." Fitz dragged his finger over a trio of scars near the widest part of his calf. "These ..."

Bile rose in the back of his throat at the memory that crept to the forefront of his mind.

The leg of his uniform trouser was soaked with blood, the fabric torn in a dozen places where the shrapnel had ripped into it. The dark, twisted pieces looked like thorns—metal, he assumed—but there was something else, shards of something chalky sticking out of his calf. At first glance, he wondered if his leg was broken, and if what he was looking at was the fractured end of his fibula sticking out of his calf. But that didn't make sense. If he'd broken his leg, he couldn't walk, and he'd stumbled from the rear of the patrol up to the front where Peterson and the others had been.

He swung his head wildly from left to right, looking around for his friend and senior medic. But all he saw was blood everywhere—in the dirt, in the thin clumps of grass along the road, and on the walls of the building that flanked the narrow road. Bloody things were scattered for thirty, forty feet in every direction, every one of them broken, burned, and torn beyond recognition, so much so that he could only tell what the pieces had once been or who they belonged to by the pattern of the charred fabric.

A sick swirl pulsed in Fitz's belly. "These are where they pulled out fragments of bone."

Ryan's eyes widened. "Bone?"

"Yes."

The boy stared at the scars as the significance of the revelation became clear.

"From your fr—?" Ryan couldn't finish his question. The pained look in his father's eyes gave him the answer. His mouth hung open as he tried to process what he'd heard. "I'm sorry, Dad."

Fitz's features hardened as he held himself together, not wanting to fall apart in front of his son. He closed his eyes and tried to set aside the memory of Peterson's last seconds and the image of the medic walking some forty feet ahead, his flax-colored hair concealed underneath a Kevlar helmet, his laughing blue eyes shaded behind impact-resistant, wrap-around Oakley sunglasses.

"Me, too," he whispered. "Me, too."

CHAPTER 27

Tension hung in the air between Fitz and Jenn when they retired to their bedroom that night. That tension remained even after they made love.

She knew by the way he held her, his arm curled around her possessively as she tucked herself snug against his side, her head resting in the crook of his shoulder, that something was bothering him. His eyes shifted from side to side, blinking then narrowing then blinking again as he deliberated in silence. She watched him for a minute then finally rubbed her hand against his chest, ruffling his sweat-damp hair as she turned and pressed a kiss against his skin.

"What's wrong?"

He looked up, then pressed a long, lingering kiss against her forehead.

"I kinda don't want you to go. It's been nice having you two around again, and just the thought of being alone again, well, I guess it's just been so great to have you back, I don't want to give you up again." He closed his eyes, relaxing into the sensation of Jenn's fingers gently threading their way through the hair on his chest. Opening his eyes, he smiled. "Not just you, and not just this…" He squeezed her a little tighter against his side. "But Ryan, too."

Jenn fiddled with a tuft of hair as she thought about what he'd said.

"We don't have to go back. I mean, I can have Mom and Dad pack up our stuff and send it to us. If you think that—"

"No." Jenn tensed in his arms and he quickly clarified. "I mean, I'd love for you two to stay—there's nothing I want more than to have both of you back home with me, you know? But …"

His voice trailed off and this time, it was Fitz whose muscles stiffened.

"We can stay, Fitz. We can stay. I can call the airline to cancel our flight and—"

"No. I can't, Jenn." He pressed his lips together in a firm line. "I mean, I've taken enough from him already, burdening him with my problems—you and him both. I can't take any more away from him. He's got two more weeks of summer hockey, right?"

"Well, yes, but—"

"He should finish that up," Fitz insisted. "I just— I already ruined his birthday, ruined his spring, drove you both halfway across the country with my drinking and everything else. I can't take hockey away from him, too. I want you two home more than anything, and for us to be a family again, but I can't be the reason he misses out on one more thing he deserves, you know? So, when he's all done with hockey, then you guys can come home."

The last few words fell sloppily from his lips as Jenn sensed the conflict, the anguish and the uncertainty roiling inside of him. Slipping free from his grasp, she turned onto her side and sat up slightly so that she was at eye-level with him.

"You're a good father," she whispered against his skin.

"But I wasn't." The faint shadow of the Ponderosa pine swayed along the bedroom wall. "Not for a long time."

"You can't unring the bell, Jacob." Jenn kissed his cheek and

Fitz shrugged a little, then turned his head and pulled away. She followed his eyes across the room.

"Ryan told me what you two talked about at the pool."

"He did?"

"Yes." She slid back into her preferred spot, tucked against his side. "I don't think he knew what to make of it all."

"Neither do I," Fitz admitted, nuzzling her hair as he snaked his arm around her shoulder again.

His comment hung between them, unexplained and unchallenged, as they lay in silence. Their bodies were curled together and even their breathing fell into sync as the cool night breeze blew against their still-damp skin.

"He feels torn, too," Jenn said quietly, finally breaking the silence between them.

Fitz cocked a brow. "About?"

"Going back to Oregon." She looked into his eyes. "He's afraid you'll think we're abandoning you."

"Really? I'm afraid he'll think I'm trying to push you away again by wanting you two to go back."

"It's just for a couple of weeks."

"Are you saying that for his benefit or mine?"

His brow furrowed and Jenn knew he immediately regretted the sharpness of his tone.

"Both. But I told him that you'll be fine on your own. It's just a couple of more weeks, then we'll all be together again."

Fitz wrapped his arm more snugly around her and dropped a kiss on the top of her head.

He'd held her like this a thousand times, her skin sticking to his as they cuddled after making love. How many times had they had "one last night together" before he went away, whether for a training course or a field exercise, or for an overseas advising mission or combat deployment? Jenn wasn't sure. But all those other times, *he* was the one to go, knowing each time he kissed her and Ryan goodbye that they would be waiting for him when he came home.

This time, he was the one left behind.

"You never really get used to it," Jenn said wistfully, watching the gauzy drape flutter in front of the open window.

The first time he came home to her after an extended absence was after spending three weeks in the field for *Robin Sage*, the field exercise that served as the final exam at the end of Fitz's sixty-two weeks of Special Forces training. She remembered that night like it was yesterday.

"Jenn," he said, his voice low and raspy as he brought his hand up to stroke her hair. "You need to understand something, you know, before you decide."

"Before I decide?" she asked breathlessly. "Before I decide if I want to quit my job and follow you out to Colorado, or to Germany, if that's where they send you? I made my decision before you even walked through that door tonight."

He closed his eyes and pressed his lips to her smooth brown hair. "I just want to make sure you understand—"

"What is there to understand?" she asked, exasperated. "I love you, you idiot. I'm willing to uproot myself and move halfway across the country—hell, halfway across the damn planet for you. I understand, Jacob."

"What I'm trying to say is, Green Berets aren't garrison troops. Even if there isn't a war going on, I'll be sent on advising missions, a lot of times to places I can't even tell you about. I'll be gone a lot. And if there is a war—and at this rate, having been through two in the last five, six years, there's no doubt there'll be another one or two or God knows how many more before I retire. You just ..." He sighed. "You

just need to understand that I'll be gone a lot and—"

"I know," Jenn interrupted, tucking an errant lock of hair behind her ear. "I know I'll have to share you with the Army. I've had to do that for the last six months and I know I'll have to do that for however many years you stay in." She placed her hand on his, curling her fingers around the thick, veiny top of his hand. "But I'd rather share you with the Army, and have whatever life I can make with you, than think about not having you at all."

Fitz pulled her hand to his lips, kissing it and gazing deep into her eyes. "Are you saying you'll marry me?"

"Only if you stop trying talk me out of it," she replied with a laugh. "Yes, you knucklehead—of course I want to marry you. Do you want to marry me?"

"Are you kidding?" Fitz pulled her toward him, lowering his legs as she let herself be yanked on top of him, her legs straddling his thighs. "As soon as fucking possible."

Fitz shifted beneath her, drawing her back into the present.

"What do mean you never get used to it?" he asked.

Tracing her finger from the notch at the base of his neck into the nest of hair below, she thought about how it felt, walking into the house and turning on the lights, trying desperately to ignore the emptiness that came with knowing he'd be gone for weeks or months to come.

"It never gets easier—being alone, waiting for you to come back—no matter how many times we go through it. After a while, you learn what to expect and you slip into a mode where you adapt. But it never gets easier."

"I hate it," Fitz whispered. "Maybe it sounds stupid, and I know it's just for a couple of more weeks, but I hate being alone."

She kissed his chest and murmured against his skin. "I know you do."

"Being alone gives me a whole new appreciation for what you've had to deal with."

Jenn closed her eyes and wondered if things really were as good as they felt. They would never be able to go back to the way things were before—before the IED, before the drinking, before the anger and the corrosive silence. But she wondered if the changes Fitz was making meant that they were on their way to a better place, one that would be safe and stable enough to let all three of them begin to heal. She felt a flutter of optimism at the thought.

She wasn't sure how to put any of that into words, or if it even made sense to try, so she let it go. Instead, she settled into the quiet comfort of his embrace, listening to the sound of his slowing breaths until she, too, fell asleep.

CHAPTER 28

Though it had only been a few hours since he'd dropped Jenn and Ryan off at Denver International Airport, it seemed like they had already been gone a week.

For five weeks he'd lived without them: eating dinner by himself (except for the two or three nights a week he and Remy went out after AA), sleeping and waking in an empty bed, and spending his evenings alone in a house empty of any other sound but his own footsteps and the blaring TV.

For four days he'd had them back in his life, and being alone again promised to be even more miserable than it was before. Fitz knew it was the right thing to let them go back to Oregon so his son could finish out the last two weeks of summer hockey. But knowing it was the right thing to do didn't lessen the misery of their absence.

Although it hadn't kept the nightmares or flashbacks from waking him, there was no question that sharing a bed with Jenn again made it considerably easier to fall asleep. But as wonderful as it was to be able to love her that way again, sex wasn't the only thing that helped him fall asleep. There was something about holding her, and being held by her, that made him feel safe and decidedly less alone, and it was *that*, above all, that soothed him enough for sleep to overtake him.

They'd exchanged a dozen text messages while she and Ryan made their way from Denver to Salt Lake City to Portland, and he answered his BlackBerry on the first ring when she called after they landed in Portland.

"I miss you already, Jenn."

"I miss you, too." Her voice crackled as the signal faded in and out.

"I wish I could sleep with you tonight." His tone was hushed as he stood by the window and listened to the breeze swish through the needles of the Ponderosa pine. "I didn't realize how much I missed it. How much I missed you. Being with you."

"I know." The disembodied voice of the airport's public address system warbled in the background. "But we'll be back in just a little more than two weeks. Two weeks from Sunday."

"But I want to hold you now. To make love to you."

Jenn made a sound halfway between a murmur and a whine. She couldn't answer him the way he wanted her to—the way he knew she wanted to—because their son was right beside her. But, for now, knowing was enough.

"Two weeks, Fitz. Two weeks and we'll be together again. We'll be a family again."

He closed his eyes and nodded. "When you go to bed, just remember I'll be here thinking about you, and wishing you were here. With me."

"I will." A smile brightened the edge of her voice. "We'll talk to you tomorrow, okay?"

Fitz ruffled the longest part of his closely shorn hair. "Okay. I love you. Tell Ryan I love him, too."

"I will." He heard her smile again. "I love you, Jacob. Have a good night."

"You, too," he said, just before the line disconnected with a beep.

He dropped the phone onto the nightstand and listened to it clatter against the base of the lamp. His eyes fell on the framed picture on top of the chest of drawers. In it, he and his parents stood in front of the bleachers at Fort Benning after his graduation from Ranger School. He wore freshly pressed green-and-brown Woodland camouflage fatigues, his bright yellow-and-black Ranger tab safety-pinned to his left sleeve.

Fitz glanced at the faded Ranger tattoo on his left bicep, rubbing his fingers over it as he remembered the night he walked into a Columbus tattoo parlor. Emboldened by the two-for-one pitchers at the bar down the street, he had slapped cash on the counter and walked out with fresh ink. He'd been little more than a kid then—young and proud, strong and lean after sixty-one days of grueling training, walking around with his Ranger qualification tab and a bright new tattoo feeling like he was a foot taller than he'd been when he was just ordinary "leg" infantry.

A decade and a half later, he was a different man.

The only non-uniform item he owned with the Special Forces insignia on it was an old white mug etched with indelible coffee stains that he kept in the team office at the HQ building. Fitz didn't brag or advertise what he was, where he'd been, or what he'd done. He didn't tell people that he could drop a man at a thousand yards with a single shot; that he could snap a man's neck with his bare hands; or that he spoke fluent Arabic, Turkish, and two dialects of Persian. At thirty-nine, Fitz was quiet about his competence and expertise in a way that he never was as a brash young Ranger.

He went into the Rangers a cocky twenty-one-year-old who cut his teeth fighting in a short, decisive war. Less than a year after earning his Ranger tab, he went to war again. But this time, American forces achieved a tactical victory only, withdrawing from Somalia having lost far more in blood, equipment, and prestige than was gained in the disastrous seven-week operation.

Fitz left Mogadishu a changed man. In Somalia, he saw that money and massive firepower weren't enough to triumph over spirit, determination, and guts. America and its allies had helicopter gunships, laser-guided munitions, and the best-trained light infantry in the world—the U.S. Army Rangers—but in the end, the Rangers were pounded into retreat by a ragtag militia of men in T-shirts and flip-flops armed with AK-47s, RPG-7s, mortars, and old Soviet machine guns mounted on the backs of twenty-year-old Toyota pickups.

Somalia taught Fitz that it wasn't enough to be strong—you had to be smart, too.

Six months after returning from Mogadishu, Fitz reported to Fort Bragg to attempt the Special Forces Qualification Course. It was at Bragg, at the base hospital, that he met Jenn, and in Bragg's Main Post Chapel that they were married, just days after Fitz finished sixty-two weeks of training and earned his Green Beret.

Somalia had been a crossroads for him. If he closed his eyes, he could still hear the militia's rallying cry, *Kasoobaxa guryaha oo iska celsa cadowga.* "Come out and defend your homes." The Rangers heard those words bellowed over megaphones from the back of the rusty old pickups that wove through neighborhoods trying to rouse the locals against the foreign interlopers. Fifteen years later, the memory of that haunting call still sent a chill down Fitz's spine. Yet out of the debacle of Mogadishu came the best things in Fitz's life—his marriage, his son, a career in the Special Forces, and the chance to return home to Colorado.

Home.

While it pained him to be without his family, this time, there was no question: they were coming home. Fitz knew he needed to get some shut-eye. After brushing his teeth and stripping down to his boxer briefs, he crawled into bed, frowning at the expanse of cold, empty sheet next to him as he pulled the covers over his shoulder.

Fitz struggled to relax. He felt twitchy, unable to shake the anxious, restless feeling that made his legs squirm between the sheets. He got up and took two more melatonin capsules and another Benadryl, hoping that the little extra would be enough to silence the buzzing in his brain. He climbed back into bed but after another five minutes of tossing and turning, he threw the covers off again.

"Fuck," he whispered.

He pulled his legs up and crossed his arms over his knees. He sat like that for a while, trying to empty his mind by focusing only on his body's sensations: the slow rise and fall of his breath, the murmur of blood in his ears, the summer breeze that tickled the hair under his arms. But as soon as he thought about trying to sleep, the buzzing in the back of his head started up again. With a growl of frustration, Fitz arched his head back and bumped the headboard against the wall with a dull thunk.

"Shit." Annoyed, he grunted and leaned forward again. "I just want to get some fucking sleep," he muttered to the empty room.

He glanced at the clock on the bedside table, saw that it was only a quarter to one in the morning—not quite midnight in Oregon—and considered texting Jenn. As he reached for his phone, his hand fell on the small brown leather volume sitting next to the lamp.

Fitz flicked the light on and picked up the book. He felt the cool, smooth leather between his palms. It was a small book, slightly larger than the paperback romances Jenn devoured on her days off, and its cover was held firmly closed by a leather thong that wrapped around it twice and was secured with a loose half hitch knot. The tie was so old and dry that Fitz was hesitant to open the book. However, curiosity got the better of him and he carefully loosened the knot, letting the stiff leather thong fall onto the sheet next to him.

Fitz turned the book over in his hand, rubbing his thumb across the cover, its grain buffed to a smooth shine by what he imagined were years of handling. The well-worn leather reminded him of the Western saddle he'd used at a Boy Scout camp in the Laramie Mountains the summer before his thirteenth birthday.

He'd stumbled on the book by accident when he ventured into his parents' unfinished basement the morning after his father passed. Roger Fitzgerald kept boxes of his old Army papers in the space behind the stairs, and Fitz needed a copy of his dad's form DD-214, his "Report of Separation from Active Duty," so he could prove his father's eligibility for military funeral honors and order a headstone from the VA.

He knew by the yellowed tape that the cartons had probably been sealed since the late 1970s. When he opened them, it was like unlocking a time capsule. They were full of photographs, including his father's ROTC commissioning portrait, a picture of him in sweat-stained jungle fatigues sitting on the front of an M48 Patton tank in South Vietnam, and one (obviously taken from the inside of a jeep) of a sign that read "No Photography Beyond This Point," with the last *t* partially obscured by the barrel of an M16 rifle.

There were certificates, awards, and letters of commendation, and three small boxes—two of them contained Purple Heart medals, and the third, a Bronze Star with a *V* in the middle of the ribbon indicating that the award had been given for valor. Fitz never knew his father had been decorated for heroism. The Bronze Star citation describing the circumstances of the award was stuffed in a manila folder near the bottom of the carton along with the sought-after DD-214 form.

A second carton contained more of Roger's military memorabilia, but also photos and papers from Roger's father's time in the military. Fitz's grandfather served as a Marine flamethrower operator in World War II and came back from the island-hopping campaigns in the Pacific with emphysema, likely as a result of continuous exposure to burning gasoline.

It was in the second box, in the middle of his grandfather's Marine Corps records, photos and keepsakes (including his "piss-cutter" garrison cap with the eagle, globe and anchor), that Fitz found the leather-bound book. The tome seemed oddly out of place amid the papers, pictures, and uniform items, so Fitz tucked the volume under his arm and left the rest of the papers and things to be sifted through another time.

Kicking his feet free of the blanket, he studied the book, tapping his thumb on the front cover and wondering what he'd find inside. A faded red fabric bookmark dangled between the pages but the book seemed too slender to be a Bible. Perhaps it was a prayer book or hymnal, but that seemed unlikely because there was no imprint of any kind on the spine. Fitz held the book up to his nose and sniffed. It smelled musty and he guessed it hadn't been opened in several decades.

Outside, an owl called out into the night, drawing a smile from Fitz as he opened the book.

The paper was a warm sepia color, thick and slightly warped by moisture. On the first page, inscribed in tall, angular script above the pre-printed word *Journal,* was the owner's name:

Pte. Thomas R. Fitzgerald
14th Bn, Royal Irish Rifles

Fitz stroked a finger over the name, which was written neatly with what he assumed was a fountain pen. A strangeness washed over him as he looked at the name. His Marine grandfather had been Thomas Ryan Fitzgerald, Jr. This man, then, the one whose diary Fitz held in his hands, must have been Thomas Ryan Fitzgerald, Sr.—his *great*-grandfather.

Fitz knew little about his great-grandfather except that he'd immigrated to the United States from Ireland after World War I with his wife, and that his son—Fitz's grandfather—was born in a dilapidated tenement in Hell's Kitchen a few months after they passed through Ellis Island. Thomas Fitzgerald, Sr., died before his grandson, Roger Thomas Fitzgerald, was born, so Fitz's father never knew him. Beyond that, Fitz had no idea what kind of man his great-grandfather was, or what his life was like.

He felt a twitter of excitement and curiosity as he turned the page.

21st September 1915

It was not yet dawn when the sergeants summoned us up by platoon and had us march down to the South Quays for embarkation. Though we were a bit weary from the late night and having got up early to break camp, the lads and I were in high spirits as we made our way down to the quayside.

A part of me wished we had more time in Dublin, but by that point they were not giving out passes to anyone (not wanting to tempt desertion, I suppose). Besides, though things have tamped down a bit since the war began, I am not sure I would want to wander round the streets of Dublin since the moment I tried to order a pint or ask for directions, my speech would give me away and they would know I was an Ulsterman. Back home, people know what county or side of Belfast you come from and what you are by the way you speak. My name may sound Catholic but to one who knows Belfast, my speech would have given me away, so it was just as well I stayed in barracks.

The journey from Dublin to Holyhead was longer than I had expected. Once disembarked from the boat, a train took us to Bramshott, to the south and west of London, but the train was very slow and ground to a halt round Bordon, forcing B, C, and D companies to get off the train and tramp the rest of the way on foot, eight miles to our camp. The lads of my section were in a foul mood by the time we got to the barracks in Bramshott (which some of the lads had taken to calling Bramshite).

Fitz stared at the yellowed page with its angular script and an odd chill shuddered through him. Nearly a century had passed since his great-grandfather, a soldier fighting under a different flag an ocean away, had scribbled these words. He smiled as he reread the passage about the train breaking down and how the men had to go the rest of the way on foot. It reminded him of the time he had to hump his gear back to camp when a Humvee broke down during a training exercise in the California desert.

He wondered what Private Tommy Fitzgerald had looked like in uniform. He found a photo in the box in the basement, taken a few months after Pearl Harbor, with Tommy Fitzgerald, Sr., standing next to Tommy Fitzgerald, Jr., who was in his Marine Corps uniform, presumably while the latter was home on leave. Assuming Tommy, Sr., was in his late teens in 1915, he would have been in his mid-forties in the photo.

Glancing at the picture on the top of the bureau, he wondered what his great-grandfather, Tommy (who, he realized, actually *was* a Tommy) would have thought of the wars his grandson and great-grandson fought in, and the places where they fought them. The jungles of Vietnam and the mountains of Afghanistan were a far cry from the muddy trenches of the Western Front.

Fitz looked up at the photo of him and his parents at Fort Benning and tried to remember his father talking about Tommy, Sr., but his memory came up blank. He remembered hearing now and again about Grandpa Fitz fighting with the First Marines at Guadalcanal, Peleliu, and Okinawa, but not once had he heard about Great-grandpa Fitz serving in the First World War.

Shrugging, he brought his attention back to the rest of the entry for September 21, 1915:

It's now nine o'clock and they have finally just let us duck into our huts to get some rest. Tomorrow promises to be a long day, so I best call it a night. It will be good to finally get aboard the boat to France and start to go about the business of fighting a war. The life of a barracks soldier is nothing short of grim.

Fitz smirked and wondered if this was his ancestor's way of nudging him to get some sleep himself.

"Is that what you're trying to tell me, old man?" He rubbed his finger over the ink, as if by touching the letters he could somehow hear Tommy, Sr.'s voice more clearly. "Fine."

He tugged the faded red ribbon out from between the pages in the middle of the book and marked his place. Fitz set the book on the bedside table and turned off the light, then slid his legs under the covers again.

He nuzzled into the warm down pillow with a yawn, imagining for just a moment that he was curling into another kind of soft warmth.

CHAPTER 29

"Whatcha got there?"

Fitz stood behind Peterson and peered over the tall Swede's shoulder with a mischievous grin. He noisily cracked open a can of Coke and watched Peterson slide a finger under the flap of an envelope. Aware of Fitz's leering, the medic turned around and rolled his eyes.

"What?" Fitz chuckled, his brow creased in feigned innocence.

"You are such a fucking pain in the ass," Peterson said, hunching over his lap as he ripped the envelope open.

"Anything good?" Fitz leaned forward in a half-hearted bid to peek at Peterson's mail.

Slapping the envelope and letter face-down against his thigh, Peterson's eyes swiveled toward the barracks door to make sure no one was standing outside.

He glanced over his shoulder and squinted at Fitz. "Are you so desperate you wanna read my love-letters now? Though ..." He bobbed his head from one side to the other, as if weighing whether or not to reveal a secret, then shrugged. "Cody did tell me once he thought you were kinda cute. A bit too furry, but definitely cute. You know, in a bearlike sort of way." The medic stuck his tongue out and gave Fitz a teasing once-over. "If only you were a little taller."

Fitz grunted out a laugh and smirked. "Low center of gravity makes me a good mule. And a smaller target, of course. A tall Aryan Youth poster child like you can be seen a half-mile away."

"Yeah? Well, your short legs means the enemy doesn't have to lead as much. I'm a bigger bulls-eye, but your short, slow ass is a much easier shot to make, especially with iron sights."

"Yeah?" Fitz grinned and raised his hand with his middle finger firmly extended. "Fuck you, Doc." Peterson puckered his lips and made a kissing sound, then shook his head and returned to his letter.

A couple of minutes passed in silence before the medic took one last longing look at Cody's letter, folded it back into its envelope, and stuffed it into the thigh pocket of his fatigues. He ran his hands over his head with a frustrated growl and looked up to find Fitz sitting on a foot locker a few feet away.

"I've never done this before," Peterson confessed, a frown tugging at the corners of his mouth. He scratched the edge of his bearded chin with his thumbnail as his icy blue eyes met Fitz's. He swallowed hard and looked down at his lap. "I don't know how you do it."

Fitz studied Peterson's tired face.

"Do what? This isn't your first rodeo, Doc." Fitz was puzzled by the comment, given that Peterson had served two six-month deployments to Iraq and Afghanistan and shorter stints as an advisor in Mali and Georgia since joining the detachment four years earlier.

"I know. But I never really left anybody behind before. Know what I mean?"

"Yeah." Fitz's voice softened as he noted the sad slump of his friend's shoulders. "I know exactly what you mean."

"It's hard." Peterson glanced away, unnerved by Fitz's gaze. "I just ..."

The medic stared at the criss-cross of his bootlaces and began to stroke the tufts of his red-tinged beard, tugging them between his thumb and forefinger.

Fitz watched Peterson fuss with his whiskers as his expression morphed from frown to smile to pout. He sympathized, remembering the first time he deployed overseas after finishing Special Forces school and the palpable ache he felt in his chest each night when he rolled into his rack alone.

"It's hard," he admitted. "It was hard the first time I did it, and no matter how many times I do it, it's still hard. It doesn't get any easier. If anything, it gets a little harder."

"It doesn't? Get easier, I mean."

Fitz crossed his arms on top of his thighs. "Bosnia was my first." He turned his hand over and studied the way the light reflected off the white gold of his wedding band, which was dotted with tiny gouges and scratches from years of wear. "Me and Jenn had just moved to Carson when I got orders to ship out to Bosnia to help with the transition from IFOR to SFOR in December '96." Peterson's eyes narrowed and Fitz smiled, quickly recognizing the source of his friend's confusion. "Because I learned Turkish in the Q-Course, they assigned me to be the liaison between Task Force Eagle HQ and a Turkish mechanized battalion. I was overseas for half of the first year we were married."

"Fuck. That's brutal."

"Yeah." Fitz shrugged. "I was there about a month when I caught her for our once-a-week phone call and she told me she was pregnant."

"Really?" Peterson laughed. "You two didn't waste any time, did you?"

"Guess not. And let me tell you, man. What they say about pregnant women and their crazy sex drive—it's totally true, especially when you come home from an overseas tour and she's seven months along."

"She jumped your ass the minute she got you in the door, huh?"

Fitz winked. "More or less. She'd have wore my ass out if she hadn't have gone into early labor six days after I got home."

Peterson rolled his eyes, drawing a chuckle from Fitz.

"Seriously, though—there's no two ways about it. It sucked. It seemed like just when we'd settled into a nice groove, me and her, and got our little hovel in enlisted housing all squared away the way Jenn liked it, I got shipped off." Fitz paused for a moment as he thought about the long months in Bosnia. "She had the worst of it, though."

"Well, obviously. She was pregnant and you were overseas."

"Yeah, but that's not why." The humor that had twinkled in Fitz's eyes faded. "I mean, of course, I'd worry about her—especially her being pregnant and all—but the way I'd worry about her wasn't anything like the way she'd worry about me. Jenn had always been a total newshound, but once I deployed to Bosnia, she stopped watching the news. She told me it was hard enough thinking about me riding around roads lined with land mines without having to hear on the news about what was going on over there. To this day, she can't stand TV news. She reads the paper, but there's something about seeing it on TV that she'd just rather not deal with."

Peterson thought about that for a minute.

"There was this one night," he began, patting his pocket where he'd stowed the letter. "Me and Cody'd been dating for a few months, and we were just sittin' there on the couch and he said somethin' about maybe us moving in together. And I was, ya know, kinda not sure about it. Not because I didn't want to. I did, but ..." He hesitated for a moment and shrugged. "I wanted to make sure he knew what he was getting into, with the deployments and overseas missions and all the time I'd spend in the field training. I told him I'd be gone a lot, a lot of times on short notice. And that there was always a chance, you know, that I might not make it back."

Fitz smiled, recalling the almost identical conversation he and Jenn had the night he asked her to marry him. "They know," he said. "The people who love us, Doc, they know. They're braver than we'll ever be, I think, 'cause even though there's that chance that we might not make it, they love us anyway. We're the crazy motherfuckers who make a living this way, but it's the crazy people who love us—Jenn and Cody—who're the brave ones. Not us."

A soft smile curved Peterson's lips as he pictured Cody back home. "Yeah," he said dreamily. "They are, aren't they?"

Fitz threw off the sheet and sat up, his breath heaving as he felt for Jenn beside him. He was met with a flash of disappointment when he found the bed cold and empty. The night air hit his sweat-slicked skin and he shivered as he blinked away the image of Peterson and his shiny white smile, made all the brighter by the reddish-blond scraggle of beard surrounding it.

"Fuck," he whispered into the dark.

CHAPTER 30

Fitz was standing in the checkout line with his mother when it occurred to him.

He hated grocery shopping. He really, really *hated* it.

It hadn't always been that way. He used to like doing the shopping. When he wasn't in the field training, deployed in Iraq or Afghanistan, or overseas on an advising mission in far-flung places like Mali or the former Soviet republic of Georgia, Fitz was the one who did the grocery shopping. But after he came back from Afghanistan, he was too badly injured to do it. Even after his physical wounds healed, the headaches, fatigue, and forgetfulness caused by the severe concussion he suffered in the blast made shopping almost impossible, so Jenn continued to do it. And since he'd lost his license and Jenn had been gone, he relied on Remy for a ride. Now, every trip to King Soopers reminded him how much his life had changed.

Fitz watched with a frown as the teenage clerk bagged his purchases. He was so caught up in the mire of his own thoughts that he didn't hear the checker ask if he wanted cash back.

"No," his mother answered for him. The checker glanced at her and then shot Fitz a puzzled look.

"Mom," Fitz growled.

"Let's just get these groceries home, hmm?" She spoke gently but with enough of an edge that Fitz didn't argue, though the quick flare of his nostrils left little doubt that he thought about it.

"Fine." He hit the "OK" button on the keypad to accept the total and stuffed his hands into the pockets of his jeans. He didn't give the checker or the bagging clerk a parting glance as he brushed past them on his way out the door.

"It's been a rough week for us," Diane explained to the checker, smiling apologetically as she took the receipt and tucked it into her purse.

She found him standing outside, his brows sloped low and hard over his eyes as he scowled at the darkening sky. A late afternoon storm was rolling in off the plains and by the feel of it, the skies were about two minutes from opening up along a squall line some ten miles to the east. He grabbed the cart and pushed it toward her car.

Once the groceries were loaded into the trunk and the cart returned to the corral, Fitz jerked the door open and slumped into the passenger seat. He didn't turn to look at her or say a word. The only sound that signaled his readiness to leave was the click of his seatbelt.

But Diane Fitzgerald was no stranger to silence.

When Roger came back from his second tour in Vietnam, he was prone to wild, unpredictable mood swings. One minute he would be sweet, loving, and mirthful. The next, he'd be angry, bitter, and brooding, often without a discernible trigger to explain the sudden shift. As the months and years went by, his mood swings leveled out somewhat, but there were still times when his temper flared and his mood soured without any hint as to why.

Diane knew she was one of the lucky ones. She had friends— women she knew from their time at Fort Campbell and Fort Carson—who were widowed by the war. Another of her closest friends, a woman whose husband served with Roger in the 101st Airborne, was left to raise four children on her own when her husband took his life with a shotgun behind the wood pile on a cool November morning. She remembered attending his funeral ten years after the fall of Saigon, and considered him no less a casualty of the war than her other friend's husband, who died in a rocket attack at Khe Sanh in '68.

Knowing that other women had it worse didn't offer much comfort when Roger's brooding silences stretched from hours into days, and it didn't make her feel any better—or better-prepared to deal with the situation—when it became apparent that her son, like his father, came back from war with emotional wounds more difficult to heal than the physical ones that scarred his skin.

Diane glanced over at her thirty-nine-year-old son. He sat in the passenger seat in stony silence, his thick arms crossed in front of his chest as he chewed on whatever emotion was eating away at him. *Oh, Jacob.* She sighed, curling her fingers around the steering wheel and staring at the lazy red glow of the traffic light.

"A man's gotta figure his own way out the other side of it," Roger once told her when she asked him to speak to their son, who had seemingly fallen off the face of the earth after returning from his last deployment. Jacob's weekly phone calls had all but stopped, and when she did manage to connect with him by phone, it was because she called him—never the other way around. The conversations were terse and forced, and his voice more often than not was quiet, distant, and, sometimes, slurred.

As if it weren't enough to hear her son's distress, it was obvious from speaking to Jenn, who reported, "He's doing as well as can be expected," and Ryan, who simply told her, "He's okay," and hurried to get off the phone, that Jacob was anything but okay.

So it was no surprise when she opened her door the morning

after Roger's death to see how much Fitz had changed in just a couple of months. When he finally admitted to her how he'd lost his driver's license, her reaction was more one of resignation than disappointment.

"It'll be fine," she told him as they pulled into their neighborhood. "Don't worry. This time tomorrow *you'll* be driving us home."

Fitz turned and glowered at her, giving her the first eye contact since stomping out of the store in a smolder.

"It's fucking embarrassing. Getting chauffeured around by my mom and an Army chaplain, and having to take my driver's test again after I've been driving for twenty-three fuckin' years."

She heard his anger and knew, despite the sharp edge to his voice, that his frustration was not with her, even though she was the one burned by the blowback.

"What is, is." She held her breath and waited to see if the comment would further rouse his anger. "There's no point rehashing any of it, Jacob. We can't undo what's been done. You can't turn back the clock. All any of us can do is move forward."

He unfolded his arms and shook his head, the tension in his arms and shoulders slowly uncoiling as he stared down the street.

"Your dad always loved John Wayne." A flash of sadness tickled the back of her throat. "And he always liked that saying of his: 'Courage is being scared to death but saddling up anyway.' I don't remember which of his movies that's from."

Fitz's brows, which had been knit low over his eyes, suddenly arched. "I'm not really sure that's from a movie, Mom," he said, reaching up and scratching at the two days' worth of stubble that roughened the edge of his jaw.

Diane smiled faintly as she turned onto their street.

"Well, anyway." She conceded the point with a tiny shrug.

"What I'm saying is, there's nothing heroic about doing what's easy. You know that better than anyone. What you're doing is hard, honey—some of the hardest stuff there is. I just …" Her voice trailed off when a swell of emotion tingled high in her throat. "I wish your father had been able to be here for you, and to have been able to see what you've done, just in the last week, to bring your family back together." She drew a long, steadying breath. "I'm not sure he'd ever have been much help for you in all of this, but I know, as God is my witness, that your dad's looking down at us and he's proud of you for doing what you're doing."

Fitz's lip curled in disdain. "You mean for getting my driver's license back after losing it because I'm an asshat?"

"You're not an asshat. You made a mistake—granted, a big one—but you're trying to make things right, to make life better for yourself *and* your family. Step by step, you're doing it. Tomorrow is the next step. You've done the hard parts already. Tomorrow will be a snap."

"I don't know," he said with a sigh. "I've fucked up so much, it's like I'm waiting for things to turn to shit all over again because I fuck something else up."

Diane frowned. "You won't. And if somehow you stumble, you'll get back on your feet and dust yourself off again. I know you will."

"I dunno."

"I do." She threw the car into park and set the brake. "You're the strongest man I know."

Fitz's eyes widened and deep creases formed on his forehead. "Really, Mom?"

She smiled and studied him for a moment, then reached her hand over and patted his knee.

"Come on. Let's get these groceries in before the rain starts, okay?"

CHAPTER 31

26th February, 1916

It was about one in the morning when the three of us—me, Hughes, and Brown—finally arrived at the number 5 listening post to relieve the men on duty. We had each a cartridge loaded into the breach of our rifles and a box of grenades that sat on the ground between me and Brown. Our orders were to meet any intruder that approached the wire with a Mills bomb, without calling out a challenge.

Unlike the previous entries which had been written in ink, this one was scrawled in pencil and Fitz could feel the impression left in the paper by the writer's own hand. As he stroked his finger across his great-grandfather's words, Fitz wondered what it would have been like to fight a war that was static, with battle lines dug into the earth as the warring sides stared at one another across a no-man's land dotted with mines, coils of barbed wire, unexploded shells, and dead bodies lying where all could see them but no one could retrieve them.

He considered himself lucky that most of the times he'd gone to war, he and his men spent their days on the move as they carried out missions in their area of responsibility, rather than entrenching themselves in fixed fortifications for weeks or months at a time. While Fitz and his men frequently ventured outside the wire in search of the enemy, risking contact each day they went out on patrol, he never felt trapped in quite the same way soldiers like his great-grandfather were in the trenches of the Great War.

It was so cold with the wind blowing and whipping around, biting at our cheeks even though the trench itself provided a windbreak of sorts, that all we wanted to do was huddle up in our post and do what we could to keep warm. It was dark and we could scarcely see a thing beyond our own wire, which made for a bit of nerves as we hoped that the Hun on the other side there was suffering as much as we, and had the sense to stay in his post on the other side of the wire.

Fitz wondered what his great-grandfather would have said if the old Tommy had seen him in northern Iraq in the winter of 2002, six months before the U.S. and its allies invaded. Picked for the fact that he was fluent in Turkish, Arabic, and Farsi, he was one of a handful of men from the 10th Special Forces sent to assist the CIA in organizing the Kurdish militias, the *peshmerga,* into a formidable fighting force. He spent the winter of 2002 and early spring of 2003 traveling from village to village in the rugged mountain districts along the borders with Turkey and Iran, securing the trust of Kurdish tribal leaders and assessing the readiness of the local militias.

He spent a half year in a hostile country 7,000 miles from home, a temperamental satellite phone his only link to the outside world, but as he held the diary in his lap, Fitz decided he would rather have wintered with Kurdish guerrillas on the Iraqi frontier than be trapped in a maze of muddy trenches along a static front.

Had he been forced to serve in conditions like Private Fitzgerald did, he was certain he'd have lost his mind.

All I could think as we watched and listened at the sap-head was how dreadful the cold was and how much my toes hurt. As the night wore on, the pain stopped, and they just went numb. Oh, what I would have given to lay in a hot bath under a roof with a good fire going in the other room and a warm cup of tea in my hands. Though it seems like torture to think of, somehow it made me feel a bit less cold to daydream of being warm rather than muddle about in my own thoughts about how bloody cold it was. So I listened and watched and idly imagined splashing around in a piping hot bath as I waited for our watch to be over.

Shortly before dawn—I'm not quite sure when because with all the gloves and mittens it was nigh impossible to dig into my pocket to find my watch, and in any case it would have been too dark to read it anyhow—we were relieved by another team of three and made our way back to the dugout in time for breakfast and, thank God, some sleep.

Fitz smirked at his great-grandfather's timely, if not subtle, reminder. Stroking his finger one more time across the paper to feel the grooves where the pencil embossed it, he slipped the ribbon between the pages to mark his place, set the journal on the bedside table and turned off the light.

He pulled the covers over his shoulder as he rolled onto his side and stared out the window at the faint gray light cast by the waxing moon. The Ponderosa pine swayed in the breeze, reminding Fitz of the wind that howled outside the old stone houses where the *peshmerga* hosted him the winter before the invasion of Iraq. He remembered their voices bidding him goodnight in their language—"*şew baş, Feetz*"—and how they'd smile when he tried to speak their tongue.

An eight-week crash course at the Defense Language Institute had taught him enough rudimentary Kurdish to get by in the isolated mountain villages of Iraqi Kurdistan. An Iranian language, Kurdish was related to Farsi, and sometimes Fitz found the words for things were similar (like "*bread*," which was *nān* in Farsi and *nan* in Kurdish). Many times, though, the words were so different (like "*evening*," which was *begáh* in Farsi but *êware* in Kurdish) that he struggled to understand and be understood.

One night he found himself switching between Arabic and Kurdish as he explained to one of the *peshmerga* what sushi was and how it was eaten. "You would eat cold, raw fish?" a gray-bearded Kurd had asked him, his sun-wrinkled brow creased in confusion as Fitz sipped his tea. "With a pair of tiny wooden sticks? This is the strangest thing I have ever heard."

Fitz stared out the window, remembering how his mind would buzz with exhaustion at the end of a day spent communicating with people whose language he scarcely knew. After a couple of months among the Kurds, he managed to pick up enough of their tongue that he only needed to rely on Turkish, Farsi, or Arabic as crutches when explaining complex or obscure ideas. But still, the task of navigating an unfamiliar language and culture was hard work, and each night, for however many hours of sleep he managed to get, he slept like a log.

"*Yek ziman her bes niye,*" one of the elders told him after Fitz apologized for misunderstanding something the man had said. "One language is never enough."

The other tribesmen in the meeting had laughed, giving the sheepish American a reassuring clap on the back. Though Fitz was far from fluent in Kurdish, he spoke three other languages besides his own, he understood and respected them, and he told them the truth, even when it was discouraging. The Kurds knew he would do all he could to help them and lead them well in the coming war, and so they trusted him almost as they would one of their own.

As his mind loosened and began to yield to the murmur of sleep, Fitz thought how weird it felt when he and the CIA team finally reunited with the larger American force in the days following the invasion. After months of hearing little of his native tongue, it was strange to be suddenly surrounded by English-speaking voices again. It took days to stop thinking in the muddled patois of Kurdish, Farsi, and Arabic that had been his lifeline during the months he spent in the mountains of Kurdistan.

Fitz arched his head back and yawned, remembering how the relief of coming home and being able to hold his son again, whose little arms wrapped around his waist as he hugged the six-year-old with one arm. He came home with a broken shoulder and shrapnel wounds in his hip and thigh, but his son's embrace had filled him with a euphoria that no painkiller could match.

"Hey, buddy," he said, holding the boy against him as he ruffled Ryan's silky hair.

"We missed you, Daddy." The boy's words came through in a snuffle as he hugged his father's waist. Fitz winced and bent over slightly, rubbing his free hand over Ryan's back as he felt his son's silent, shuddering sobs.

"I know, buddy," he whispered, blinking away tears as he looked up and met Jenn's gleaming gray eyes. "I missed you guys, too."

Fitz stroked his jaw with his fingers, remembering how warm Ryan's little hand felt palming his bearded cheek when they reunited on the tarmac. A few moments later, he pulled the blanket over his shoulders as his eyes fluttered shut and sleep finally overtook him.

CHAPTER 32

Fitz stripped down to his boxer briefs, cracked open the window, and crawled into bed. He frowned at the empty half of the bed next to him and sighed, reminding himself that each night alone put him another day closer to being reunited with his family. Steeled by the thought that he had less than ten days left to go, he reached for the leather-bound book that had become his nighttime companion.

Though he'd have done anything to have his family back home and his wife in his bed, a part of him was grateful for the solitude that afforded him the opportunity to read the diary each night before bed. The ordinary pace of family life, with Jenn's work schedule, his work and training schedule, and Ryan's school and hockey commitments, left little quiet time around the Fitzgerald home. But if there was a silver lining to the way things were and the circumstances of his finding the diary, it was that it gave Fitz a chance to hear his great-grandfather discuss his wartime experiences in a way his father or grandfather never did.

Unable to contain his curiosity any longer, he opened the diary and began to read.

30th June, 1916

There's a charge in the air today. The camps are thick with throngs of men and equipment, many of them newly arrived these last two or three months. Another lad said that there are here arrayed eighteen full divisions of thirteen battalions each—which, if I figure the maths right, means round-about one and one half million men on our side of the line. A major push is upon us, no doubt about it, and the lads and I are looking forward, not to the fighting itself exactly, but to the prospect of finally being done waiting.

I never would have imagined that the life of a soldier at war would involve so much lying about doing nothing. When I first joined the Young Citizen Volunteers in the fall three years ago, we did marching drills, practised with batons and sticks, first aid, long-distance signals and such. The pace of things picked up even more when the YCV became part of the Ulster Volunteer Force—though I was sad to see the Catholic lads, most especially my friend Jack McNeil, go their separate ways. It was after that we became the 14th Battalion of the Royal Irish Rifles.

They have already once postponed the infantry attack. It was supposed to have gone yesterday morning, but midway through the morning on the 28th, they sent word that we were to stand down, which did little but wind up our nerves even more than they already were.

There is a constant cacophony of noise—wagons and equipment being moved in and out and about at all times of day and night, plus the mind-numbing pounding of the artillery, which has been raining shells onto the German lines for the last couple of days, though after the call came to postpone, the rate of fire slackened off quite a bit, I imagine because they want to make their shells last longer.

I know I should be sleeping, but I cannot, what with the noise and the nervous chatter of the lads around me, and the low, dull buzzing that's been in my ears since the last two days. I have cleaned my rifle and reorganized my kit four times in the last two days. I've mended all the holes in my socks and a rip in the sleeve of my coat. The postponement of the assault just makes the waiting all that worse, and the time drag along even more painfully slow than it would otherwise. If it were up to me, I would just as well be done with all the waiting, head back out to the trenches and go over the top. The waiting is killing me.

The sergeant just came round and gave us a stern look. "Get some rest, lads," he says. Rest—cause he knows there will be no sleeping at this point. All we can do is rest and wait.

Fitz swore he could hear the tension in his great-grandfather's voice as he read the messy scrawl and felt how hard the pencil had pressed into the paper.

He knew that feeling. He'd experienced it countless times in the days and hours leading up to a major operation: an indescribable swirl of anxiety mixed with an impatience that left him twitchy and unable to sleep when he knew he needed it most.

He remembered sitting in a hangar in Saudi Arabia holding a fully loaded rucksack between his legs and his rifle across his knees as the sweat soaked into his fatigues underneath his body armor. Tension crackled through his limbs as he waited to queue up with the rest of his platoon into their assigned "chalks" and head out to the tarmac to board the Black Hawk helicopters that would ferry them into Iraq.

He always felt that same sort of tension when he was sitting in the back of a helicopter waiting to fast-rope down to *terra firma*, or riding in a stiff jump seat in the back of a C-17, his main chute strapped to his back and his reserve snug against his belly, or waiting on the ground for reinforcements, air support, or resupply.

For the most part, Fitz didn't mind the uncertainty. Hell, the uncertainty was part of what made his work exciting and interesting—but he hated *waiting*. He never felt more anxious or impotent than those times when he had done all he could to prepare and was left with nothing to do but wait. The wait gnawed at him, nibbled at his confidence until his bowels turned to a churning swirl of anxiety. It was everything he could do to hold himself together until the waiting was over and the need for action saved him from the maddening monotony of helplessness.

Fitz drew the old red ribbon along the crease between the pages to mark his place and closed the book, setting it on the bedside table next to his BlackBerry, wallet, and keys. He reached for the light but hesitated as his eyes fell on the square-headed key to the Scout. His shiny, newly reinstated Colorado driver's license was tucked inside his wallet. In the morning, he would head back down to Fort Carson and, after a visit to the base hospital to get the orthopedist's written confirmation that his wrist had healed and that he was fit to return to full duty without restrictions, would formally assume his position as the senior weapons sergeant of his detachment.

He flicked off the light and stared out the window at the old Ponderosa pine, its sparse, sagging branches a graceful silhouette as it swayed in front of the moon.

CHAPTER 33

Fitz found it strange to be behind the wheel again—wonderful and satisfying, but also strange.

The '76 Scout looked and felt every bit of its thirty-three years. The sharp-angled, squared-off dash with its fake wood laminate had none of the smooth, rounded shapes of a modern car. The steering wheel was large but had a slender rim that gave it an almost delicate feel, and while the original vinyl seats had held up well, but they, too, had begun to show their age, evidenced by the cracks had opened up along the seams. The windshield, pockmarked by years of gravel and grit, was only the Scout's second. The venerable off-roader had only two modifications to its original factory configuration: a new stereo with a CD player, and the electronic ignition interlock Fitz had to install to get his driver's license reinstated.

He merged onto the interstate, letting the throttle open up after passing through Denver's southern suburbs and into the rolling pine-covered hills that marked the way to Colorado Springs. He rolled the window down, the wind tickling the hair on his arm as he grinned and let the newer, faster cars zip by him.

With a temperature in the low sixties and not a cloud in the sky, it was a gorgeous morning for a drive. It had been almost two months since he'd last driven. He held his breath when a Colorado State Patrol car pulled up close behind him, hugging his rear bumper for a few seconds before backing off and zooming past on the left.

Fitz leaned his head to the left, enjoying the feel of the cool morning air against his scalp. These mornings—crisp summer days like this when the air was clear and Mount Evans loomed large along the western horizon—were his favorite. As he felt the breeze on his face, Fitz thought about the diary entry he'd read at breakfast, and the cool, clear morning his great-grandfather woke up to on the day that 120,000 British soldiers attacked German positions along a twelve-mile front:

They always talk about the calm before the storm. Our ears had grown used to the near-constant pounding when, at half seven on the 1st of July, the guns went quiet. It was a beautiful day—the morning air was pleasant and crisp, the sun was shining, the sky was a bright, clear blue, and the birds were chirping happily in the trees. One of the lads, Lawton, made a quip about it being a perfect day for an easy Saturday stroll.

A semi changed lanes, pulling right in front of Fitz and forcing him to slam on his brakes. The Scout's brakes grabbed hard and the truck's nose dipped as it slowed. Fitz eased off the brake and brought the Scout back up to speed. The wind that had been blowing steadily against his arm and face had faded when he slowed down, and the cloudless sky suddenly reminded him of the morning he and Peterson set off on their last patrol.

That cool February morning, the turquoise sky was so striking that he and two of the Afghan corporals had been talking about it as they waited for Peterson and the others to finish gearing up. It was one of the most beautiful mornings Fitz had seen since arriving in Kunar Province in late October. Spring seemed to have come early to the Korengal Valley and the change in the weather had Fitz and the others feeling particularly upbeat that morning.

For Fitz, just as it was for Private Thomas Fitzgerald the morning of the first day on the Somme, the beauty and quiet didn't last long.

As we made our way to take our places behind the brigade's other battalions that had already queued up in the trenches, the bombardment began again, and the sweet silence soon seemed like a distant memory. By the time me and the lads went over the top, the sound of our pounding guns and the Germans' own was loud in our ears. The field was littered with the dead and wounded—who could be distinguished from one another chiefly by whether or not the man moaned when you stumbled over him.

We put our heads down and kept moving, bayonets-first like we'd been trained. Each time the German guns started combing our way again, the corporal shouted for us to come round and follow him. We took cover where we could in the defilade offered by shell craters. When we heard the machine guns go quiet as the enemy had to reload his ammunition or clear a jam, we stumbled out and ran to the next crater hole before the guns began sweeping across the field again.

Fitz leaned hard into the accelerator, passing the lumbering semi and growling as a wave of lightheadedness passed over him. The thought of Tommy, Sr., hunkering down in a blast crater in the middle of No Man's Land, reminded him of the first time he was trapped under fire.

It was in Mogadishu, as the men of his Ranger platoon attempted to make their way to the crash site of a Black Hawk helicopter that had been shot down. He and a half-dozen other

Rangers had huddled against a wall on one side of a residential block as the distant crackle of small arms fire came closer and louder. Soon the Rangers came under heavy fire. The Somali rounds kicked up dirt and stones just a few feet away from where Fitz crouched, and a bullet ricocheted against the wall behind him. A couple of men began firing in the direction the gunfire seemed to be coming from. Another burst sounded in the distance and a round zinged over Fitz's head, flinging a chunk of concrete against the back of his neck. Seconds later, another shot rang out from the other end of the street and the Ranger next to Fitz fell face-first into the sand, his head shattered by a bullet to his temple just below his helmet.

Realizing that the round had come from the opposite direction as the rest of the gunfire that was peppering their position, Fitz had swung his rifle around and barked at his comrades to lay fire on a pair of structures a hundred meters behind them. As the air filled with the punchy clatter of the Rangers' return fire, he heard the militia's haunting call echo in the distance:

"Kasoobaxa guryaha oo iska celsa cadowga," the Somali voice bellowed. "Come out and defend your homes."

Blinking at the memory, Fitz settled into the right hand lane, reaching back to scratch his neck as he recalled the Somali heat and how the sweat pooled under the collar of his Kevlar vest.

He grunted at the memories and images, wanting nothing more than to send them on their way. Unable to flush his mind of the sight of the Ranger lying face-down in the blood-soaked sand, he reached into the pocket of his cargo shorts and retrieved his BlackBerry. He pressed a button to display the time above a picture of Jenn and Ryan sitting on his parents' deck. His thumb hovered over the green call button as he wondered if she would be awake yet.

After a moment, he decided it was too early and slipped the phone into his pocket.

CHAPTER 34

It was late afternoon when Fitz finally called them—late enough that he knew Ryan would be through with hockey for the day, but early enough that Jenn wouldn't yet be tied up cooking dinner. He sat on the front porch and leaned against the pillar, tapping his foot as he waited for her to answer.

"Hey," she answered, her voice sweet and liquid in his ears. He missed her—and Ryan, too—even more than he had while he was deployed, and more so than in the five weeks after they first left.

"Hey." Fitz found himself at a loss for words. More than anything, he'd called simply to hear the sound of her voice.

"So, you're back on post?"

"Yeah." Fitz rubbed his calf, letting his fingertips skim gently over the bumpy skin before ruffling the hair and wiggling his foot as a distraction. "Just came down this morning. Gotta report for a team meeting at 0800 tomorrow and then hit the range at 0930. Feels like it's been ages since I've thrown lead downrange but I gotta get back in the swing of things before we head out into the field next month."

Static hummed on the line between them. Fitz knew she hated that he had to leave for a field exercise just two weeks after she and Ryan returned home, but they both understood that nothing could

225

be done about it. With the mission in Iraq still winding down but no end in sight to the war in Afghanistan, Fitz's team followed a strict twenty-four month rotation schedule—spending six months deployed in theater, followed by eighteen months to recuperate, reequip, and train before deploying again. The operational cycle was relentless and while they tried not to think about it, the family was constantly aware of where in that cycle they were and how close he was to having to deploy again. It had been that way since 9/11, and they accepted that it might be that way until the day Fitz hung up his boots and left the Army.

"I miss you, Jacob."

Warmth pooled in his gut when she called him by his Christian name. Most times he was Fitz, but when she wanted to get under his skin, or when she wanted to let him know he'd gotten under hers, she called him Jacob.

"I miss you like crazy, Jenn," he whispered. "I'm glad you and Ryan are staying there so he can finish out hockey, but God—having you two back again, even though it was just for a few days, was amazing. The next week's gonna feel like a fuckin' eternity."

"I know." She drew a breath and he sensed that there was more she wanted to say, but that she was constrained by time and place. "Ryan's here. Do you want to talk to him?"

"Umm." Fitz swallowed, a flash of anxiety washing away the warm, happy feeling that had filled him just moments before. "Yeah, I mean, if you think he wants to."

"Of course he does." There was a shuffling sound as she handed off the phone.

"Hello?" Ryan's voice was slightly huskier than it had been before Fitz deployed to Afghanistan, but still sounded boyish. For some strange reason, the change seemed more noticeable on the phone. "Dad?"

"Hey, buddy. How're you doin'? You done with camp for the day?" Fitz winced at his own awkwardness as he tried to make conversation with his son. He'd been disconnected from the daily rhythms of the boy's life for so long it was like they lived on separate planets.

"Yeah." Ryan's voice wavered slightly, then steadied again. "We had a team scrimmage today and I got a hat trick."

"Really? That's awesome, buddy. I wished I'd have been there to see it."

"Me too, Dad."

Ten more days, Fitz reminded himself, trying to focus on his son's success and not on the fact that he'd missed it. "I got my driver's license back," he offered, bracing for a snarky response. A moment passed with nothing but static on the other end of the line. "I'm back home, you know—on post. Going back to the range in the morning. Docs released me for full duty." A few seconds passed but Ryan still didn't say anything. "House sure feels empty without you guys."

Please say something, Fitz begged silently. The two outings to the pool had narrowed the distance between him and Ryan, leaving him optimistic that maybe, just maybe, he'd find a way to make things right with his son. But every passing second of silence nibbled at his optimism and left Fitz questioning whether he'd been fooling himself all along.

"Are we still gonna go camping?" Ryan asked abruptly. "St. Mary's Falls Trail? You know, when me and Mom get back?"

Fitz smiled, vaguely remembering suggesting the outing weeks ago. "Yeah, definitely. I'd like that a lot."

"Cool." Voices in the background began chattering. "I gotta go, Dad. Nana says I have to take a shower before dinner."

Fitz laughed. Ryan's sweat had begun to take on a more adult-like rankness in the last six months. "Yeah, you better. Nana doesn't want anything stinky in her kitchen." The clatter of dishes in the background made Fitz suddenly feel very far away from his family. "What's for dinner?"

"Beef stew." The downward lilt in Ryan's voice left little doubt of his opinion of the evening menu. "Hey, Dad, I gotta go."

"Okay. I love you, buddy. I miss you and can't wait to see you again."

"Yeah," the boy said with a sigh. "I love you, too, Dad."

Fitz closed his eyes as his son handed the phone back to Jenn.

"I have to go, too. Call me later tonight? Maybe ten-ish?"

Fitz's pout curved into a crooked smile. "Yeah, sure. Give my best to Frank and Lois, okay? I love you."

"I will. Love you, too, Jacob."

Hours later, Fitz turned off the TV, tossed the remote on the coffee table and dumped his empty soda cans in the sink, frowning at how the clatter echoed in the empty house.

After brushing his teeth, he dropped his toothbrush in the cup next to the faucet and leaned over the sink to look at himself in the mirror. Having given himself a trim the night before the funeral, his hair was still regulation-length. But one stroke of his fingers over the edge of his jaw reminded him of how long it had been since they laid his father to rest. He was scruffy, though nowhere near as scruffy as he'd been when Jenn came into his room at Brooke Army Medical Center in Texas after he was medevac'd from Afghanistan.

He'd only been half-awake, thanks to the cocktail of drugs they'd given him, but he remembered the look on her face when she saw him lying there with an oxygen tube in his nose and an IV in his arm, smiling at her behind a ragged brown beard. Fitz recalled her smile and the way she touched the top of his hand, stroking the vein over his wrist to his knuckle. Too drowsy and scramble-brained to speak, he turned his hand over, capturing her finger with his thumb and giving her hand the best squeeze he could manage under the circumstances. The last thing he remembered from that night was her whispering his name as she kissed his forehead.

He closed his eyes, taking a moment to savor the memory of Jenn's soft lips brushing against his skin before he shut off the bathroom light. Climbing into bed, he propped the pillows behind his back and reached for the diary. He stroked the leather cover, appreciating its smooth grain before opening the diary to the passage where he left off.

6th July, 1916

Although I would be a fool to say it is the worst part of being in hospital (though as far as I'm concerned, I'm loathe to complain at all about having been wounded given how many fallen men I stumbled over that first day), I hate being out of touch with my mates. I have no idea where the men of my section or my company are, and given the sheer number of wounded men who have passed through this and a half dozen other casualty clearing stations since the fighting began on 1st July, there seems to be no one here who can tell me.

Fitz flipped the diary over onto his thigh and leaned back against the headboard.

He knew the feeling of having survived, but not knowing what happened to one's comrades. In the minutes after he woke up at Landstuhl, everything was hazy—his vision, his hearing, and, above all, his memory—and he wasn't sure where he was or what day it was or what had happened to him. He'd looked down and saw the IV in his left arm, then turned and saw the right half of his body swaddled in bandages. When he tried to move his right arm and leg, he felt a dull tightness. The discomfort made him wince and a similar tightness tugged at the side of his neck. *Where am I?* he'd wondered, unsure in those very first moments if he could even speak, or if any of it was even real.

"Doc," he'd called out as soon as he realized he wasn't intubated. "Where are you, Doc?" When there was no answer, panic fell over him like a curtain. "Doc, where are you?!"

He recalled the look on the attending nurse's face when she ran in and found him squirming in his bandages, his heart monitor beeping and lighting off because his heart rate had shot up as the panic overtook him. Afraid he would tear open his sutures, the young lieutenant quickly administered a sedative, and soon everything faded to black again. He remembered nothing until the afternoon, several days later, when he awoke from a nap and saw his wife's smile and shimmering gray eyes. The confusion he'd felt at Landstuhl was still there, but her presence blanketed him with a sense of safety that took the edge off his fear.

Fitz drummed his fingers on the diary's hard leather cover and picked it up again.

There is a lovely nurse, a sweet, dark-eyed angel from Belfast who has tended to me these last few days, and when I asked her about the fate of my company, she apologized and told me she did not know. When I asked if she could find out, she looked at me with her beautiful doe eyes and told me there was no way for her to do so, then pulled the sheet to the side and set about to changing the dressings on my leg and head.

Fitz laughed out loud. *So I'm not the first Fitzgerald to fall for his nurse,* he thought. He smirked, recalling the morning he sliced open his shin on the obstacle course and how he distracted himself from the pain by plotting how he was going to get the sexy gray-eyed nurse's phone number.

Though it is not a pleasant thing to have one's bandages unwrapped, his wounds poked at, and wrapped again in fresh gauze, I have come to look forward to my dressing changes nearly as much as to meal times, perhaps more so, because I get to have her all to myself for a few minutes of time, and feel her touch. Oh, her touch—it is so gentle, and her voice so soft and sweet, I truly think that she is an angel of God sent to take care of me in this hell I now find myself in.

Fitz imagined Tommy Fitzgerald lying in a crowded field hospital in France, gritting his teeth in pain and beside himself with worry for his comrades. He guessed that his great-grandfather had heard whispers of the casualty reports as they came in and it became clear that the assault on July 1st had been extremely costly. By the end of that day, British forces had advanced one mile to the east but at a cost of over 19,000 men killed or missing in action and another 38,000 wounded. That his great-grandfather, who chose his words carefully, called his situation *hell* left little doubt how horrible it had been for him. He was glad that the young private stumbled upon a woman whose kindness gave him comfort when he needed it most.

Maeve McGinty is her name, and she hails from North Belfast. She's a VAD—a volunteer who answered the call for young ladies to join the Volunteer Aid Detachments. She came to France as a sort of junior nurse, helping out with various tasks so that the experienced nurses can assist the surgeons in treating the more difficult cases. Her brother Michael is a lance corporal in the 12th Rifles, which is part of the 108th Brigade that took the northern flank of the assault on the Schwaben Redoubt.

He has been missing since 1st July, and I know by the look in her eyes that she knows he is gone. She is so beautiful and gentle and sweet, I feel my heart breaking for her, knowing she has lost her brother, but also I feel as if my heart is wrapping around her, or wants to. When she touches me, a shock runs all through me, crackling up from the bottoms of my feet all the way up my spine and through my shoulders. When she holds my hand, or touches my leg, I feel my entire body, my whole being, come alive in a way I have never felt before.

Reading of his great-grandfather's burgeoning love for the young nurse made Fitz smile, suddenly realizing why Jenn so adored the romance novels she read on her days off and before bed. He wanted to know how Tommy and Maeve's story ended. Was Maeve his great-grandmother, or just a passing fancy whose affection and companionship comforted Tommy when the wounded Belfast lad needed it most?

Last night, when she came round with my tea, Maeve sat with me as I ate. Once I was finished, she drew her chair up close to my bed and clasped my hand in hers. "I'll miss you terribly," I told her, pulling her hand up and pressing her knuckles to my lips. Her cheeks flushed a lovely pink as she smiled at me.

"I'll miss you, too," she said. "It's not that I don't want you to go, but rather that I wish I'd be going with you."

I was quiet for a minute as I held her hand to my lips. "I love you," I told her. The words slipped out of me without any forethought at all. It had not been my intent to tell her in such a way, or at such a time. I was sure my heart was going to explode out of my chest. I was about to say something else, but I so stammered about, I had no chance to get it out before she leaned in close and kissed my cheek, which was all rough with beard, since I had not been able to have a proper shave since taking shrapnel to my ear on the 1st.

"I would leave this place today," she whispered to me, "if I knew I could leave here with you."

Fitz's chest swelled with warmth as he read of his great-grandfather's love for Maeve. Fitz found himself rooting for Tommy, loving Maeve for no other reason than because Tommy loved her, and because she loved Tommy back.

It was everything I could do not to turn my head and kiss her. One of the senior nurses was just then passing by, and I saw from the jaundiced look in that stern old nurse's eye that she would have had my head had I so much as pecked Maeve on the cheek.

"If I could take you with me," I told her, "I would. We'd go home together, you and I."

Maeve closed her eyes and a tear fell onto her round, pink cheek. I squeezed her hand and brought it once again to my lips, kissing her fingers since there was no way to kiss her beautiful lips. "As soon as I can leave this place, I will," she said. "And as soon as I am home, I will find you."

Fitz closed the book with a snap and set it on the bedside table. He drew the covers back and slid his legs between the sheets, pulling the thin, waffle-weave blanket over his hip. Grabbing his BlackBerry off the table, he pressed the speed-dial button and nuzzled into the pillow as he listened to it ring. He smiled when her husky voice answered.

"Hey—"

"I love you," he whispered.

CHAPTER 35

Remy acknowledged the waitress with a soft jerk of his chin. She handed them their drinks and offered to give them a minute to look over the menu.

"You doin' okay there?" Remy sipped his Coke, then hid his mouth behind his glass as he waited for Fitz's response.

Fitz shrugged as he squeezed four lemon wedges, one by one, and dropped them into his iced tea. "I'm okay. I miss my wife and kid, you know, and I'm worried about my mom. She hasn't lived alone since the Nixon administration."

"She seems like a tough little lady to me," the chaplain observed.

Fitz grinned. "Don't let the 'little' part fool you. Mom's all of ninety pounds soaking wet, but she kept my dad in line all those years. And lemme tell you, that was no easy task. I mean, if you think *I'm* a pain in the ass ..."

Remy smiled, glancing over to the bar where his eyes met the waitress's long enough to inform her with a slight shake of his head that they weren't yet ready to place an order. He looked back to find Fitz staring at his iced tea, dunking the lemons by poking them with his straw. Remy watched his companion's jaw tighten then relax, before tensing again.

The chaplain was used to Fitz's constantly shifting moods. One minute, the sergeant would be bright-eyed and smiling, full of quips, jokes, and pithy observations, and the next, he fell silent and sank deep into himself, his eyes hardening or glazing over as he turned inward. The reasons for the sudden shift were often indiscernible, but Remy knew that sometimes, a bit of gentle probing was enough to get Fitz talking again.

"So you got things all squared away up there in Littleton?"

Fitz gave his lemons another couple of stabs, then shrugged again.

"Yeah, I guess."

He resumed his straw-borne attack on his lemons. Remy watched in silence as Fitz fussed with his tea. Having already pressed once to penetrate Fitz's deliberative quiet, the chaplain decided to sit back and wait as he wondered what exactly was going on in Fitz's head.

"So I was going through my dad's stuff," Fitz finally said. "You know, looking for his DD-214. I don't know why he didn't keep a copy of that shit handy for Mom, but ... well, anyways, so I had to go through all these boxes in my parents' basement full of Dad's Army stuff to find it. There were boxes and boxes of crap, not just of my dad's, but also some of my grandpa's stuff from when he was in the Marines back in World War II."

"Oh, wow. That had to have been kinda cool, though."

"It was, in a way." Fitz's voice wavered as he glanced out the window. "Weird, though, too. There was all kinds of stuff in there—old medals, photos, commendations, and all. Found out stuff I never knew about my dad, and his dad."

The chaplain heard a faint shadow of something, gravity perhaps, darken Fitz's voice.

"Really?" Remy's brows arched in curiosity as he hoped a gentle verbal nudge would keep Fitz talking.

"Like, I knew my dad got wounded a couple of times in Vietnam, you know?" Fitz's gaze was dim and unfocused as he stared at his tea, poking at his lemons. "He got shot once in the arm at Song Be, about twenty miles from the Cambodian border, back in '68. I knew about that one. And I knew he got hit with shrapnel on his second tour, in the A Shau Valley in '71." He fell silent but didn't look up as he watched the lemons bob among the melting ice cubes.

"But?" Remy prompted him again.

Fitz dropped his straw in the glass and looked up with a sigh.

"I'd always thought he caught a bit of shrapnel in the thigh. Never knew 'til Mom told me that he actually caught it in the groin."

"Ooof." Remy hissed and gritted his teeth as he imagined the injury.

"Yeah. Tore him up bad enough they actually had to remove one of his balls. Found out that's why him and Mom never had any more kids." He shrugged and resumed his assault on the lemons. "NVA mortars as contraception, you know?"

"Wow. I bet it was strange finding that out."

Fitz stilled his fidgeting. "It was."

He reached for the backpack sitting next to him, unzipped it, and retrieved the leather-bound diary, which he'd slipped into a quart-sized Ziploc bag. "Check this out," he said, sliding it across the table.

"What is it?"

Remy carefully opened the Ziploc bag and pulled out the journal. He ran his finger over the smooth leather cover and tugged gently at the red ribbon place marker before gingerly opening it. Fitz watched him read the inscription on the inside.

"It's my great-grandfather's," Fitz told him. "He was in a British regiment called the Royal Irish Rifles, which was part of the 36th Ulster Division, at the Battle of the Somme. He kept this diary from the time his youth group became part of the Ulster Volunteers until he and my great-grandmother, Maeve, left to come to the U.S. in 1919."

Remy's mouth fell open in a broad, toothy smile.

"Are you serious? That's amazing."

"Yeah," Fitz said with a proud flash of his brows. "It was kinda hard to read at first, because of the handwriting, and the language itself is more formal and stilted than we use today."

Fitz sat quietly as the chaplain read. He poked at his lemons from time to time until the ice had mostly melted and the cubes no longer tinkled against the glass. A few times he started to speak but hushed himself. Instead, he leaned against the back of the booth and watched the restaurant's patrons come and go.

"Have you two decided what you want?"

The waitress stood with her notepad pressed against her chest as her eyes swiveled back and forth between Fitz and the red-headed chaplain, who looked up from the book with a sheepish grin. The two men exchanged glances and with a quick nod Remy prompted Fitz to go first.

"I'll have the carne asada." Fitz elicited a faint smile from the server with his flawless Spanish pronunciation. "Medium well. Extra jalapeños and *cebolletas*, please. Do *tortillas de harina* come with?" The server nodded. "Awesome. Plus, a side of guacamole and some more chips."

The chaplain laughed. "I'll have the combo with two enchiladas and a beef taco." The waitress jotted down their order, thanked them, and walked away. "Where'd you pick up the Spanish accent?"

"I'm good with languages." Fitz said with a smirk. "Plus, I grew up around here, and there are a lot of Mexican taquerias and *carnicerias* around town if you know where to look. You, on the other hand, order like a total gringo."

"I *am* a total gringo," Remy admitted. Pushing his half-empty glass of Coke toward the edge of the table where it could be readily refilled, he quickly brought their conversation back to the diary. "This is really amazing, Fitz."

Remy continued to peruse the volume while they waited for their food. He was fascinated by the diarist's intelligence and wry sense of humor, which he supposed was a family trait—like great-grandfather, like great-grandson. He moved through the diary, reading passages here and there as Fitz shared vignettes of some of the more interesting entries he'd read.

When the waitress arrived with their plates, Remy closed the book, slipped it into its protective sleeve, and gently set it aside. Grinning as Fitz's carne asada was placed in front of him along with a plastic dish of warm tortillas, Remy sat back to make room for his own plate.

"You've really been getting into this, huh? I mean, the diary."

"I've been up every night reading it, sometimes until the wee hours of the morning. It's just so interesting I can't put it down. It's like this entire family history nobody bothered telling me about."

The chaplain tapped his finger on the cover of the book and slid it toward the middle of the table.

"Still having trouble sleeping?"

Fitz's hazel eyes narrowed and his jaw tensed.

"I just don't understand why nobody ever told me this stuff," he said, ignoring the question as he tucked the diary into his backpack.

"I never knew my great-grandmother was Catholic, or that her and my great-grandfather came to America because people were vandalizing their parents' houses, busting up their windows, splattering paint on their front doors, and harassing them on the streets. Which is ironic since a couple of generations before that, a Fitzgerald man married a woman who was Church of Ireland and he ended up leaving the Catholic Church for her, which is how us Fitzgeralds came to be Protestants in the first damn place.

"I didn't know any of that. All I knew was that my dad's grandparents came over from Ireland right after the First World War. I never knew that my great-grandfather lost half his toes and part of an ear to a shell blast on the first day of the Battle of the Somme. I mean, why didn't my dad ever tell me any of this stuff?"

"About his grandfather, you mean?" Remy asked.

"Yeah."

"Maybe he didn't know," the chaplain suggested. "Maybe your dad didn't tell you because your great-grandfather didn't tell *him* all of those things. Maybe Great-grandpa didn't tell his son or grandson about all the things that happened to him because it was too unpleasant to think about."

Fitz kneaded the inside of his lip between his teeth but said nothing. Glancing over at the bar to make sure the server wasn't on her way with refills, Remy took a deep breath and turned back to his friend. His eyes narrowed and he studied Fitz for a moment, trying to gauge whether or not to press harder. Fitz's eyes flicked up to meet the chaplain's and they held one another's gaze for several seconds.

"How come in all the time we've known each other, you've never told me anything about what happened to you over there?"

Fitz's eyes flashed and Remy felt a flicker of unease as the Green Beret's hands clenched into tight, veiny fists.

"Or about the buddy of yours you lost?"

Fitz's nostrils flared wide as he glared back in anger. "Because it's not something I want to talk about."

Remy shrugged, then reached for his Coke and took a long, measured sip.

"Maybe your great-grandfather didn't want to talk about those things either. Maybe he felt guilty for having made it back alive, mostly in one piece, when so many other men didn't make it back at all."

"What are you trying to say, Padre?" The two Spanish syllables dripped with sarcasm. Remy saw it for what it was—a way of pushing him away, of keeping him at arm's length as the discussion edged toward a sensitive, painful place.

Remy leaned over the table, crossing his arms in front of him as he looked deep into Fitz's hard, shimmering eyes.

"I think you feel guilty for having survived that IED." The chaplain's voice was soft and steady. "That you made it home alive when your friend didn't."

Fitz's jaw turned rigid as he looked away, his gaze settling on his glass of watered-down tea.

"That's not why." His voice was barely above a whisper, his gaze narrowing as he chewed the inside of his lip. "That's not—"

Fitz's long lashes fluttered as his temple pulsed and his Adam's apple dipped low in his throat. The chaplain began to speak but hesitated as he saw Fitz roll his thumb in circles over the side of his forefinger, over and over again. As he watched Fitz grind his teeth and stare into his glass, Remy wondered what memories were grinding away in his friend's mind.

Fitz looked up at the ceiling and shook his head, squeezing his eyes shut as a low, rough sigh rattled in the back of his throat. "We flipped for it." His voice was raspy and distant. He opened his eyes and met Remy's sympathetic gaze.

The chaplain's brows furrowed slightly as he struggled to follow Fitz's non sequitur. "What?" He tempered the tone of his voice as he prompted Fitz to explain. "I don't know what you mean."

Fitz looked away for a second as he stared out the window, then shook his head as if to shuttle an unwanted image from his mind.

"We flipped a coin. I'd walked point the last two times we'd done a dismounted patrol through that particular area and I told him it was his turn. He gave me a hard time about it, because he was always a pain in the ass like that, so we flipped for it." His voice cracked on the last word, and he lowered his gaze, closing his eyes for a moment and swallowing hard before looking up again.

"They set off the IED right as Doc and his fire team walked past, and ..."

Tears welled up in Fitz's eyes as the memory played out in his mind.

"It tore him apart," he croaked. "We'd just passed between two little stone houses, and it went off in the space between them. They just—" He blinked, freeing a tear that he quickly wiped away with his thumb. His mouth hung open for a few seconds, then as he gritted his teeth and rubbed the side of his calf under the table. "The surgeons pulled chunks of his pelvis out of my leg at Landstuhl."

Remy's mouth went dry and he watched Fitz rub his hand over his scar-pebbled leg, something he'd seen him do dozens of times before. And while Remy had long known that his friend carried the guilt of his comrade's death, he'd never imagined that Fitz had actually had literal pieces of his comrade surgically removed from his body. He struggled to wrap his mind around the gravity of it.

Remy took a sip of his Coke, worried by the pinched, anxious look on Fitz's face.

"Look," he said. "It was a chance thing—a flip of the coin. And had he simply taken his turn, it would have been him anyway, right?" His brows knit low over his eyes as he shook his head firmly. "No, I took point two days in a row, see? Had he gone the time before, it would have been *me* that day. I went the two days before that, so—"

"It's not your fault. You can't own this."

Fitz clenched his teeth as he rotated his glass back and forth against the table. "He shouldn't have been there. I should've—"

The chaplain reached across the table, touching Fitz's wrist as Remy tried to still his hand. "Come on, Fitz, you can't—"

"Don't." Fitz jerked his hand away, knocking his glass over in the process. He slid out of the booth before the spilled tea began to drip onto his seat. He grabbed his backpack, fished a twenty-dollar bill out of his pocket, and dropped it onto the table.

Remy stood up and called after him as he headed for the door.

"Fitz, wait. Listen—"

But before the chaplain's words reached Fitz's ears, he was already out the door.

CHAPTER 36

Fitz glanced in the side mirror, half-expecting so see the chaplain come running out of the restaurant. His hand trembled as he scraped the edge of the key against the Scout's steering column.

"Fuck."

He tried again, jabbing the key into the ignition and turning it, but all he heard was a lifeless click. Growling in frustration, he ripped the interlock's handset off the dash, breathing hard into the device and glaring at it as he waited for it to beep its approval. When it finally did, he turned the key with a jerk, clenching his jaw as the truck's electrical system woke with a quiet murmur.

The instruments on the dash flickered as Peterson's bright eyes smirked at him from the edge of a memory.

He'd been the last one to report to the team room that morning. Fitz was sitting in the back nursing his third cup of coffee when he looked over the rim of his mug and saw the newcomer acknowledge the officers with a nod before taking a seat. Fitz's eyes narrowed as he studied Staff Sergeant Matthew Peterson, the new medic whose file he'd reviewed the day before.

Fitz's lip curled when the blond-haired, blue-eyed medic with the high cheekbones turned to say something to Ramirez, the engineering sergeant next to him. He found it hard to believe that the new pretty-boy medic would fit in with the rest of the team. Ramirez's broad nose scrunched at whatever Peterson whispered to him.

He knew from the file that Peterson had an impressive resumé—deploying to Bosnia in 1997 with the 1st Infantry Division as part of the NATO peacekeeping mission, and later serving with the 82nd Airborne before earning his Green Beret in April 2001. Not six months after moving to Böblingen, Germany to join the 10th Special Forces Group's 1st Battalion, the planes hit the Twin Towers and the forward-deployed teams of the 1st Battalion were sent to Afghanistan. In the four years since then, Peterson had served deployments in both Afghanistan and Iraq before transferring to 2nd Battalion and Fitz's team.

Bringing his mug up to his lips, Fitz resolved to give the kid a chance to prove himself before passing final judgment. He sipped the strong, God-awful Army coffee and winced as the team's officers, Captain Farr and Chief Young, called the meeting to order. Fitz watched with a smirk as Peterson sat up straighter in his seat and the goofy smile vanished from the medic's lips.

Fitz's ears filled with the roaring sound of blood as the Scout surged to highway speed and merged onto the interstate with a throaty growl. He cranked the window down just to feel the wind on his face, to help the present seem more *present* as he prayed for the obtrusive memories to go away. He tried to focus on the loud hum of the pavement underneath the Scout's tires.

But no matter what he tried, the memories continued to flicker on the edge of his awareness.

"That Ryan?" Peterson smiled when Fitz swiped his thumb over the photograph, as if by so doing he could actually reach out and touch the boy's face.

"Yeah." Fitz pursed his lips and held the wallet-sized school picture up to the light.

"Can I see?" The medic's wispy blond brows arched high over his eyes. Fitz handed over the photograph, his forehead creasing as Peterson held the tiny photo between his thumb and forefinger. "Good lookin' kid," he said with a wry grin. "I mean, he's a real good lookin' boy. You sure he's yours?"

Fitz rolled his eyes. "Very funny, Doc."

He snatched the picture out of Peterson's hand and carefully slipped it into his left chest pocket, patting it to make sure it was secure. "That's Ryan. He's eleven. He's on the honor roll at school—a smart cookie just like his mom."

Peterson cocked a brow at the remark. "You're not exactly a flunkie yourself, Boss."

"Well, thanks," Fitz said, scratching the edge of his bearded jaw. "But Ryan and Jenn are head and shoulders smarter than me. My boy's got my wife's mind for science and math."

"Your wife's an R.N., right?"

"Licensed nurse practitioner, actually." Fitz made no effort to conceal the pride in his voice. "She got her master's at UCCS a couple of years ago. She's a shift supervisor in the ER at Penrose—you know, over there on Nevada Avenue?"

Peterson laughed. "Yeah, I know it well. Cody's station's not too far away. He takes patients to Penrose all the damn time. Him and Jenn probably know each other." His eyes narrowed as a mischievous grin lit up his face. "You know how ER nurses are with their favorite paramedics."

"Why would you assume that Cody's her favorite? Just because he's your favorite? I'm afraid it doesn't work like that, pal."

"What are you talkin' about, Boss? Chicks always dig the gay guy."

The memory of Peterson's glittering eyes and toothy smile cut

Fitz to the quick. His fingers curled around the steering wheel. His chest tightened so much it hurt to breathe and his shoulders tensed until they ached.

He tried to ignore the swelling roar of conversation around him as he polished off his fifth beer of the afternoon. A couple of kids from Colorado College with black and gold CC baseball caps sat down next to him and ordered a bucket of Bud Light longnecks. The bartender came by and asked if he was ready for the second of his two-for-one Sierra Nevada drafts, and Fitz answered with a quick jerk of his chin.

A few beers later, Fitz tore his gaze from the game on the TV and turned his heavy, wobbly head to the kids next to him.

"Yeah, I know," one said to the other. "I mean, that's the dumbest-ass T-shirt design I'd ever fuckin' seen. So then I told him, 'What, you think we're all a bunch of fags?' Shit, I wouldn't be caught dead wearing that fuckin' thing. Looks like it was made for a fuckin' sorority, and—"

Fitz stood up roughly and kicked his stool away from the bar. "You got some kind of fuckin' problem?" He angled his head as he appraised the young man with a dark glare.

The young man took an apprehensive step back. "Look, I wasn't even talking to you, mister. Really, man, just chill out and mind your own business, all right?"

The kid's voice was liquid and murky in Fitz's ears, and everything around him seemed fuzzy—everything except the feeling of indignation and rage that bubbled inside of him. It was when the second kid muttered, "Maybe he's a fag," that Fitz's entire body released like a tightly coiled spring and both of the kids hit the floor. By the time somebody pulled him off the second kid, Fitz's knuckles were split and bleeding, through nowhere near as profusely as the kid's busted nose and lip.

His knuckles were still throbbing when Jenn bailed him out of the

El Paso County Jail a couple hours later.

Fitz grunted. His arm shot out and he flipped the radio on, nearly twisting the knob off in a bid to drown out the sound of his own recursive thoughts. A familiar guitar riff bellowed out of the truck's speakers—the local hard rock station was playing one of his favorite Metallica songs. He tried to lose himself in the song's bass line while the main riff came across as a low, almost syncopated growl, but he found himself slipping away from the present as the radio, too, faded into the murmur of memory.

"Hmmph." Peterson leaned on the open door with a crooked, open-mouthed grin.

Fitz's brow furrowed as his senior medic gave him a long, head-to-toe look. "What?" he groused, glancing down at his loosely-laced Nikes. "You told me it was casual."

Peterson snorted and gave Fitz another, somewhat quicker, once-over, then finally opened the door all the way. "Get in here." He shut the door behind them and turned the deadbolt.

Fitz's jaw dropped as he walked into the apartment. The place was immaculate—which alone didn't shock him, because Peterson was known for being fastidious both about his appearance and the way he kept his rack and gear squared away in the field—but the apartment was more than neat. The place was, for lack of a better term, very cool.

"Nice digs," he called to Peterson who had disappeared into the kitchen.

Left to his own devices, Fitz set about reconnoitering the public areas of the apartment. The furniture was like nothing he had ever seen before—ultra-modern with smooth, simple shapes, but crafted from a rustic, western-looking wood that he guessed was some kind of stained pine. A modern western theme dominated the living room, the walls of which were painted a deep chestnut that reminded him of the time his Boy Scout troop went to Monument Valley, Utah. A framed photograph over the couch caught his eye, but it took him a few moments to recognize the line of craggy peaks rising up behind a mist-covered flatland. It was the Trialeti mountain range in Georgia. He remembered the warm summer day Peterson snapped the photo during a break in training maneuvers near Krtsanisi.

Fitz's living room reconnaissance was cut short by the creaking of the oven door. No sooner had he turned around than his nostrils were struck by the rich, smoky smell of tomatoes, cheese, basil, and oregano emanating from the kitchen. Peterson inspected the bubbling pan of lasagna inside, then, satisfied with its progress, took it out of the oven and flipped the dial to turn it off.

"I hope you're hungry," he said as he tossed the oven mitt on the counter and reached for the open bottle of Chianti next to the sink. "We've got enough lasagna to feed a whole platoon and Cody got called in at the last minute to cover an extra shift so it's just the two of us. Vino?" He held up the bottle of wine but Fitz waved him off as the medic took a small sip from his own glass.

"You got any beer?"

Peterson snickered, biting his lip to keep from spewing a mouthful of wine. "How thirsty would you have to be to defile your gullet with a glass of wine?" He set his glass on the counter. After a bit of clinking around in the fridge, he pulled out a bottle of beer.

Fitz rolled his eyes.

"Fat Tire work, Boss, or is that too trendy for your tastes?" He retrieved a bottle opener from the drawer and popped the beer open without waiting for a reply.

"Smart-ass," Fitz muttered, snatching the beer out of Peterson's hand and inspecting the label of the Fort Collins microbrew. "Hell, had they had this shit when I was up at CSU, I might not have dropped out of college."

"*Really?*" *Peterson's brow arched with curiosity as Fitz tipped his bottle back and took a long sip.*

"*Nah, probably not.*" *They both knew that the shortest way to a foul-tempered team sergeant was stick him behind a desk for more than two consecutive days.* "*So.*" *Fitz waggled the bottle in his hand as his eyes drifted toward the stove.* "*Anything I can do to help with dinner?*"

"*Nuh-uh. Lasagna's done, and the salad's already made, so we're pretty much good to go once the lasagna sets.*"

Fitz's stomach growled, reminding him that the only thing he'd eaten since breakfast that morning was a package of strawberry Pop-Tarts he grabbed from the vending machine in the HQ building before his 1300 team sergeants' meeting.

"*Works for me. Mind if I—?*" *He gestured toward the living room sofa.*

"*Not at all. Go ahead.*"

Peterson drew a deep breath as Fitz wandered into the living room, then walked back over to the open bottle of Chianti and refilled his glass, giving himself an extra inch of the sour red wine.

Fitz sat where he could rest his beer on the end table and take full advantage of the leather sofa's wide, plush arm. Peterson toed off his Sanuks and sat down on the other end, curling one of his legs underneath him as he sat back and cradled his glass of wine in his lap.

"*Hey, Boss?*"

The waver in Peterson's voice drew Fitz out of his daze. The medic's normally upbeat voice was softer, breathier, heavier somehow and as soon as Fitz heard it, he knew Peterson's dinner invitation wasn't just about showing off his Italian cooking and new apartment.

"*What's up, Doc?*"

Peterson pressed his lips together in a firm line.

"*I need a favor.*"

The medic's pale cheeks sat high and his face seemed rigid, as if he were bracing himself for something. In the three-and-a-half years since Peterson joined Fitz's team, the two had grown fairly close, and they'd helped one another out now and again—like when Doc bummed a ride to work because his truck was in the shop, or when Fitz needed someone to help move the new sectional into the living room. But Fitz knew from the expression on the medic's face that this wasn't one of those kinds of favors.

"Okay. What can I do?"

Peterson looked down into his Chianti and stared at his own rosy reflection.

"You know how my mom died last spring, right?"

Fitz frowned. "I know, man, I'm sorry." Peterson had been devastated when he got the call from his aunt that his mom had passed away. Fitz sensed that the medic's had an especially close relationship with his mother, and losing her hit him especially hard.

"Thanks," Peterson whispered, a faint smile crossing his lips before fading. "My dad passed about ten years ago—not that we were ever close, really. I had a sister but she died of leukemia when we were kids."

Fitz reached for his beer but just rubbed the edge of the bottle's crimped glass bottom against his jeans. "I'm sorry, buddy."

"I don't really have any next of kin. My closest living relative is my mom's sister, Cindi—she's still in North Dakota. Her and my uncle have a farm near Huff, about twenty minutes away from Mandan, where I grew up. My uncle drives a cement truck for a company in Bismarck."

Fitz nodded but said nothing, unsure of where the conversation was going.

"I need you to promise me something," Peterson said.

"Okay." Fitz's forehead creased at the seriousness in the medic's voice.

Peterson closed his eyes and sighed, then turned and looked out the window, taking a moment to admire the faint orange glow behind the mountains.

"If something happens to me over there—you know, when we deploy—I need you to call Cody. He's the only thing I have left in this world ..."

Peterson's voice trailed off as he looked down and stared into his wine again. Fitz watched him chew the inside of lip, his broad shoulders slightly hunched as he gently swirled the wine in his glass.

"I don't want him to find out on the TV news. He deserves to get the news personally, but with Mom gone and the fucking rules being what they are, the Army's not gonna tell him. It's gotta come from one of the guys. And—" He rubbed his eyes, then shrugged. "I didn't know who else to ask. Captain Henley is damn near Jerry Falwell's mini-me, and Chief Young isn't much better. And Bruniak—well, you know what he's like."

"Yeah," Fitz said with a snort. "Bruniak is like the fuckin' Associated Press *wire service."*

Peterson looked up from his wine and grinned. "Well, that's one way of putting it."

For a minute, neither of them said anything. Peterson finished off the last of his Chianti in two swallows, then stood up and walked back into the kitchen.

"I'm sorry for putting you in a spot like this, but I didn't know who else to ask. My aunt—she's my next of kin, but she doesn't know about ... I mean, she's just a country girl from North Dakota, just like the rest of my family. I'm not sure how I was supposed to tell her that her high-speed, low-drag soldier nephew's actually a raging queer who's living with another man who, oh, by the way, would really appreciate the courtesy of a telephone call should said queer soldier end up coming home in a flag-draped casket."

Peterson punctuated his rant with a grunted-out laugh as he grabbed the open bottle of Chianti and poured himself another glass. "I'm sorry." He corked the bottle and set it in the corner next to the toaster. "I just ... Fitz, I really tried to think of someone else who—"

"Don't," Fitz said as he stood up and walked into the kitchen. "It's not a problem."

Peterson smiled and nodded, then breathed out a long, relieved sigh that ended in a laugh. "I wasn't really sure. I mean, it's just—well, it's hard to know sometimes. You know, how people are going to react." He paused, then looked up at Fitz with a lopsided grin. "And don't take this the wrong way, Boss, but you're not exactly easy to read."

"Really?" Fitz set his beer on the counter with a hard clank. "Ah, right. You two making goo-goo eyes at the bar was a bit of a tip-off. Come on, Doc. If I had an issue with this, you'd've known about it long before now." He reached for his beer and brought it to his lips, then set it down again without taking a sip. "I never understood all that crap anyway. I've seen more problems with unit cohesion because some NCO is fuckin' some other NCO's wife than I ever have 'cause there's a gay guy in the unit. The whole 'Don't Ask, Don't Tell' thing is stupid, if you ask me."

"Ugh." Peterson groaned and leaned back against the counter, swirling the wine in his glass. "Stupid doesn't even begin to describe the idiocy of the whole policy. Remember when they bounced those nine soldiers from the Defense Language Institute at the Presidio? There are more queers at DLI than you can shake a stick at. And who gives a fuck if they're gay or not? Their job is to learn foreign languages with an emphasis on tactically useful conversation. Six of those guys were learning Arabic. And bouncing six Arabic students from DLI in 2002 was a real brainiac idea. To hell with prepping the troops to invade Iraq—there's queers at DLI! I mean, shit."

Fitz tilted his beer back and took a long sip. "As far as I'm concerned, I'd just as well have the best-lookin' guy on the team be the gay guy. I sleep better at night knowing you're not going to go chasing after my wife."

Peterson looked up from his wine with a wicked flash in his blue eyes. "How do you know I won't?"

Fitz crossed his arms and shot the medic a pointed look.

"Because Cody would kick your goddamn ass if you did."

He read the signs that hung over the freeway and debated whether to continue on to Garden of the Gods Road, trying to ignore the sound of Peterson's voice murmuring at him from someplace in the back of his mind. He growled at the niggling presence and clenched his teeth hard enough that his molars ached as he mashed his foot down on the accelerator, sending the truck surging toward the next exit.

He jerked the blinker on as he swerved into the far right lane and onto the off-ramp. He leaned into the steering wheel as he turned and looked left, squinting into the headlights of the oncoming cars, scowling at them as each one whooshed by. Finally, a small space opened up and he gunned it, dismissing the angry honk of the Honda behind him with a firmly extended middle finger as the big white Scout lumbered into the left hand lane.

It seemed, though, that no matter how loud the Scout's engine roared, he could still hear Peterson's deep voice pleading with him.

"I need you to promise me something ..."

A Diamond Shamrock gas station sat on the left but Fitz saw it too late to make the turn. Wanting nothing more than to silence the memories that roiled in his mind and the slow, loping Dakota drawl that came with them, he turned and saw a 7-11 a block down on the right. Without even looking, he slapped his right turn signal on and the truck lunged forward, barely missing the rear bumper of a Chevy.

"Fuck you," he snarled at the blaring horn as it rushed by on the left. "Stupid motherfucker."

He pulled in front of the red brick convenience store, threw the truck into park and stomped on the emergency brake. His brows sloped low and hard over his eyes as he reached for the key and saw the black handset of the ignition interlock.

"If something happens to me over there—you know, when we deploy—I need you to call Cody. He's the only thing I have left in this world ..."

Fitz twisted the key and silenced the rumbling diesel, then climbed out of the truck.

CHAPTER 37

Gravel crunched beneath the Scout's off-road tires as Fitz pulled into the scenic overlook. The half-moon had climbed high enough in the sky to cast a cool, gray glow over the red cliffs of the Garden of the Gods, leaving long shadows where they rose up from the valley floor.

He fished his phone out of his pocket and stared at it for a second, then set it face-down on his thigh.

"I had to get out of Mandan."

Peterson tugged at his reddish-blond beard as he sat next to Fitz in the observation post. "Let me tell you, 15,000 people ain't much, okay? And while I wasn't the only queer guy in town, I might as well have been. And across the river in Bismarck? Well, that wasn't a whole hell of an improvement. 50,000 people, but it's still like a gay fuckin' wasteland there. I was sure I would die if I had to stay." He raised the binoculars and moved them in a slow arc as he surveyed the rocky, tree-dotted hills in the distance. "I mean, I didn't mind my folks, really, or the farm." He paused, then lowered the binoculars, propping them on his lap as a faint smile crossed his lips.

"We grew flax and canola—seed crops that get made into vegetable oils. The crop looks real pretty when it blooms. Imagine entire fields

full of blue and yellow flowers. Reminds me of the big fields of poppies you see down in Helmand."

The medic brought the binoculars back up to his eyes and resumed scanning the hillside.

"So, anyway, summer after I graduated from high school, I popped smoke and moved down to Kansas City. My cousin Kevin lived there and agreed to sublet me the extra bedroom in his apartment. I liked it there. There was a gay community, so I wasn't really alone like I was in Mandan, but still, after a while, I got bored. I took classes at the local junior college. I was most of the way through the coursework I needed to take the exam to be an LPN. You know, a licensed practical nurse—"

"I know what an LPN is." Fitz grinned. *"My wife's a nurse, remember?"*

Peterson laughed. *"So yeah, I was just about done with my LPN coursework when I met a guy in a bar—a country western bar called Sidekick's Saloon. It's one of those places where all the cowboys are lookin' for other cowboys, right? Strong drinks, good jukebox. Anyway, he was on leave, passing through on his way to Fort Riley. He told me all about how much he loved being a medic. I went down to the recruiting station and signed my enlistment papers two days later."*

"And the rest is history, huh?" Fitz's right eye narrowed as he stared down the scope of his rifle at movement downrange. Once he was satisfied that the movement was non-hostile, he relaxed and sat back a little from the scope.

Peterson set the binoculars back on his lap again. *"It's funny, I guess. In a sense, I'm in this line of work because I'm gay—'cause of that guy I met and chatted up in Sidekick's. But I love what I do. Getting to work with guys like you, saving lives, and making a difference. I would never want what I am to get in the way of being able to do that. I love this, and while I can't fucking wait for the day when all this stupid bullshit stops and I can finally be myself and a soldier, too, I don't want to lose this."* He turned to Fitz with a soft smile and scratched at his beard. *"This is as much of who I am as ... as who I am. Know what I mean?"*

Fitz picked up his phone again and hit redial.

"Come on," he whispered as he listened to the ring on the other end of the line. "Come on, come on. Pick up."

"You've reached Jennifer Fitzgerald," the voice crackled. "I can't take your call right now, but if you leave a message, I'll get back to you as soon as I can. Thanks."

Fitz hung up before the beep and tossed the phone onto the passenger seat where it clattered against the six-pack of beer. Even in the dim glow of the truck's dome light, the big block letters *BUD LIGHT* could be read through the translucent white plastic of the 7-11 bag.

"I need you to promise me something ... "

He reached across the seat, hooking his fingers in the flimsy handles of the plastic bag as he pulled it across the vinyl seat toward him.

"If something happens to me over there ... "

Fitz curled his fingers into a loose fist and touched the side of one of the cans with the top of his knuckle. The cool metal felt smooth and slick as he swiped his trembling thumb over the flat lever of the pop-top and swallowed drily. He pushed the six-pack away and leaned back against the headrest, unable to look at the object of his temptation. Squeezing his eyes shut, he gritted his teeth and prayed for the hum of memories to let him be.

His eyes traced the distinctive outline of Peterson's broad shoulders and narrow waist as the tall Swede led the patrol along the dusty path that was the main road through the little mountain village of Kelalbat. For a month, the village had been the focus of their efforts in that part of the Korengal Valley. Peterson's smooth, long-legged gait slowed as he pivoted at the waist and turned, the barrel of his rifle swinging into view as everything was swallowed into a bright flash that knocked Fitz to the ground some forty feet away.

With a frustrated grunt, Fitz reached for the phone again.

He pushed the green dial button and it called up the list of his last ten calls. *Jenn, Jenn, Jenn, Jenn*—each one followed by a little upward arrow showing that all four calls were outbound, each one ending in a voice mail greeting. He clenched his fingers tightly around the phone's cool plastic handset and stared at the delicate calligraphy etched in deep black ink on his forearm. When he loosened his grip on the phone, the muscles in his arm shifted beneath their names.

He knew this place.

It had been a month since he stood in front of the kitchen sink with forty milligrams of powdered Percocet in his palm and deliberated whether to give in, enticed by the prospect of a night of solid sleep free of the plaintive howls of the dying and the sight of stone walls splattered with the shredded remains of his medic.

He'd been here before.

But if the months since the explosion in Kelalbat had taught him anything, it was that no matter what he did, the memories would come back again, and again, and again.

"I need you to promise me something ..."

Fitz looked at the six-pack and wondered if, after nearly two months of complete abstinence, six beers would be enough to hammer the memories into submission and give him four or five hours of peace. Maybe he'd become a lightweight after going that long without a drink.

"If something happens to me over there ..."

He wanted nothing more than for the memories to go away—to never have to think of that day, or what happened over there, ever again—but Peterson's twinkling blue eyes and impish grin refused to be forgotten.

Fitz reached across the seat and grabbed the phone, staring at it for a minute before scrolling through his favorites and pressing the dial button.

"Come on, come on, come on." The syllables of his whispered plea were sloppy as the tears welled up in his eyes. "Come on."

After five or six rings, a voice on the other end of the line finally picked up.

"H'lo?"

Fitz wiped his eyes and sniffed.

"Remy, it's me."

He opened the door and swung his legs around to the side. He leaned forward and covered his eyes with one hand as he held the phone with the other.

"Are you okay? Where are you?"

"I messed up man," Fitz croaked, his voice cracking on the word *up*. "I shouldn't have done it, but I just ..." His voice trailed off and he wiped the moisture from his eyes with the callused heel of his hand. "I really fucked up."

Several seconds of static filled the line between them.

"I'm having trouble hearing you, Fitz." Remy's voice grew louder as he tried to make himself clear. "Where are you? Are you okay? Tell me where you are."

"I just want it to stop," Fitz muttered. "It's too much. I can't take it anymore."

"Where are you?" The chaplain's voice peaked with concern. "Fitz, tell me where you are."

Fitz's eyes narrowed and he looked around, suddenly unsure where he was. After buying the beer, he'd shoved the change in his pocket, climbed in the truck, and drove west toward the hills. At the time, he just wanted to be *away*, wherever *away* took him.

"Tell me what you see," Remy said, his voice reedy and a little hesitant. "I'm gonna come get you, okay? But you've gotta tell me where you are."

Fitz glanced around and saw enough spaces for perhaps a dozen cars. The parking area was hemmed in on the west side by fifteen boulders, each one nearly as wide as a car, to keep people from driving into the ravine below. "Mesa Road, I think. West of I-25, I guess. I can see Garden of the Gods from here. It's like a little overlook. Drove past all the subdivisions with the fancy custom homes. All I see in front of me are the rocks."

Fitz heard shuffling and a soft metallic click in the background.

"I'm gonna come and get you, okay?" Remy said. "Stay where you are. Don't go anywhere. I'll be there in ... I'm on post now, so I've gotta shoot up there. It'll be like twenty minutes, all right? Just hang in there and I'll be there in a little while." The chaplain fell silent for a moment. "Just promise me you'll stay right where you're at, okay? Everything's going to be okay."

CHAPTER 38

Remy Daniels's mind was buzzing as he merged onto the interstate.

He had seen Fitz vulnerable before, both in AA and otherwise, but the brokenness in the sergeant's voice alarmed him. Glancing up at the rearview mirror, he flipped the lever on the mirror to redirect the headlights of a fast-approaching semi. He cringed at the speeding trucker's horn, which reminded him of the last time he ran this kind of errand.

Remy's gut churned as he remembered the night he answered an early-morning call from a young private first class in his battalion at Fort Hood. When he picked up the phone, the reception was faint, each word laced with heavy static, and the soldier's voice was thick and raspy, but what he gathered from the muddled call left little doubt that the young infantryman was deeply despondent. Remy had counseled PFC Hendrick a couple of times before, when he'd told Remy about an incident at a checkpoint in Taji where a driver failed to stop as ordered. Nervous after having just lost a comrade in an attack on that same checkpoint a week earlier, Hendrick and the others fired on the vehicle, killing the driver and the two passengers. Afterward, they discovered that the occupants—a middle-aged Iraqi man and two school-aged boys—were unarmed. When the other two soldiers involved in the shooting were killed by a roadside bomb a week before the end of their deployment, Hendrick became convinced that their deaths were some kind of cosmic punishment for the checkpoint killings.

Hang in there, Fitz, Remy mouthed silently as he raced up I-25, passing slower-moving cars one by one as he wove his way from Fort Carson up to the northern edge of Colorado Springs.

He blinked, trying to flush away the image of PFC Hendrick sitting cross-legged on the floor at the foot of a motel bed in Pflugerville, an hour south of Fort Hood. When the motel manager opened the door, they found Hendrick with a .38 revolver in his lap, his head tipped back against the bed, half its contents spilled on the bloody bedspread.

Remy opened his eyes and drew a deep breath as he passed a smoking Ford Torino and prayed he would have better timing for Fitz. His thoughts were so scattered with worry, he found himself heading west on Uintah Street but couldn't remember exiting off the interstate.

In the months since he'd met Fitz, he'd come to admire the wry, snarky Green Beret, not just for his intelligence and work ethic, but also for his resilience and for his big (if often well-hidden) heart. The chaplain knew he'd made a mistake pushing Fitz at dinner on the subject of survivor's guilt. As he reached the bottom of the hill and turned right onto Mesa, he grabbed his phone out of the center console and dialed Fitz.

"Come on, pick up," he whispered as he listened to one, then two, then three unanswered rings.

"Hello?" came the gruff voice on the other end.

"It's Remy. I'm almost there. You okay?"

"I'm still here, aren't I?"

Remy smiled faintly. Despite Fitz's distress, he was still enough of himself to respond with sarcasm.

"Yeah, you are. Hey, I don't know why I didn't think of this before—your phone, does it have a maps feature?"

"Umm, yeah." Remy could hear the gears turning. "Oh, uh. Wait."

The chaplain noted the slowness of the normally quick sergeant's thinking and speech. After a few seconds and some faint clicking in the background, he prompted him. "Where are you, Fitz? What street are you on?"

"Uh, Mesa, I think. Before it hits Thirtieth Street, looks like. I guess that's right."

Remy exhaled with relief. "Okay." He accelerated and flipped his high beams on. The houses along the left side of the road had thinned out. "I'm one, maybe two, minutes away, okay? Just hang tight."

His heart stopped when he pulled into the small parking area overlooking the entrance to the Garden of the Gods. The driver's side door of the Scout hung open but there was no sign of Fitz. A closer look found the sergeant sitting on a boulder with his feet propped up on the truck's front bumper, rubbing his hand anxiously over the back of his head. The chaplain pulled his Highlander next to the old Scout and cut the engine, taking a second to admire the moonlit edges of the red sandstone hogbacks below.

Remy walked around the back of the truck, glancing inside and saw a six-pack of beer on the passenger seat. Relieved to see no sign that Fitz had a weapon or any suicidal intent, or that he'd opened any of the cans of beer, the chaplain sighed and leaned against another boulder a couple of feet away.

"Here." He held out a twenty-ounce bottle of Diet Orange Crush he'd picked up at a gas station on the way.

Fitz looked up, his red-rimmed eyes bleary and unfocused as he accepted the drink. "Thanks." He held the bottle in his hands for a minute before twisting the cap off with a sharp *whoosh*.

"Hey." Still propped against the boulders, Remy folded his arms and crossed his legs in front of him as the gravel crunched loudly beneath his heels. "I'm sorry about earlier. I wasn't trying to—"

"Naw, look." Fitz waved his hand. "Don't."

The chaplain studied Fitz's face, which was dimly illuminated by the half-moon and the headlights of the cars that passed by every minute or so. Fitz's cheekbones seemed sharper in shadow, his temples pulsing as he ground his teeth.

"It's not your fault. You aren't responsible for Peterson's death."

Fitz tipped the bottle back and gulped about a quarter of the soda in two big swallows, shaking his head as he screwed the cap back on. "You're wrong, Padre. I'm totally responsible. If it weren't for *me* and the decisions *I* made, Peterson would still be alive. That's the bottom fuckin' line."

Remy sighed. "Come on, Fitz. It doesn't matter whether you did or didn't take point the day before he died, or whether you flipped for the point position that morning. It was just random chance that your friend lost the coin toss and walked point that day. Hell, it wasn't either of your doing that the insurgents set the IED off when they did, hitting the front of your patrol as opposed to waiting to let it go when the middle of the patrol was passing by. Had the Taliban done it right, you'd both probably have been killed. But none of that's your fault, Fitz."

Fitz leaned forward and set the soda bottle on the hood of the truck. "No. You don't understand, okay?"

Remy's brow knit in frustration as Fitz stared at the houses on the other side of the road. "Listen to me. You didn't do anything wrong."

"You really think so?" Fitz turned and stared at the chaplain, his lip curled in disgust. "Because I'm pretty fucking sure that I broke the rules when Doc asked me to promise to contact his roommate if something happened to him over in Afghanistan since the Army wouldn't do it because gay lovers don't count as next of kin under the casualty notification regs."

Remy blinked and shook his head in confusion. "What?"

"Yep," Fitz said with a purse-lipped nod. "That's right. My senior medical sergeant was a queer, and while I'd pretty much figured that out, I didn't know for sure until he outed himself a couple of weeks before we deployed last fall. Had I followed the rules, I'd have had to tell my captain, who'd commence the process of having the best medic I've ever served with administratively discharged because it's more important to the Army what hole a guy puts his dick in than that he be good at keeping other guys from getting their dicks shot off."

"He asked you not to tell." Remy's voice was low and quiet as he hesitated, wary that Fitz might clam up completely if he pushed him too far. "Didn't he?"

Fitz closed his eyes. "More or less," he admitted with a tired sigh. "My duty, per the regs, was to turn Peterson in. Had I done my duty and followed the stupid goddamn rules, Peterson would never have deployed with us, and he would never have been on that patrol that morning in Kelalbat. He'd never have been in the path of that IED and he'd still be alive. It's a straight line, Padre: I broke the rules and did what Doc wanted me to do. He's dead because of me."

Remy didn't say anything and just watched Fitz's eyes as the cool night air hung between them. Finally, the chaplain drew a deep breath and nodded, kicking the heel of his sneaker against the gravel a couple of times before looking up again.

"I have an aunt," he began, watching as Fitz rubbed his hand back and forth over his head in a dazed, distracted rhythm. "My Aunt Michelle. She's my mom's sister, right? She and my uncle live in Carrollton, outside of Dallas. She spent twenty years working for American Airlines as a reservationist. Sounds to me like it'd be the most boring job imaginable, but she really, really liked it. She's a real Chatty Cathy, so she loved spending all day on the phone with people talking to them about the vacations they were going on and the trips they were taking and all that. Occasionally she'd talk to people who really, I don't know, struck her.

"There was this one time she had this young woman call. Lady was, I guess, I don't know, maybe twenty-four or twenty-five years old. From Providence, Rhode Island, right? She was getting married and she was calling to make a reservation for a flight to take her and her fiancé to Hawaii. They were going to spend their honeymoon at a resort on Kauai. Apparently figuring out the flights took a bit of work, so she and my Aunt Michelle were on the phone for quite a long time."

Fitz scrunched his nose as his brows sloped hard over his tired eyes. "Yeah, okay." His voice was edgy, and Remy watch as his friend struggled to figure out what an airline reservationist had to do with his medic getting blown apart by an IED.

"Apparently Providence to Kauai was a complicated mess of flights with lots of connections," Remy explained. "But it's not too bad a drive from Providence to Boston, so Michelle ended up putting them on an American Airlines flight from Boston to L.A., with a connection at LAX to Honolulu."

The chaplain paused, twisting the ball of his foot into the gravel.

"She booked them on American Airlines Flight 11—the one that the hijackers flew into the North Tower of the World Trade Center."

"Oh, damn." The grimace on Fitz's face melted into a frown. "Shit, that's terrible."

"She gave notice the next day," Remy said soberly. "Aunt Michelle heard the news that morning and she knew, just as soon as they said that the plane that hit the North Tower was an American Airlines flight from Boston to L.A., she knew that the newlyweds she'd helped get on that flight were gone. In her mind, she'd put them in the line of fire, putting 'em on that flight. She felt responsible for their deaths. Still does."

Fitz's gaze hardened and his lower jaw shifted forward as he sat in stony silence.

"She was no more responsible for that couple's death than you are for your medic buddy's. Your friend Peterson knew the risks. He'd been in the Army for a long time, right?"

"Fourteen years."

The chaplain pushed off the boulder he'd been leaning against and walked toward the truck.

"He knew the score," he said, grabbing the bottle of Orange Crush off the hood. "He knew the risks, and loved his job in the Army—same as you do, right?" Remy twisted the cap off and leveled a narrow-eyed stare at Fitz before he raised the bottle and took a sip. "He knew he might die, but he stayed in anyway. He loved his work and all it entailed."

"I guess."

"You guess?" Remy set the soda bottle back on the hood. "You *know* that's how this works. It's why guys like you stay in. You love the job you do, and you feel it's important work. Hell, it's why I do what I do, ministering to a flock of crazy bastards like you instead of finding myself a nice quiet congregation in the suburbs somewhere."

"That's not the point, Remy." Fitz gritted his teeth and shook his head. "He's dead because of me. If it weren't for me, he'd still be alive."

"No," Remy said firmly. "You didn't take his life. You were a friend, and by honoring the trust he placed in you, you let him live the way he wanted to, which meant risking dying for his country. That was *his* choice, not yours. You let him choose the life he wanted, even though in the end that choice meant he died."

Fitz wiped the moisture from his eyes with his thumb and forefingers. "He's still gone."

"He is," the chaplain said with a sober nod. "Like many of the men and women you and I have served with, he's gone. But what you did—letting him keep serving the way he wanted to—was an act of friendship, Fitz. And to hell what the Army's rules say. What you did was a damned decent thing, to let a man choose his own path and to continue to serve the country he loved."

A long, rough sigh rattled in the back of Fitz's throat as he rubbed his hair, scraping his fingernails against his scalp.

"I promised to call him. Cody—Peterson's boyfriend." He looked up at the moon and winced as he fought back tears. "But, you know what? I didn't. After Doc coming out to me and everything, I didn't do the one fuckin' thing he asked me to do."

"You couldn't, right?" Remy cocked his head to the side and squinted one eye as he studied his friend's blurry gaze. "You were in the hospital for how many weeks after the IED?"

"A few days at Landstuhl," Fitz replied. "And another couple weeks at Fort Sam Houston when I got back stateside. First week and a half I was so doped up I didn't even know my own name. Barely recognized my wife when she walked into my room at

Brooke. And ..."

Fitz's voice trailed off as he stared at his lap.

"I'm sure the local TV reported it while I was still doped up at Landstuhl. But even after I got home, I thought about calling him, to tell him about how much I liked Peterson and what a great guy he was, and tell him, you know, all the stuff you tell a guy's wife or mom when he dies."

Fitz looked up again, his hazel eyes narrowed and gleaming with tears.

"But?" Remy prompted him.

"But I didn't." He looked as if he might say more, but instead simply shut his mouth and leaned forward to retrieve his soda. "I should've, I could've, but I didn't."

Remy hesitated before asking the obvious question.

"Why not?"

"Because," Fitz said grimly, "I didn't think he'd want to talk to me. If I was him, I'm not sure I'd want to talk to me, either."

Remy pursed his lips and pondered that for a moment. "How long were Peterson and Cody together?"

Fitz's gaze swiveled up and to the right as he thought about it. "They met after we got back from Tblisi in '07, but moved in together before our last deployment, so, I dunno, maybe a year and a half."

"What's he do? Cody, I mean. He's not a soldier, obviously."

Fitz's forehead creased as he tried to understand what Remy's question was getting at. "He's a paramedic for the Colorado Springs Fire Department."

The chaplain smiled. "So he's no dummy. And no stranger to what it means to be in a dangerous occupation."

Fitz frowned and looked down at his feet.

"I'm an idiot."

"No, you're not. But I'll tell you this. Seems to me you and Peterson had a good friendship. And if I had to guess, I bet Peterson looked up to you. I mean, you've been living this Army life, with all the deployments and time away from home and all the risks that come with a job where you get shot at for a living." The chaplain paused, smiling faintly as he drew a slow, reluctant smirk from Fitz. "If you were important enough to him to trust with the secret he told you, I think he probably told Cody of that trust."

"I don't understand."

"Go talk to Cody. Peterson trusted you with the most important thing in his life—or, perhaps, the second-most important thing in his life. His *career*. I think he thought the world of you, and I bet Cody thinks pretty highly of you, too. He won't blame you, Fitz—not for losing Peterson, and not for you not being able to call him when you were in Army hospitals doped up six ways to Sunday."

"But what if he doesn't want to talk to me?"

"He will." Remy's voice was firm and unwavering as he waited for a protest. None came and another soft smile crept across his face. "You need this, Fitz. You need it and Cody needs it. Go. Go talk to him."

Fitz closed his eyes and breathed a long sigh, then nodded.

CHAPTER 39

Even after stopping for a latte on the way up from Colorado Springs, Fitz found himself in the terminal a full twenty minutes before Jenn and Ryan's flight was due to land.

Jangling his keys in his pocket, he surveyed the broad, sunlit atrium. There were two brewpub restaurants, a handful of newsstands, two bookstores, an electronics store, a small salon offering manicures, pedicures and chair massages, and a pair of coffee shops. Glancing down at the empty coffee cup in his hand, he shrugged and tossed it into a nearby bin.

Shoving his hands into his pockets, he made his way from one side of the atrium to the other, remembering the glass-walled smoking lounges he saw at the airport in Frankfurt. He drew his hand into a fist inside his pocket, craving something, anything, that would relax the twitch in his muscles. He recalled with a smirk how he chased away the boredom in the Saudi desert during the lead-up to Desert Storm, spending hours playing cards, listening to music, and smoking cigarettes. The nicotine soothed him as weeks turned to months with no break in the monotony of the war that seemed like it would never begin.

He'd come to regret the decision when he went to try out for the Rangers and found the rigors of Ranger School compounded

271

by nicotine withdrawal. Blinking away the memory, Fitz ducked into a café in search of caffeine—the only real crutch he allowed himself now that nicotine and alcohol were off the menu.

Armed with a large caffè Americano, he wandered into a bookstore to while away the time until his wife and son arrived. He scanned the titles in the Current Affairs section, half of which he'd read, either during his last deployment or the six weeks his family was away. None of the remaining titles caught his eye, so he moved to the next shelf, which was stuffed full of romance novels. He recognized a couple from Jenn's nightstand and quietly snorted at the extremely muscular and very hairless chests of the men on the covers. Jenn, who laughingly called them her "smutty" romances, read two or three a month. Browsing the shelves, he saw one on the bottom shelf portraying a clothed man—one of the few, he noted—in what looked like a British Army uniform from World War II, embracing a woman in a sundress. The image reminded him of his great-grandfather's diary and its narrative of the burgeoning love between Tommy and Maeve. He skimmed the teaser on the back and guessed that Jenn hadn't read this one, so he grabbed it and went to the counter to pay.

Fitz tucked the book into his backpack next to the novel he'd brought to pass the time, a copy of Orhan Pamuk's *Snow* in the original Turkish. Glancing up at the arrivals board, he felt an odd swirl in the pit of his belly as he saw that their Frontier flight from Portland had landed early.

Making his way to the far end of the atrium, he passed one of the brewpubs. His steps slowed as he saw a soldier in fatigues sitting at the bar. The soldier picked at his French fries as he chatted with the well-dressed woman seated next to him. Fitz noted the 173rd Airborne patch on the soldier's sleeve and wondered if the kid was on his way to or from Afghanistan. The businesswoman reached over and touched the soldier's hand as she looked up and signaled the bartender for her check. The airport P.A. barked a stern warning to passengers about unattended bags, and the soldier looked over his shoulder at the sound, his eyes meeting Fitz's for a fleeting second.

Embarrassed at having been caught staring, Fitz turned away and walked toward the middle of the terminal, halfway between the escalators at each end of the floor. His BlackBerry buzzed in his pocket. He fished it out, using his hand to shield the screen from the glare of the skylights.

Just got off the plane, the text message read. *See you in a few.*

Fitz drained the last few sips of his Americano in a single swallow and tossed the empty cup into a wastebasket. He parked himself near the middle of the arrivals hall, leaning against a column as he watched the escalators at both ends of the floor. Every couple of minutes, as a train arrived from the concourses with a load of passengers, the escalators flooded the atrium with another wave of people whose wide, tired eyes scanned the boards to learn which carousel would deliver their bags. All of the Frontier flights flew in and out of the A Concourse, the nearest one to the terminal, and as the minutes passed, Fitz kept checking his watch, wondering what was taking them so long.

Finally, he spied a familiar head of floppy brown hair among the long line of people on the escalator. Pushing himself away from the column, Fitz walked toward Ryan, his gaze briefly meeting Jenn's as she stepped off the escalator a few passengers behind her son. Fisting his hands tightly in his pockets, Fitz drew a deep breath then exhaled it in a long sigh.

Jenn reached out and placed her hand on Ryan's shoulder as they approached. The boy looked up, uncertainty in his arched brows as she gave his shoulder a gentle squeeze.

"Hey, guys." Fitz said softly. Jenn acknowledged him with a smile. "You're early. Must've had a pretty good tailwind this morning, huh?"

Ryan tugged the straps on his backpack, snugging them tightly against his shoulders as he raised his eyes to meet his father's expectant gaze.

"Hey, Dad."

The two stood awkwardly for a few moments, each waiting for the other one to close the distance. Jenn's fingers brushed across her son's back, silently encouraging him. He finally stepped forward, his head low as Fitz drew him into a hug.

"It's good to have you home," Fitz whispered into Ryan's ear. "I've missed you guys so much."

Ryan pulled away from the embrace, curving the brim of his cap as he pulled it low over his eyes. He pressed his lips together and Fitz's gaze widened as he waited for Ryan to speak, but the boy just nodded and stuffed his hands into his jean pockets.

Cocking his head to one side, Fitz took a moment to drink in the sight of his wife. She wore a light sweater over a tank top and khaki crop pants, and he couldn't help but smile at the apple-green polish on her toenails. Her calves were tanned, something he hadn't noticed when they came in for the funeral two weeks before. It pleased him to know she'd made time for herself in Oregon, rather than spending the whole time in arenas watching their son play hockey.

"Oh, Jenn." His voice rumbled as he hugged her to his chest and cupped his hand around the back of her head, stroking her silky hair with his fingers. "Missed you."

"I know," she whispered back. "I know."

The ride home was quieter than Fitz had expected, and he found himself stealing glances at Ryan in the rearview mirror every few minutes. Each time he'd look up at his son, Jenn would pat his thigh in silent reassurance. Her fingers stroked the hair on the side of his thigh, letting her fingertips trace the dips and contours the shrapnel had carved into his skin. His muscles initially tensed, then relaxed as her fingers continued their soothing ministrations. Fitz let himself sink into her touch, his hands loosening their grip on the steering wheel as he focused on the road.

By dinner, the awkward tension had eased somewhat. Fitz had made sure the refrigerator and pantry were fully stocked, and on Remy's advice, picked up a premade pizza crust at King Soopers along with all the toppings. After the monotony of a two-and-a-half hour flight from Portland, plus a two-hour layover, Ryan jumped at the chance to take charge of the pizza while Fitz made a salad and Jenn slipped upstairs to begin unpacking.

Dinner was a quiet affair. The three of them ate in silence, each consumed by their own thoughts. Fitz found the lack of conversation both a little unnerving and strangely comforting. For two months, the house had been filled only with the sound of his own footsteps and the ever-blaring television. Now, Jenn and Ryan were back, but as much as he'd missed them while they were gone, he found himself at a loss for what to say. Every so often, he would look up from his plate and into Ryan's green eyes, but when he opened his mouth to speak, his breath hitched and his mind went blank.

At eight o'clock, Ryan asked permission to go to bed early, something he didn't even do when he was sick. Fitz watched his son jog upstairs after a quietly murmured *goodnight,* then turned to Jenn with a shrug.

An hour later, Fitz came in from taking out the trash to find Jenn waiting for him at the base of the stairs. The house was quiet except for the whispery swish of the dishwasher, and all of the downstairs lights had been turned off except for the warm, dim light over the stove.

"Fitz."

Her voice was low and soft and he felt it like a caress as he neared the stairs. She followed him, pressing her hand gently against the small of his back as he rounded the banister and entered the bedroom.

Fitz's breath caught in his throat as he saw the blue suitcase in the middle of the bed, empty but for a couple pairs of sandals and her polka dot sundress. He stared at the dress, remembering the afternoon he came home to find her packing.

"I'm sorry," she whispered. "I'll just ..."

She brushed past him and stuffed the old suitcase into the closet without bothering to put the last few items away. When she flicked off the closet light and turned around, he was frozen in place, watching her.

Jenn smiled as she approached, hesitating for a moment before reaching up and running her finger over the patch of chest hair exposed by his unbuttoned Henley. He gasped at the contact, then lowered his head to kiss the top of her hand.

"I'm glad you're home."

She smiled, her finger stroking the fuzzy triangle of skin before she placed her palm over his heart. Fitz clasped her hand to his chest, closing his eyes at the warmth of her touch.

Her eyes narrowed. "Are you okay?"

Fitz swallowed, his Adam's apple bobbing low in his throat as he let go of her hand.

"Yeah." He took a deep breath and rubbed his hand over the back of his head. "I'm fine, really. It's just ... I don't know."

Fitz stood there for a moment with his lips parted, then shook away the thought and peeled off his shirt, tossing it in the hamper on his way to the bathroom. He felt her eyes on him while he brushed his teeth and he smiled into the foam, relieved to finally not be alone anymore.

He climbed into bed, propping his head on his hand as he watched Jenn wash her face. She splashed the warm water on her cheeks to rinse away the soap, then stood up, her forehead framed by damp little wisps of hair. Fitz's gaze traced the outline of her shoulders, from the straps of her lilac cotton nightgown down her sides to the round flare of her hips. There was a curious novelty in watching her nightly ritual, even though he'd her seen do it a thousand times before. He knew it was stupid, but he couldn't look away. She patted her cheeks dry with a towel and turned around, chuckling at the sight of him lying there, staring.

Jenn turned off the bedside lamp and pulled the covers back, the mattress sinking a little when she slipped between the sheets. Rolling over to face him, she slid toward the middle of the bed until her roving hand tickled the crisp curls on the top of his thigh.

"Hey," she whispered, cocking her head to the side as she studied his face in the faint light of the waning moon.

Fitz looked down at the sheets with a shy smile.

"Hey."

Deep grooves formed across his forehead as his brows worked up and down while his fingernail scraped the sheet in nervous preoccupation.

Mirroring his pose, she propped her head on one hand and reached for him with the other, her finger dipping into the crease between his pectoral muscles to stroke the downy patch of hair there.

"You've been quiet all afternoon. You and Ryan both." She paused for a moment, but when no reply came, she pressed him again, stroking his chest as if she could pry open his heart with a fingertip. "Are you sure you're all right?"

He shrugged a little, turning away from her touch to roll onto his back. When he felt the evening breeze fill the space between them, he extended his arm, encouraging her to tuck herself against his side as he stared at the ceiling.

"It's just been a rough couple weeks." Fitz punctuated his words with a sigh, pressing his fingers into her skin as he hugged her close. "Not just with you guys gone, but …" He swallowed thickly and hugged her tighter to his side. "Remy wants me to go talk to Cody. You know, Doc's boyfriend."

The term hung heavy in the air. It was only the second time he'd uttered the word in this particular context and he felt a flutter in his belly at the prospect of facing his fallen comrade's partner.

"You met him once, I think."

Jenn laid her hand on his chest, resting her fingers gently against his skin.

"I think Remy's right." She stroked his skin with the edge of her thumb. "I mean, if it had been you and not Peterson that day …" The rise and fall of his chest stilled as her voice cracked on the word *day*. "Then I'd want to hear from him. You two grew close during that last deployment, and if I'd …" Her words trailed off again as her voice broke, unable to name what Fitz knew was her worst fear. She closed her eyes and sighed. "I'd want to talk to your friend. If I were Cody, I'd want to talk to you."

Fitz bit his lip, replying with a noncommittal shrug.

Jenn touched his jaw, gently turning his face so she could see his eyes. "You're going to talk to him, right?"

He nodded. "Yeah. I will."

Fitz looked away again, focusing his gaze on the pale moonlight shining through the wood blinds, casting a striped shadow on the wall across from the bed. Jenn's fingers traced circles on his chest and he listened to the sound of her breathing. They lay in silence for a while as they familiarized themselves with the intimacy that had evaded them for so long.

When Jenn stirred against him, he turned away from the shadows to find a serious expression on her moonlit face.

"There's something else," she said vaguely as she rolled away from him, her soft skin peeling apart from his. The sudden loss of her warmth left him feeling a little raw at the separation.

"What?"

Fitz braced himself, wondering what he'd done wrong. He'd tried to make the house feel as much like a home as possible, even though it had stopped feeling like one the moment their taxi pulled out of the driveway. He didn't know how to close the distance that had formed between him and Ryan in the months since he came home from Afghanistan. The silence lingered, but he didn't know what to say.

"You need to talk to somebody."

The statement rang in Fitz's ears like a thunderclap, the buzzing in his mind drowning out all other sound in the room. He grunted and pushed himself up to a sitting position.

"I can't talk to an Army shrink." The tension in his jaw made the words come out more harshly than he had intended. "I just can't. I'm lucky they haven't bounced me already. If I get chatty with an Army shrink, I'll get chaptered out for being mentally unfit and my career is over."

"You don't have to talk to an Army counselor," she said, sitting up and pulling her knees to her chest. "There are people right here in the Springs you can talk to. I did some research and got the names of some counselors you can talk to. Maybe Remy can get you some other names."

Fitz rubbed his eyes. "I don't know, Jenn."

"Listen to me." She placed her hand on his shoulder, her fingers curving gently against his skin. "Screw Tricare. We don't have to use insurance. We can pay out-of-pocket if you're not comfortable talking to someone on-post. But I want you to talk to someone."

Fitz laced his fingers together behind his head, pressing his forehead to his knees as a rough sigh rattled from the back of his throat.

"I tried."

"I know you did."

"I wanted it to be perfect for you guys, you know, so when you guys got back here, everything could be the way it was before. But it's like no matter what I try, it's—"

"Fitz, listen—" She rubbed her hand over his calf, letting her fingers press against the bumps and divots, frowning when his muscles clenched against her touch. "Listen to me."

He grabbed her hand, squeezing it as he pulled it to his chest. "No, see? You were right. I can't bring us back to what it was like before. No matter what I do, I can't fix it." He released her hand. "I screwed it up, Jenn."

He waited for her to speak, for her to tell him that he hadn't, but after a few moments of her silence he knew she wouldn't disagree because, on some level, what he said was true.

"This isn't like replacing a worn belt on the Scout," she said. "Or re-machining the engine thingy whatever-it-was you did last year."

He couldn't help but smile a little. "The engine cylinder head."

Jenn smirked. "Well, that, too. But maybe the trouble is all the focus on trying to fix this." A flash of panic pulsed in his gut, but the warmth of her reassuring hand on his quickly settled him again. "I don't think we can get back to like it was before. But it's better today than it was before. And we can make it better still, right?"

Fitz nodded. "Yeah, I guess."

"See?" She patted his calf and gave him an encouraging smile, her gray eyes narrowing as a thought came to her. "Maybe we're like that old Scout, after all. You always say how it's a work in progress. That's what *we* are. All these years, you've never given up on that truck."

Fitz smiled sheepishly, unable to deny that she'd tolerated him doting on the boxy old off-roader over the years. She brought her hand up to his cheek, her fingertips caressing the rough stubble. His eyes flicked up to meet hers.

"I'm not ready to give up on us, and I don't think you are either."

CHAPTER 40

"I don't think you fussed this much over what to wear before our first date."

Jenn smirked at Fitz, who stood in front of the mirror, three shirts crumpled at his feet while he tried on a fourth. He frowned as he looked in the mirror, assessing how much of his arm the sleeve covered.

"You're not helping," he groused.

Fitz stroked the grooved scars on his forearm that, thanks to body hair, were less visible than the one that ran from his elbow up his bicep. Satisfied that the sleeve of the madras shirt hid enough of his longest scar, he tucked in his shirt and stepped into a well-worn pair of canvas Sanuks. After some deliberation, he chose his favorite belt buckle, a pewter piece embossed with a charging bighorn ram—a gift from his Special Forces team after their 2006 deployment, during which the Afghan troops they'd been training came to call him *Qoch-e* (the ram) because of his gruff manner, his fearlessness, and his sure-footedness in the mountains.

"I'm sorry." She sidled up behind him and kissed the sensitive spot behind his ear. "You look nice."

"Thanks." He turned around enough to plant a kiss on her cheek. He closed his eyes and sighed, bringing his forehead to meet hers. "I don't know how I'm supposed to act, you know? I don't want to look like I'm dressing for a date, but I don't want to show up looking like a fucking slob, either."

Jenn smiled, took a step back and gave him a long once-over, then hooked her finger into his belt loop, pulling him toward her again.

"You don't look like a slob." She cocked her head, leaned in and gave him a quick peck on his clean-shaven cheek. "You look cute."

Fitz arched a brow and frowned. "Cute?"

Rolling her eyes slightly, she tried again. "You look like a guy who works his ass off during the week and knows how to kick back on the weekends."

She traced her fingertips along the line where the half inch of hair on the top of his head faded to just a sixteenth of an inch. "Mmmm. And I love it when you've just gotten a haircut."

A quiet growl rumbled low in Fitz's throat. "Easy, woman," he warned her with a crooked grin. "I got an important mission to carry out tonight. But afterwards ..." His eyes gleamed brightly as he gave her a once-over of his own. "I'll probably need some R&R."

"Hey." She gently pressed her fingertips into his shorn scalp and she pulled him in for another kiss. "It'll be fine, all right? Ryan's spending the night at Brandon's, so call me if you need anything, okay?" He nodded and Jenn patted him on his hip. "I'm serious."

"Thanks." He swiped his wallet off the top of the dresser and stuffed it into his back pocket, and was halfway out the bedroom door when she called out to him.

"Fitz." A smile curved her lips when he turned to face her. "I'm proud of you." She watched his cheeks rise in a boyish grin. "More than you will ever, ever know."

"Thanks." He gave her a waist-high wave before he disappeared down the stairs.

They had agreed to meet at the local Buffalo Wild Wings, where there would be too much noise and bustle around them, even on a Saturday afternoon, for anyone to pay much notice to a couple of guys talking over a basket of wings. The Rockies' home game against the Diamondbacks was already underway by the time Fitz found Cody in a corner booth in the back of the restaurant.

Fitz glanced up at the TV.

"Holy shit!" he said, momentarily forgetting himself as he read the score on the screen. "Up two runs already. All right." He tore his gaze away from the game to find Cody staring at him with an amused glint in his eyes.

"Hey." The tall, well-built paramedic laughed as he stood up from his seat.

"Hey."

Fitz shook Cody's hand and noted with a sheepish grin how smooth and uncallused it felt compared to his own. The paramedic brought his other hand around to clasp Fitz's between his, holding the gesture for a moment before letting go.

"It's nice to see you again. It's been a while." Cody scanned the area for a passing server. "You want a beer?"

"Nah," Fitz said with a wave of his hand, noting the surprised quirk of the other man's brows as he sat down. "I, uh … I gave up drinking a while back."

"Ah," the paramedic said with a smile. "Good for you. It's the only vice I have left anymore, but you're probably right. Who needs it?"

"Don't abstain on my account, though. Really, I've been sober for months." Fitz held his breath for a moment, trying to shake the strangeness he felt being back in a sports bar after so long. "If you want a beer, have a beer. Doesn't bother me."

"Okay." Cody waved down a server. When a young redhead with long, dark lashes stopped at their table, he gestured toward Fitz with a soft jerk of his chin.

Fitz smirked at the waitress, whose gaze was clearly focused on Cody as she slowly turned to take Fitz's order. "I'll have an unsweet tea with extra lemons," he said, ignoring her scrunch-nosed look. In the months since he gave up alcohol, he'd grown accustomed to people's surprise at seeing a soldier *not* drinking in a bar.

"And for you?" She turned to Cody with an obvious swing of her hips, prompting Fitz to roll his eyes.

"I'll have another Corona with lime." Cody winked at Fitz. "And a couple of menus, please. My buddy and I are definitely going to be ordering some wings."

"No problem, hon," she said, returning the wink she'd assumed was for her. "I'll have your drinks right up." Fitz watched the waitress sashay toward the bar to drop off their order.

Cody sat back and draped his arm over the back of the booth, studying the man across the table. He and Fitz had met a few times before, so it was with a hint of poetic irony that he suggested that they meet at the same winghouse where they first met the evening Cody stopped by after a softball game.

Fitz fidgeted with the spiral-bound drink menu, unable to make eye contact as he simmered in discomfort.

Cody watched him for a moment before clearing his throat and breaking the silence.

"I'm glad you called. Surprised, but glad."

Fitz drummed his fingers on the table. "I should have called you months ago, I guess," he said, finally bringing his gaze up to meet Cody's. "I let you down. I let Peterson down."

Cody heard the ragged edge to the other man's voice and reached across the table to place his hand on Fitz's, stilling his nervous drumming. His hand was leaner than Fitz's, but his broad palm and long fingers seemed to dwarf the hand underneath his.

"Don't." He curled his long fingers around Fitz's palm as their eyes locked. "It was me who let *you* down."

"What?" Fitz shook his head, flummoxed by the unexpected reply. "No."

Cody smiled and released Fitz's hand.

"There was nothing I could do for Matt." His voice broke on his late partner's name. "I should have reached out to you and your family, but—well, I wasn't sure it was my place. I'm sorry for that."

"No," Fitz said, his Adam's apple dipping low in his throat. "*I'm* sorry because—" He reached up and scratched the back of his head. "Because I wasn't able to make sure you found out about ..." He looked up at the hanging light fixture, trying to will away the tears. "He made me promise to call you if anything happened to him, but I was so out of it for the first few days after ..." He sighed and gave a sad half-shrug. "My wife says it wasn't until a couple of days after I got to the hospital at Fort Sam Houston that I could even string a sentence together. I got my bell rung pretty hard over there and they had me pretty doped up to let my brain and body rest."

Cody's gaze swiveled down to Fitz's chest, where his open shirt revealed the edge of a faint scar across his collarbone. The paramedic's well-trained eye noted the pattern of fading pockmarks and the pair of longer, jagged scars on Fitz's forearm that he knew were from shrapnel.

"Embedded metal fragments," Fitz said with a sardonic lilt to his voice. "The gift that keeps on giving."

"How many?" Cody asked, his voice soft and devoid of the judgment that Fitz heard with most people's sympathy.

"Just a couple, actually, in my thigh. My wife and the docs tell me they may work their way out eventually. The surgeons at Landstuhl and Fort Sam Houston were able to get the rest of 'em out."

"That's good." Cody sipped his beer, draining the last quarter of it in a couple of swallows, then set the bottle on the edge of the table. "Seems you've mended pretty well, considering. Army docs did a good job patching you back up."

Fitz shrugged. "Yeah, I guess."

The hum around the bar swelled with cheers as the Rockies drove in two runs to take the lead over Arizona. Distracted by the noise and the game, the two men fell into an uncomfortable silence, made even more so as Cody reached for his beer, only to realize he'd finished it already. Fitz's eyes remained on the flat-screen TV over the bar that replayed the two-run RBI, his jaw tense as he avoided Cody's gaze.

"It's not your fault, you know."

Fitz closed his eyes and slowly turned away from the TV, opening them again to meet Cody's warm brown gaze. He opened his mouth but before he could think of what to say, the younger man spoke again.

"I just want you to know that what you did for Matt—keeping his confidence the way you did—meant the world to him. To both of us."

Swallowing thickly, Fitz looked away, blinking the moisture from his eyes. "He was the best of us. Had the biggest heart of any man I ever served with. I'm sorry I—"

"No," Cody insisted. "In all the years he spent in the Army,

Matt never had anyone he could really, really trust the way he trusted you. It's hard to explain, I guess, but he always felt like he had two lives that he could never really reconcile. Fitz, you gave him a kind of freedom—the freedom to be out, to be open, with someone who knew and understood both halves of him."

Fitz turned away again, sighing as he stared dazedly out the window. "Thing is, had I been less understanding, Matt would still be alive."

Cody shook his head. "What good is it to live if one is not free? You and Matt both dedicated your lives to fighting for freedom. By letting him trust in you and not turning him into the brass, you gave him the freedom to be himself—to live the life he chose when he raised his hand and took that oath."

"An oath I violated when I—"

"You didn't take Matt's life." Cody's voice dropped slightly, his words falling slowly and softly as his eyes shimmered in remembrance. "You let him live it. He chose that life, same as you did. You can't blame yourself, Fitz. It's ..." His voice trailed off for a moment. "It's just one of those things. We can't own what happened. Matt wouldn't have wanted us to. He died doing what he loved, and, well, we have to love him for that and keep on living."

Fitz took a deep breath and nodded. Silence fell between them again, but after a minute, their reverie was interrupted by the waitress arriving with their drinks.

"Here you go." She had a happy twang to her voice as her eyes quickly met Cody's. "And some menus," she added, setting both menus on the firefighter's side of the table. Detecting the unspoken gravity between them, she nodded and took a step back. "How about I give you guys a couple of minutes to decide?"

Fitz shot her an irritated glare.

"Yeah, sure," the paramedic said with a soft smile. "Thanks." As soon as she turned away, he reached for his fresh beer and set about to tucking the thick slice of lime into the bottle, glancing up only briefly at Fitz, who'd turned to watch her walk away.

Fitz blushed when he realized Cody had caught him looking. The silent laughter in the firefighter's eyes lit off something inside of Fitz that dissolved the heaviness that hung between them.

"It's really not fair, you know," he said, his feigned indignation belied by his smile. "Letting that poor girl make a run for you when she doesn't realize you play for the other team."

Cody laughed and leaned back in his seat. "At least I give her hope, right?" His eyes drifted to Fitz's hands. "I saw her checking you out before you even sat down, but one look at that shiny gold doodah on your finger and she knew you were off the market."

"Oh yeah?" Fitz arched a brow. "Well, don't be fooled. There's a lot of women out there—and men, too, for that matter—who don't give a shit about whether the person they're chasing is wearing a ring."

"That's true. I had this one call, a couple years ago, I guess. A motor vehicle accident. Bad single vehicle DUI crash. Lady wrapped her Lexus around a tree, and both her and the guy in the passenger seat were real banged up—she had a fractured hip, two broken ribs, and a broken wrist, and the guy ruptured his spleen, had a greenstick fracture of the clavicle, and a dislocated shoulder."

"Ouch." Fitz grunted, blinking away the still-hazy images of the night he wrapped his Jeep around a utility pole. "That's not good."

"Yeah, right?" Cody glanced down at his beer with a smirk. "Anyway, I was checking her over after we cut her out of the vehicle, you know, and when I looked at her left hand, it was obvious from the tan line and the little indentation in the skin that she'd taken her wedding ring off recently. Suffice to say, the guy she was with wasn't her husband."

"Ooof. I'm guessing *that* was an awkward moment at the hospital."

"I can only imagine. It was one of those times I was very glad I'm a paramedic and only have to hang around the ER long enough to hand the patient off to the nurses and docs."

Fitz sighed as the word *doc* refocused him on the reason for his errand.

"Matt was the best damn medic I ever had. Hands down." A smile spread across his face as a memory washed over him. "He actually helped deliver a baby by radio once. Mother and baby would've both probably died if it weren't for him."

"Really?" Cody's face lit up and a thin-lipped grin spread wide across his faintly stubbled face. "He never told me about that. What happened?"

For the first time since sitting down, Fitz leaned back in the booth, propping his arm on the windowsill.

"We were in the Korengal Valley, right? There was a Civil Affairs team doing infrastructure work in the next valley over, the Shuryek. They were basically on the other side of this mountain, Sawtalo Sar. So, this one night in January, we were in our racks trying to keep our asses warm because the temperature had dropped ten, fifteen degrees since sundown. A storm had blown in and the snow was really starting to pile up—three or four inches per hour—when we got a call on the radio. Our combat outpost got cold as shit because it sat on a ridge with no cover or windbreak, overlooking a piece of the Korengal, but the upside of that position was that we usually had pretty good radio reception."

Cody reached for his beer and took a long sip, flinching a little at the tartness of the lime, then set the bottle aside.

"Matt always talked about how damn beautiful it was there, in that part of the country. Kept saying how that, and also how nice the people in the countryside were. Made it all seem that much more tragic seeing how chaotic and fucked up the place is."

"The Korengal is gorgeous," Fitz agreed. "It always reminded me of the Roaring Fork Valley, especially that area around Glenwood Springs." He paused, recalling a rafting trip he took with Ryan down the Roaring Fork the summer before.

"So we get this radio call, right?" he continued. "The reception was readable but still pretty shitty given the weather and, we soon realized, because it was coming from a position in the next valley. It was from a sergeant in Bravo Company, 96th Civil Affairs Battalion. They'd been summoned to the home of a farmer whose wife was in labor and having trouble with the delivery. The local midwife had died just the week before, and the weather was too bad to send anybody to the next village to fetch someone else to help."

The glimmer of excitement in Cody's eyes brightened as his medical mind honed in on the facts of the case. "How long had she been in labor before you guys got the call?"

Fitz tried to remember. "A few hours, I think, but I'm not real sure. My memory of the month or two before—" He suddenly fell silent, unsure of how to refer to the IED attack. "It's sometimes kinda sketchy, even now."

Seeing Fitz's obvious discomfort, Cody dismissed his own question. "So, anyway, what happened?"

"Right," Fitz said with a grateful smile. "There were two women in this particular CA platoon, and they'd both gone into the house together. The segregation of the sexes over there is so strict that even if we'd have been able to hop in a Humvee and drive over, none of us would've been able to go in and tend to the lady because women aren't allowed to have physical contact with males outside their immediate family. It's part of why women's health and infant mortality is such a problem over there. They don't exactly have a lot of women doctors, or even midwives, and female patients' own families won't allow them to have contact with doctors they're not related to."

"Maybe you could've put Matt in a burka," Cody suggested. "Though his size-thirteen feet would probably have given his ass away."

Fitz laughed. "Well, yeah. That and the fact that he was six-four, which is a foot taller than any Afghan woman I ever saw."

"Well, there's *that*. So, what was the issue with the labor?"

Fitz nodded and slid his tea to the side. "Neither of the CA sergeants were medics, but they spoke Pashto, so by asking the woman questions and having the answers relayed to him, Matt was able to figure out that the baby was breach. He sat there on the radio and coached the two sergeants and the Afghan patient through the process of turning the baby, and then stayed on the line while the lady went through the rest of her labor. About an hour later—" He paused and smiled at the memory. "You gotta imagine me, Matt, and ten other soldiers all huddled around the radio listening to this whole thing go down. We're listening to all of this and hear all the women talking in the background—our women, the pregnant lady, and the lady's sister or mom—and then finally, all of a sudden, we hear a baby cry."

"Aww." Cody wore a sloppy grin as Fitz remembered Peterson pulling the handset of the wideband radio away from his ear so the others around him could hear the sounds of the birth.

"We all had tears in our eyes," Fitz admitted. "I did, especially after the CA sergeant told us the new mother had asked the name of the soldier on the radio, and when Matt told her, the sergeant came back and told us that the baby would be named Mattā, which is 'Matthew' in Farsi. Matt was crying, but laughing, too, joking about how after all this it sucked he didn't get the payoff of seeing the baby."

"It's funny." The paramedic's voice was dreamy and reflective as he glanced up at the TV to check the score. "Matt loved delivering babies—he got to do it a couple of times when he had that hospital rotation at Tampa General as part of his Special Forces medic course. He talked about how maybe when he got out, he'd finish his nursing degree and be an obstetrics nurse."

Fitz couldn't help but smile at the idea of the tall, broad-shouldered Swede working in the delivery room.

"He'd have been a great obstetrics nurse. Though you've gotta admit it's a hell of an image—a big handsome gay Viking running around helping deliver babies." Peterson's voice echoed like laughter in his mind. *Chicks always dig the gay guy.*"

"What about you?" Cody asked. "I mean, you're no spring chicken. Are you going to stay in?"

Fitz shrugged. "I don't know. I hit my twenty next spring, but I'm not really sure what I'm gonna do after that." He thought about how much things had changed for him in the seven months since his return from Afghanistan. "I lost my team sergeant's job. You know, with my drinking and all. Don't think I'll ever get it back. I'm lucky they didn't bounce my ass out with a court-martial." He looked into Cody's eyes but saw no judgment, just sympathy and something unexpected—acceptance.

Cody frowned a little and reached across the table, stopping short of making contact with Fitz's nervously tapping finger.

"Hey, I've got a buddy—he's on the SWAT team here in the Springs—and he was telling me about this class he took a couple of months back. It was some kind of advanced course in tactics, put on by this Denver-based outfit that does tactical training for state and local law enforcement all over the western U.S."

"Huh." Fitz grunted, scrunching his nose with skepticism. "Okay."

"I know," Cody said with a smile. "But this guy from the training company gave my buddy the hard press, trying to recruit him. I bet an outfit like that would love to get ahold of somebody like you, with the background you've got."

"I don't know." Fitz rubbed his fingers over the dark Gothic letters inked into the silky skin of his inner forearm. "I was thinking about maybe getting a transfer to Fort Bragg—maybe see if I can land a gig as an instructor at the John F. Kennedy Special Warfare School. I've been SF for thirteen years and spent almost my whole time focused on the Middle East and central Asia, except for a tour in Bosnia and those stints me and Matt did in Georgia and North Africa. I think I stand a decent chance at getting a gig with the training cadre there."

"Matt always told me you were a great teacher." Fitz's brow crinkled at the compliment, drawing a smirk from Cody. "He did. Said you were tough and you pushed people, but that you were patient, and always met people at whatever level you found 'em. I think you'd be great at the SF school. Or wherever you end up."

"Well, thanks." Fitz blushed at the praise.

"But…" Cody held up his beer, waggling his index finger for emphasis. "You've gotta promise something, though."

Fitz blinked as Peterson's words echoed in his ears. *I need you to promise me something.* His breath caught in his throat, but he slowly exhaled as he tried to dismiss the flutter in his belly.

"What's that?" he asked, his voice casual despite the butterflies.

The paramedic reached across the table again and grinned as he patted the top of Fitz's hand.

"Just don't be a stranger, huh? I'm serious."

The slight narrowing of Cody's gaze conveyed a vague plaintiveness to the request. For a fleeting second, Fitz swore he saw a flash of icy blue in Cody's dark mahogany eyes. Unsure if it was his mind playing tricks on him or one last practical joke played on him by the impish Swede, he decided it didn't matter. He smiled and clapped his hand over Cody's.

"I won't. I promise."

CHAPTER 41

Jenn leaned over the deck railing, smiling at the breeze that tickled her arms as the men below opened up the badminton set.

Her son and husband stood side-by-side, their brows creased with nearly identical skepticism as Cody ripped open the box and dumped its contents on the lawn. Fitz reached down and grabbed the torn box, heaving it to the side as the broad-shouldered firefighter unfolded the instructions and silently inventoried the poles, stakes, rackets, and birdies that lay next to the carefully rolled net.

Fitz snorted out a laugh as Cody skimmed the setup instructions. "So we're seriously going to play badminton here?" He grabbed a racket and twirled it in his hand, amused at how light it felt compared to the twenty-five pound machine gun he'd lugged around for six days during his team's last field exercise.

Cody folded up the instructions and tucked them into the back pocket of his jeans. "Sure, why not? It's a nice fall day and it's an excuse to finally put this backyard to good use."

Fitz's expression suddenly turned rigid and the slender-handled racket stilled in his hand, and Jenn knew he was lost in a memory. She wondered what it was that drew him in so deeply in that moment. Was he thinking about the fall afternoon a year ago when

296

he and Ryan tossed a baseball around the backyard of their Fort Carson home while she tended to the burgers on the grill? She thought about that afternoon—their last perfect day together as a family before he left for Afghanistan—and how much things had changed since then.

She looked around, her gaze passing over the soft Kentucky bluegrass and the bed of gravel underneath the deck before settling on the cedar shake roof as she traced the outline of the modest three-bedroom house. After vacating the apartment he and Peterson had shared, Cody bought a house in Fountain, a couple of miles east of Fort Carson's gates, where a third of his neighbors were active-duty military. And while Fitz and Cody had gotten together over wings and a ballgame several times since their initial meeting, this was Fitz's first time visiting him at home. A wave of sadness swirled low in Jenn's belly as she watched him stare at the house, his eyes glazed and his jaw slack as the badminton racquet dangled loosely in his hand.

Sensing the shift in his father's mood, Ryan reached for the racket, plucking it out of his father's grip with little resistance.

"We played this last year in P.E.," he said, twirling the flimsy aluminum racket in his hand as his father had done and letting it spin against his palm. "It was okay. Reminded me of wiffle-ball in a way."

Ryan's observation drew his father's attention from the goings-on in his head long enough to hear the fence gate swing open with a loud creak. Fitz glanced over his shoulder, his sullen expression brightening as the newcomers made their way around the side of the house.

"Padre!"

Fitz stepped forward with open arms, nearly tackling Remy as he drew him into a snug embrace. The chaplain patted Fitz on the back as he returned the hug, gasping for breath when the burly soldier finally released him. Remy turned and reached for his wife's hand, tugging her closer and snaking his arm around her waist as Fitz's toothy smile softened into a sheepish grin.

"Hey, Lakshmi." His greeting was awkward, almost bashful. Fitz's thick, tanned fingers curled around Lakshmi's dark, slender ones, swallowing her grip in his for a moment before she brought her other hand around, gently patting the top of his.

Lakshmi smiled. "It's nice to see you again, Fitz." She gave his hand one last pat, slipping from his grasp as she greeted the boy behind him with a nod. "And you must be Ryan. Remy's told me so much about you."

Ryan looked up with a shy smile. "Yeah, hi," he said shyly, poking his fingertips between the racket strings. Fitz elbowed him, and Ryan quickly tucked the racket under his arm and offered his hand to Lakshmi. "Nice to meet you."

As soon as Lakshmi released his hand, Ryan stepped back, retreating to the edge of the gathering. His shoulders slumped under the collective gazes of five adults, but he relaxed as the introductions continued and the attention passed over him again. While the boy's brooding spells seemed to occur less often since their return from Oregon, it was his tentativeness and lack of confidence that seemed hardest to shake. Jenn had hoped that, too, would ease as he began a new school year and hockey started up again, but an unshakable reticence still clung to him.

Remy's voice called up to her from the lawn below and snapped her out of her thoughts.

"So, since you already know the man in charge, it's time you finally met the woman who knows what's *really* going on."

Jenn laughed at the introduction. She glanced down to find the ginger-haired chaplain standing there with a broad grin as his wife squinted, shielding her gaze from the mid-afternoon sun.

"Why don't you two join me up here?" Jenn beckoned them with a wave of her hand. "I'm not sure how many people it takes to set up a badminton game but I can't imagine it takes five."

Lakshmi tapped Remy's wrist and nudged him toward the stairs the led up to the deck. Jenn and the chaplain shared a quick hug before Remy stepped back and made introductions.

"Jenn, this is my wife Lakshmi. Lakshmi, this is Jenn, Fitz's better half."

"It's nice to finally meet you. Remy's been an absolute godsend these last few months and—well, it's good to finally meet you."

Lakshmi winked. "Likewise."

Fitz called out from the lawn below. "Hey you up there! Porch peeps!"

Jenn turned to find Ryan looking up them expectantly, a racket in one hand and a plastic birdie in the other. "We, uhh, we're gonna need another player for our game. Do any of you guys want to play?"

Remy and Lakshmi exchanged glances, and after a silent conference comprised of widened eyes and faint nods, Lakshmi set her purse down next to the cooler.

"I'll join you guys," she announced. "That'll give you two a chance to catch up."

Remy's rusty brows knit over his eyes. "Are you sure, Laksh? I mean—"

"Pffft—of course I'm sure. It's been a while since I swung a racket. It'd be good to see if I still have the touch." Seeing a lingering doubt in the creases cutting across his lightly freckled forehead, Lakshmi leaned in and kissed his cheek. She turned to Jenn with a soft smile. "I'm sure you two have plenty to discuss."

Jenn and Remy watched the foursome make final adjustments

to the net before choosing sides. What originally appeared to be a grossly lopsided matchup, with Fitz and Cody squaring off against Ryan and Lakshmi, proved surprisingly competitive. Ryan's hand-eye coordination proved every bit as good as his father's as he used his natural quickness and his well-honed hockey skills to capitalize on his opponents' momentum and drop the birdie just beyond his father's reach.

"She's a bit of a ringer, isn't she?" Jenn smirked as Lakshmi's quick backhand saved her team from Cody's smash.

Remy chuckled. "She lettered in tennis in high school—used to play quite a bit when we were up in Chicago."

"Is that where you two met?"

"Yeah—back in '03. We met in grad school." Jenn's brow ticked up in interest and Remy laughed, knowing she'd insist on hearing the whole story. "We were both students at Meadville Lombard Theological School. I was in the Unitarian-Universalist seminary program, wrapping up my third and last year of my MDiv, and she was midway through her master's in Community Leadership. We met in a class—'Community Outreach in the Post-Denominational Age.'"

"You know, I didn't even realize the Army had Unitarian chaplains," Jenn admitted. "Fitz and I ended up getting married by a Methodist chaplain at Fort Bragg, even though I was brought up Catholic and he was Episcopalian."

Remy's eyes narrowed slightly at her use of the past tense in reference to Fitz's faith.

"There aren't very many of us," he explained. "Just six UUs on active duty at the moment, and another four in the Reserves. Wish there were more, to be honest. A lot of non-UU soldiers come to me who've avoided chaplains in the past because they were afraid of being judged or proselytized. Being a UU chaplain makes it easier to serve the needs of all the soldiers in my flock, regardless of faith or denomination."

Jenn looked at him for a moment. "I'm glad you are what you are."

She paused, kneading her lip between her teeth as the badminton game continued on the lawn below. Fitz leaped up and smashed the birdie with his racket, but the shuttlecock buzzed low over Cody's head and landed under the net. Ryan laughed at his father's gaffe and Jenn closed her eyes, savoring for a moment the simple sound that was still far rarer than it should be.

"Fitz didn't really need someone to tell him what to do," she said quietly. "He knew what he had to do. Between the colonel's ultimatum and us—"

She stopped, her breath catching in her throat as she remembered his expression as the taxi pulled out of the driveway the afternoon she and Ryan left.

"Sometimes I wonder if I made a mistake, you know—leaving when I did?" Her voice had faded to a croak, her words falling wetly from her lips as she blinked away the tears in her eyes. "I mean, what kind of wife leaves her husband when he needs her most? Who gives up on him when he's hurting?"

Remy cocked his head. "The kind whose husband was so out of control he nearly killed himself and your son the night before." He pressed his lips together in a firm line. "You didn't give up on him, Jenn. Giving up would've been walking out the door and never coming back. Leaving your wedding band on his nightstand and letting his CO serve him with divorce papers. That would've been giving up. You leaving was a shock to his system, for sure. But one he needed."

She shrugged and shook her head with a sigh. "I was at the end of my rope. It had gotten so bad, and I'd been thinking about leaving, but kept talking myself out of it. But it got worse and worse, week after week, that by the time it happened, I was hanging on by a string. I just couldn't take it anymore. So I left."

"Listen." Remy reached for her hand. "You never gave up on him. That very first day I met him, in our AA meeting, I could hear in his voice how close he came to rock bottom. But I heard something else, too."

Jenn looked up, curiosity shimmering in her gray eyes.

"Hope."

Remy leaned on the railing and watched the players switch sides of the net for their next game.

"As angry as he was, as alone as he felt, you left him with the hope that things could change, that they could get better and he'd be able to get his family back. That hope sustained him in the weeks after you left."

Jenn nodded mutely.

"As dark as things got, Jenn, it never went totally black for him. Even at the worst, there was always that glimmer of hope that you guys would be a family again if he could find his center." A cheer rang out from the lawn below as Ryan scored a point. "Hope is a powerful medicine. You guys have come a long way because nobody gave up. Nobody lost hope."

Jenn pushed away from the railing and looked down at her sandaled feet with a sigh. "I'm not sure sometimes. I watch the way they are together, and it's like they're walking on eggshells all the time. It's like they're both afraid that this thing—the way things are now—might fall apart at any second. And I feel like that's because of me, because of what I did when I decided to leave. That it's my fault things feel so precarious right now."

Remy answered with a noncommittal shrug. "I'm not much for rehashing the past. We all do it—grinding on about past decisions like a cow chewing its cud—but I've never seen the benefit of it. We are where we are, right?" He waggled his brows, trying to tug a tiny grin from Jenn's worried pout. "Sure, you guys have a ways to go yet, but seems to me that all the pieces are in place. The fundamentals? They're all there. You guys will be all right."

She grunted out a laugh. "You sound awfully sure about that."

Remy cocked his head and smiled. "You're a nurse. Your job is to heal bruised, broken bodies. My job is much the same. I heal bruised, broken spirits, or at least do what I can to help them heal themselves."

His smile fled and the sparkle in his bright blue eyes dimmed a little.

"I've worked with a lot of soldiers and families since I've been in the Army, and even lost a couple 'patients' along the way …" He hesitated for a moment, and she saw his gaze wander as if watching a memory fade into the distance. Closing his eyes, he chased away the thought with a shake of his head. "I know it may not seem like it sometimes, but you guys are going be okay. I've got faith."

Silence fell between them as the boisterous game continued on the lawn below. When she noticed Ryan's hair clinging to his forehead and temples in thick, sweaty strands, Jenn whistled the game to a halt, summoning all of the players to the porch for a hydration break. She and Remy cracked open the cooler, handing out bottles of water and soda to the flush-faced players, who accepted the refreshment gratefully as they caught their breaths.

Fitz sat back and quietly sipped his soda as Ryan spoke animatedly about the hat trick he scored in hockey camp in July. A proud smile hung from Fitz's lips but there was a wistful haze in his eyes as he listened to Ryan talk about the summer they spent apart. Jenn noticed the look on his face and hoped Remy was right about them.

Once Fitz, Ryan, Lakshmi, and Cody resumed their game, Jenn and Remy slipped into the house to prepare to put the food on the grill once the coals were ready.

"Oh!" Jenn gasped with surprise when she opened Cody's refrigerator, expecting to find two pounds of ground beef and a package of bratwurst. Along with the usual grill fare, she found a tray of preassembled vegetable kabobs and a pan of cubed tofu in a spicy marinade of citrus, chili, and ginger.

Remy peeked over her shoulder. "Awww, that's sweet of him."

She turned and shot him a puzzled look. "What?"

"Looks like Fitz made sure Cody had some vegetarian options available for Lakshmi," Remy explained. "Which just proves your husband's a total genius."

Jenn's brows scrunched over her eyes. "You completely lost me, Remy. What are you talking about?"

He set the kabobs and the tofu marinade on the counter and turned to her with a sly grin. "Fitz's genius as a soldier isn't because he's lethal as a sharpshooter or talented with explosives, or good at navigating in the desert with nothing more than a map and the stars. Even if all of those things are true." Jenn leaned against the counter and crossed her arms as she listened. "We had Fitz over for dinner a few days before you guys came back. Lakshmi made her jackfruit curry with sweet and sour deep-fried fish and she told him about how her parents moved the family from Sri Lanka to New Jersey in the mid-eighties after the civil war started there."

He dipped his fingertip into the marinade and brought it to his lips, shrugging at Jenn's disapproving look.

"See, Fitz pays attention to details—where people are from, why they come or go, what's important to them. He's got an intuitive ability to understand people in the context of their culture and circumstances and to make inferences based on the kinds of clues most people miss.

"I didn't need to tell him that Lakshmi is more or less a vegetarian because of how and where she was raised. He guessed from her name that she was Hindu and knew from our discussion that she was Tamil, and at dinner he noticed that she eats fish but otherwise eschews meat. So, after figuring all of that out, he made sure that this afternoon's barbeque includes things she can eat besides coleslaw and potato salad, made in a style that'll appeal to her Tamil palate. And he did it all without being asked. When Lakshmi finds out she's going to love him forever. That's what I mean by genius. Your husband is a cultural sponge."

Jenn couldn't help but chuckle. "He tried to teach me a little Turkish on our first date."

"Impressive. Did it work?"

"Heavens no," she laughed. "I've never been very good with languages. I took French in high school. I could memorize the vocabulary and verb forms all day long but no matter how hard I tried, my accent was absolutely pathetic. I actually got laughed at on a choir trip to Montreal when I was a junior. It amazes me that Fitz can pick up languages like that and sound like a native without even trying."

The chaplain looked at her for a moment, a flicker of amusement in his eyes.

"It's an uncommon gift, to be sure."

The two eased into a companionable silence as Remy disassembled the veggie kabobs and reassembled them, slipping the marinated tofu chunks onto the skewers while Jenn went to work turning the shapeless pile of ground beef into burgers.

After a few minutes, Jenn paused in her patty-making, her greasy hands in midair as she gave him an appraising, narrow-eyed look.

"So, why did you choose chaplaincy? You know, as opposed to finding a nice, low-key congregation in the suburbs somewhere."

Remy looked up from his kabobs, holding an empty wooden skewer like a rapier as he considered her question.

"I did a ministerial internship in 2003 at a UU church up in Palatine, about forty minutes northwest of Chicago. Like most Unitarian congregations, it was a liberal community and relatively affluent. Parking lot full of Volvos, Subarus and Audis, right? We'd just invaded Iraq a few months before I started my internship, and the congregation as a whole opposed the war. There was a woman in the congregation—one of the Sunday school teachers, actually—whose son had joined the Marines after high school. He participated in the invasion as part of the 3rd Battalion, 1st Marines, and was wounded in Nasiriyah."

Jenn remembered vividly how the war's first days had ticked by in a surreal slow-motion as she waited anxiously for news from Fitz, who had deployed on a classified mission months earlier in support of what later became the northern front of the invasion. She'd felt an unexplainable twinge in her gut the morning CNN reported that a Kurdish/American convoy in northern Iraq had been hit by friendly fire when a Navy F-14 mistakenly dropped a laser-guided bomb on their position during a battle near Mosul. Later that night, she received a phone call informing her that Fitz had been seriously wounded during combat operations and was on his way to an Army hospital in Germany.

"Chet, her son, caught some shrapnel in his back," Remy explained. "They patched him up at Walter Reed but when he came home, he was lost."

He paused, glancing down at the plate of kabobs, his brows knitting together as he thought about his congregant's troubled son.

"I met him once, at a church yard sale his mother somehow managed to coax him into attending. He had this empty, faraway look in his eyes. It wasn't until after he hung himself a few weeks later that I found out how bad things had gotten after he left Walter Reed. His wasn't the first funeral I helped arrange as a ministerial intern, and it wasn't my last. But seeing what Chet's mother went through, and seeing how lost he'd been after he came home—well, it got me thinking. By then, Lakshmi and I were dating. Being from a family that came to the U.S. fleeing a civil war, she wanted to work with refugee assistance programs that would help immigrant families in crisis adjust to a new life and a new home. After seeing what Chet and his family went through, I knew I wanted to minister to military families, who in a way endure some of the same struggles that Lakshmi's refugee families deal with."

Jenn pondered that similarity for a moment. "How did Lakshmi feel about your decision to join the Army?" She smiled, recalling the morning she met Fitz and his bloodied shin at Fort Bragg's base hospital. "I kinda knew what I was getting into when Fitz and I started dating. But with you two—seems like you joining the Army might've been a bit of a game-changer."

Remy laughed, glancing out the sliding glass door just as a shuttlecock sailed over the net. "Not in the way you might think," he replied. "There are two UU seminaries in the U.S.—one in L.A. and one, Meadville Lombard, in Chicago. The probability that I was going to find a full-time gig in Chicago was basically nil, so we knew we'd have to move. To be honest, I wasn't sure how she'd feel about me joining the Army when her family fled Sri Lanka, where the army is known for whisking people away in the middle of the night who'd never be heard from again. But shame on me for doubting her, you know? Lakshmi's got a big heart, the biggest

I've ever known. She knew I wasn't joining the Army because I believed in war as a policy or violence as way of solving problems. I joined the Army because soldiers and their families are people, too—people whose hearts and souls need taking care of just as much as the rest of us."

"If not a little more, now and again," Jenn added, slapping another hamburger patty between her palms as the sliding glass door opened with a *whoosh*.

Remy acknowledged her with a tip of his head. "Amen to that." They looked up as Fitz walked into the kitchen, wiping the sweat off his face with the hem of his shirt.

Suddenly aware that he was being stared at, Fitz stopped in his tracks and let his shirt hem fall over his belly. "What?"

Jenn shot Remy a knowing if somewhat exasperated look and snorted, then handed Fitz a plate of hamburger patties and chicken breasts.

"The coals are ready," she told him with a grin. "Here—go make yourself useful."

CHAPTER 42

It was the most sedate going-away bash Jenn had ever attended.

In the nearly fourteen years since she became an Army wife, she'd watched a lot of soldiers receive Permanent Change of Station orders and enjoy one last hurrah with their comrades and their families before heading off to a new assignment. Some parties were so wild and out of control it was a wonder no one ended up in the hospital. Jenn used to enjoy such hail and farewells, but after Fitz's return from Afghanistan a year earlier, she approached such gatherings with caution.

She wasn't sure what to expect when Master Sergeant Bruniak offered to host the farewell barbeque at his house in Fountain. The men of Alpha 0227 were work-hard, play-hard kind of guys, and Jenn had seen enough of Fitz and his comrades at family picnics to know they were more than capable of turning any casual get-together into a full-on riot, especially when beer was involved.

Jenn sat back and watched from a distance as Fitz and Bruniak exchanged barbs in a steadily escalating duel of ball-busting one-upmanship, but she could tell they keeping it dialed back a bit. Fitz's teammates recognized that a party to celebrate his leadership and accomplishments before he headed off to his new gig as a Special Forces instructor had to respect Fitz's decision to give up drinking. So while there were beers and sodas in the cooler and a bottle of Stoli for the junior commo sergeant who didn't like beer, the mood was happy without being over the top.

"How you doin' there, Cap'n?"

Captain Clark nearly spilled his Sprite all over the front of his jacket in surprise.

"Jenn." He greeted her with an awkward smile, switching his soda from one hand to the other and shaking his soaked, sticky hand in the air before wiping it on his jeans.

She smiled and tucked a strand of hair behind her ear. "Fitz always said I'd make a good sniper. He hates it when I sneak up on him. I can't help that I walk quietly, though—guess it's a result of too many years spent working in hospitals around sleeping patients and grouchy residents who get cranky when roused mid-catnap. Plus, the whole tooth fairy thing. Ryan never made a peep when I did it. Fitz on the other hand? Let's just say we had a couple of very close calls."

Clark laughed. "Well, I'll have to keep that in mind when the time comes."

"It'll come."

The captain gave her a puzzled look. He scanned the backyard. "Where's your son?"

Jenn laughed. "Oh, he's inside." She nodded toward the sliding glass door behind a trio of weather-worn Adirondack chairs, each one occupied by a bright-eyed, beer-drinking soldier.

"He went inside to play Xbox with Cody, Spaz's son Max, and Staff Sergeant Swenson. Guess you might say he's in there tanking up."

Clark coughed. "What?"

"On video games," Jenn clarified with a grin. "Fitz decided this PCS was our big chance to 'drive across America,' as he put it, so we're road-tripping it from here to Fayetteville. You should've seen the look on Ryan's face. Three days without his Xbox—you'd have thought we told him we were amputating his thumbs."

"Poor guy. A week without *Assassin's Creed?* That's some serious deprivation there."

She shook her head and laughed. "Don't encourage him."

For a minute or so, the pair stood on the edge of the yard watching through the glass as her son, another boy, and two grown men played what appeared to be a very competitive car racing game. At one point, Ryan must have done something well, because Cody reached over and tousled his hair, then patted him on the back.

The therapist she and Fitz had been working with told them that their son would likely seek out a strong male figure in the wake of losing his grandfather and due to the lingering effect of Fitz's difficulties. Jenn smiled, grateful that in the five months since Fitz reconciled with Cody, not only had a friendship grown from their shared loss, but Ryan had acquired another strong male role model.

As if reading her mind, Clark smiled. "I bet you're happy to get Fitz off the deployment rotation. You know, to have him around more. A boy needs his father around, especially at that age."

Jenn saw Ryan turn to Cody and laugh, his green eyes bright as a smile spread across his face. She thought about the angry, scowling youth she dragged back from Oregon to his grandfather's funeral the summer before.

"I nearly lost both of them. Not just a year ago when Fitz was wounded. But when he ..." She jerked her chin toward the grill where Fitz stood with a couple of his teammates exchanging stories. "When he pulled away, Ryan became bitter and angry. For a while, I couldn't reach either of them, no matter what I tried."

"I'm sorry." He waggled his mostly empty soda can and looked down at his feet.

"Don't be. What you did—taking the team away from him, forcing him to get help—you saved him." She looked into the captain's dark eyes, holding his gaze for a long moment. "You saved him, and you saved us. I don't think he'd have woken up had I just taken Ryan and left. Losing his team and being threatened with an Article 32 and a bad conduct discharge, on top of us leaving—all of it, all at once—that's what made him see how bad things had gotten." She sighed, remembering the afternoon she packed their suitcase and fled halfway across the country with their son. "That was the kick in the ass he needed."

"I don't know," the young officer said with a blush. "I mean, I—"

Jenn's eyes narrowed and met the captain's molasses-brown gaze. "Without you, Captain, we wouldn't be here."

Clark swallowed thickly and shrugged. Though he didn't acknowledge it, Jenn knew he'd seen the photos the MPs took of Fitz's mangled Jeep at the accident scene and knew as she did that Fitz, who'd survived countless brushes with death over the course of his career, very nearly lost his life that night.

"All right, everybody!"

Bruniak's booming voice shook both of them from their thoughts.

"Coals are just about ready, so I figure this is as good a time as any to do the formal bit before we throw the steaks and burgers on. Figure once you'ns all been fed, you're not gonna want me interrupting your meat-comas to listen to a bunch of ceremonial claptrap."

Jenn and Clark joined the crowd around the porch where Bruniak presided over not one but three charcoal grills, which cast an eerie orange glow on his and Fitz's faces.

Once most of the guests had made their way back to the porch, and the four video gamers dropped their controllers on the coffee table and stepped outside again, Bruniak clapped Fitz on the back and stepped forward.

"So, I guess I should say a few words here." The tall, thick-necked sergeant glanced over at Fitz, who draped his arm around Ryan's shoulder and urged the boy to stand in front of him. "You know, just so you'ns don't think I just give away a couple hundred bucks' worth of New York strip steaks on a regular basis for the hell of it."

The crowd chuckled as the Pittsburgh-born Pole turned and gave his friend a crooked, affectionate grin.

"I first came to Carson almost exactly nine years ago this week," Bruniak began, scratching the close-cropped hair on the back of his head as he tried to remember the speech he'd thrown together the night before. "And when I got here, they assigned me to 0227 as the assistant weapons sergeant working underneath some jagoff everybody called 'Fitz.' He rode me like a fuckin' racehorse for the first six months I was here."

Fitz looked back at Bruniak with a smirk as the crowd laughed.

"Well, it was a good thing, because six months after I showed up here and joined the team, those fuckin' bastards flew those planes into the Twin Towers and the Pentagon."

Bruniak suddenly blanched. He glanced at Fitz and Ryan next to him, then shifted to his wife and Jenn with a shrug and a sheepish grin. "Sorry, ladies." His eyes flicked over to Remy, meeting his gaze with a wince. "And Chaplain."

The audience chuckled at Bruniak's inability to contain his obscenity even for a formal hail-and-farewell presentation.

"We didn't get sent into Afghanistan for the first round," he said. "But me an' Fitz got detailed over to Iraq the next year to spend the winter with the Kurds and help 'em get their collective shitskies together so they'd be able to hold open a northern front when the big machine roared in from the south in the spring."

Fitz snaked his arm around the front of Ryan's chest and hugged him close. He remembered the months spent moving from village to village in the rural hinterlands of northern Iraq's Kurdish frontier, and the heartache of not being able to regularly communicate with his family during that time. But even the misery of those months didn't begin to compare to the six long weeks he spent exiled from his family after his DUI. The memory of it sent a chill down his spine worse than any he'd felt in the Zagros Mountains that cold, lonely winter. Fitz blinked away the thought as he looked at Remy, who nodded in solemn understanding.

"And so anyway," Bruniak continued, his lips quirked with a faint smile. "We got over there, and a'course kicked some major ass, thanks in no small part to Fitz, who approached our mission there the same way he does everything else: total effort, all business, attention to detail, all the while keepin' sight of the big picture. Hard core all the way, but with a creativity and flexibility that got us out of some seriously sticky situations, especially in those first few crazy-ass months over there."

"I didn't do it alone," Fitz said, looking out to the crowd. He saw his team, a couple other guys he knew from Bravo Company and 2nd Battalion, plus Remy, Cody, and some of the wives, kids, and girlfriends of the guys on the team.

Bruniak chuckled, not surprised that even at a party in his honor, Fitz chafed at the idea of public praise.

"Things moved pretty quickly for Fitz after that. We got back from Iraq and he got promoted to Operations and Intel Sergeant the next year, and after a couple more deployments to Anbar and

Kandahar, he got the bump again—this time to Team Sergeant. He kept the team squared away through tours and advising missions in Mali, Senegal, Georgia, and Kunar before he finally burned through all his good-luck tokens and got himself torn up pretty good in Kelalbat last year."

Bruniak fell silent for a moment as he thought about Peterson. He had arrived at the scene minutes after the blast, only to find that there was very little of the medic left for the mortuary affairs unit to piece together at Bagram and send home. With a sigh, Bruniak crossed himself in Peterson's memory and continued.

"Fitz had a bit of a rough go for a while there, what with him getting banged up pretty bad and us losing Doc." His words were oblique as he braced himself for the response, but the gathering didn't even murmur. Every one of them, even the rookie medic Swenson, knew that the outgoing sergeant had struggled to recover after the IED attack. "But, tough bastard he is, he soldiered through it and came through on the other side."

Bruniak looked out over the crowd with a bittersweet smile.

"I think I speak for every one of us when I say we're sorry to see you go, but wishing you all the best as you make your way back to Bragg. I can't think of a better man to teach the young pups the Special Forces way than you, Fitz."

The *hooahs* that grunted out from the crowd drew a wide, proud smile from Fitz and a laugh from Ryan.

"*Hooah*," Bruniak grunted back. "If those little baby snake-eaters come outta there one-tenth the soldier that you are—that you've always been since the day I met you and got my ass handed to me—then we're gonna be damn lucky to have 'em. All's they gotta say is they trained under you, and that'll be enough for me to let 'em have my six any day."

Applause welled up from the crowd, punctuated with a few

more *hooahs* and whistles.

Bruniak's broad, gap-toothed smile suddenly wilted as he scanned the group with a furrowed brow.

"Swenson!" he snapped, his grin returning in a crooked, lazy form as his eyes met those of the young medic, who looked up with a start, breathed a silent *oh,* and double-timed it into the house.

Sensing what was coming, Fitz patted Ryan's shoulder and let him go. He smiled as the boy made his way toward his mother, who stood near the back of the assembled crowd. "All right," Bruniak barked. "Guess you know how this part goes, eh, boss?"

Fitz laughed and stepped forward, his eyes narrowing at Swenson, who emerged from the living room holding a large framed, matted plaque.

The top of the plaque was adorned with a wide arch comprised of the flags of Saudi Arabia, Iraq, Somalia, Turkey, Bosnia-Herzegovina, Jordan, Iraqi Kurdistan, Georgia, Mali, Senegal, and Afghanistan—all places where he'd deployed over the course of his career, first with the 101st Airborne, then later as a Ranger, and, finally, as a Green Beret. Below, on the left side, was a sepia-toned map of Africa, the Balkans, the Middle East, and central Asia, with each of those countries highlighted in a different color with the years of his service there written in a calligraphic script. On the right side was a pen-and-ink caricature of Fitz with an overgrown buzz cut and the shaggy beard he wore when he served in Afghanistan and with the Kurds in Iraq.

Fitz searched the crowd for Sergeant First Class Kim, who wasn't just a skilled medic, but a talented amateur cartoonist who whiled away the hours drawing comic books that he published on an internet blog. Fitz met Kim's shy gaze and mouthed a silent thank you.

"Wow." Fitz studied the caricature, which showed him with slight scowl as he looked down at the aluminum canteen cup in his cartoon hand. "Must be the end of the month—runnin' low on coffee. It was rough waitin' for resupply over there."

He looked up and over at Jenn, who winked at him. She'd sent him care packages once a month during his last deployment and always included his favorite brand of instant coffee and, for those times when he really needed a turbocharged caffeine boost, a box of *mate* tea. She knew from her years as an ER nurse the difference a good cup of coffee or tea made when working long hours under pressure.

Bruniak gave the picture an approving nod. "Not a bad likeness, actually. Though I think Kim made your beard look a bit too Kenny Loggins rather than Charlton Heston in *The Ten Commandments,* which is how I remember it."

Fitz snorted. "You're just jealous because you could never grow a decent beard. Private Wahidi had a better-looking beard than you did and he was barely seventeen."

The crowd laughed.

"Whatever you say, Moses," Bruniak snickered. "At least I wasn't getting my whiskers snagged in my chinstrap."

Between the map and the caricature was a rectangular bronze inset with an inscription, which Bruniak read aloud to the gathering as Swenson held the plaque up high enough so everyone could see.

"Presented to Master Sergeant Jacob 'Fitz' Fitzgerald, in honor of ten years of outstanding service as a member of Operational Detachment Alpha 0227, Bravo Company, 2nd Battalion, 10th Special Forces Group. Every man who has served with you is a better soldier for having trained and fought in your company. It is with gratitude and pride that we commend you to your next duty station, where you will help forge a new generation of America's finest fighting men. *De oppresso liber.*"

Fitz reddened, flattered and proud but a little embarrassed by the recognition. He stepped forward and shook Bruniak's hand, gazing into his old second-in-command's dark, brimming eyes before the sergeant pulled him into a bear hug that nearly swallowed him up.

"Hey." Bruniak pulled away and studied Fitz's face, then squeezed his shoulder with an intimacy born of years of shared struggles and losses. "You deserve this, all right?" His voice was little more than a rumble. "None of us have put as much on the line—or left as much of ourselves behind—for as long as you have, buddy. You and Jenn and your boy—you'ns deserve this, understand?"

Fitz saw the gentleness in Bruniak's usually stern features, softened by the warm glow of the hot coals.

"I mean it," Bruniak told him. "You've given enough. Go do us proud."

EPILOGUE

February 16, 2010
Fort Logan National Cemetery
Denver, Colorado

It was a cool but pleasant winter day, the kind that made Jacob Fitzgerald love the state that had been his home most of his life. The sun burned bright in the clear sky, but the morning chill left a frost on the grass that blanketed the long rows of white granite markers that stood like sentinels over the men and women resting beneath them.

Fitz knew by heart what section and row to find the man he was looking for, and with the sun warming his shoulders, he marched quietly, mindful of the crunch of crisp grass beneath his hiking boots and of the footsteps of his wife and son behind him. He slowed as the familiar name came into view, pausing to read the inscription before he crouched in front of the grave and speared a miniature American flag into the soft, grassy earth.

He bowed his head and closed his eyes, and for a moment simply sat in solemn silence. When he looked up again, he placed his hand on the cold stone marker, skimming his fingertips over the letters carved into its smooth face.

MATTHEW ARON
PETERSON
SFC
US ARMY
IRAQ
AFGHANISTAN
JAN 16, 1974
FEB 15, 2009
PURPLE HEART
LOVED DEEPLY
DEEPLY LOVED

"Hey, buddy," he whispered to the gravestone. "I'm sorry it's been a while since I last came by."

He heard the soft shuffle of shoes on the frost-kissed grass and a smile crept across his lips as he visualized his son standing behind him, his hands stuffed in his coat pockets.

"It's been kind of a crazy time for us," Fitz said with an apologetic shrug. "Lots of things changing, and pretty quickly, too. Good changes, mostly, but you know how it goes—even good changes can be stressful as all hell when it slams down on you all at once."

Fitz paused the way he always did when he came to visit Peterson. He knew there was no point to it, but for some reason, he felt less strange talking to his dead friend if he gave the medic a chance to answer, even if the reply came in the form of a gust of wind or the swift-moving shadow of a hawk flying overhead.

"I'm leaving the team," he said. "Been thinkin' about it for a while, to be honest. It was time, Doc. After losing you over there, then coming home and losing my shit and damn near everything else that matters, I—" He swallowed thickly, tapping his fingers on Peterson's name.

"I … I just needed to make a move, you know. My boy's thirteen now. His voice is starting to change, he's filling out, and growing like a goddamned weed—four inches since I got back from the 'Stan. And he's …" Fitz's voice dropped to a whisper again. "He's getting stinky the way teenage boys do. He's becoming a man, you know? I've been gone a lot—too much—while he's been growing up, and he needs me to be around now, and I need to be here for him. The deployment tempo is too much. Even though we're drawing down in Iraq, it hasn't reduced the operational demand on SF units like ours."

He breathed a sad sigh. "I damn near ruined everything, Doc. I gotta put everything I have and everything I am into building it back up again, even stronger and better than it was before. I've given the Army twenty years—twenty long years where the needs of the Army took priority over the needs of my family. Can't do that anymore. Not like before."

Fitz raked his fingers through the cold, stiff grass at the base of the headstone and smiled.

"Cody said you told him I was a good teacher." He ruffled the grass again, blushing the way he always did when praised. "But, you know, it's time to let the young Turks rise up and lead. Time for old guys like me to sit back and let the young guys do the ground-pounding now. Besides, I'm not sure how much more wear and tear this old body of mine can take, anyway. There's a reason war's a young man's game."

He paused, frowning at his choice of words. Peterson had been three years his junior, and as far as Fitz could tell still had several years before the ravages of time—arthritis in the knees, lower back, and anywhere else affected by the cumulative pounding on old injuries—would have caught up with him.

Fitz's own knees creaked as he shifted his weight from one hip to the other. "It's gonna be a while before I'm able to come see you next. We're heading back to Bragg. Back to where it all began, right? Back to where you and me got our green berets, and where Jenn and I met." Fitz smiled and laughed. "God, you should've seen me back then, Doc. I was freakin' relentless. Wouldn't take no for an answer. I pestered her until she agreed to go on a date with me."

He hesitated again, wishing his slain friend could speak up and razz him the way he always used to.

Bouncing lightly on the balls of his feet, he leaned closer to the headstone. "I'm transferring to the 1st Special Warfare Training Group at Fort Bragg. They're going to have me teaching Dari for Phase II of the SF qualification course."

He traced his fingers across the deep-carved letters that named the place where Peterson gave his life. The gravity of the loss washed over him, tingling in the back of his throat and burning in his eyes like the dust that hung in the air after the blast. He felt the sharp edges of the letters that spelled *AFGHANISTAN*. Fitz thought about telling Peterson how he hoped that somehow he could teach a young Green Beret, PsyOp or Civil Affairs candidate something about Afghanistan and its mixture of peoples, tribes, and clans that would save that soldier's life someday, or perhaps the life of an Afghan peasant over there.

But he didn't. His fingers stroked the letters again, but he said nothing, sensing that somehow his friend knew why he wanted to teach language and culture rather than the advanced fighting skills that Army Special Forces were renowned for. *He knows why,* Fitz thought, letting his fingers slip down the slick, cool surface of the stone.

"There's this pilot program where instead of just having a native teacher teach the language, the course is taught by a team of two instructors, with the hope that the increased student/teacher interaction will improve how fluent the students are at the end of the process. I'm excited about it. It's gonna be good to get off the deployment merry-go-round. My family's been through enough, I think."

He looked down at the ground, seeing how the thick, toothy tread of his boots had flattened the grass in front of Peterson's grave.

"I don't know. Maybe it's selfish of me, but after all these years of putting the Army ahead of my family, I think it's time I put my family first for once. I don't know how much longer I'll stay in, but we'll see how it goes."

A sigh and the sound of feet shuffling behind him reminded Fitz that, unlike some of his other visits to Peterson's grave, he wasn't alone this time.

"Ryan wasn't too keen on the idea. With me being in the 10th Special Forces all this time, we've been at Carson for thirteen years. He's one of the rare Army brats who hasn't had to move around."

Fitz heard a quiet murmur behind him, but couldn't tell if it came from Jenn or Ryan.

"He was afraid they wouldn't have hockey in North Carolina," Fitz said with a grin. "Turns out there's a youth league in central Carolina and a team in Fayetteville that plays at the ice rink at Bragg. I didn't remember there being a rink at Bragg when I was there, but hell—any free time I had back then was spent chasing Jenn around."

Jenn chuckled behind him and he laughed.

"They're called the Fire Ants, can you believe it?" Fitz rolled his eyes and shook his head in feigned disbelief. "Which Ryan of course thinks is a bad-ass name. Whenever I hear 'fire ants' I think of the swamp phase of Ranger School and how I stepped in a mound of those nasty little fuckers on a road march and how goddamn much my ankle swelled—"

"Jacob."

Hearing his whispered name startled him, jerking him back to the present. He turned to see Jenn watching him with a sympathetic smile as her fingertips skimmed along the edge of his shoulder.

He closed his eyes and nodded. "I know."

The levity that had brightened his voice just seconds before darkened as the prospect of leaving became a reality. He took a long, deep breath, then rocked forward on the balls of his feet until his forehead rested against the cold stone of Peterson's grave.

"Goodbye, Doc."

He pursed his lips and dragged his fingers over the letters of Peterson's name one last time. He scraped his fingernails against the granite as his hand curled into a fist. "I love you, brother." He closed his eyes, letting the grief wash over him the way the counselor had told him he could. After a moment, he looked up and pressed the flat of his knuckles against the stone. Nodding once, he rocked back on his heels and pushed himself to his feet.

"Wish us luck, Doc," he said, patting the side of the gravestone.

It was with a quiet sigh and one last nod that Fitz bade his friend farewell and turned to his family with a tired smile.

"Let's go."

Acknowledgments

Writing a novel is a strange thing. It's a fundamentally solitary activity that depends on the contributions of many who lend a hand at key milestones during the process. There's no question that *The Road Back From Broken* would not have been possible without the help and support I had along the way.

While much of this story is set at Fort Carson and in my hometown of Littleton, Colorado, my research took me as far as to Northern Ireland to fill in the gaps in Fitz's family history. To that end, I want to acknowledge the assistance of the wonderful people at the Somme Heritage Centre in Newtownards, County Down, who answered my questions about Volunteer Aid Detachment (VAD) nurses at the Somme, and the two veteran volunteers at the Royal Ulster Rifles Museum on Waring Street in Belfast, who pointed me towards resources on the Young Citizen Volunteers.

My research also took me to several U.S. Army posts (Fort Hood, Fort Benning, Fort Lee, and Fort Bragg), and to the small regimental museums that document the history of individual Army units there. I'm especially grateful for the time I spent at the John F. Kennedy Special Warfare Museum at Fort Bragg, which is tucked away in a small standalone facility amid the cluster of buildings that house the 1st Special Warfare Training Group

(Airborne) and the John F. Kennedy Special Warfare Center and School.

I wish to thank my editor, Jessica Swift. In Jessica, I found a partner who immediately connected with my book and its people, and who understood my passion for the story. I'm grateful for her help in making *Road* a stronger and tighter tale than I could make it on my own.

Effusive praise and all the props go to my cover artist, Mark Aro of Hyperactive Studios, whose talent and patience transformed the swirling muddle of Garden of the Gods photos and Army dog tags into stunning cover art with a sense of place and purpose.

I owe a huge thanks to my colleagues in the Military Writers Guild, a diverse assembly of men and women who welcomed me with open arms and who've been a constant support over the last year. I'm especially grateful to Ty Mayfield, Jessica Scott, and Phil Walter for their help and encouragement along the way.

There's no doubt that I couldn't have done this without the community of readers, writers and friends who provided alpha/beta feedback at various points along the way: Lisa, Dana, Angie, Jocelyn, Amy, Missy, Debra, Paula, Maryssa, Kirsten, Nicholas, Vania, Steph, Catherine, Wendi, and Michele. Their input made this story better and and their enthusiasm for Fitz, Jenn, Remy and gang kept me going when the going got tough.

When I decided to forego the traditional channels and publish this book myself, I leaned heavily on the advice and experience of people who have done it before. Special thanks go out to my friend and fellow novelist A.C. Dillon, who patiently coached me through the process, talked me away from the edge more than a few times, and shook her proverbial pom-poms when I needed it. A, you are a champion.

Last but definitely not least, I'm grateful for the support of my husband Lars, an Army veteran himself who challenged me to make 2014 the year I would sit down and write the book that had been percolating inside of me. And so I woke up on New Year's Day 2014, sat down on our sofa with my MacBook, and began to write the story that became *Road*. Lars has been there every step of the way, cheering me on, offering feedback, and in general being my pillar of strength amid the emotional ups and downs that punctuate the writing/publishing process. Without his steadfast support and unfailing encouragement, this book would never have happened.

Connect with me!

I love to hear from my readers. Connect with me on Twitter
http://twitter.com/C_T_Morgan
and Facebook:
https://www.facebook.com/CarrieMorganAuthor,
or at my website,
http://wages-of-war.com.

If you liked *The Road Back From Broken,* I would love it if you would take a moment to leave a review on Amazon or Goodreads. Writers, especially indie writers like me, depend almost exclusively on word of mouth and reader reviews. So, if you have the time to leave a little review, I'd be grateful for the feedback.

Book club readers

I would absolutely love to talk to your book club about *The Road Back From Broken*. If your book club meets in central Florida, I'll gladly drop by in person. Otherwise, we can do it via Skype or a similar video chat technology. Either way, contact me and we'll figure something out.

Made in the USA
San Bernardino, CA
19 October 2015